MURDER
AT THE
NATIONAL
CATHEDRAL

MARGARET TRUMAN

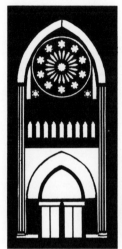

MURDER AT THE NATIONAL CATHEDRAL

RANDOM HOUSE 🏠 NEW YORK

To Wesley Truman Daniel
with love
from Gammy

THIS LARGE PRINT BOOK CARRIES
THE SEAL OF APPROVAL OF N.A.V.H.

Excerpt from the hymn on page 81 is from
Hymnal 1940, published by the Plimpton Press.
Copyright 1940 by the Church Pension Fund.

Library of Congress Cataloging-in-Publication Data

Truman, Margaret,
Murder at the National Cathedral / by Margaret Truman.
p. cm.
ISBN 0-679-40044-3
I. Title.
PS3570.R82M7545 1990   813'.54—dc20   90-53342

Manufactured in the United States of America
9 8 7 6 5 4 3 2
First Large Print Edition

Book design by Oksana Kushnir

Murder at the National Cathedral is a work of fiction.
The characters in it have been invented by the author,
and any resemblance to actual persons,
living or dead, is purely coincidental.
The story is also fictitious, and no such crime
as is described has taken place at the National Cathedral.
The National Cathedral had no participation
in the creation of this book.

"This church is intended for national purposes
  . . . and
assigned to the special use of no particular
  Sect or
denomination, but equally open to all."
            Pierre L'Enfant
            1791 Plan for the City of Washington

". . . a national house of prayer for all people."
            The Congress of the United States—
            1893

"Here let us stand, close by the cathedral.
Here let us wait. Are we drawn by danger?
Is it the knowledge of safety, that draws our
  feet
Towards the cathedral? What danger can
  be . . . ?"
            T. S. Eliot
            Murder in the Cathedral

"Someone has been murdered in the cathedral."
            The Right Reverend
            George St. James,
            bishop of Washington

MURDER
AT THE
NATIONAL
CATHEDRAL

chapter
1

The National Cathedral, Washington, D.C.— A Very Hot Morning in August

"Dearly beloved, we have come together in the presence of God to witness and bless the joining together of this man and woman in Holy Matrimony."

Mackensie Smith, contented professor of law at George Washington University, formerly discontented but preeminent Washington, D.C., criminal lawyer, told himself to focus on what was about to happen. He'd been thinking moments before about what an ambivalent structure a cathedral was, even this relatively new addition to the world's cathedral population. So much majesty and awe—so much stone—so much bloodshed in the older ones over centuries. How inspiring these Gothic monuments to the simple act of believing in something greater and good, and how dangerous, as with all religion, when in the hands of creatures who get carried away and misuse the potent metaphor of faith.

Those thoughts banished, Smith glanced to his left. The stunning, mature woman who would become his wife in a matter of minutes turned to him and smiled. Annabel Reed had reason to assume that his thoughts at that tender moment were only of his adoration and love for her. She was largely correct, although her husband-to-be had room in his capacious mind for less romantic contemplations. He was also wishing that the priest conducting this ceremony in the Bethlehem Chapel of the National Cathedral weren't compelled to be quite so formal. Smith understood, of course, that there was a certain amount of religious boilerplate that had to be indulged. Still, he would have preferred something a little less stiff, perhaps something between an elaborate high mass in the cathedral's nave, and a last-minute midnight, minimal, bread-and-butter ceremony in an Elkton, Maryland, justice of the peace's home.

The priest, Paul Singletary, paused after intoning the tender words from the Book of Common Prayer, and smiled at Smith and Reed. The couple had known him for a time; Smith went back six years with him. Mac Smith was a close friend of the cathedral's bishop. George St. James was out of town that week, which was not the reason Smith hadn't asked him to officiate. It had more to do with what Smith termed "a reasonable level of modesty." Asking the bishop to marry them would have smacked of a certain overkill. Just a priest would do fine, thank you, especially one known to them.

Smith again looked at his bride. A tiny drop of perspiration was proceeding on a slow but steady descent down the right side of her lovely aquiline nose. Should he reach over and remove it? An affectionate gesture certainly, but probably not good form, so he didn't. Outside, the final days of August in the nation's capital had turned, characteristically, viciously hot and humid. It was cooler here in the chapel below ground-level, but even God's natural stone air-conditioning was wilting under the meltdown that Washington called summer. Carved figures of King David with his harp and Ruth with a sheaf of wheat looked down from their niches on the south wall as though they, too, might begin perspiring at any moment. The Bethlehem Chapel, one of four in the cathedral's substructure, was the first to be completed. Since 1912 it had been the site of many services, and was the church home over the years for the services of various denominations—Polish Catholic, Jewish, Russo-Carpathian, Serbian, Greek Orthodox. A *national* cathedral.

Reverend Singletary looked once again at the Book of Common Prayer. Smith looked into the priest's eyes. Was he amused at something? He seemed to be, Smith decided. Marriages made later in life always had a different aura from that accompanying the ritual of officially coupling the young for the first time.

Smith was widowed; his wife and only child, a son, had been slaughtered on the Beltway by a drunk driver. Annabel Reed had never married, although, God knows, more than a few attractive and successful men had energetically pursued the idea. That she had decided upon Mac Smith was flattering to him. But not humbling. No false modesty here. Smith was a handsome man by any standard, slightly taller than medium, stocky and strong, hair receding slowly and within acceptable limits, face without undue deficits.

Annabel's beauty was even less debatable. Playing the whom-do-you-look-like game, which Smith detested (his least-favorite version of it being "Which of us do you think the baby looks like?"), it was inevitable that Rita Hayworth was mentioned. Yet Annabel was more beautiful than any actress, at least in Smith's eyes. She was, to put it simply, the most beautiful female creature he'd ever seen, not much at acting, for she never put up a false front, and rather nice to boot. By virtue of the ritual being performed here today—all day?—she would be his wife. Let's get on with it, he thought. Enough.

Though any clergyman could make a determination as to whether the lawfulness of a proposed marriage was in question, Smith was surprised when Singletary chose to invoke that medieval section of the marriage ceremony. "If any of you can show just cause why they may not lawfully be married, speak now or else . . ." he said, allowing scant time for the clearing of a questioner's throat, much less speech, "forever hold your peace."

There was a silence that Smith hoped was not pregnant. The Bethlehem Chapel seated 192 people; thirty of their close friends, including a few former members of Smith's law firm who had forgiven him for closing it down following the deaths of his wife and son, were clustered up front.

Mac's thoughts were on only one person, however—Tony Buffolino, a disgraced and dismissed former Washington MPD vice-squad cop whom Mac had once defended, and who'd become an unlikely friend in the best odd-couple tradition. If anyone pretended to raise an objection to the marriage just for kicks, it would be a character like Buffolino. Mac turned his head slightly, saw Tony, who winked at Mac, started to raise his hand, brought it down, and lowered his head.

Paul Singletary smiled at her as he said, "Annabel, will you have this man to be your husband; to live together in the covenant of marriage? Will you love him, comfort him, honor and keep him, in sickness and in health; and, forsaking all others, be faithful to him as long as you both shall live?"

"Oh yes, I will," she said with unmistakable cheer in her voice.

Singletary repeated the vow to Smith, who replied, "I will," in a surprisingly gruff, emotional voice.

Smith looked to the choir loft, where four members of the cathedral's boys' choir—the few who preferred music to baseball in August—had gathered to sing. Later in the service they would perform Annabel's favorite hymn, "Wilderness," the choice of which had pleased Father Singletary because of its humanistic, contemporary theme.

Singletary read the verse beginning "Love is patient; love is kind" from I Corinthians, and the four boys got through "Wilderness" rather quickly; the usual tempo seemed to have been accelerated by a third. Mac Smith approved. He was also impressed, as was everyone else in the chapel, with the strong, bell-like voice of one of the boy sopranos, whose tones rang out above the others.

Soon, it was time to exchange rings. Annabel had virtually no family. She had friends, of course, but her hectic schedule as an attorney-turned-art-gallery-owner and almost constant companion to Mac Smith had severely limited time to cultivate and nurture friendships. She was being given "away" as a wife by his mother, Josephine Smith, as spry and sparkling as a split of champagne, a tiny woman who lived in the Sevier Home for the Aged in Georgetown, a facility operated by the Episcopal church, and who often said that she considered Annabel as much a daughter as she did Mac a son, and sometimes more. Smith's best man was the new dean of GW's law school, Daniel Jaffe. Josephine Smith and Jaffe handed the rings to their respective charges.

Mac and Annabel Smith slipped the gold bands on their ring fingers, and Singletary blessed them, concluding with the familiar "Those whom God has joined together let no one put asunder."

"Amen," said their friends.

As Mac and Annabel knelt (It's always the knees that go first, Smith thought), Singletary intoned the final blessing of their union. They stood. They kissed. Eyes met eyes.

"The peace of the Lord be always with you," said the priest.

"And also with you," came the reply.

After the ceremony everyone went outside, where friends took quick point-and-shoot photographs, delivered quick point-and-kiss greetings to Annabel, and grasped the groom's hand, with an occasional teary kiss for him, too. Properly, they congratulated Mac, who said in mock modesty, "It was nothing," and added, "Just a four-year chase."

"Going on a honeymoon?" one of Smith's colleagues at the university asked him.

"London, but not right away. Somehow it seems you don't take an instant honeymoon at this stage in your life."

Another professor laughed. "You two have been on a honeymoon for years."

"I suppose we have," Smith said, not precisely caring for the innuendo in the comment.

Tony Buffolino came up and extended his hand. He was accompanied by his third wife, Alicia, a waitress he'd met at the Top of the Mark in San Francisco, where he, Smith, and Annabel had gathered while solving one phase in the murder of a presidential aide at the Kennedy Center. Afterward, Smith had got Buffolino a job as a security guard at the university. But Alicia came along with grander ideas. They now owned what Buffolino fondly referred to as the only Vegas-type cabaret in Washington, minus slot machines, of course.

"You did good, Mac," Buffolino said, in his best congratulatory style. Alicia kissed them on their cheeks. "Such a beautiful couple," she said.

"Frankly, I'm glad it's over," Smith said. He looked at Annabel. "You?"

"Frankly, I'm glad we've begun. Besides, I love weddings," Annabel said. "Maybe we could do this every couple of months. Don't forget, Mac, I've never been a bride before."

Father Singletary joined them. It was said that many women in the parish were in love with him. He was a tall, fine-looking man with a shrewd gentleness to his eyes and a wide, smiling mouth that women naturally responded to, a man self-assured without much—though with just a touch of—vanity. Singletary seemed, as Ralph Waldo Emerson had written, created of "God's handwriting." He took Smith's and Annabel's hands and grinned. "I was certain somebody would protest this marriage," he said.

"Who would protest it?" Smith asked.

"Me. I've been mad about this woman ever

since I met her." Singletary smiled down at Annabel. "I suppose the fact that you've chosen a lawyer rather than a man of God says something about you."

"In God we trust, all others pay cash," Annabel said.

"If this distinguished legal beagle doesn't work out, Annabel, call me," the priest said.

"Don't wait by the phone, Paul," said Annabel, laughing. "And thank you for making us one."

"My pleasure. Well, excuse me. I have a funeral to prepare for. The cycle of life."

"Birth and death," Tony Buffolino said, pleased that he was able to contribute to the conversation. He always felt awkward around clergymen.

"Yes," said Singletary. "And marriage and . . ."

"Divorce?" said Smith.

"Fortunately, the church doesn't have a ceremony for divorce," Reverend Singletary said. "Maybe someday. Or the rite of blessed separation." He laughed.

"Not for us, thank you," Annabel put in.

"Better not be," said Singletary. "If you do, find another priest."

"No divorce," Smith said. "No separations. Just ordinary, routine bliss." He hugged his wife.

"All best," Singletary said. "I'm off to do the funeral. Then London tonight. I have to go there often."

As the man who had married them walked away, Smith's thoughts returned to where they'd been at the beginning of the ceremony. Odd. He looked up at the graceful portal above the flight of broad steps leading to the cathedral's south entrance. The carved, dominant figure of Christ stood with His disciples at the Last Supper. Death? Resurrection? Fact or fiction? No matter, not if one believed—or didn't.

A black cloud crossed the sun.

Mac was glad they'd eschewed any suggestions of a party following the ceremony. He wanted them to be, as the song says, alone together.

"Come on, Mrs. Smith," he said, "let's go home."

chapter
2

Lambeth Palace, London—
Two Months Later. A Windy, Cold, and
Wet October Tuesday.
"Decent Day," the Locals Said.

The Reverend Canon Paul Singletary looked
up at the library's hammerbeam ceiling, then to
a faded, coarse beige-and-red tapestry that
covered much of one wall. On the tapestry was
the inwoven cross of the archbishop of Canterbury—*primus inter pares,* first among equals—
whose seat of power as head of the worldwide
Anglican Communion was the medieval
Lambeth Palace, to which Singletary had come
this late October afternoon.

A window on the west wall afforded a view
across the Thames to Westminster and its

Abbey, and to the Houses of Parliament. A twelfth-century primate had bought the land on which Lambeth Palace sat in order to be close—but not too close, God forbid—to the Crown.

Towering fuscous cumulonimbus clouds over Westminster unleashed a brief, brilliant shaft of white lightning as the door to the library opened and the Reverend Canon Malcolm Apt entered. Nice timing, Singletary thought. He sat in the chair and scrutinized Apt as he approached, not because he didn't know him, but because he always found Apt's face to be interesting. It was as though Apt's features had been pasted on the flat plane of his face slightly off-center, which created the effect of eyes, nose, and mouth out of alignment, pointing in a slightly different direction than the face itself. He wore a white surplice over a purple cassock; the cassock reached the floor. Apt was a short block of a man whose salt-and-pepper hair was the consistency of wire; he'd lost few wires in his fifty years.

Singletary stood without energy. "I didn't expect to be kept waiting this long," he said.

Apt ignored the comment and the tone in which it was delivered. "Come," he said, "we'll

talk in the archbishop's study." He led Singletary along the Great Corridor, where portraits of
all the archbishops from Victorian times hung,
then into a large, comfortably furnished room.
Apt went to the windows, looked out over the
river as though to assure himself it was still
there, and drew on a cord that caused heavy
drapes to slide closed with a soft whoosh.

"Well?" Singletary said.

"He won't be able to see you, I'm afraid."

"Are you serious?"

"Some people think I'm too serious."

Singletary looked at his watch; it was seven
o'clock. Seven peals of a church bell confirmed
it. "I've wasted my time then."

"If you choose to view it that way, Paul," Apt
said. "Sit down. The archbishop asked me to
discuss certain aspects of this with you."

Singletary was not interested in discussing
anything with Malcolm Apt. He'd wanted to see
the archbishop of Canterbury himself. Apt was
the archbishop's suffragan bishop, or VP in
charge of . . . well, public relations. At least
that's what his title would be in the secular,
business world. His official title was director of
church information.

Apt sat behind a highly polished cherrywood

table. Singletary sat across from him. Although dusk was starting to fall outside, the open drapes had permitted some light to enter. With them closed, the efficacy of the study's interior lighting seemed to have been diminished by half.

"Paul, the archbishop is growing increasingly concerned about this Word of Peace thing."

Singletary laughed crisply enough to make his point, but not enough to indicate disrespect to the archbishop of Canterbury. Apt continued, and Singletary knew that he was speaking words that had been carefully considered, perhaps even written prior to his arrival at the library. "You must understand that when the archbishop gave his support to Word of Peace, not a great deal was known about it. Frankly, I tried my best to dissuade him from involving us in it." Apt smiled—not much of a smile, but because it tended to stretch his mouth slightly, it enhanced the feeling that the paste-up job had been hasty. "I must admit that you were very effective when you presented the Word of Peace program to the archbishop. How long ago was that, Paul, a year?"

Singletary shrugged.

"Of course, there was the weight of the others with you, especially the African bishop. What's his name?" Apt asked it with seeming sincerity, but Singletary knew that Apt was well aware of the African bishop's name. He'd seen Apt do this before, degrade someone by pretending to have forgotten the name.

"Bishop Eastland."

"Ah, yes, Bishop Eastland. Certainly one of our high-visibility bishops. Nasty mess, that apartheid. We'll all be happy when that's resolved. How is Bishop Eastland?"

"Fine, and still fighting apartheid, according to what I read in the press."

"A most impressive man. As I was saying, the archbishop's enthusiasm for Word of Peace has waned, although he has not withdrawn his support. Has your Bishop St. James's enthusiasm back in Washington been sustained, or has it waned, too?"

"Heightened might be a more accurate way to describe it," Singletary said flatly.

Apt sat back and clasped his hands on his belly. "Heightened. Interesting."

"Malcolm, you said the archbishop wanted you to discuss something with me about Word of Peace. Is this it, that his enthusiasm has waned?"

"In a sense, yes, although there is more behind it. He is, of course, not only charged with the administration of the church; he is equally responsible for how we are viewed by others. That is also my particular responsibility, one I take very seriously. You will admit that some of those who have become involved with Word of Peace seem self-seeking, or political, and many are controversial at best, including yourself."

Singletary laughed again; this time it was more genuine, and with less concern for the archbishop. "Controversial? We pray each night to a highly controversial figure."

"Prayers are our leveling factor, Paul. What we do between prayers is another matter."

"You mean, of course, to what extent we become involved in . . ." He thought before finishing. "To what extent we become involved in things not very *churchy.*"

"I'd rather not be told what I mean, Paul, although that is your prerogative . . . and bent." Apt smiled.

They'd had this conversation before, especially since Singletary had become a conspicuous leader of the worldwide and nondenominational Word of Peace movement, in which the world's clergy were to use their collective weight and individual pulpits to spread the word of peace. Apt, and the archbishop of Canterbury, whose religious philosophy Apt shared (genuinely or because it was good for tenure? Singletary often wondered) were advocates of the Anglo-Catholic division of the church—the "Oxford movement"—archconservative (he was not called "*arch*bishop" for nothing, Singletary thought in a whimsical moment), rigid, authoritarian, puritanical, and intolerant of the more liberal wing that did not, in Anglo-Catholic eyes, adhere strictly enough to *Catholic* doctrine, of all things. They were *for* peace, to be sure, but not for disturbing it.

Singletary, on the other hand, was very much part of what was called the Broad Church (in political jargon, the Episcopal "liberal party"). There was also the so-called Evangelical movement, claiming to represent a middle ground of philosophy but firmly sin-based, Luther- and Calvin-influenced, and without much respect from either the conservative or the liberal wing of the church.

Word of Peace was a distinctly liberal movement, aggressively intermixed with Singletary's widely publicized work with drug addicts, runaway teens, the homeless, and a score of other social causes back in D.C. And nationally. Truth was, it was not those social causes but politics that prompted criticism of the Word of Peace movement. The movement stood for boycotting South Africa until it rid itself of apartheid, and for getting out of Ollie North's Central America and dissociating from its so-called freedom fighters. The olive branch in place of the B-1. Politics!

Singletary looked at his watch again. He said, "You know, Malcolm, you and I are both canons because we serve bishops and cathedrals. I will give you that your boss holds higher rank, but mine, George St. James, is not exactly, as some of my friends would say, 'chopped liver.' I would also remind you that in both Luke and Matthew Our Lord calls for the church to feed the hungry, clothe the naked, heal the sick, be the harbinger of comfort and caring and hope."

"I am familiar with Matthew and Luke."

"Wasn't it from the gate I entered this afternoon that the Lambeth dole was practiced?" Singletary frowned as he pulled from his memory the words " 'Every Friday and Sunday, unto every beggar that came to the door, a loaf of bread of a farthing price.' "

Apt stretched another thin smile.

"And you're also familiar with what Canon Casson told the executive council," Singletary said. "That the Gospel isn't believable unless the church relates to its neighborhoods—including the larger neighborhood called the planet."

"So endeth the lesson!" Apt stood. "I have another appointment."

"So do I. I'm already late."

"Safe journey home, Paul."

"Yes. Please tell the archbishop how disappointed I was not to be able to see him on this trip."

"You didn't come to London just to see him, did you?"

"You know I didn't. Still, first things first . . ."

"You'll be staying a few days?"

"One more day. I have a meeting tomorrow in your limpid countryside. Then back to Washington on Thursday."

Singletary picked up his black raincoat from the chair. Apt opened the study door. And began to accompany him. Singletary said, "It's okay, Malcolm, I know my Luke, Matthew, and the way out."

Singletary had been provided a car and driver by the London Word of Peace Committee for his visit to Lambeth Palace. It was at his disposal for the evening. He climbed in the back of the navy-blue Ford and gave the driver an address in Mayfair, near Berkeley Square. When they reached it, the driver slowed to read numbers. Singletary said, "This will be fine."

"Shall I wait?" the elderly British driver asked.

Singletary wrinkled his brow and pursed his lips in thought. "No, Bob, I think I'll be here awhile. I'll take a cab back to the hotel or walk. It isn't far. Thank you very much for your courtesy."

Singletary waited until the car had been driven away. Then, after looking left and right, he walked back to the corner of Charles Street and went up Davies Street. At number 418 he climbed the short set of steps and announced his arrival with three brisk raps of the brass knocker on the red door.

"Paul?" a voice asked from behind the door.

"Yes."

The door was opened by a tall and slender,

broad-shouldered woman of thirty-one. Clarissa Morgan possessed what Singletary considered a rare combination—black hair and eyes with milky-white skin. She wore pink silk lounging pajamas. "Come in," she said, her accent edged with a touch of Welsh clarity. "I was about to become worried."

Singletary stepped into the foyer, and she closed the door behind them. "He kept me waiting, didn't even see me," he said.

"Poor dear," she said, taking his coat. "Hardly the sort of behavior one would expect from the archbishop of Canterbury."

"Exactly what one would expect of *this* archbishop of Canterbury, considering the fact that he's to the right of Thomas Cartwright." Realizing that she didn't understand the reference, he muttered, "Another puritanical right-winger of the faith."

He walked into a small, tastefully decorated parlor and went directly to a cupboard, opened its doors, and pulled out a metal bottle of Danska. Clarissa came to his side carrying a bucket of ice. "You?" he asked as he put ice and the vodka into a glass and removed his jacket.

"I prefer wine."

They touched glasses and sat on a very contemporary-looking leather sofa, a jarring note in the midst of the room's antique furnishings. She touched his cheek with slender fingers tipped with nails the color of dusty roses, smiled, and said softly, "You look older when you're angry. Don't be angry, at least not to-night."

He managed to smile, downed half of his drink, and removed his clerical collar. "Where are we eating?"

Her voice now had a softer quality. "I thought we'd eat right here. If that's all right with you, of course." She looked into his eyes. "It *is* all right that we stay here, isn't it?"

His face said that the anger he'd felt since leaving Lambeth Palace was fading fast. "Yes, it's all right with me. Very all right. What are we having?"

She smiled and stood. "Cold tarragon chicken, a simple salad with raspberry dress-ing, rolls and butter, and a peach tart for des-sert. How . . . hungry are you? All of it will keep nicely. But will you? Will I? Do you know how sinfully handsome you are?"

He stood and embraced her. The smell of her hair and perfume filled his nostrils as he touched his lips to her neck. His hands slid slowly down her back. The only words spoken between them as they entered the bedroom came from Clarissa. "If you'd like to unleash a little bit of that controlled anger now, Reverend," she said, "I'd love it."

As the Reverend Canon Paul Singletary communed with Clarissa Morgan, the driver called Bob pulled up in front of the Red Lion pub in Mayfair. He told the barmaid that Mr. Leighton's car was waiting. She disappeared into the back dining room while Bob returned to the Ford. A few minutes later a tall, gray-haired gentleman with a Burberry raincoat neatly folded over the sleeve of his brown tweed suit left the pub. He carried an umbrella, and walked with an odd slight leaning to the left, as though too many years of toting a heavy briefcase had bent him that way. Bob opened the back door of the Ford, and the man got in.

"Home?"

"Yes."

After driving a block, Brett Leighton asked, "Well, did you take our clerical friend someplace interesting?"

"To the house in Mayfair with the red door. Actually, to a nearby address—but he walked to his final destination."

"Yes." Leighton smiled to himself. "A most beautiful altar at which to pray."

Bob said nothing.

"His plans?"

"He said he would be going out of town tomorrow."

"Out of town. You'll be driving him?"

"Not likely. The dispatcher said nothing about it."

"Let me know if you do."

"Of course, sir."

Bob dropped Leighton in front of a white townhouse in Belgravia. "Thank you, Bob," Leighton said.

"My pleasure," said the driver. "Will there be anything else tonight?"

Leighton handed Bob a sealed envelope, which, after Leighton had disappeared inside his house, the driver opened. He put the hundred-pound note in his pocket and drove to the Lamb and Flag on Rose Street in Covent Garden, a pub formerly known as the Bucket of Blood, where he ordered a clanger and a Directors bitter and joined his friends at a round corner table.

"Good day?" Eddie asked.

"A bloody bore 'cept for the traffic. I swear it gets worse every day," Bob said. "Can 'ardly see where you're going. Have to keep your eyes open for sure. Bloody Americans everywhere. No idea how to drive."

After eating his pastry roll of bacon, onion, and herbs, Bob considered leaving. His wife would be angry that he was late again, but what did she know? He deserved his relaxation, with the important work he did. Couldn't tell her. Just as well.

He bought the next round. And another. And the hundred-pound note became smaller in proportion to Bob's growing expansiveness.

chapter

3

The National Cathedral, Washington, D.C.— The Next Night, Wednesday

Joseph Kelsch idly pulled sheet music from a large pile on the table in front of him. The choir-boy knew there really wasn't any need to refile the music. Ordinarily, the cathedral's vast collection of religious music was meticulously maintained; Joey had been assigned the unnecessary task as punishment for having disrupted that afternoon's rehearsal of the boys' choir. What was especially annoying to him was that he was ten years old, it was nine o'clock at night, and he'd been told by the choirmaster, Canon Wilfred Nickelson, that he was to continue with this make-work until eleven, after which he'd surely be twenty years old, and which also meant he would be unable to partici- pate in the Ping-Pong contest that was going on at that moment back in the boys' dormitory. Joey was one of the better Ping-Pong players in the school and had advanced to the final round, the winner to be decided that evening. Canon Willy Nickelson has caused him to lose his opportunity to be the winner.

If Joey Kelsch, the boys' choir's finest young voice and biggest cutup, had been honest with himself, he would have admitted that the worst thing about his punishment was having to be alone in the choir room at night. He'd turned on all the lights. Still, there was something murkily forbidding about being here alone, about being alone *anywhere* in the vast cathedral after dark. Every sound was magnified and caused him to stiffen. His eyes darted from window to window. Thoughts of the tournament took his mind off his fears for a moment. That nerd Billy would probably win, now that Joey couldn't compete. A series of black thoughts about choirmaster Nickelson filled Joey's head as he lazily shuffled another piece of paper onto a pile. He was *better* at Ping-Pong than Billy. This wasn't fair. He hadn't done anything terrible during rehearsal, just talked too much after Nickel-Pickle had twice told him to stop.

As he sat at the long table in the choir room, Joey heard voices a few times when people passed in the hallway outside the door. He recognized Bishop St. James's rumble on one occasion, and he considered going into the hallway to voice a complaint to the bishop about his punishment. "The punishment doesn't fit the crime," he would say to St. James if he went into the hallway. He didn't; Bishop St. James was a nice man, but he would say, "I suggest you take this up with Reverend Nickelson."

Joey sighed and looked at a clock on the wall. Another whole hour and a half to go. Though he wasn't always on the side of the angels, in the soft, subdued light he resembled one. "Crap!" he muttered.

Across the hall from the choir room, behind the altar in the Bethlehem Chapel, which had been Mac and Annabel Smith's wedding site, a man stood in the shadows. He cocked his head at the sound of footsteps on the hard stone floor. They became louder, then stopped. A figure appeared at one side of the altar, paused, looked down at the vault in which the Right Reverend Henry Yates Satterlee, first bishop of Washington, and his wife, Jane Lawrence, had long ago been interred, looked up at an alabaster tomb bearing a recumbent likeness of Bishop Satterlee, and then, through narrowed eyes, peered at the man in the shadows. They began to talk, their tones low, their anger soon evident. The one who'd been second to enter the chapel closed the gap between them; they were only a few feet from each other now, their voices rising in intensity and volume, their words coming back at them in fragments off the hard walls.

"Ssssssh, keep your voice *down.*"

"You won't get away with this."

"How dare you . . . ?"

". . . too far. You went . . ."

The tall man who'd been in the shadows made a sound of disgust and began to walk toward the small door at the front of the chapel that led to the hall. The other quickly turned to the Satterlee vault. Two large, heavy brass candlesticks used during Communion services had been left there by a member of the Altar Guild; they would be polished the next day by another of the guild's devoted, reverent women.

A hand grabbed one of the candlesticks by its top. A few quick steps after the man from the shadows. The candleholder was raised in the air, then swung down and around in a wide, vicious, and accurate arc. As the base of the candlestick caught the man in his left temple, there was the sound of bone being crushed, followed by a low, pained moan when the man hit the stone floor as if driven into it like a flame-hardened nail.

Joey Kelsch stiffened as the noises from the chapel reached him. The choirboy had been listening, had heard only one voice, but not the other. He hadn't been able to make out the words, but he knew the speaker was very angry. Other people's anger was always frightening. Besides, he had heard enough of it from the choirmaster. Still, Joey went to the door that led to the corridor and pressed his ear to it, heard footsteps in an irregular pattern, heard laborious breathing, heard what sounded like something being dragged along the floor, a large sack of flour, maybe, or a big cardboard carton. The sounds faded in the direction of the stairs that led up to the north entrance to the cathedral, where the tiny Good Shepherd Chapel remained open twenty-four hours a day.

Joey carefully pushed the door out an inch; its hinges made some noise, but not much. He continued opening it until there was room for him to poke his head into the corridor. Looking to his left, he saw empty corridor. Looking to his right, he saw a figure, nothing more than a black shroud really. He thought it a statue until he saw that it was about to turn the corner and go up the stairs with whatever was being dragged behind.

Joey closed the door, felt his heart threatening to beat through his chest wall. He waited, unsure of what to do. Then he heard footsteps returning. The door was open just enough for him to peek through the crack. Now it was not just a form in the distance. There was, for a split second, a face. The hands belonging to the face were carrying two red hand-crocheted kneeling pads from the chapel, their faded renderings celebrating Bethlehem and the birth of the Baby Jesus.

The face returned to the Bethlehem Chapel and disappeared from Joey's field of vision.

Joey quietly pulled the door closed, tiptoed across the choir room, left through another door leading to the outside, and ran as fast as he could to his dormitory. Other students were finishing the Ping-Pong tournament in the room, but Joey didn't stop to join them. Trembling, he raced up the stairs, went into his room, quickly got into his pajamas, climbed into bed, panting, and pulled the covers over his head.

Until then, he hadn't cried.

chapter

4

The Next Morning,
Which Would Be Thursday

Although the sunrise was only a suggestion,
the Right Reverend George St. James, bishop
of Washington and dean of the National Cathedral, had already completed his daily contemplative stroll, had ridden his stationary bike, and
had said his morning prayers. Now, as he
stepped from the shower and vigorously began
drying himself, he focused on the day ahead.

The major event was to be the funeral of
Adam Vickery, a former attorney general of the
United States, scheduled for nine o'clock in the
cathedral's nave. Vickery and his wife, Doris,

had been active in cathedral affairs for many years. Vickery had sat on the cathedral's chapter—its "board of directors"—for the past seven years, and as head of the building fund had received deserved accolades for his deft handling of it. His death had been sudden and unexpected. Seemingly in the best of health, he'd been found slumped inertly over his desk three nights before, the victim, apparently, of a massive coronary.

Now toweled dry, the bishop looked at his naked image in a full-length mirror in the rectory's second-floor master bedroom. The enticing aroma of coffee drifted up from the kitchen. St. James heard his wife, Eileen, singing along with a popular song of another decade that came from a radio, a song the bishop began to hum although he couldn't put a title to it. His wife would know the title *and* the words and carry the tune. He looked at himself in the mirror again and smiled; God had a reason for everything, even personal tragedy and sociological disaster, but what could possibly have been on His mind when He—okay, or *She,* the bishop reminded himself—decreed that in middle age weight must settle in the midsection? St. James was the same weight he'd been while attending the Yale Divinity School almost thirty years before, but the same number of pounds had found an unwelcome redistribution center between his chest and his hips. Maybe I'd better start riding more of it off—or up—on the bicycle that goes nowhere, he thought.

He dressed, joined Eileen in the kitchen, kissed her cheek, and ate the scrambled eggs and dry toast she'd set before him. *The Washington Post* was beside his plate at the table. No need to look for the Religion section; it wasn't Saturday. Then again, politics was the city's religion, and there was always plenty of *that* in the *Post* each day. Which was not to say that religion—the spiritual variety—didn't play a role in the nation's capital. Lord knows there were enough prayer breakfasts every morning in Washington to save a regiment of souls. Prayer breakfasts in the White House were very much in vogue with the new administration, and the Cabinet, the House, the Senate, myriad governmental agencies, and even the military kicked off their days with a few words to a Higher Authority.

St. James had once delivered a sermon based upon the theory that religion played less of a role in Washington than in almost any other

city in the world. He used the numerous guidebooks to Washington as an example, pointing
out that they scarcely mentioned the city's religious life, and suggested that an interdenomi-
national committee be formed to encourage
better coverage in future editions. Nothing ever
came of it, which did not surprise him.

What really bothered him (although he did
not give a sermon on this) was that Washington's churches were usually better known for
whom they attracted rather than for the quality
of salvation being offered. President John F.
Kennedy virtually put St. Matthew's Cathedral
"on the map" because of his frequent attendance there, and because it was where his funeral Mass had been conducted.

Directly across from the White House, on La-
fayette Square, stood St. John's Episcopal
Church, known as the "Church of the Presidents" because virtually every American president showed up there at least once, including
Gerald Ford, who privately and understandably
asked for divine wisdom while contemplating a
pardon for Richard Nixon. Nixon, of course, enjoyed having the church and clergy come to
him at the White House, as opposed to Presidents Carter and Truman, who frequently

prayed at the First Baptist Church, only a few minutes' walk from the White House.

Teddy Roosevelt had worshiped at Grace Reform Church, but his wife and her family went to St. John's Episcopal. Grace Reform rewarded TR's allegiance by creating a collection of memorabilia from the Roosevelt White House. St. John's did not create such a memorial for the rest of his family.

The Eisenhowers preferred worshiping at the National Covenant Presbyterian Church, which lost its location to a modern office building and was moved to new ground near American University, where tourists could browse its Chapel of Presidents.

Of course, there had been the snide references to *Christian* Dior, cattily referred to as First Lady Nancy Reagan's religion. St. James had thought that a cheap shot, but had laughed when first hearing it.

Churches everywhere, he mused, but only throwaway mentions of them in the guidebooks. A pagan city, if one used the travel literature as one's criterion.

He scanned the *Post*'s front page, was more thorough as he went through the Style section, finished his second cup of coffee, and kissed his wife good-bye on the other cheek. "I'll be home this afternoon," he said. "I need some quiet time to work on the presentation." He was to address the National Association of Asphalt Contractors that night—he gave many such speeches in the continuing process of raising money for the cathedral's building fund. What had begun for him as a quest for God too often translated into a quest for checks. It seemed never to end, this need for money. The cathedral, sixth largest in the world, was an insatiable devourer of cash, its completion so near yet so far away; just another ten thousand for an additional gargoyle, forty thousand to reinforce a corbel in the north entrance, a hundred thousand to repair water damage in the Children's Chapel. Adam Vickery would be missed, St. James reflected. Despite his unpleasant demeanor, Vickery knew how to shake money loose.

The bishop strode with purpose across the fifty-seven-acre close and looked up at the Gloria in Excelsis Tower soaring more than three hundred feet into the cerulean October sky. Given its supporting hill, the tower was the highest structure in Washington, so inspiring, so majestic, and so expensive. St. James felt good, but he always felt good in the early morning. Morning was the time his internal clock ticked at optimum speed. By the time he addressed the asphalt contractors, his clock would have slowed, and he'd have to wind it up a little to make it through. How much he disliked having to ask for money! Praying for it was one thing; asking was another.

A group of men milled about the south entrance. One of them, Idris Porter, chief of the Washington Cathedral Police, was leaning against his white Ford Bronco talking to a man whom the bishop didn't recognize. The man was bulkier than Porter, and wore a gray suit.

"Good morning, Idris," St. James said. "Ready bright and early I see."

"Yes, Bishop," Porter said with a smile. He was a very dark black man with sparse, unruly gray hair. "Bishop, this is Agent Lazzara, Secret Service."

"Good morning," St. James said, extending his hand. Security at the cathedral for events such as Vickery's funeral necessitated the involvement of other agencies besides the cathedral's small security force. Which agencies, and the number of personnel assigned, depended upon many factors—anticipated crowd size, the deceased's position and level of controversy, rumors, threats. There hadn't been any threats regarding the funeral as far as St. James knew. When attorney general, Adam Vickery had been controversial, as most attorneys general are, considering that they're appointed more for past political favors and fund-raising than for legal insight, but controversy hadn't followed him into private life.

"Nice day," Lazzara said.

For a funeral, St. James suspected Lazzara was thinking. "Yes," the bishop said. "How many agents will be here?"

Porter, who was always a little disgruntled when his domain was intruded upon by other officials, answered with curt, controlled precision: "A dozen from the Secret Service uniformed force, four plainclothes, nine MPD officers. FBI is supposed to have six men assigned, too."

"Well, it looks like with you all, including the Metropolitan Police, we're all safe for another day," the bishop said, a chuckle in his voice. "Glad you're here." He bounded up the steps and entered the cathedral's south transept. To his immediate right was the War Memorial Chapel, dedicated to the men and women who'd lost their lives in defense of the country. St. James entered it, looked for a moment at a huge needlepoint tapestry called "Tree of Life" on which the seals of the fifty states were done in petit point, then continued through another door leading into the Children's Chapel, his favorite of the cathedral's nine chapels.

"Suffer the little children to come unto me," he said softly, looking at a reredos of carved wood overlaid with gold portraying Jesus when he'd spoken those words. Children and small four-legged animals, the most vulnerable and dependent of all creatures. Everything in the Children's Chapel was child-size—a small organ, scaled-down seats and low altar, miniature needlepoint kneeling pads featuring family pets and wild beasts, including those that had boarded Noah's Ark. A statue of the Christ Child stood near the entrance, its arms open wide in welcome. St. James did what he almost always did upon entering the chapel. He took the Christ Child's extended bronze fingers in his own and squeezed, as thousands of visiting children did each year. The statue itself had burnished with age, but the rubbing of so many tiny hands kept the fingers bright and shiny, a glow from children to Child. The bishop went to the altar, genuflected, gave thanks for the glory of another day of service, and crossed the cathedral to the narrow, winding stone steps just inside the north entrance and across from the Good Shepherd Chapel. A sign at the foot of the steps said CLERGY; an arrow pointed up. Good direction, he thought once again, and took the steps two at a time.

He'd no sooner entered the bishop's dressing room and closed the door behind him when there was a knock. He opened the door to admit one of his canons, Jonathon Merle. "Good morning, Jonathon."

"Good morning, Bishop," Merle said dourly, in a tone which mirrored his general personality. The canon was considerably taller than the bishop, his body lean and angular. His face matched his body; hawklike, eyes sunken and ringed with puttylike flesh, nose a bit of a beak. His face had an overall grayness to it that went perfectly with the rest of him. A sincere man but, sadly, a somewhat sour one.

"Everything in order?" St. James asked, referring to preparations that would be taking place downstairs for the funeral.

"Yes, I think so." The Bishop would be present during the ceremony, but Father Merle would conduct the service.

"Is Father Singletary back?" St. James asked absently.

"He's due tonight, I think," Merle said.

"I wonder how his meeting with the archbishop went." St. James said it not so much because he wondered what the answer would be but because he knew any mention of Paul Singletary nettled Jonathon. That these two canons disliked each other was no secret, and while St. James did what he could to keep their mutual animosity from getting in the way of cathedral business, there were times when he took a certain private delight in the conflict. The truth was that he, too, disliked Father Merle, a failing for which he often asked forgiveness during his prayers. He was confident that Merle had no inkling of his feelings, thank the Lord. The canon's devotion to God and to his priestly duties at the cathedral were indisputable. If those criteria were ever foremost in the bishop's mind, it would be Singletary's devotion he would question, not Merle's. The problem with Canon Merle was his personality, or lack of it. A rigid, dogmatic, and humorless champion of the church's conservative element, he had little patience with those who did not embrace his views. Heading that list was the Reverend Paul Singletary.

"What did you think of the article last Saturday?" St. James asked as he disappeared behind a folding screen. The article in the Religion section of *The Washington Post* was an update about the Word of Peace movement, to which Bishop St. James and the cathedral had pledged considerable support. There was no answer from Merle. "Did you hear me, Jonathon?"

"Yes. I didn't think very much of it."

"Really? What did you find lacking?" He knew the answer; a considerable portion of the article dwelt upon Singletary, and a picture of the handsome liberal priest dominated the page. The photo had been taken in an AIDS hospice in the Adams Morgan district that had been established through Singletary's untiring fund-raising efforts.

"It misrepresents the purpose of this church," said Merle.

"Interesting," the bishop said as he came out from behind the screen. "What *is* the mission of this church?" He was instantly sorry he'd asked. These conversations usually went nowhere; Merle would deliver a sermon on the spot. The bishop sometimes thought he himself had become a missionary cause for Merle, a potential convert to the canon's view of the Anglican role in the world.

Merle said, "You'll forgive my impudence, Bishop, but it has been my concern from the beginning that the lofty and holy purposes of this cathedral could be tarnished by overinvolvement with the Word of Peace."

"Why would I consider you impudent, Jonathon, for raising such a thought this morning? You've been saying it with some regularity for over a year."

"My concerns grow each day," Merle said gravely. "I find some of the leaders of the movement to be distasteful. I find the movement itself, despite its professed aims, to be distasteful." His usual pinched voice became more so.

"You find seeking peace in this world to be distasteful?"

There was silence, and St. James realized he had gone too far. He smiled broadly and said, "It is to my benefit and this cathedral's as well that we have Father Jonathon Merle to keep his eye on the till and his hand on the tiller. Perhaps we should discuss Word of Peace in a less busy, more contemplative atmosphere. In fact, I would be delighted to have dinner with you this evening, Jonathon, just the two of us. I've been thinking a great deal lately about China. More specifically, I've been craving Chinese food for a week. We can indulge my craving and spend some quiet, focused time discussing this." He clapped Merle on the arm.

The canon did not smile or respond to the invitation. Instead, he said in the same sober voice, "I think it's time for the reins to be pulled in on Father Singletary."

St. James had heard this comment before, too. "Could be you're right, Jonathon, although you must admit that Father Singletary's seemingly inexhaustible energy when it comes to helping the sick and the poor invites a rather positive image of our ministry. Wouldn't you say?"

"He seeks only his self-grandiosity, not the glory of the church."

St. James laughed and said, "I know, I know, Paul Singletary has a remarkable gift for—and interest in—self-promotion. He *is* grandiose at times, and seems to have a great deal of trouble practicing the sort of humility that we are expected to demonstrate. Still, as Hooker said, let us not attempt to unscrew the inscrutable. Tonight, Jonathon, I'll treat you to hot-and-sour soup and General Tsao's chicken. Shall we make it the Oriental Gourmet? My goodness, even talking about it has my mouth watering. Eileen has a meeting and—" He slapped his forehead. "Oh, sorry, I can't do it tonight. I have to talk to a business group. A raincheck? Meanwhile, Jonathon, let's get on with the business of the day—namely, to bury Adam Vickery. I think it's fitting that you conduct the service. You and he were quite close, shared common views."

"Well, not close, but we saw many things eye-to-eye."

"I'll see you downstairs," said the bishop.

Merle left, leaving St. James to put on a purple cassock, over which he slipped a white rochet with embroidery at the bottom. A black silk chimere with white lawn sleeves and cuffs came next; his stole hung straight down from his neck, befitting his status as a bishop. A pectoral cross rested comfortably on his chest. As he donned these holy garments, his thoughts were less than holy. There was no escaping politics, not even in the house God built. Even early in his career, when he was a simple parish priest, there had been the squabbles between parishioners, some seeking God, some seeking ego-gratification, others looking for the enhanced possibility of salvation through increased influence in church matters. As he rose through the ranks, political considerations had increased proportionately. He'd become the National Cathedral's bishop and dean after serving as suffragan, or assistant bishop, to the previous bishop, John Walker, a brilliant and passionate black man who seemed to walk easily between the lofty demands of his position and the humbler demands of using the nation's house of worship to feed the hungry, clothe the poor, and minister to the sick in the ghettos of the capital. A simple devotion to Christ was not enough, not in the nation's church in the most politically fueled city in the world, Washington, D.C. Politics! The least pleasant aspect of his duties, although he knew he was good at it; St. James had learned much about the art of negotiation and diplomacy from Bishop John Walker.

The bishop frowned as he gave himself a final check in the mirror, not because of what he saw but because of the invitation he'd extended to Merle. Now he'd have to go through with it another night. An evening with Jonathon over a Chinese meal was like the old joke, he thought, a contest in which the winner received one week in Philadelphia, the second-place winner two weeks. He looked up, crossed himself, and said with a wry smile on his face, "I do this only for You." *And because I do like hot-and-sour,* he added silently. Come to think of it, that describes my two canons.

As he opened the door and prepared to descend the steps, he thought of a dinner he'd had a month ago with Mac Smith and Annabel Reed, now Mr. and Mrs. Mackensie Smith. He'd been away from Washington when Paul Singletary celebrated Mac's marriage to the beautiful redheaded woman with whom Mac had been intimately involved for some years. The first thing St. James had done upon returning was to call and invite them to dinner. He wished Smith would be willing to take on a more active role with the cathedral chapter now that Adam Vickery was gone. Smith, like Vickery, was an attorney, which gave him a unique way of looking at problems. As the bishop started down the stairs, he realized he'd never met anyone who had Mac Smith's innate ability to be involved with so many people and so many things, yet maintain a safe distance from all of them. A lawyer. A very good lawyer—and, oh yes, a professor.

St. James had rounded the final turn and was about to step into the north entrance's foyer when the scream erupted, reverberating off the cold stone walls, ceilings, and floors. He stopped and felt his stomach tighten. Screaming again; a woman, close by. St. James swung to his right; the shrill, piercing voice seemed to be coming from only a short distance away—from the Good Shepherd. He went to the door and looked in.

Three two-person pews were empty. He stepped inside and looked left, to the small altar upon which a tiny vase of wilted flowers stood in front of the Salisbury pink granite sculpture of Christ cradling a lamb in His arms. Standing there was a woman, her eyes wide with fright, her screams now reduced to smaller sounds of anguish and pain. She was trying to speak, but the words were caught in her throat. She turned and stared down to a pew just large enough for one person, and almost hidden from St. James's view from the door. The bishop saw an arm. Another step and he saw more of the figure slouched in the pew. A crude sign taped on the stone wall directly in front of the body said PLEASE NO SMOKING.

The woman started to scream again. St. James held up his hand against the noise, put his hand on her shoulder, and took a final step that allowed him a full view of the occupied pew.

"My God," he said as his eyes fixed upon the crushed skull and lifeless body of the Reverend Canon Paul Singletary.

chapter 5

That Same Morning—A Splendid, Sunny, Temperate October Day

Mac Smith returned from a brisk walk with Rufus. He steered the Great Dane into the kitchen and set about squeezing two glasses of orange juice, heard the shower going, heard Annabel singing "When You Wish Upon a Star," which seemed to have become her favorite tune to lather by since their wedding. Prior to that she'd been partial to Gilbert and Sullivan and the Beatles. Good: he preferred the Disney song.

Smith was about to take a sip of juice when the phone rang. He glanced at the kitchen clock—7:10. Early for a casual caller. He headed for his small study at the rear of his—their—house in Foggy Bottom, which he'd shared until recently only with Rufus.

"Mac, it's George St. James."

"Good morning, Bishop," Mac said. "You're doing God's work early. What prompts a call at this hour?"

St. James sighed before he said in a low, breathy tone, "Mac, a terrible thing has happened here this morning." Before Smith could ask, St. James said, "Paul has been murdered."

"Run that past me again, George."

"Paul Singletary has been murdered. Right here in the cathedral. I found his body a half hour ago."

"Christ! I just saw him . . . well, no, it was August, but he married us."

"I know, Mac. It's a dreadful shock. I can't begin to tell you how terrible, to, find his body . . ."

"Where?"

"In the cathedral. In the Good Shepherd Chapel."

"The tiny one."

"Yes."

"How was he killed? How do you know it was murder?"

"The side of his head is bashed in. Someone struck him a wicked blow."

"*You* found the body?"

"Yes. Well, a woman actually did."

"What woman?"

"I don't know her name. She's distraught, beside herself. I have her here with me in my dressing room."

"Have you called the police?" Smith asked.

"No. I wanted to speak to you first."

"George, I think the police should have been first on your list."

"Please, Mac, can you come here right away? I want to explore things with you before I call the authorities."

"What about the cathedral's legal counsel?"

"They're money lawyers, Mac. You've had experience with criminal matters. I know this is an imposition, but . . ."

"I'll be there as quickly as I can. Annabel and I were getting ready for breakfast before coming to Adam Vickery's funeral. I'll tell her."

"Don't mention this to her, Mac. Not to anyone until we've talked."

"George, this can't be kept a secret." Smith

didn't want to sound annoyed, but his voice reflected what he was feeling at that moment. "Who else have you told?"

"No one. I pushed a piece of furniture up against the chapel's door."

"The body is still in there?"

"Yes."

"You'll be in your office?"

"Yes, I . . . no. Can you meet me in the Bishop's Garden?"

Smith looked at a clock on his desk. "I'll be there in twenty minutes. But you should call the police."

He hung up and stuck his head into the bathroom, where Annabel was drying her hair, a huge pink towel wrapped around her nakedness. "Who called?" she asked.

"George St. James. I'm heading for the cathedral now to meet with him. We'll have to scrap breakfast."

"Why?" she asked.

"There's been a . . . an accident at the cathedral. George wants to discuss it with me . . . from a legal point of view. I said I'd meet him in twenty minutes."

"What kind of accident?"

Smith looked into her large green eyes and

had a sudden burst of recognition, which had been happening with some regularity since the wedding. They *were* married. She *was* his wife. No secrets. Right? Right! "Look, Annabel, this will be a shock, but Paul Singletary is dead."

She slumped back on a stool, the hair dryer blowing hot air on her feet. "Paul? How? What happened?"

No secrets. "He's been murdered. Somebody hit him in the head, at least according to George. He's . . . he's dead."

"I'll be ready in ten minutes," she said, standing and redirecting the hot air at her thick, wet red hair.

"No. Right now, George is concerned about people knowing, for some reason. It's got to come out, of course. I'm meeting him privately, in the Bishop's Garden. You hang out here, take any other phone calls, and meet me at the back of the cathedral at quarter of nine, near the statue of George Washington."

"Mac, I . . . You're not going to get involved in another—"

"Please. I've told you all I know. I'll do better at quarter of nine."

Smith drove his blue Chevy Caprice up Wisconsin Avenue and stopped at Church House

Road, the first small access road to the cathedral close. He saw the gathering of security people, and decided to continue on Wisconsin until reaching another road that would take him to the north side of the cathedral, where there should be less activity. He parked in a designated visitors' space and walked briskly around the North Cloister and the administration building, turned right, the College of Preachers on his left, and followed the road south past the library and the deanery until reaching the Norman Arch, the main visitors' entrance to the lovely Bishop's Garden. He paused and looked back; a Cathedral Police white Ford Bronco, its yellow lights flashing on top, sped by. Had the bishop changed his mind and informed the authorities? Smith hoped so.

He didn't know where in the gardens George St. James would be waiting, but decided to head for the Rose Garden, where floribundas and hybrid tea roses would be in full bloom in Washington's mild October weather. His hunch was right. St. James, now dressed in simple clerical collar and black suit, stood at the end of the Rose Garden beneath an old pear tree. Next to him, surrounded by rare Kingsville dwarf box, stood Heinz Warneke's statue of the

Prodigal Son. The scent of roses hung thick in the still morning air.

St. James spotted Smith and waved him over, as though directing the relocation of a piece of heavy furniture.

They shook hands. What had happened that morning was written all over the bishop's face. It was drawn and sallow, a pleading quality in his ordinarily bright blue eyes. "Thank you for coming," he said.

"I saw some activity," Smith said. "Did you change your mind, notify the police?"

St. James shook his head. "I told you I wanted to wait until—"

"All right, tell me again what occurred this morning."

St. James quickly recapped the events, culminating with the discovery of Singletary's body in the Good Shepherd Chapel.

"Who is the woman who found him?"

"I don't know her name. Eileen is with her in my dressing room."

"Eileen knows?"

"Yes, I had to tell her. I mean, she is my wife."

"Of course. . . . I understand. When did you last see Paul?" Smith asked.

"A few days ago, just before he left for London." St. James stopped, as though having been struck by a revelation. "He wasn't due back in Washington until today."

"Looks like he cut his stay short. George, you do know that we must advise the authorities and do it now."

"Can't we wait a few hours, at least until the Vickery funeral is over?"

"Why do that? What would that accomplish?"

St. James let out an exasperated sigh and turned away, took a few steps, then turned again. "I don't know, Mac," he said, "it just seems to me that a few hours wouldn't matter. A funeral is about to be held here of a man who has been important to this cathedral. Does it have to be interrupted by police sirens and television crews?"

Smith jammed his hands in his pockets and looked at the ground before saying, "One, there is always disruption when someone is murdered, whether it's in this cathedral or elsewhere. Two, it is illegal to withhold from the police the fact that a murder has been committed. Three, to postpone notification not only puts you and the cathedral in a bad light, it could have an adverse influence on the eventual investigation. No, George, the time to tell them is now."

St. James's mind seemed to wander into a less tangible realm. He spoke not to Smith but to an unseen person: " 'Puts the cathedral in a bad light.' That's what I want so desperately to avoid."

Smith said brusquely, "The light is going to shine here whether you want it to or not, George, and it's going to be a lot hotter if you don't do the right thing and do it now."

Smith's hard words snapped the bishop back to the garden. He nodded. "Yes, of course you're right, Mac. That's why I called you. I knew you would know the right thing to do, and would see to it that I did it. Is it possible . . . well, I also wondered: would *you* call the police and ask them if they could be as discreet as possible while the funeral is going on?"

St. James's concern for the funeral irritated Smith, but he didn't vent it. He simply said, "Yes, I'll call them now."

Smith followed the bishop across the gardens, through the Norman Arch and into the cathedral and the hallway outside the door of the Good Shepherd Chapel. A large armoire had been pushed against it. A scribbled sign hung from it: CLOSED FOR REPAIRS. Smith stifled a wry smile. What could possibly have been running through the bishop's head to go to this trouble? Confusion, obviously, and some well-meaning fear—more likely *hope*—that the reality of it could be postponed indefinitely. But sealing off the chapel would help the investigation.

"He's in there, exactly as you found him?" Smith asked, his eyes fixed upon the armoire.

"Yes. Maybe you should take a look before you make your call, Mac."

Mac silently debated it, then decided to do it quickly. "You said the woman screamed. Didn't anyone else hear her?"

"Yes, a parishioner looking for a bathroom, but I said someone had fallen, twisted her ankle."

"And with Security people within earshot, no reaction?"

"Not that I know of. They were all outside, at some distance. Sound sometimes travels here; sometimes it's, well, buried."

Smith looked left and right, pushed the armoire, and slid it far enough so that he could squeeze through into the tiny chapel. St. James stayed outside as Smith took the few steps to the pink granite altar. A window was open; Smith looked out onto the garth and its flowing fountain before turning and looking down on the body of Paul Singletary. "Jesus," he muttered, glancing up quickly at the sculpture above the altar of the Good Shepherd holding the baby lamb. Feeling sickened and saddened, Smith forced himself to do what he perceived at that moment to be his duty. He looked once again at Singletary, leaned forward to more closely examine the wound on the side of the slain priest's head. It hadn't been a flat object that killed him. The murder weapon obviously had a sharp and heavy edge to it, judging from the way the skull was cut open.

Smith came out of the chapel and joined the bishop in the hallway. "Horrible. Shall I call from your office?"

"No, upstairs, right above here. My dressing room."

Eileen St. James was nervously pacing the floor when they entered. "Eileen, Mac Smith is here," St. James said.

She spun on her heel and had the look of someone reacting to a very loud and sudden sound. "Oh, Mac, yes! George said he had called you."

St. James said, "Where is the woman?"

"She left."

"Left?" St. James and Smith said in unison.

"I couldn't stop her. She kept crying and moaning. I went to get some towels and cold water. When I returned, she was gone."

"Damn!" Smith said.

"Did she ever tell you who she was?" the bishop asked.

His wife shook her head.

Smith sat at the desk, his hand poised over the telephone. He looked up at the bishop and his wife and said, "Now look. No matter what happens, you must promise to be totally honest with the authorities. Whatever problems this may cause the cathedral can't be helped and will soon pass."

"The press will have a field day with this," St. James said. "One of our own, probably our most visible priest, murdered right here in the National Cathedral. I can't believe it."

"I had trouble believing it, too, until I saw the damage done to Paul's head." Smith's hand rested on the telephone. He looked at them before picking up the receiver and putting it to his ear. Before he could punch in the number of Washington's MPD Homicide Division—a number he'd never forgotten from his days as a lawyer who had handled many criminal cases—the sound of sirens was heard outside.

Smith slowly lowered the receiver into its cradle. "I think someone beat us to it."

chapter
6

Minutes Later—Clouds Moving In

Mac Smith went outside. Six Washington MPD squad cars had arrived; they'd parked in pairs outside the three main entrances to the cathedral, their uniformed officers fanning out over the cathedral close. An unmarked car had also arrived, and Smith recognized one of the men getting out of it. Chief of Homicide Terrence Finnerty was a lean-cheeked, wiry little man with a nasty cast to his face, and once-yellow hair discolored with age. He wore a cheap green raincoat, and black shoes sufficiently scuffed to make you notice them. The two other detectives who followed were bulky, heavy men. The black man carried a two-way radio, the white man a notepad. As Finnerty came up the steps leading to the south entrance, he spotted Smith and said in what could pass for a near-falsetto, "Mackensie Smith. I didn't know you were a daily communicant."

"Only on special occasions," Smith said. "The funeral of a friend of mine is taking place this morning." It wasn't true that Adam Vickery was a friend. Smith and Vickery had certainly known each other well enough when Vickery was attorney general and Mackensie Smith was Washington's most respected and successful criminal attorney. But it wasn't friendship. Smith had found Vickery to be shrewd, tough, and unpleasant. Compounding that evaluation was Smith's conviction that Vickery was not the most honest of men, and that the conflict-of-interest charges leveled at him had sufficient substance to ensure that had they been aggressively pursued, the result could well have been a finding of actual conflict, not just the appearance of conflict that had become a popular rationale for the sleazy behavior of some public officials. Still, Mac Smith had his reasons for attending the funeral, including the adages "Once you're dead, all bets are off" and "Everyone is entitled to be remembered for his best work."

Smith glanced at the squad cars and their uniformed occupants. "Heavy artillery, Terry?"

"Got a call about a murder here. Know anything about it?"

"Yes."

Smith's abrupt answer caused Finnerty's face to tighten. A muscle in his right cheek pulsated, and his small black eyes narrowed. "Tell me about it. Why didn't you call?"

"We were about to. Who called you?" Smith asked.

"Anonymous female."

"What did she tell you?"

"Hey, Mac, I ask, you answer. Who got it?"

Smith motioned for Finnerty to follow him up the steps and into the cathedral. The other two detectives followed. Smith stopped and said to Finnerty, "Have them wait outside for a few minutes." Finnerty obviously wasn't sure whether to honor Smith's request, but he did, holding up his hand to halt the progress of his colleagues.

Smith led Finnerty through the transept and into the empty War Memorial Chapel. "What the hell am I about to get, confession?" Finnerty asked.

"Not unless you need it. Look, the funeral of Adam Vickery, the former attorney general, is about to start. A priest, named Paul Singletary, has been found murdered. Somebody put something heavy to the side of his head."

"Singletary? The do-gooder?"

"The same. The bishop is concerned that this place not be turned into a zoo while the funeral is going on. Can you give orders to your officers to be less conspicuous? I'll take you to the body and to the bishop. Once the funeral is over, the place is yours."

"Give me a break, Mac. You're telling me that this priest gets wasted here in the Washington Cathedral, and I'm supposed to ice it until Vickery gets planted?" His laugh was silly. "Vickery ain't going to know what's going on."

"But his family will. Look, Terry, do what you want, but if you find it necessary to play war games for the TV cameras, count me out. I'm just a parishioner grieving at a friend's funeral. I know nothing about murder. Nice to see you again." Smith started to walk away.

"All right," Finnerty said, "as long as you and I move on this now. Wouldn't look good to sit through a funeral while a murdered priest lays around, but I'll do my best to keep things quiet until the funeral's over. It ever occur to you that the murderer could still be here?" Smith pointedly ignored the question, and Finnerty sensed his annoyance. "Okay, Mac, we'll move as quiet as possible. But we have to move."

"Good. This is, after all, a place of worship," Smith said, not proud of himself.

Finnerty went back and told his detectives to brief the uniforms while they began to look around and to guard exits. He then fell in with Smith and they walked across the nave toward the north transept and Good Shepherd Chapel. They'd almost reached it when a television crew—a cameraman with a large VTR on his shoulder, a sound man wielding a microphone, and a black woman reporter, Rhonda Harrison, with whom Smith had been friendly since she arrived in Washington eight years before— came through the north entrance. Rhonda flashed Smith a large, warm smile. To Finnerty she nodded: "Detective Finnerty." The smile was gone.

"Hello, Rhonda, how are you?" said Smith.

"Who was murdered?" she asked. A powerful light on top of the VTR came to life and flooded Smith, Finnerty, and Rhonda in blinding white light.

"Turn that thing off," Finnerty said.

"Can't talk this minute, Rhonda," Smith said.

"Come on, Mac, what's going on?"

"Later, Rhonda. Sorry. Come on," he said to Finnerty.

Two of the cathedral's uniformed security police had just entered through the north doors. Smith stopped them. "I'm Mac Smith, and this is Detective Terry Finnerty. There's been a problem here this morning, and I'm representing the bishop in this matter." He turned and saw the television crew approaching. "Keep those people out of this area until you're told otherwise." He could see ambivalence on their faces. One of them said, "I'll check with Captain Porter."

"Go ahead, but one of you keep that crew out of here."

As the remaining cathedral cop moved to block the TV crew, Smith led Finnerty past the armoire and into the Good Shepherd Chapel. "There he is, Terry. We were friendly. He married my wife and me a couple of months ago."

Finnerty glanced at Smith and smiled. "I didn't know you got hitched."

"It was time," Smith said.

"So she said, I'll bet."

Finnerty approached Singletary's body and bent down. He screwed up his face as he leaned to within inches of the wound. "Didn't bleed much," he said, more to himself than to Smith.

"I noticed that, too," said Smith.

"Any idea how long he's been here?"

"No. The body was discovered by a woman an hour or so ago."

Finnerty looked up from his kneeling position next to the body. "An hour ago? Jesus! What woman?"

Smith shrugged. "She came in here, probably to pray, discovered the body, and started screaming. The bishop heard the screams and came in. He took her to his dressing room upstairs and called his wife to come over and stay with her. She's disappeared."

"Who?"

"The woman who discovered the body."

"Wonderful. How come?"

"The bishop's wife went to get some . . . It doesn't matter. She's gone."

"Wonderful."

Finnerty touched Singletary's eyelids and

lower jaw. "He's pretty rigid. He didn't get it this morning, more like last night. We'll get a better fix on it at the autopsy." He stood and stretched. "Who has access to this chapel?"

"The world, I think. It's open twenty-four hours a day."

"It is? Just this chapel, or the whole cathedral?"

"I think just this chapel, although you can confirm that with the bishop."

Finnerty shook his head and looked out the open window onto the garth and its large, abstract, siliconed bronze fountain. "Where is the bishop?" he asked, his words mingling with the gurgling water from the fountain and the faint, sweet sound of choristers rehearsing.

"Upstairs with his wife."

"Let's go, before she disappears," Finnerty said.

Smith led him up the narrow stone stairs to the clergy's rooms and into the one reserved for Bishop St. James. After Smith made the introductions, Finnerty said, "Mac told me you wanted to keep this quiet for a while, Bishop. I can't do that. I got to move my men in right now, get Forensic over here. There may be a funeral for a dead big shot, but my concern is the dead guy—sorry, Reverend—downstairs."

St. James nodded. "Yes, of course, I understand. I just thought—"

"Yeah, yeah, I know what you thought, but it can't be. Smith asked us not to make a circus of it, and we'll try. What about this woman who found the body?"

Eileen St. James explained that the woman had disappeared.

"You spent some time with her?"

"Well, yes, a little."

"I'll have somebody get a description from you."

The bishop vacated his chair behind a desk and pointed to the phone.

Finnerty shook his head. "Thanks, but I'll coordinate this from downstairs. I'm going to need a list of everyone who was in this building last night and this morning."

"Last night?" Mrs. St. James said.

"Yes. Can you get me that list right away?"

"I suppose so. I'll assign someone," the bishop said.

"Good." Finnerty turned to Smith. "You coming with me?"

"I'll walk down with you, but I'm attending the funeral. My wife is probably here by now."

"Check in with me later."

"If you want."

"Yeah, I want. Looks like you're in the middle of this mess, a friend of the corpse, here before we get here, delayed notification."

Smith looked at Bishop St. James as Terry Finnerty left. He certainly hadn't intended to be in the middle of anything. His plans for that day were to attend a funeral and work on some lecture notes for class. St. James's call had changed all that.

"Mac, what do we do now?"

"Concerning what?"

"Concerning the murder and the service for Adam Vickery. Do I mention during the service what's happened here?"

"I don't think you have any choice, George. You've got marked squad cars all over the place, and the TV crew we ran into downstairs will only be the first of many. You have to say something and do it right up front. It may be shocking news to the congregation, but speculation and rumor are worse."

St. James's expression was one of abject despair. He knew Smith was right, yet making

such an announcement was anathema to him.
He looked into Smith's eyes and said, "Of
course, you're right. I'll announce it early, get it
over with. Thank you, Mac."

Smith patted his friend on the shoulder and
managed a weak smile. "I'll look in on you
later," he said glumly, his concern not for
St. James's difficult task but for the dilemma
into which he himself had suddenly been
thrust. Annabel would not be happy.

Annabel was indeed waiting downstairs
when Smith arrived. So were hundreds of people who had gathered for Adam Vickery's funeral, members of the press, and police
everywhere. "Is it true?" Annabel asked. "Murdered?"

"Yes."

She gasped, her eyes flooded. "I can't believe it."

"Believe it, Annie. I saw his body."

They joined others in the pews. The bishop,
accompanied by Reverend Jonathon Merle
and other members of the cathedral's clergy,
slowly ascended to the high altar, known, too,
as the Jerusalem altar because the stones of
which it was constructed had come from quar-

ries outside Jerusalem. St. James climbed up to the Canterbury pulpit. He surveyed the faces before him. A closed casket containing the remains of Adam Vickery stood alone on one of the risers leading to the altar. "Ladies and gentlemen, this is a sad day in the history of this cathedral. Not only have we come to mourn the death of a man whose record of public service to the nation and dedication to the goals of this cathedral were exemplary, we must also mourn the sudden and brutal death of a man of God who was loved by all, a man of God who reached out to the disenfranchised of our society in a way that our Lord Jesus intended, a man of God who served mankind and his church with vigor and sensitive devotion." His voice broke. "I speak of the Reverend Paul Singletary."

Annabel's earlier gasp was now a chorus echoed by many in attendance. Suddenly, it was clear why so many law-enforcement officers and press were milling about in the outer aisles. Most mourners had assumed they represented normal security precautions and press coverage of the Vickery funeral. Now they knew better.

St. James continued, "Unfortunately, we live

in violent times. Not only has our dear col-
league and friend Paul Singletary been brutally
murdered, but it has happened right here in this
House of the Lord, in the tiny Good Shepherd
Chapel that is open day and night for the bereaved and troubled to seek solace through
silent prayer. The shock, which you share, is
considerable. Yet, in the cycle of life, we must
continue. The life of our departed friend Adam
Vickery must be celebrated here today, and his
transport to a gentler place, carried there in the
hands of Our Lord, Jesus Christ, must not be
delayed. I ask all of you to do your best to
concentrate on this solemn and necessary ritual. I can tell you nothing else about the death
of Father Singletary. That is in the hands of the
proper authorities." He swallowed, blinked his
eyes, and said, "Let us pray."

The mood of most people following Vickery's
funeral was more soberness at the news of
Singletary's murder than grief for the former
official whose obsequies they'd just attended.
A hearse and a dozen long black limousines
were lined up outside the south entrance.
Smith and Annabel went up to Vickery's widow,
Doris, and extended their condolences. If Mac

had never particularly liked Vickery, Doris at least had a fairly pleasing and open personality.

Vickery had once approached Smith about taking a job in the Justice Department as an assistant attorney general for civil rights. Smith had turned him down. Vickery—the Justice Department itself, for that matter—had come under considerable pressure from civil-rights groups to modify his views and policies. Gains in civil rights for minority Americans, which had been hard-won over the years, stood in jeopardy during Vickery's time in office. Smith knew that his appeal to Vickery lay in his record and reputation as an attorney concerned with defending the rights of minorities, which would have given Vickery and the administration something—someone—to crow about. Smith was not about to give them that. Besides, Mac Smith had always been impatient with bureaucracies.

It was Doris Vickery who'd managed to bring Mac closer to the family. It happened in the midst of her husband's troubles over his alleged influence peddling. Doris had called Smith at home. She sounded distraught, which Smith assumed was the result of the pressure on her husband. He reluctantly agreed to meet with them. When he did, he was told it was their daughter, Pamela, who was the focus of their concern.

Pamela Vickery was a beautiful, bright, and rebellious young woman who'd begun running with "the wrong crowd," according to her father. She was with her friends in California when the house in which they lived was raided by local drug-enforcement agents. Adam and Doris Vickery swore to Smith that Pamela did not use drugs, and was a victim of circumstance, in the wrong place at the wrong time. It had been a minor-league drug bust—some marijuana, Quaaludes, small amounts of both—hardly destined to pique vast media interest. But it did, of course, given that Pamela was the daughter of the nation's attorney general.

Adam Vickery's initial reaction was to let her take the rap: "Maybe it's what she needs to straighten herself out," he told his wife. But Doris Vickery was not about to see her daughter, troublesome as she might be, have a serious mark against her in her young life for something Doris was convinced Pamela had had little to do with. That's why she called Smith, to ask him to intercede with the right people in California legal circles and try to extricate Pamela from the ramifications of the incident. Adam Vickery could have done so with ease, but his intercession would not have been viewed as an appropriate action by America's number-one attorney.

Smith promised merely that he would look into the situation. He did, became convinced that Pamela's parents had accurately characterized the level of their daughter's involvement, and worked through a California lawyer to see that charges were minimal against the young woman. Smith had one conversation with Pamela Vickery, after she was put on probation. He suggested to her that she return home and pursue her education. She told him three thousand miles weren't nearly far enough away from her father. No thanks, she'd stay in California.

Now, outside the cathedral, Doris Vickery squeezed Smith's hand. "Thank you for coming, Mac. How horrible about Father Singletary." She turned to Annabel and managed a tiny smile. "Congratulations on your marriage."

"Thank you, Mrs. Vickery," Annabel said. "I'm so sorry about your husband."

Doris Vickery sighed. "Yes, thank you. How

ironic that Adam's funeral should occur on the same morning that a priest is slain in the cathedral. It's probably just as well that Adam wasn't here to experience it. He loved this place, Mac, put his heart and soul into it after leaving government service. It gave him . . . a new lease on life, a fresh start. We needed that."

"Yes, I know, Doris," Smith said. She was right; Adam Vickery, despite his previous personal shortcomings, had done a remarkably good job for the cathedral and its building fund. That's why Mac Smith had said to Annabel, "Cloud over his head or not, we go to the funeral. Washington is like the Mafia. I shoot you dead, but I turn up at the church." To Doris, he said, "He'll be missed."

They were joined by Jonathon Merle, whose conduct of the service had been in his usual colorless, matter-of-fact style. Doris Vickery said to him, "Thank you, Father Merle, for your kindness. It must have been very difficult for you, knowing what happened to Father Singletary."

"Yes, very upsetting. I suppose it's only just begun, the scandal, the publicity, the nasty reports."

"It may not be as bad as you think," Smith

said. "We can hope that they'll find who did this and put it quickly to rest."

Merle grimaced. "I've been saying for years that Good Shepherd shouldn't be open night and day. We have the dregs of society coming in here at all hours—addicts, alcoholics, criminals. This is the result I feared."

They were joined by the talented choirmaster, Wilfred Nickelson, whose boys' choir had performed ably during the funeral service. "Excuse me," Nickelson said to the others. He asked Merle, "Have you seen Joey Kelsch?"

"No."

"He didn't show up this morning. I was worried." Then to Mac, Annabel, and Doris Vickery he said, "Our best young singer, flighty but extremely talented. Not like him to simply not be here." He turned again to Merle. "Well, I thought I would ask. I'll call his parents. Perhaps he took ill and went home without informing anyone. A breach of the rules, but Joey is a difficult boy." Nickelson went off to the phone.

The Smiths stood on the steps of the south entrance and watched Doris Vickery join other members of the family at the limousine.

"Free for lunch?" Annabel asked.

"Lunch? At a time like this?"

"It's not the food, Mac. I want some time to sit down with you so you can tell me what's gone on here this morning."

"Of course I will, but let me find out a little more before we do that. Why don't you go home. I'm going back in to talk with the bishop and Terry Finnerty. I'll meet you there in an hour or so." She was disappointed at being excluded, but he said that he felt it better, at least at the moment, to pursue this alone.

"I'll stop by the gallery," she said. He kissed her lightly on the lips.

"Mac," she added, "don't get roped in."

He knew she was referring to his involvement with the case of the Kennedy Center murder the past year. He'd pledged to her—more to himself—that despite his excitement and commitment when getting involved, he would remain forever esconced happily in academia as professor of law at George Washington University.

"Mac." She didn't need to say more.

"I know, I know, but I do owe the bishop a little more of my time, considering that he brought me into this thing this morning—and that the man who was murdered married us. Go home. I'll join you soon."

Her look said it all.

It was always easy getting into something, a lot harder getting out.

Of anything, including debt, affairs, marriage, murder . . . *especially* murder.

chapter

7

That Afternoon—Mostly Overcast Now

Smith never did make it home for lunch with Annabel, and she would not be pleased. He called twice from the cathedral to say he was still involved in sessions with the bishop but would return as quickly as possible. She responded to his first call with understanding and kindness. His second call was met with the start of the Irish iciness of which Annabel was capable, although she seldom displayed it, making its infrequent use that much colder.

Eventually—it was sometime after three—he walked into their Foggy Bottom home. "Sorry," he said cheerfully. "I didn't expect to be there so long."

"Evidently," she said.

"Don't be angry, Annabel. I couldn't simply walk away from George and this situation he's in. He's very distraught, as you can imagine. He needed a sympathetic ear."

Annabel looked at him for a moment, then said, "And what do you need?" before walking into the kitchen. Smith followed, came up from behind, placed his hands on her shoulders, and said gently, "I don't understand your anger, Annabel. Most of all, I don't understand your not understanding." He almost added that his immediate concern was that the cynical adage about good relationships being ruined by marriage might be about to take place in his own life. Now that he was a *husband,* did that change the rules? Was he now involved in greater accountability to Annabel than had been the case when they were simply going together? They had never lived together because, for both of them, that would have represented a tactical mistake if nothing else. Did she have to approve his every act?

He didn't have to ask. She turned and said in

a steady, well-modulated voice, "Mac, has marriage changed us already?"

Her taking the words out of his mouth left him without words. For a moment. "Of course not," he said. "Why would you think such a thing?"

"Because you're acting different. Before . . . before we became man and wife, you involved me completely in everything you did. When you got suckered into the mess at the Kennedy Center, you wanted me at your side. You even dispatched me to New York to talk to that slimy lawyer, and I was with you every step of the way. Now a friend of ours is murdered; another friend—who also happens to be bishop of the National Cathedral—asks for help, and you send me home to make a tuna-fish sandwich for my man when he returns from the wars!"

He coughed, stepped back, and frowned the way he usually did when a student in his advanced criminal-procedure class asked a question he was not prepared to answer. "You know, Annabel," he said, "one of the things that attracted me to you was your independence. After all, you are the owner of a flourishing gallery. Murder . . . law is really my domain."

It was a mistake, and he knew it the minute he said it. Annabel Reed had been a successful matrimonial attorney in Washington before chucking it for her primary passion in life— aside from Mac Smith, of course—her gallery of pre-Columbian art in fashionable George-town.

She said nothing, but a hint of a smile indicated what she thought of his comment.

"Yes, I know," he said, "you are an attorney. But you didn't deal with criminal matters. George is seeking my counsel because the ramifications of Paul Singletary's murder are substantial. George is primarily concerned that someone from the cathedral staff might have killed him, not a drifter or drug addict, as most people are speculating. I understand his concern, and want to be helpful. I'd think you would expect that of me. Both of us have been involved, at least to some extent, with the cathedral."

She sighed. "Of course I want you to help. I just don't want you to get in too deep. I just . . . I just don't want . . ."

He stepped close to her again and placed his strong hands on her shoulders. "You just don't want *what*?"

A mist formed in her large green eyes. "I just don't want to be treated like a disposable wife, or see you throw away your own new life."

He couldn't help but laugh. "But you *are* my wife. As for my new life: in no way disposable. How would you prefer I treat you?"

"I meant the law school, and I mean the way you used to treat me, like an object of your affection, your mistress, your concubine, your *fille de joie.*"

He listened patiently. "You didn't mention 'partner,' " he said.

"I don't want to be your partner, not exactly."

"But you said you wanted to be involved in Paul's case. That makes you a partner."

"A limited partner."

"Meaning what?"

"Meaning that I don't want to spend my day dealing with murder, but I would like to spend *part* of my day being at your side, being useful. Besides, I make lousy tuna-fish sandwiches, and you know it."

"Done!" He cocked his head, narrowed his eyes. "To be honest with you, Annabel, it's easy for me to give in. Now that I've spent time with George and others at the cathedral, I really don't see much need for me. Okay, I am once

again a college professor, and you are my ob-
scenely beautiful, talented, brilliant, and successful wi—uh, wanton harlot.'' He was
tempted to turn her toward the bedroom, but
there was something unseemly about that idea
for the moment. Would he have hesitated
before they were married to dismiss the nasty
brutish business of murder and then act upon
his carnal, lover's instincts? *Had* marriage
changed them?

Hell, no, he decided, wishing he were more
convinced.

For the rest of the afternoon he graded papers, while Annabel went back to her gallery to
pay some bills. She returned at six, and they
settled in front of the TV to watch the evening
news.

Singletary's murder was the lead story. The
police issued a terse statement—the priest had
been murdered by an unknown assailant, the
method of death a blow to the head. His body
had been found in a chapel of the National
Cathedral. There were no leads at the moment.
The body had been discovered by a woman,
identity unknown, whereabouts unknown. The
tag line on the newscast: ''Former top D.C. at-

torney Mackensie Smith, now a professor at George Washington University, has been retained by the cathedral in this matter. Stay tuned."

"Damn," Mac said, pouring himself a small glass of Blanton's bourbon over ice.

Annabel was sitting on a couch. She'd changed into a Kelly-green silk robe over nothing else, and was flipping through the latest issue of *Art in America* while watching the news. In her hand was a delicately shaped balloon glass with a small amount of white wine. She looked up. "Have you been retained by the cathedral?"

"Can't they get anything straight? Of course not."

"Have you told George that you would do more?"

"No. Well, I did say that I would do what I could to make his life a little easier . . . give some advice, that's all."

Annabel smiled, the sort of smile Mac could do without and this for the second time that day. "Uh-huh," she said with deliberate sweetness, returning her attention to the magazine.

The phone rang, not an unwelcome interruption for Smith. It was a reporter from *The Wash-*

ington Post, who wanted to confirm a rumor that Smith had been retained by the cathedral to defend one of its clergy in the Singletary murder.

"Nonsense!" Smith said.

Other calls came over the next hour, each an attempt to run down a rumor concerning Smith's involvement, or a likely suspect.

"Let's go out for dinner," Smith said after hanging up on yet another caller.

She shook her head. "Put the answering machine on. I'd just as soon bring something in from the American Café."

"All right. What'll you have?"

"Mac."

"Yes?"

"Reality has set in. You are going to be up to your neck in this, aren't you?"

"An overstatement, but yes, I do feel I have to help find the murderer of the man who married us."

She smiled gently and genuinely. "I understand. What will you do first?"

Smith sat down next to her and shrugged. "I told George I'd make some inquiries here and also while we're in London."

"Inquiries about what?"

"About Paul's movements there prior to his returning to Washington. About whatever we can learn here about motives and such."

"The trip to London is our honeymoon. You are aware of that?"

"Of course. And remember that we decided to combine business and pleasure. I have to address that group of barristers, and you wanted to trace down leads on those Tlatilco female masks. I'm not suggesting an extensive investigation of what Paul did in London, just some questions. Jeffrey Woodcock should be helpful. I'm eager for you to meet him. He's a nice guy." Woodcock was a highly respected London solicitor, whose firm's clients numbered, among others, the Church of England. He and Smith had been friends for many years, and when Smith and Annabel were planning their honeymoon, Smith had called Woodcock and arranged for them to meet for dinner.

Annabel continued to browse through the magazine. She lowered it to her lap and said, "I've been thinking a great deal about Paul Singletary."

"So have I. Hard not to."

"I've been thinking about his death, of course, but there's more. He was so charming, and so committed to good deeds . . . but that's really all we knew about him."

"What else would you like to know?"

She shrugged.

"We never know everything about anyone. If we did, no one would ever get along, or marry."

She laughed. "How true. Maybe I'm just naturally suspicious . . . no, skeptical, or at least wary, of anyone in the limelight here in Washington. How much do we really know about the whole life of Paul Singletary?"

"Wary? Even of me?" Smith said.

"Especially of you."

Smith grunted. "I'll have to ponder that. What's your pleasure?" he asked as he pulled a restaurant takeout menu from a drawer.

She tossed the magazine to the floor and sat up straight, the folds of her robe falling loose and exposing the slope of one lovely white breast. *"You're* my pleasure, Mr. Smith."

"Are you about to make conjugal demands on this aging body?"

"To the contrary. I am abandoning my role as a wife, and reverting to the whorish role that I enjoyed for so long *before* we got married."

"You're sure this is the time for sex, Annabel? There's been a murder in the national place of worship, of all things."

"And nothing will change that. If I am going to lose you so early in my marriage to your need to meddle in murder, I insist upon due compensation."

"What about dinner?"

A tall woman, she stood up and allowed the robe to fall in a soft green pile around her feet. Nude, she looked down at him and said, "Somehow, I don't think we'll be hungry. But if we are, I'll play wife again and whip up a sandwich for my dear husband. I make excellent tuna-fish salad. Or hadn't you heard?"

With a rolled-up magazine, they convinced Rufus to vacate the king-size bed, and for twenty minutes or so—neither was counting—forgot about everything except themselves. Murder would just have to wait.

chapter
8

**Friday Morning—
Sunny, but Rain Forecast**

Long before the automatic coffee maker had a chance to trip on, the phone started ringing. Two calls were from press people; the other was from the bishop, who asked if Smith had time to meet with him late that afternoon. Smith said it looked like a full day, with two classes, one a seminar, but that he would find an hour. They settled on four o'clock at St. James's home.

"What should I tell others who call?" Annabel asked sleepily. She stood near the front door in robe and slippers as Smith prepared to leave for the university.

"Tell them I expired," he said, slipping into his raincoat.

"Don't even joke about something like that," Annabel said.

"Tell them there is no sense in calling me, because I have no official connection with the investigation of Paul's murder." He kissed her on the cheek, then changed his mind, found her lips, and pressed hard. "I wish I had time to stay around. You exude a certain heightened sensuality early in the morning."

"Don't feel you've missed anything," she said. "I exude a certain exhaustion but I'll be out of here in a half hour. Lots going on at the gallery today, including a meeting about the fund-raising exhibition we're doing for St. Albans." St. Albans was the Episcopal church on the cathedral grounds that served a local congregation. Annabel had recently taken over a vacant store next to her gallery in Georgetown and promptly committed the new space to St. Albans's mission fund for a showing of artists who had some connection with the church. It would take a month for renovations on the gallery's addition to be completed; the exhibition was scheduled to be hung in six weeks.

Smith took Rufus for a long walk before going to his class. Rufus needed the exercise and Smith needed to think. They wandered Foggy Bottom, an area of Washington defined by Eighteenth Street on the east, Constitution Avenue on the south, the Potomac River and Twenty-sixth Street on the west, and Pennsylvania Avenue on the north. Originally a malarial marsh incorporated as Hamburg but called Funkstown after Jacob Funk, who'd purchased the original land, it eventually became known as Foggy Bottom, an unkind reference to the foul emissions produced by the many industries that once had been settled within its boundaries. Today, it is an attractive neighborhood that is home to the Kennedy Center for the Performing Arts, George Washington University (the second-largest landholder in Washington after the federal government), and the departments of State and Interior. It had been Mac Smith's home ever since his wife and son were killed and he'd left his luxurious Watergate apartment suite and bought the narrow two-story taupe brick house on Twenty-fifth Street, its trim, shutters, and front door painted

Federal blue, its rooms devoid of painful memories that had started to suffocate him as a Watergate widower.

He returned Rufus to the house, and after carefully checking his briefcase, which he had checked and repacked the night before (he could not go to sleep without having prepared his briefcase for the following day), and taking his raincoat from the closet, as rain was predicted, headed for Lerner Hall. A reporter from the *Post* was waiting on the front steps, along with two uniformed officers from the MPD.

"Mr. Smith, could I have a word with you?" the reporter asked. One of the officers motioned Smith to approach them. Smith excused himself with a word to the reporter and went to where the officers stood. "Mr. Smith, we tried you at your home, but your wife said you'd left."

"Yes, I took a walk. My dog and I, that is. What can I do for you?"

"Chief Finnerty would like a word with you."

"Now? I have a class to teach."

"He said for us to bring you to him as quickly as possible."

"You'll just have to tell him I won't be available for the next two hours."

"I'll call in," the other officer said. He returned from the squad car and said, "The chief says we should wait for you, Mr. Smith. He says you should teach your class, but that he would like to see you right after it."

Smith looked at his watch. "All right, but you have two hours to kill."

"No problem, Mr. Smith." Of course not, Smith thought. Cops were experts at killing time. They had to be.

Smith headed for the door, but the reporter intercepted him again. "Mr. Smith, I'm Mark Rosner from the *Post.* Give me a few minutes?"

"Sorry, I can't. I'm already running late for my class. Besides, I have nothing to talk about."

"The Singletary murder," Rosner said. "Aren't you serving as counsel to the cathedral?"

"No."

"But it's my understanding that—"

Smith flashed a broad smile. "I think you should find better sources. I'm a college professor who happens to be a personal friend of the bishop of the cathedral. Excuse me, I don't want to be rude, but I'm afraid I'm about to be." He walked away, leaving the reporter with an expression on his face that indicated both annoyance and ambivalence.

When Smith entered the lecture hall, most of his students were in their seats. They were a decent lot for the most part, with a few exceptions. That they were bright went without saying; you didn't get into GW's law school unless you could demonstrate as much. The problem, Smith often thought, was that, as with medical schools, intelligence and grades were virtually the sole determining factor for admission to law schools. But how do you judge a young man or woman's sense of humanity, commitment to decency, to social justice, to using an excellent legal education to give something to the world and not just to take from it? When he dwelt too much upon that subject, as this morning, he became depressed, so he pushed it from his mind, went to the lectern, unloaded his carefully arranged briefcase, and wished the students a good morning.

"Professor Smith," Bob Rogers said, "anything new on the murder of the priest?"

Smith had expected questions about Paul Singletary's murder, and had decided during his walk to dismiss the subject as quickly as possible. He looked at the questioner over half-glasses and asked, "Have you read the news-papers, watched television?"

"Yes, sir."

"Then you know as much as I do."

There was a ripple of sarcastic laughter.

"What's funny? No, sorry, that's not true. Father Paul Singletary was a friend of mine."

Another student, Joyce Clemow, retorted, "Which is why we thought you'd know what was going on."

Before Smith could answer, another aspiring lawyer, Joe Petrella, said, "I heard you're going to defend whoever in the cathedral murdered Father Singletary."

Smith placed his glasses on the lectern and shook his head. "What kind of attorney will you end up being, Joe, if you're content to go with rumor that has no basis in fact?"

Petrella sheepishly lowered his head. Beside him, Smith's best student, April Montgomery, a thin, pale young woman with a facial tic that made it appear that something had lodged temporarily in her nose, said, "Do you believe it was an outsider who killed Father Singletary—say, a homeless person who came into the cathedral early in the morning?"

"I have no idea," Smith said. "The police have just begun their investigation."

"Have they found the woman who discovered the body?"

"Not that I'm aware of," Smith said. Other questions sprouted until he threw up his hands in a gesture of surrender. "Look," he said, "we have a great deal to cover here this morning, but okay, since the only thing on your minds seems to be the Singletary murder, let's take fifteen minutes to discuss it." He leaned on the lectern, thought for a moment, then said, "Here is what I do know. Father Singletary was killed by a blow to the side of his head. It appears upon casual observation of the wound that the object was heavy, and that it had a lip or ridge that caused considerable compression of the skull. MPD's Forensic Unit did a thorough job of analysis of the crime scene, which was the tiny chapel known as Good Shepherd. Singletary was found sitting in a single pew, his body slumped against a wall. There appears to have been little bleeding, which has caused those who were on the scene to raise a question." He paused. They looked at him. "Which is—?"

April Montgomery said, "Whether he might have been killed elsewhere and moved to the chapel."

"That's interesting," Joy Collins said. She was the most exuberant of Smith's students. "They didn't have *that* on TV or in the papers."

"It will be, as soon as enough of the right questions are asked and facts digested. An autopsy is being performed or has been performed on the Reverend Singletary, and perhaps that will determine a number of things, including—what?"

Several raised their hands.

"The approximate time of his death, lividity, the advancement of rigor mortis, body temperature, the level of potassium in the eye fluid, rate of decomposition," said Bob Rogers, who usually had such lists at his command.

"Right. All will be taken into consideration. Many color photographs were shot, and detailed sketches were made. Each of you, of course, is familiar with the techniques used to evaluate a crime scene." He surveyed their faces; he'd become a forensics expert when he was practicing criminal law. It was vitally necessary to understand forensic medicine in order to mount a credible defense for a client. Some of his students didn't seem to be interested in such things, aside from morbid curiosity.

"Any speculation on motive?" April asked.

"No, but there soon will be. That will all be part of the criminal profile that develops once more information has been gathered by the authorities." Smith knew that as scornful as Terry Finnerty (like most local law-enforcement officers) was of the FBI, he would need the help of the bureau's Behavioral Science Unit—now part of the National Center for the Analysis of Violent Crime (NCAVC)—in developing a description of the type of person who might have committed the murder, using both psychological and investigative input. He told them so.

"Maybe it was somebody who hates the church and clergy, somebody who flunked out of a seminary, or who was brought up in a repressive religious household," Petrella offered. Joe Petrella seemed to especially enjoy the drama of law.

"Maybe."

"Was Father Singletary married?"

"No."

"Was he . . . gay?"

"Why would you ask that?" Smith asked.

"Well, you know clergy, they have—"

"Paul Singletary was an Episcopal priest, not a Roman Catholic. Episcopal priests are free to marry and to have children. Why would the fact that he was a priest raise a question of his sexual orientation?"

"Homosexuals are free to be homosexual, or to be heterosexuals, or to be bi-, to marry, and to have children," said April.

She was right, of course, and Smith ignored that line of conversation. He said, "The basic supposition at this moment is that Father Singletary was murdered by someone whom he confronted in the chapel, most likely an outsider. This unknown person would fall under the category of an unorganized murderer. All signs point to a lack of premeditation since no knife, gun, or other formal weapon was used. It is also safe to assume at this juncture that Father Singletary did not know his assailant, and was taken by surprise."

"But if he was murdered elsewhere, as you suggested was a possibility, Professor Smith, and brought to the chapel, that would certainly indicate a more organized murderer," Joyce Clemow said. "If that happened, the murderer didn't just swing something at Father Singletary and run. He thought about it, and spent time with his victim."

"You are correct," said Smith. He looked at his watch. "Our fifteen minutes of diversion are up. I would now like you to turn to the cases assigned on writs of habeas corpus."

Chief of Homicide Terrence Finnerty sat in his office with six other detectives assigned to a task force to investigate Paul Singletary's murder. Smith waited outside until the detectives left, and Finnerty invited him to come in.

"Sorry to screw up your day, Mac," Finnerty said as he poured himself a cup of black coffee from a battered Thermos. "Want some?"

"No, thank you. The British knew what they were doing when they named cop coffee 'tonsil varnish.' "

"Hey, this ain't bad coffee, Mac. My wife makes it fresh every morning."

"That's different. Thank you anyway."

Seemingly pleased that he'd set *that* record straight, Finnerty leaned back in his chair, put his scuffed black shoes on the edge of his desk, and squinted at some papers in a file folder.

"Any word yet on the autopsy?" Smith asked.

"No," Finnerty answered without looking up. "I'll get a prelim from the M.E. this afternoon. It'll take a while for the blood and urine samples to be run. We're busy in the chop shop." He glanced up at Smith. "Any ideas?"

Smith laughed. "Is that why you had me brought down here, to ask if I have any ideas? Why would I have ideas? Once you and your people took over, I was out of the picture, still am."

"Not in the papers."

"I just know what I read in the newspapers."

"Bull! After the funeral for Vickery you hung around the cathedral a long time, holed up with the bishop for at least a couple hours."

"Who told you that?" Smith asked, knowing the answer. Obviously, Finnerty had had one of his people keep an eye on his movements.

"What did you talk to the bishop about?"

"About having lost a friend," Smith replied.

"Two hours to talk about that? Must have been a hell of an interesting guy."

"He was. You know his reputation. Paul Singletary was probably the most involved and visible clergyman in Washington."

"Yeah, I know, but that's just the public side. Tell me about Singletary, his private side. You knew him pretty good, right?"

Smith thought of Annabel's comments. "Probably not as well as you're assuming. I wouldn't call him a *close* friend."

"You asked him to marry you."

"No, I asked him to officiate at our wedding, which doesn't necessarily indicate closeness. We wanted to be married in the cathedral. Bishop St. James was out of town. We knew Paul, and asked him to conduct the service."

"How come you were the one the bishop called the minute the body was discovered?"

"I keep asking myself the same question. Annabel has been active in church affairs for a number of years, and I've been involved in a few aspects of the cathedral's activities, been called upon to give some legal advice on occasion. I guess the combination of knowing the bishop fairly well and being an attorney was good enough for him to think of me first. I wish he hadn't."

"He like girls?"

"Father Singletary?"

"Yeah."

"One of my students assumed Paul might

have been gay because he was a single clergy-man. Are you making the same assumption?"

"No, Mac, not at all, but I have a feeling we're going to have to get to know the *real* Father Singletary if we're going to have any chance of solving this case."

Finnerty was right, of course, especially if Singletary's killer turned out not to be a total stranger. In order for an effective profile to be drawn of the murderer, the police and the FBI's Behavioral Science Unit would need knowl-edge of how Singletary lived, his friends, his hobbies, his haunts, everything about how he lived his intimate life on a daily basis.

"Paul was an attractive and engaging man," Smith said. "He was dedicated to helping the disenfranchised of our society, and worked hard on their behalf, sometimes to the conster-nation of his peers and colleagues. I know he also found time for some semblance of a social life. Yes, he did like girls. I recall two occasions when he was accompanied at social gatherings by a woman."

"Same woman?"

Smith shook his head. "No, two different women, both very attractive, I might add."

"He was in London just before it happened, right?"

"So I understand." Smith remembered George St. James's mentioning that Singletary had returned from London a day earlier than scheduled. Why? That was one of the things he told the bishop he'd try to find out when he went to London on his honeymoon. Should he bring it up with Finnerty? He decided not to. Probably had no significance, but let Finnerty earn his money.

It dawned on Smith that he was rapidly shifting into the defense-attorney mode—maybe not officially, but certainly psychically. This both interested and dismayed him.

"We got a description from the bishop's wife. Not a very good one, but it was the best she seemed to be able to do. Here." Finnerty handed Smith a typed transcript of what Eileen St. James had given the interviewing officer.

White female—somewhere between 40 and 60—reddish hair that probably was dyed because there were a lot of black roots—short, maybe five feet, maybe a few inches taller—kind of a narrow little face—

pale complexion—had a black mole on her
cheek (couldn't remember which cheek)—
wore a skirt (doesn't remember color)—a
black (or dark blue) sweater with buttons—
another sweater, color unknown, under-
neath, maybe a white blouse under
that—no recollection of shoes—no distin-
guishing marks other than the black mole—
nervous personality (but Mrs. St. James
said that could be because she discovered
a body)—high voice (but she was crying all
the time, so hard to tell what her voice was
really like)—no accent—twisted her hands
around each other a lot—used terms like
"Dear Jesus" and "Father in Heaven"—
maybe had alcohol on her breath but can't
be sure.

Smith looked up from the page into the small
black pupils of Finnerty's eyes. "I think it's surprisingly detailed, considering the circumstances. The bishop's wife is observant," he
said.

"Or the cop asking questions was good."

"Are you asking whether I know this
woman?"

Finnerty shrugged. "She doesn't sound like

either of the women I saw Paul Singletary with on those social occasions, if that's what you're getting at."

"Not his type, huh?"

"No, not his type."

"You ever get involved with any of his knee-jerk work?"

Smith found the term offensive, but didn't respond to that. He said, "Just once. Father Singletary was having a legal problem running a soup kitchen. Some of the neighbors hired an attorney and brought suit to have the place closed down. Singletary didn't ask me to help. He brought it up at one of those social occasions I mentioned earlier, and I went to bat for him, talked to the neighborhood attorney and got him to understand that he didn't have any legal basis upon which to demand the closing of the kitchen. I don't think I've been involved in any other aspect of Paul's . . . 'knee-jerk' . . . projects."

Finnerty grinned, obviously pleased that he had annoyed Smith, which only annoyed Smith more. "Any truth that you're going to defend whoever murdered Singletary if it turns out he's from the cathedral?"

"No truth whatsoever," Smith said. "Is that it,

Terry? If it is, I really would like to get back home. I still have a busy day ahead of me."

"Including spending a little time at the cathedral again?"

"Maybe."

"Careful, Mac, don't get too religious."

"No need to worry about that, Terry. Call me anytime. I'm as anxious as everyone else to see you resolve this. Good luck."

"It's sickening what's happened to this city," the woman standing outside the Georgetown townhouse said to the uniformed policeman guarding the front door. "Animals, nothing but animals," she said. "He was such a good man, and they killed him. They should rot in hell, whoever killed Father Singletary." The officer responded with a series of "Uh-huh"s.

Inside, two of the six detectives assigned to the Singletary case took photographs of the apartment and made notes. Its furnishings and decoration were eclectic, unconcerned Early Bachelor. The sofa and chairs were thread-bare. The walls needed painting, and two cheap area rugs were stained and curled at the corners where double-faced tape had dried out and let loose.

"Nice VCR," Joe Johnson, a black detective, said. It was a new model with many advanced features, and was hooked up to a large NEC video monitor. A wall of videotapes framed the equipment.

"No books," Vinnie Basilio said.

"These Bibles," his partner said.

"Whattaya expect a priest to have, porn?"

Johnson laughed. "Could be." He started to tell of a case he'd worked on just after he'd been promoted to detective, a story his partner had heard too many times. He cut him off. "What I don't figure is the security system."

"Say what?"

"The security system on this place. *Every-*thing is wired, and this kind of system costs big bucks. What the hell would a priest have that's so important he'd put in such a system?"

Johnson laughed again, a pleasant rumble from deep inside. "A good VCR and TV."

The Italian American shook his head and grimaced. "Nah, this security system had to cost ten times what he was protecting. I don't figure it, a priest doing this."

"Hey, man, he was no ordinary priest, right? I mean, this guy was in the papers every other day, walking the mean streets with the crackheads, feeding bums, stealing teenybopper hookers from their pimps. Maybe *that's* why he's got this system in here, to protect his neck."

"A lot of good it did him."

Detective Johnson responded to a knock. Finnerty stepped into the living room and closed the door behind him. "Anything?" he asked.

They recounted what they'd been discussing. Finnerty did not seem as impressed with the security system as Basilio had been. "Files, letters, anything like that?"

"We didn't look yet," replied Johnson.

"Well, get to it quick," Finnerty said. "We're about to lose the place."

The two detectives looked at him.

"The feds are coming in," Finnerty said, his disgust obvious.

"How come?" Basilio asked.

"Beats me. As far as I'm concerned, it's strictly a D.C. murder, but I got the word that when the feds get here, they run the ball club, so you remember that, too."

"Sure. No skin off my nose. They'll just screw it up like they usually do," Basilio said.

Johnson laughed.

Finnerty and the two detectives quickly started going through a small desk in the bedroom. There was very little in it—a drawer for paid bills, a drawer for unpaid bills, some blank stationery and envelopes, pens and pencils, no personal address or phone book, no photographs except a few of Singletary with dignitaries that hung above the bed.

"You wouldn't figure he'd live here in Georgetown," said Detective Basilio.

"Why?" Finnerty asked.

"Because he's big in the ghetto. How come he doesn't live in the ghetto? What was he, one of those liberals who beats it back at night to where the decent folk live?"

Neither Finnerty nor Johnson had a chance to comment because there was another knock at the door. Finnerty opened it to two young men with short, neat haircuts who wore inexpensive but nicely fitted and neatly pressed suits. One of them, who had a round face with red cheeks, said to Finnerty, "Can I talk to you?"

They went out into the hallway, where the agent showed Finnerty his identification. "We're going to be spending time in the apartment, and we need to be left alone. I'd like you to move your uniformed man up to this floor and have him take a position outside the door. We'd appreciate somebody on that duty twenty-four hours a day.''

Finnerty was tempted to tell them to provide their own personnel now that they were coming into it, but he didn't. He'd learned long ago that shooting off his mouth in these situations accomplished nothing. Worse, it often got him in trouble, the kind of trouble he didn't need with two years to the pension. Instead, he returned to the apartment and told his detectives it was time to leave.

The two agents stood in the center of what had been Father Paul Singletary's living room. The one with the round face, who was in charge, removed his suit jacket and carefully draped it over the back of a chair that was beside a small, cheap Formica table. ''Might as well get to work,'' he said to his partner, who had blond hair and a large mouth defined by thick lips. He, too, had removed his suit jacket, exposing beneath his white shirt a body that had pumped a lot of iron. ''What's first?'' he asked his superior.

''The tapes. Looks like we're in for a long night at the movies.''

■ ■ ■

At three o'clock that afternoon, Bishop George St. James received a visitor to his office in the cathedral's administration building. His name was Jin Tse, and he was a heavyset Korean who wore a suit that said Savile Row.

"Good of you to see me on such short notice," said Tse, settling himself in a comfortable chair facing the desk.

"Frankly, I would have preferred to see no one today," St. James said, "but I do respect your reasons for wanting to meet as quickly as possible, Mr. Tse. If my mind seems to wander at times, please forgive me. The full impact of what has happened here, and to Father Singletary, is just beginning to sink in. It's like being run over by a sixteen-wheeler, if you understand."

"Yes, of course, and I offer you my deepest sympathy. His death has been a terrible shock and loss to us at Word of Peace, too."

"As I can well imagine," said St. James. "Actually, we've been dealt a double blow here. Not only is Father Singletary gone, but Adam Vickery, who performed wonders for us in managing our building assets, also died."

Tse nodded.

"Ironic, isn't it, that two men who supported the cathedral should die so close together? Of course, Adam Vickery's death was natural, part of the order of things. As for Father Singletary . . . well, being murdered is never natural."

Tse cleared his throat before saying, "Bishop St. James, the reason it was necessary to meet with you as quickly as possible was to alleviate the fears many of the leaders of Word of Peace have been feeling since Father Singletary's murder. Our goals depend a great deal upon the continued support of such institutions as this cathedral, and the church it represents. Paul . . . do you mind if I call him Paul?" The bishop shook his head. "Paul was always so proud that his bishop had committed himself and the church with such vigor and determination to Word of Peace." Tse spoke perfect English; to hear him on a telephone would lead a listener to believe that a native-born American who'd studied elocution was speaking. "As you might be aware, our movement has its detractors. With the unfortunate death of such a leader, it gives them what they might perceive as a golden opportunity to increase their attacks upon this crusade. What I need to be able to do is immediately inform my people that Paul's death has not weakened our cause but, in the tragic but time-honored tradition of martyrdom, has actually enhanced our efforts to bring peace to this world."

What St. James had apologized for at the beginning of the meeting was now happening. He was having trouble concentrating on the well-formed words of this Korean gentleman sitting across from him.

St. James had heard of Jin Tse from Paul Singletary, although as he reflected upon the priest's comments, he realized Singletary had offered little information about the man. Paul had told him that Tse was one of the prime organizers of Word of Peace, particularly in the Washington area, where the Korean was engaged in intense lobbying of politicians who might throw their weight behind the movement. The bishop was sorry that he had agreed to meet with him, not because of the crush of cathedral business or out of his deep sense of loss, but because he really didn't like Tse. He couldn't pinpoint why. Tse was pleasant enough, courteous to a fault, and had been respected by Singletary. Yet something bothered St. James about him, and he decided to end the meeting.

"Mr. Tse, it is difficult for me to devote much thought at this moment to Word of Peace, although I do believe in it." (Did he? He'd never been sure. He did believe in its goals, however.) "It's a matter of priorities at this point. We have Father Singletary's funeral coming up as soon as his body is released by the authorities, and there is the continuing need to cooperate with those authorities in bringing to justice the individual who committed this deplorable act of violence. I can tell you, however, that whatever support I offered Father Singletary in his work with your movement has not changed. If that puts your mind and the minds of your people at rest, then I am pleased to be able to express it to you."

Tse realized that the bishop was ending their meeting. He stood, smiled, and extended a hand laden with heavy rings. St. James took it. "Your generosity, Bishop St. James, is exemplary. I could ask for nothing more than to have heard the words you have just said. The spiritual and financial commitment made to Word of Peace by this shrine of national worship will be instrumental in bringing about a just and lasting peace for people all over this globe. You are truly a man of God."

St. James was now even more uncomfortable. He withdrew his hand from the Korean's metal-wrapped fingers and escorted him to the door. "You'll be at Paul's funeral?"

"Of course," said Tse. "Indeed, hundreds of supporters of Word of Peace will be there to pay a final tribute to one of the most gentle and committed men I have ever had the pleasure of knowing."

"Yes, well, thank you for coming here today. Good-bye."

Tse was driven away from the cathedral in a large gray Mercedes sedan that had been parked at the doors of the south transept. The driver turned left onto Wisconsin Avenue, which took them in the direction of Georgetown. A nondescript green Ford Fairlane that had been parked across the street fell in behind them. Two young men with close, neat haircuts were in the second car. The man on the passenger side dialed a number on the vehicle's car phone. A female voice answered, "NIS."

"Samuels."

"One second."

A male voice came on the line.

"Samuels. We're continuing contact with Buddha by vehicle."

The man on the other end, who managed the surveillance unit, said, "Report again when mode of contact changes."

"Right," the young man named Samuels said. He hung up the phone and said to the driver, "Are Marsch and Williamson picking up from us later?"

The driver said, "No, they're over at the priest's apartment. I don't know who's spelling us, and I don't care, as long as I get to go home by eight. If I don't, someone will kill me and you'll have another investigation. Look for my wife. It's our anniversary."

The Mercedes pulled up to the entrance of the Watergate Hotel, and Tse emerged. His driver pulled away. "I'll pick up Buddha," Samuels said, jumping out of the car. As the driver was about to follow the Mercedes, Samuels said through the open window, "If you don't make it home for your anniversary, my couch opens up. See ya."

chapter

9

Monday Morning—Overcast and Chilly; Funeral Weather

The Right Reverend George St. James, bishop of Washington, looked out at the thousands of faces of those who'd gathered in the cathedral's nave to mourn the loss of Canon Paul Singletary. His mind wandered for a moment. He peered down the more-than-five-hundred-foot aisle leading from the altar to the west entrance and, distracting himself from the unpleasant task at hand, observed once more with interest that the aisle wasn't straight, that it did a little jig at approximately the halfway point, a deliberate act by the architect to avoid

the "narrowing railroad track" visual phen-
omenon.

He cleared his voice and said from the pulpit,
*"They do rest from their labors and their works
do follow them."* His words rang out through
the cavernous cathedral.

Joining Bishop St. James at the high altar
were other members of the cathedral's and St.
Albans's clergy, including Jonathon Merle and
a young priest from St. Albans, Carolyn Armstrong. Annabel, who'd come to know Reverend Armstrong while planning the forthcoming
show in Annabel's gallery, had remarked to
Mac after first meeting her that the young
woman was striking, and all the more so because of what she represented. She was one
of those fortunate women who need no
makeup, and the fact that she could present a
bare and unadorned face to the world worked
perfectly with her calling. An aura of sweet divinity surrounded her. At the same time, she
was a woman who could hardly be missed. She
was tall and had thick black hair that she rarely
wore loose; when attending to her priestly duties she caught it up into a casual chignon. Her
skin was flawless, and the contours of an amply

endowed body were only partially obscured be-neath her vocational garb.

Mac and Annabel held hands as they sat in one of the forward pews. Their thoughts some-times coincided, other times were far afield. Naturally, visions of their wedding day in the Bethlehem Chapel kept returning, Paul's hand-some, smiling face bestowing God's grace upon their union, the implied playfulness in his voice and the twinkle in his eye, his easy banter with them outside the cathedral. As those pleasant thoughts ebbed and flowed, there was also a natural anger. How senseless, how wrong, for this dynamic man to have his life end in such a brutal and wanton fashion.

Smith looked around. Two distant cousins of Singletary's sat together at the far end of a pew. Chief of Homicide Terrence Finnerty was in the crowd along with what Smith assumed were other representatives from the MPD. The Word of Peace contingent numbered in the hundreds. Whole inner-city classes of school-children, mostly black and Hispanic, had been brought to the service by their teachers. The vice president of the United States had made a last-minute decision to attend, which had thrown the security people into turmoil. He sat quietly with his wife and two Cabinet members, a dozen Secret Service agents surrounding their entourage.

Most of the other mourners, Smith decided, were people who probably had had no direct contact with Paul Singletary, people who were saddened and outraged by his murder and who'd come to pay their simple respects to a man they didn't know but whose reputation for good works had touched each of them in some unspoken, intangible way.

The choir was a combination of the cathedral's boys' and men's choirs. They lined both sides of the aisle of the chancel and sanctuary that led to the high altar. From outside came the constant whir of a helicopter hovering above. Barked orders through a bullhorn on occasion added yet another alien sound.

Reverend Armstrong read a section from the Scriptures, its words acclaiming all who carry out the Lord's good work on earth by comforting the sick and ministering to the poor. The message was so fitting that as she reached the end of the verse, her voice broke and it was apparent that she had to fight for control to complete the reading. Her near-breakdown brought sobs from people throughout the congregation.

Jonathon Merle was next. In contrast to Canon Armstrong, he was more patrician and steely than ever. He read from the Gospel in a flat, businesslike tone, his eyes never leaving the printed page, his cadence that of a man getting through a ritual as coolly and perhaps even as quickly as possible.

Bishop St. James sat in the great carved stone Glastonbury Cathedra, "the bishop's chair." When Merle had completed his duties at the pulpit, St. James slowly stood and walked to take his place. Mac Smith noticed the fatigue in his friend's gait. It was confirmed when he started to speak, his voice heavy and weary, a sense of profound sadness clinging to every word.

"Reverend Canon Paul Singletary loved many things in this life, but mostly he loved the God he served so admirably. He was a man whose spirit could be lifted by music, and there were always favorite hymns that he would listen to when in need of personal renewal. One of them speaks eloquently of the blessed rest in our Saviour's hands that he has undoubtedly found. I know he is with us today and will take delight in once again hearing this hymn that meant so much to him."

St. James returned to his stone chair as choirmaster Wilfred Nickelson conducted the combined choirs. The magnificent ringing sound of the accompanying organ seemed to lift the voices up a hundred feet to the gray shadows of the nave's ceiling.

> *"Now the laborer's task is o'er;*
> *Now the battle day is past;*
> *Now upon the farther shore*
> *Lands the voyager at last.*
> *Father, in thy gracious keeping*
> *Leave we now thy servant*
> *   sleeping."*

Joey Kelsch, who stood at the front of the boys' choir, delivered the final two lines of each verse as a solo. Early in the hymn, the words soared from his lips and throat. Then, as he began the later lines of the last verse, he faltered. People leaned forward. Choirmaster Nickelson looked sternly in his direction. Would he complete the two lines? the congregation silently wondered. Joey looked up from the hymnal he held in both hands. His gaze went from the men's choir across the chancel to the congregation, to Bishop St. James, Father Merle, and Reverend Armstrong, then back to the congregation. His blue eyes were alight with fear. He managed to sing the final words, quickly turned away, and crouched as the suppressed sounds of his vomiting nonetheless reached them and faded with the final notes of the organ.

St. James returned to the pulpit. Should he mention the unfortunate and untimely illness of the choirboy, who was slinking away in shame?

He drew a deep breath and said, "Father Paul Singletary devoted much of his life to serving his fellow man. He did this in the ghettos of this city, in the drug-rehabilitation centers, and in the kitchens where the homeless are nourished. Of course, he also served his country admirably. He was particularly fond of this prayer, often used on shipboard during storms or in times of war." St. James adjusted his glasses and began to read: "O most powerful and glorious Lord God, at whose command the winds blow and lift up the waves of the sea, and who stillest the rage thereof; we, thy creatures, but miserable sinners, do in this our great distress cry unto thee for help. . . ."

When St. James had finished the prayer, and preparations had begun for the closing portions of the service, Annabel whispered to Mac, "That poor boy."

"I know. There's lots of flu going around. Kid must be terribly embarrassed. Say, did you know that Paul was in the military?"

"No."

"I gather from what George said that he might have served in the navy, maybe on board a ship. That's a slice of his life I knew nothing about."

Their attention returned to the altar. "Let us pray" was the call. Mac and Annabel sank to their knees. Their fingers found each other's once again as they prayed along with the bishop for the salvation of Singletary's soul.

Outside, Mac introduced Annabel to Terry Finnerty. He asked the detective, "Anything new?"

Finnerty shook his head.

"Nothing further in the autopsy findings?"

"Nah. Nothing under his nails, no fight."

"Meaning he knew the person who killed him?" Annabel said.

"Maybe, maybe not. Maybe he didn't know

the person, but it happened so fast he didn't have a chance to put up a fight."

"The word is getting around, Terry, that the body might have been moved from another place." Smith couldn't be critical of such rumors. He'd helped to spread the word in his own law class. "Are you still leaning in that direction?"

Another shrug from Finnerty. "Yeah, I think it's a good possibility. What I need now is that woman who found the body. We put out a composite on her based on the bishop's wife's description. Maybe we'll get lucky. Nice meeting you, Mrs. Smith. You must be a saint to put up with this guy." He laughed to indicate he was kidding.

"I felt so sorry for Carolyn Armstrong," Annabel said as she and Mac walked toward their car. "I didn't think she'd make it."

"Neither did I," Smith said. "Did she know Paul pretty well?"

"I suppose so. They worked together. Everyone at the cathedral is broken up, except Father Merle, who is so controlled. She had trouble keeping from crying two days ago when we met about the art show. I still can't believe it."

Smith opened the door for Annabel. "As you said, she certainly is beautiful."

As they waited in a line of traffic to turn onto Wisconsin Avenue, Mac said, "I can't get that poor choirboy out of my mind. How embarrassing to throw up in the middle of your solo at the National Cathedral."

"I know. Did you see the look on the child's face just before it happened? He seemed to be searching every corner, every crevice, for something."

"Maybe for a place to hide. Let's change the subject. Did you get the feeling from Finnerty that he was a lot surer that the body had been moved than he was letting on?"

She shook her head. "No. Why do you say that?"

"Oh, I don't know, just something about him. I got to know him fairly well when I was practicing, got to know when he was lying and when he was being straight. If Paul was murdered elsewhere and his body taken to the Good Shepherd Chapel, it adds weight to the possibility that someone who knew the cathedral killed him, not just a drifter Paul stumbled into in the chapel. Good Shepherd, open all day and night, is the most obvious place if the stranger-as-killer theory is at the top of the list."

She nodded. "What I can't fathom, Mac, is why anyone would kill him even if they had met suddenly in that little chapel. Nothing was taken from Paul. The newspapers said his wallet was intact, there was money in his pockets. What could he have come upon that would warrant killing him? Two people passing drugs? I don't think drug dealers would come to a chapel in a cathedral to do business."

"Drug dealers will deal anywhere. Speaking of business, how are preparations coming for our honeymoon?"

"Good. I checked with the travel agent, and all the confirmations are back. I do want to pick up a dress and a blouse or two before we go. Other than that, I'm set. How about you?"

"I'm ready. I still have to work on my speech, and I want to talk with George before looking into Paul's movements in London. I'd say we're in pretty good shape." They were stopped at a light. He leaned over and kissed her on the cheek. "I love you very much, Annabel."

"Why this sudden gush of affection?" she asked.

"Just a spontaneous eruption of understanding of how good life can be. That is, when you're alive and with the right woman."

Later in the day, Bishop St. James held a meeting of cathedral and St. Albans clergy. He used the occasion to assure them that while Paul Singletary's murder had disrupted things, to understate, it was necessary for each of them to get on with the important task of moving forward on many missions vital to the cathedral's future. He was only slightly annoyed when Carolyn Armstrong interrupted to ask who would replace Paul.

"I'm afraid I haven't given that much thought," St. James said, "but I know it has to be addressed. Until it is, we're all going to have to assume some of the burden that Paul carried." He checked Merle's reaction. As dedicated as Merle was to his religion and cathedral, taking on additional workload would not please him. Jonathon always wished for more time (as many of the clergy did) to use in personal meditations and for sermon writing and research. In addition, he was somewhat shy, a condition covered over with bristles, and uncomfortable in face-to-face work with coy people. He *cared,* but never knew how to show it.

"Will you go outside for a replacement?" Armstrong asked.

"I have no idea what steps will be taken to replace Paul. We'll discuss that at another meeting." He took in the rest of the room. "We're so close to seeing this cathedral completed that we can't allow anything to deter us from that goal. I know how difficult it is to focus on our tasks, but Paul, like all of us, lived for the day when the final stone would be placed in the West Tower. He can't be here to rejoice in that moment, but we can deliver it to him."

The bishop left the room for a few minutes to greet a visitor.

"How unfortunate, the Kelsch boy interrupting the service like that," said Jonathon Merle.

"Much worse for him, poor dear," said Carolyn Armstrong.

Choirmaster Nickelson said, "He's a difficult young man. I've been having nothing but trouble with him since the night before the murder."

"Really?" Merle said.

"Yes. He'd been cutting up in rehearsal, and I assigned him a punishment detail in the choir room that night."

"How late was he there?" Merle asked.

"He was supposed to stay until eleven. I assume he did."

Merle grunted and looked at the door as the bishop entered. They spent another twenty minutes together before St. James ended the meeting by leading them in prayer.

Outside in the hallway of the administration building, Carolyn Armstrong said to Nickelson, "Has Joey Kelsch ever said anything about Paul's death?"

"Not to me," Nickelson said.

"He should talk to someone. He may need counseling. I was upset myself during the service, but to become physically ill might represent some deep turmoil he's going through about Paul's murder."

"Maybe. I'm not a shrink. I conduct a choir. Excuse me, Reverend, I have an appointment."

"Well, I *don't* conduct a choir," she said after him, realizing how silly her comment was. *And your mother wears army boots.* She left the building and walked to St. Albans, where she always felt more at home than in the cathedral. St. Albans was *her* church, a small country parish in the imposing shadow of the titanic National Cathedral, a true place of simple faith and worship without the destructive intrusions of power and politics, manipulation and machinations of the cathedral itself.

The meeting of the bishop and his staff had begun at noon. Simultaneously—although five hours later in London—the Reverend Malcolm Apt escorted solicitor Jeffrey Woodcock to one of the doors to Lambeth Palace. They'd been meeting for an hour.

Woodcock, who was short and round and who attempted to cover his bald pate with strands of hair from low down on his right side, energetically shook Apt's hand. "This was a most useful meeting, I do say, most useful."

"Yes, but unfortunate that it needed to take place, Mr. Woodcock. While this whole business is obviously a legal matter, there are potentially damaging ramifications where the image of the church is concerned. I feel confident after this meeting that you are fully aware of that fact, and that you understand the need to proceed cautiously in order to avoid unseemly scandal."

"Of course. I assure you that any legal maneuvering will be done with discretion. Good evening, Reverend Apt."

"Good evening, Mr. Woodcock."

Woodcock had intended to return to his office, but considering the hour decided instead to go directly to his club for a quiet drink and dinner. His family was in the country on a brief holiday, leaving him to fend for himself, something that, despite his brilliant law career, he was remarkably incapable of doing. His wife did everything for him; when she was away, he found the familiar comfort of the club to provide a sense of shelter.

Malcolm Apt, on the other hand, was supremely confident in his ability to handle every aspect of his life without the help of others. He went into Lambeth's kitchen, made himself a simple dinner of steamed vegetables and boiled chicken, and took it to his office.

At nine, he called for a taxi, slipped on his black raincoat and black rain hat, and waited near the entrance. He climbed into the black London taxi that had been dispatched and said, "The Red Lion pub on Waverton in Mayfair."

When the cab pulled up in front of the pub, Apt paid the fare and looked out through the window at a dark blue Ford parked down a narrow street a dozen yards away. He checked his watch; he was precisely on time. He got out of the cab and watched it drive off, its lights reflecting off glistening pavement that had been moistened by a brief shower. He strolled casually in the direction of the Ford, and when he reached it, climbed into the backseat.

Without a word, the driver got out and entered the pub, where he announced that Mr. Leighton's car was waiting. He returned to the car, again saying nothing to Apt.

Ten minutes later Brett Leighton, wearing his customary tweed suit and carrying an umbrella, came to the car and climbed into the back to join Apt. Bob drove slowly and without purpose through Mayfair, its small, exclusive shops closed, only an occasional person walking on the streets. Leighton and Apt spoke in hushed tones. After a half hour, Leighton said to Bob, "Home, please." He turned and said to Apt, "Bob will drive you back to Lambeth."

"No, I prefer not," said Apt. "He can take me to a busy intersection where there will be taxis."

"As you wish," Leighton said.

Leighton, about to exit the car as it stopped in front of his Belgravia home, said to Reverend Apt, "Remember, she is a real problem. We must keep that in mind at every step."

Apt was annoyed at being reminded of what he felt should have been obvious. He gave Leighton a slight, sour smile and watched the long, lean assistant director of MI5's "B" Division stop to admire a large stoneware pot of mums in front of his house before inserting a key in the door and disappearing inside.

"The nearest taxi queue," Apt said curtly. He was dropped off at Sloane Square, where he immediately got into a cab. Bob, who'd been handed an envelope by Leighton, drove to the Lamb and Flag and indulged in a dinner of a T-bone steak served heavily salted and vinegared in a brown paper bag, and a Directors bitter. His wife had told him that he could take care of his own dinner if he came home late again, which is what he was doing. Better food here than what she was likely to have left for him.

And better conversation, too. Maude always asked too many questions, while he'd made a perfectly good life by asking next to none.

chapter
10

The Following Sunday—
Outside Temperature, Minus 68 Degrees

"To us," Mac Smith said, touching the rim of his glass against Annabel's. "Airborne at last."

"To a sublime honeymoon," she said.

The Pan Am 747 had lifted into the air over New York's John F. Kennedy Airport, banked left, and reached its cruising altitude of thirty-seven thousand feet for its flight to London.

"Nice champagne, nice to be here," Smith said. "It's been a mad scramble the last few days."

It had been. Under the unwritten but well-understood law of diminishing time when preparing for a trip, Smith had found himself racing to fit everything in.

First, there had been an emergency meeting of the cathedral chapter to discuss a number of procedural questions, the most pressing of them, in the bishop's view, being what action would be taken should Singletary's murderer turn out to be connected with the cathedral. Smith had declined Bishop St. James's invitation to attend, but the bishop was relentlessly persuasive. Representatives from the cathedral's law firm were there, too, neither of whom had any experience in criminal law.

"Highly unlikely it was anyone from the cathedral," said the chapter president, "but better to be prepared."

Smith certainly agreed with that thinking. He was asked whether he had learned of any further developments from the MPD. He had; Smith had met that morning with the chief of Homicide. The final autopsy results were in, and Finnerty had given Smith a copy of the medical examiner's notes.

Pressed for details, Mac avoided them, but one nice gray-haired, carefully coiffed and garbed parishioner kept asking to know everything. Smith winced, finally said, "All right," and proceeded to read: ". . . skin and subcutaneous tissue crushed against underlying bone . . . surrounding bruising characterized by rough and uneven edges . . . hairs, tissue and damaged blood vessels, customary in such injury, at base of wound . . . wound crescent-shaped— two and three-quarter inches (weapon not blunt) . . . force of blow substantial . . . fractures to skull depressed and comminuted . . . considerable bone splinters driven into soft tissues . . . heavy hemorrhaging (blood vessels bled into space between skull and brain membrane) . . . internal bleeding collected between dura and inner surface . . . fracture and secondary radiating fissures indicate blow was delivered in a horizontal plane . . . minimal hypostatic staining of skin on lower back and back of neck . . . body temperature eighty-two degrees (subject was clothed and indoors—rate of cooling necessarily slowed by virtue of cause of death) . . . level of rigor not advanced (stiffness confined primarily to face) . . . time of death approximately ten P.M. night prior to discovery of victim . . . analysis of abdominal contents support estimated time of death . . . analysis of clothing and body indicate absence of substances other than belonging to victim . . .

clothing clean . . . no bruises on hands or arms to indicate defense taken against weapon . . . death was instantaneous . . ."

Smith looked around the table. The nice gray-haired woman went grayer still, and Smith repressed a small sense of satisfaction. The blunt, unpleasant words of the report had had their predictable effect on others, as well. Some feigned disinterest by looking away. One man's face was drained of blood; Smith wondered if he would be the latest Episcopalian to become ill. "How horrible" . . . "Sad" . . . "Barbaric" . . . "Brutal," said the chapter members.

"Do the police feel that anything in the report is useful to their investigation?" Smith was asked.

"I haven't discussed that with them at length," he replied. "They're being very cooperative with me, particularly Chief Finnerty. He and I go back a long way. He really doesn't have any obligation to share this information, but he seems to view me as having an official capacity. I haven't dissuaded him."

"You will handle the defense if someone from the cathedral is charged?"

"I haven't committed myself to that yet," Smith said. "I suppose, like all of us, in a way,

I'm hoping that it will turn out to be a stranger, or at least someone not close to the cathedral. I have promised the bishop, however, that I will be as helpful as possible. That is still my intention." Bishop St. James's smile spilled over with appreciation.

Smith and the bishop met privately following the chapter meeting. St. James handed Smith a letter of introduction to the archbishop of Canterbury as Smith had requested. "You're likely to see Reverend Malcolm Apt," St. James told Smith. "It may be difficult to see the archbishop in person, but this letter might help. I'll call Apt."

"I was intrigued with something you said during Paul's funeral," Smith said as he slipped the letter into his jacket pocket. "Was Paul ever a chaplain?"

"Yes."

"Navy, I take it."

"Right."

"When?"

"Evidently, soon after he was ordained. He rarely spoke of it. Maybe once, twice, as I recall. He did love that verse, though, and liked to use it when comforting the bereaved."

"How long did he serve?"

"I have no idea, Mac. Why?"

"Just want to know as much as possible about him. Well, I have to go. I'll call when we return."

St. James placed a hand on Smith's shoulder. "You know how grateful I am."

"Yes, I know."

"Have a safe trip, and don't spend all your time on this. Remember, it is your honeymoon."

"Annabel will see to it that I don't forget. Good night, George."

Smith's next meeting was with Tony Buffolino, the former Washington narcotics detective who'd been dismissed from the force for taking money from a South American drug dealer. A highly decorated cop, Buffolino had never touched any of the loose and plentiful dirty money available to narcs until a flood of bills for cancer treatment of a son washed him against the wall. As his attorney, Smith managed to quash criminal charges, but couldn't stave off Tony's dishonorable discharge from the MPD. For a time, Buffolino blamed Smith for making that deal. He'd loved being a cop, loved it even more than the freedom Smith had won for him. Then, after years without contact, Smith had called him in to help with the investigation of the murder of the presidential candidate's aide at the Kennedy Center, and found him a job when the investigation was over.

When Smith walked into Tony's Spotlight Room at noon, he found the cop-turned-restaurateur sitting at the bar. The establishment, sandwiched between two topless clubs on lower K Street, was open only at night. A young Hispanic swept beneath tables on which chairs had been stacked. The PA system played Sinatra. A heavy smell of tobacco and perfume hung like the red velvet drapes behind the small bandstand on which a set of drums and several electronic musical instruments stood abandoned like tools of war awaiting the next deafening battle. Illumination came from spotlights covered with red and blue gel. "Las Vegas Comes to D.C." a poster outside read.

"How goes it, Tony?" Smith asked as he joined him at the bar.

"Mezza-mezza," Buffolino said. He looked up from the copy of *Variety* he'd been reading. "How come you never come in here, Mac?"

"Here I am."

"I mean at night when the action's going.

You and Annabel come to the gala opening, then I never see you again. I got a dynamite show in here for a couple 'a weeks. The chick singer is a knockout, Mac, and I got a mimic who does the wildest obscure people you ever saw."

"That sounds safe . . . for a mimic," Smith said. "How is Alicia?"

Buffolino looked around before saying in a low voice, "Wonnerful. Loving and kind and drivin' me nuts." He sighed. "Things were good till we got married. You marry 'em, and they change."

"Ah, yes, I've heard that. And you should know, since this is not your first time around. Give her my best."

"I will. Same to Annabel. So, what brings you here? You sing? Always wanted to do stand-up comedy?"

"I was wondering if you were up to a job."

"PI stuff? Nah. Thanks, though. Too busy with the joint."

"Well, that settles that."

"You want a drink?"

"No, thanks."

Buffolino yelled in pidgin Spanish at the cleaning boy to bring them coffee.

"Not for me," Smith said, standing.

"Sit a minute, Mac. Relax. Coffee's not a drink. Good for your nerves. Keeps them hummin'. I kind of miss us talking." He grinned. Buffolino was a handsome man in a coarse, thick-featured way. He had sleepy, heavy-lidded eyes—bedroom eyes, they were once called. His was a fighter's face.

Smith ignored the liqueur Tony was offering but sipped the steaming hot mug of coffee set before him. "Too early in the day for anisette," he said.

"Might keep you awake, uh?"

"Something like that."

"What's the case, the priest?"

"Yes. How did you know?"

"When I'm not too busy, I watch a little TV. Your name came up. Somebody charged?"

"No, but on the assumption that someone will be at some point, I'm lining up what ducks I can."

"What would you want me to do?"

"Check into Father Singletary's background. Everything. Discreetly, though. I have to go out of town and don't want to lose time here. Annabel and I are leaving tomorrow for London on our honeymoon. We'll be back in a week. I have to find someone who can move on it. Need a report ready when I return."

"Yeah, well, Mac, maybe I could do it. Be good to get away from here for a while. Maybe good for Alicia 'n me, too. It's too close bein' together all the time. Yeah, I'll do it. What's a week? Besides, if I have to tell you the truth, and to you I *do* have to tell the truth, I'm not exactly what you'd call busy. Business is lousy."

"Sorry to hear it." Smith stood and clapped Buffolino on the back, then handed him an envelope. "A retainer. And the particulars on what we know so far."

Buffolino looked at the check. "This is a tenth, huh?"

"It's a third."

"Yeah? Okay, but only for you."

"Me and a house of God. Do you good to get out of this place and try another. Thanks. See you in a week."

"Ciao, baby."

Smith's last commitment before he and Annabel left for London was at the Sevier Home in Georgetown. He never seemed to find the time to visit his mother as much as he had promised himself he would, which always prompted a nagging feeling of guilt that was uncomfortable—and unnecessary, he reminded himself whenever it set in. For this visit, he had blocked out most of the afternoon.

They spent a good deal of it out in the gardens surrounded by English boxwood and huge azalea bushes, holly, and black walnut trees. Josephine Smith always insisted that her son stop and read a plaque in the ground along Azalea Walk:

The kiss of the sun for pardon, the song of the birds for mirth, one is nearer God's heart in a garden than anywhere else on earth.

These times with his mother were always peaceful. They could also be inspirational or amusing when he was depressed. His mother was an unfailingly optimistic person. Her standard response to "How are you?" was "Wonderful. I got up this morning, took a breath, and it worked. What more could I ask for?"

They finished their visit by sitting on the expansive porch that overlooked the gardens. They were alone; another resident of the home played the piano—badly—on the other side of the window behind them. "Well, how does it feel to be a married man again?"

"Good," Smith said, taking his mother's hand in his. "I'm a very lucky man to have someone like Annabel."

"I wondered how long it would take you to come to that conclusion," said his mother. "You certainly dragged your feet."

He laughed. "Mother, you and Dad sent me to law school so that I would learn to weigh all the facts and not make snap judgments."

"No matter, it makes me feel good and proud that you and Annabel are now married. I never did like the arrangement you had."

"Why not? It worked very nicely."

"I like things tidied up, Mac. And the law to go with love. Marriage does that."

"Yes, it certainly does. I really have to be going. I still have things to do before we leave."

"London," she said wistfully. "It's been a long time since I've been there."

"We'll go soon, the three of us, maybe in the spring. The weather is better then."

Each knew what the other was thinking. As healthy and vivacious as Josephine Smith was, the reality that she was in the final phase of her life could not be denied. Would she be alive to take to London in the spring? Mac mused. He dearly hoped so. Although he didn't spend nearly enough time with her, he liked the fact that she was there, alive, that her first breath in the morning continued to "work," and that she was available to him. He didn't look forward to the day when she wouldn't be.

After Mac and Annabel's plane had passed Cape Cod and they had been served caviar and smoked salmon, Mac showed her the written autopsy report. When she was finished reading, she said, "Charming prose style. Anything in here strike you as unusual?"

"Yes."

"What?"

"The item about the weapon having been swung on a horizontal plane."

"Yes?"

"Paul was sitting in the pew when he was found. It seems to me that if you're going to hit a man while he's sitting, the blow would tend to come from over his head. You'd hit him more toward the top of the head, not the side."

"Uh-huh."

"So, it also seems to me that unless the murderer was crouching, it's unlikely that Paul was seated when he was killed, as the position of the body suggested."

Annabel thought for a moment. "Or he was hit by a short person. Then again, it's possible that Paul was struck while standing and fell into the pew."

Smith shook his head. "No, he was sitting there, neat and proper. Sure, he was leaning against the wall, but his body was not in a position that would have resulted from falling there."

"What conclusion do you come to?" she asked.

"I have to assume that because the blow was delivered in a horizontal plane and not from above, you are right, that he was probably standing when he was hit. Then it doesn't make any sense that if he came upon an intruder, was hit, and fell to the floor, the intruder would take the time to prop him up in the pew. Hit-and-run assailants don't rearrange bodies, they just hit and run. It could have been someone he knew, but it was almost surely someone who knew the cathedral. When you add to this the lack of blood, it points to his being murdered somewhere other than in that small chapel and brought there."

"Even so, who would bother to do that? Why would someone do that? Wouldn't there be blood where he was killed?"

"Yes, there would be, unless the murderer did a hell of a good job of mopping up. MPD's been scouring the cathedral, but that's a lot of ground to cover and a lot of dark corners."

"Chances are it didn't happen far from that chapel. Paul was not heavy, but he certainly wasn't a wisp of a man. Maybe the garden out-side Good Shepherd."

"Maybe, although the M.E.'s report said his clothes were clean, no grass stains or dirt."

"That doesn't mean they weren't there. I re-member you delivering a lecture to one of your classes about how often routine things like that are missed during autopsies and clothing anal-ysis."

"I know, I know, and you're probably right. It's not likely to have happened far from the chapel."

She put caviar, chopped egg and onion on a crustless toast wedge and savored it. Smith disliked caviar and had given his small jar of beluga to her, a ritual they always went through when flying first class. "Did Terry Finnerty raise this when you talked to him?"

"No. He simply handed me the report. No, that's not true. He handed me the report and asked me a lot of questions. I get the feeling he's being nice to me, is cooperating because he sees me as a conduit into the cathedral. He's going to be very disappointed."

As the shiny, immaculate black Austin taxi took them from Heathrow Airport to Duke's Hotel in the heart of London, Annabel snuggled close to her husband. "I've never been on a honeymoon," she said.

"Nor will you ever be on another one," he said.

They fell silent; she knew what he was thinking, that he'd spent his honeymoon with his first wife in London many years ago. They'd stayed at the Savoy, a favorite hotel of Smith's. He'd considered suggesting the Savoy for Annabel, too, but thought better of it. Too much like bringing a new wife into the home of a former one. He and Annabel had stayed at Duke's on their last trip to London, and decided the little jewel tucked away in the middle of the St.

James's district suited them perfectly, with its elegantly furnished suites, attentive staff, and convenient location.

The driver pulled into the tiny courtyard in front of Duke's and, as London taxis are designed to do, turned around, if not on a dime, certainly on a ha'penny. They were greeted with reserved but real enthusiasm at Reception. On previous visits, Mac had always signed them in as Mr. and Mrs. Mackensie Smith. This time he did it with quiet, proud conviction, and legitimately.

It was ten o'clock at night London time, but five hours earlier by their body clocks. The hall porter took their luggage to what would be their honeymoon suite, number 25 on the fourth floor, and Mac and Annabel walked into the small, cozy lounge. Gilberto, the barman, came around from behind the bar and shook Mac's hand, kissed Annabel on the cheek.

"Meet Mrs. Smith," Mac said.

Gilberto, who'd been smiling broadly, frowned. "I have met Mrs. Smith before," he said in his Italian accent.

"No you haven't," Mac said. "We've only been married two months."

The smile returned to Gilberto's face. "Ah, I

understand. That deserves a celebration." He went behind the bar, and Mac and Annabel took the two barstools. There were three other couples at tables in the small room, and one pair had overheard the conversation. "Congratulations," the man offered.

Mac and Annabel turned and smiled. "Thank you," they said.

"Let me buy you a drink," the man said.

Gilberto placed his hands on the bar and said to the other customer, *"Grazie,* but this is my treat."

The bar in Duke's Hotel was known to many Londoners and American guests not only because of the professional charm of its barmen, Gilberto and Salvatore, but because they were supported by the hotel in an ongoing search for the rarest ports, cognacs, and Armagnacs. A dozen bottles stood on a special shelf behind the bar. There was an 1802 Napoleon cognac, an 1894 B. Gelas et Fils Armagnac, and a 1908 Ware's port. Only the port was unopened; it was on sale for £500, approximately $750. A one-third gill of the Napoleon cognac, barely enough to cover the bottom of a large snifter, cost £150, or about $225.

Gilberto took a half-empty bottle of Grahams

1945 port that sold for £40 per glass and carefully filled two small, elegantly etched aperitif glasses. He placed them in front of Mac and Annabel and said, *"Salute!* To love and marriage and to my good American friends."

Mac and Annabel held the glasses up to each other, then tasted. "Superb!" Smith said. They placed the glasses on the bar and continued to look at each other. Gilberto put the glasses on a small silver tray. "What suite?" he asked.

"Twenty-five," Smith said.

"I will take these to your room. You may prefer to be there."

Smith knew that Jeffrey Woodcock would insist upon dinner at Wilton's, a popular restaurant on Jermyn Street that served up traditional food in traditional ways in an atmosphere that was a little too stuffy and clubby for Smith's taste. Wilton's, he thought, was the sort of place that perpetuated the stereotype of British cooking as being bland, boiled, and without verve. It was precisely those qualities that attracted Woodcock to it, however. He was as clubby as the restaurant—a perfect match. There was one advantage to Wilton's for Mac and Annabel. It was within a few blocks of Duke's Hotel.

Judith Woodcock, whom Mac had met only once, was an animated woman with gray hair who doted on her husband, which he seemed to relish, and like him was given to repeating. She reminded Mac a little of his own mother, a younger version, of course—he knew Woodcock was sixty-two; Judith was probably within a year or two of that.

After a dinner that surprised Mac with its excellence, the four of them walked back to Duke's and settled at a corner table in the bar. The conversation eventually came around to what Mac called the subsidiary purpose of their visit to London—aside from honeymooning, of course.

"That's shocking, absolutely shocking," Woodcock said when Mac told him that Paul Singletary was the priest who'd married them. "Had no idea," Woodcock said. "I met the poor chap twice when he was over here discussing this Word of Peace project. Charming young man . . . well, perhaps not so young, but certainly charming. Yes, perfectly charming."

Smith pressed his knee against Annabel's

beneath the table. She was in a discussion with Judith Woodcock, but Mac knew she was tuned in to both conversations with equally clear reception, something at which she was expert.

"How did you have occasion to meet him?" Smith asked.

"As I said, this peace project he was involved with. The church was reluctant to enter into any sort of supportive posture without consulting the firm for a legal opinion. We saw nothing wrong with it, although I must say there were some individuals involved who are not the sort of chaps I would invite to the club." Woodcock laughed; Mac smiled. "No, not to the club, or to Wilton's, for that matter. Still, nothing wrong with the movement. One can't very well be critical of efforts to bring peace to the world, can one?"

Smith shook his head. "No, one can't." Now I'm repeating, he thought.

"Do your police chaps have any leads?" Woodcock asked.

"Not yet," Smith replied. "One of the things I've promised the bishop of the National Cathedral I'd do while we're in London is to attempt to trace Paul's tracks during his last visit. He evidently returned to Washington a day earlier than he'd planned."

"That so? Why?"

"I don't know. I have a letter of introduction to the archbishop of Canterbury from Bishop St. James in Washington. I was hoping to learn something from him about Paul's visit."

"I can certainly pave the way for you over at Lambeth," Woodcock said. "I was there just the other day."

"You were?" Smith said. "Do you meet often with your clerical clients?"

Woodcock laughed; it had a certain forced ring to it. "No, just on occasion. When something comes up that needs discussion."

"Any talk of Paul Singletary's murder the last time you were there?"

"No, absolutely none." He didn't repeat "None." Smith knew his friend was not being honest.

"Word of Peace?" Smith asked.

"Pardon?"

"Word of Peace. Is that what you were meeting at Lambeth about?"

"No . . . well, yes, that is a continuing topic of discussion."

"The church . . . the archbishop, that is, has been supportive of the movement, I gather."

"Yes, quite."

"Do you deal with the archbishop himself?"

"No, almost never. Frankly, Mac, I'll be surprised if your letter gains you an audience with him. He sees very few people. Rumor has it he's not been well, but I can't confirm that. No, I deal with Reverend Malcolm Apt."

"I know the name. Our bishop mentioned him to me, indicated he's sort of an information officer for the church."

"Yes, that and many other things. He seems to be directly involved in almost every aspect of Lambeth, almost all aspects, a right-hand man-of-all-seasons for the archbishop."

"I intend to call him in the morning," said Smith, "see if I can arrange an interview with the archbishop."

"Well, as I said, don't count on it. Chances are you'll meet with Reverend Apt."

Annabel turned to Jeffrey Woodcock and said, as though she'd been part of the conversation, "You can see that this husband of mine plans a busy honeymoon."

Both the Woodcocks laughed. "Very clever of you, Mac," Jeffrey Woodcock said, "working in enough business to satisfy your Internal Revenue chaps back home. Write off your honeymoon. Damned clever, I'd say."

Smith didn't bother explaining that he hadn't even thought of that until Woodcock brought it up. They finished their drinks and walked the Woodcocks to where they'd parked their Jaguar on Jermyn Street. During the short walk, Smith had the feeling that Woodcock had something to tell him, perhaps a favor to ask, but was not sure whether he should. Smith's feeling was confirmed after Mrs. Woodcock was inside the Jag and Annabel was bidding a final good night to her through the open window. Smith and Woodcock stood next to the driver's door. "Mac," Woodcock said, "I was wondering if I could impose upon you while you're here for a bit of legal consultation. Frankly, I could use the American view of things."

"Go ahead," Smith said.

"Not here, not now. Would you be able to find some time tomorrow?"

Smith glanced over the roof of the automobile at Annabel, who didn't seem to be hearing the conversation. Did he dare build another business meeting into the honeymoon? He decided to take the chance, provided it didn't take more than a little conversation with Woodcock. They agreed to meet the following day at eleven at Woodcock's office.

Back in Suite 25, and bundled up in fluffy terry-cloth robes provided by the hotel, Smith asked Annabel what she thought of the Woodcocks.

"Very nice people. Very nice. Very nice." He laughed. She asked, "What are you meeting him for tomorrow?"

"You . . . ?" Yes, she did have a remarkable ability to tune in on two conversations at once, even across the roof of a car. "I don't know. He said he needed my counsel on something, a legal matter. I really couldn't say no. He did pick up dinner."

"No such thing as a free lunch," she said.

"No, there isn't." He looked at his watch. "I suddenly am very tired. How about settling in for a good sleep?"

"Sounds lovely. Will I see you at all tomorrow?"

"Of course. We'll meet for lunch. We have theater tickets and . . ."

"Sorry, Mac, can't make lunch. Business. I forgot to tell you that I called that collector,

Pierre Quarle, and made a date with him for lunch tomorrow."

"You did. What's he like?"

"We've never met, but he sounds absolutely charming, a very cultivated French accent, almost kissing my hand over the phone."

They climbed into the king-size bed and pulled the covers up over them. "Will I see you after lunch?" Smith asked.

"Probably. Why don't we leave messages at Reception, and we'll coordinate, maybe have tea together."

"Sounds fine." He kissed her forehead and turned over.

She started to laugh.

He faced her. "What's funny?"

"Us. We are funny, funny that is, and I think we should enjoy every minute of it. Good night, Mr. Smith."

"Good night, Mrs. Smith." He rolled over again. After a moment of silence, he sat up, lifted her right hand from beneath the covers, kissed it, and said, *"Bonne nuit, ma minette en susucre."*

"What does that mean?"

"Good night, sugarpuss. And if the Frenchman kisses your hand, I'll send Tony over to break his knees."

As Smith and Annabel fell asleep at eleven o'clock London time, Joey Kelsch walked into St. Albans in Washington for his 6:00 P.M. meeting with Reverend Carolyn Armstrong. She hadn't explained why she wanted to see him and he'd tried to make an excuse, but she'd insisted. "It will only take a few minutes, Joey," she'd said. He hoped so.

They sat in the front pew of the small church. They were alone. Reverend Armstrong, who wore a stylishly tailored powder-blue suit over a starched white blouse, smiled warmly at the young boy. He returned the smile tentatively but avoided eye contact.

"Joey, I've been worried about you lately," she said. She placed her fingertips on his hand. "Are you all right?"

"Yes, sure. I'm fine."

"I was so upset for you when you became ill during Reverend Singletary's funeral."

"I'm sorry about that."

"No need to be sorry. It could happen to any of us. I was quite upset myself. Was it the flu?"

"Yes, ma'am."

"You look fine today."

"It was . . . just a stomach sickness. I think I ate something."

"Of course. Joey, I understand that you were working in the choir room the night Reverend Singletary was killed."

"No, I . . . only for a little while."

"Really? Reverend Nickelson said he'd assigned you a punishment until eleven that night."

"No . . . Well, he did, but I . . . I left."

"How early?"

"I . . . I knew Reverend Nickelson was gone that night, so I snuck out. I came in for a couple of minutes. Then I left. Honest."

"I believe you. Well, I was just wondering. You didn't hear anything or see anything that might have to do with what happened to Reverend Singletary that could be useful to the investigation?"

"No, ma'am. I wasn't there long. I left."

She sat back and smiled. "I was thinking how exciting it would be if you'd seen something that could help the police find out who killed Reverend Singletary. Wouldn't that be exciting for you?"

"No, ma'am. I didn't see anything. I swear."

"Fine. Okay, now I want you to promise that if you remember anything, or want to talk about anything . . . *anything* . . . that you'll come to me . . . first. Okay? Promise?"

"Yes, I promise."

"Good, Joey. Thank you for coming."

"Yes, ma'am."

He fairly ran down the aisle and out the door.

chapter

11

London, Monday Morning—
A.M. Precip; P.M. Partly Cloudy

After a leisurely breakfast in a tea shop around the corner from Duke's, Mac flagged a taxi for Annabel and told her he'd call for messages at three. He returned to the suite, called Lambeth Palace, and asked for the archbishop. A minute later Malcolm Apt came on the line. Apt was cordial. He'd spoken with Bishop St. James about the possibility that Smith might call, and would be happy to meet at Smith's convenience. They settled on two that afternoon.

"I'll have a car pick you up at your hotel at one-thirty," said Apt.

"That isn't necessary. I'll be happy to—"

"Please, I insist. The driver will fetch you at the hotel."

"That's very kind, Reverend Apt. Thank you."

Smith took a brisk walk along Piccadilly, stopping to browse among the books in Hatchard's and the beautifully presented fancy foods in Fortnum and Mason, and ordered something he'd been promising himself for years, a pure silk umbrella custom-crafted for his height from Swaine Adeney, Brigg & Sons. He felt superb; he always did when he was in London (or maybe just because he was away from Washington). As always, he hoped that he could carry a slice of the good feeling back home.

Jeffrey Woodcock's law firm was on Old Bailey Street, two blocks from the Central Criminal Court. His office befitted a prestigious London barrister. Other than one that housed books from floor to ceiling, the walls were paneled in wood almost black in color. The furniture, including Woodcock's massive leather-inlaid desk, were antiques. The only thing that seemed out of place with the serene, time-warp image was Woodcock's personal secretary, Miss Amill, who was decidedly modern. She offered coffee or tea. Smith opted for coffee; Woodcock took the tea.

"Had enough tea since you've been here, Mac?" Woodcock asked.

"Not really, but I suppose I will by the time we leave."

"You'll have to drink three-point-six-two cups a day to keep up with us."

"Interesting statistic," Smith said. "Where did you come up with that number?"

"Read it in *The Times* this morning. Silly. Some study commissioned by a tea company, no doubt. Silly."

"Or a coffee company about to release its next study that more than two cups of tea a day is bad for your health."

Woodcock laughed softly and lifted the cup and saucer to just below his lips. He placed his cup and saucer on the table without drinking and said with furrowed brow, "Mac, you've had a great deal of experience in criminal matters."

"I used to. I teach it now. There's a difference."

"Yes, quite, but it isn't as though you've abandoned crime to teach biology or the decline of the British empire."

"Never practiced crime, Jeffrey. I just teach how to help criminals get away with it. Do you have a criminal case you need some advice on?"

"Potentially." Woodcock carefully formulated his next words. "This is a highly delicate matter, Mac, and despite the fact that we are colleagues, I would not have brought this up with you if you had not already become involved with the church over this tragic Singletary affair."

"I'm listening."

"I indicated last night—splendid evening, by the way . . . your new wife is a ravishing creature and so intelligent, too—I mentioned that I had met Father Singletary on two occasions, both having to do with the Word of Peace movement. That was true."

"And?"

"And . . . and the second meeting—the third, actually—had absolutely nothing to do with law or the church. Mrs. Woodcock and I took a long weekend in the Cotswolds the day after my second meeting with Father Singletary. We have a favorite place in Broadway . . . Buckland, actually, but Buckland really isn't much to talk about. At any rate, we particularly enjoy a hotel there called the Buckland Manor. Lovely spot, lovely."

"Was Paul Singletary there?" Smith asked, assuming it was the connection Woodcock was getting to.

"Yes, he was. You can imagine how surprised I was to drive two hours out of London and see him again after having been with him only a day earlier."

"He was staying at Buckland Manor?"

"Yes."

"Did you find some additional time to talk about Word of Peace?"

"No, we didn't. In fact, after we bumped into him as we were coming into the hotel, Father Singletary seemed to make a point of avoiding us."

"Why would he do that?"

"I suppose because he considered his circumstances to be somewhat awkward. That's speculation on my part, of course."

"What circumstances?"

"He was spending the weekend there with an extremely attractive woman."

Smith silently wished the sexual cynics in his class were there with him to hear this.

Woodcock cleared his throat. "Of course, Mac, Mrs. Woodcock was slightly taken aback once I told her who he was. It meant nothing to me, of course. I really don't concern myself with such things."

"No, of course not."

At this point Smith was wondering why he'd been called to meet with Woodcock. Bumping into an Episcopal priest with a beautiful woman on his arm in a hotel was mildly titillating but hardly grist for the collective legal brains sitting in Woodcock's office.

"I never would have given this a second thought, Mac, until three days ago."

"What happened three days ago?"

"I received a call from Reverend Apt at Lambeth."

"I spoke with him this morning. We're meeting at two."

"Good. Father Apt's call to me sounded quite urgent. He was upset. You couldn't miss that on the phone. I went to Lambeth, and we spent an hour discussing the situation. It seems that Malcolm Apt had been visited earlier in the day by a young woman who brought him disturbing news."

Mac's mind was now drawing intriguing scenarios. Was it the same woman Woodcock had seen with Singletary at Buckland Manor? Every time he speculated on what Woodcock was about to say next, he was right. It made him feel good. If only it didn't take so much time.

"Switch to tea, Mac?" Woodcock asked.

"No, Jeffrey, thank you. I want to save my three-point-six-two cups for Annabel."

Woodcock laughed. "Jolly good, Mac. Well, this young woman's name is Clarissa Morgan."

"The same woman you saw with Father Singletary in Broadway, I take it."

Woodcock slapped his hands on his knees and leaned forward. "Exactly! Exactly!"

"How can you be sure?" Smith asked. "You only saw her once at Buckland Manor. Was she introduced to you as Clarissa Morgan?"

"No, but he did mumble her first name, which I seem to recall was Clarissa. Can't be two different women."

Smith stifled the temptation to point out that despite his friend's preeminent position in British law circles, his logic tended on occasion to be shaky. Instead, Smith asked, "Did she indicate to Reverend Apt what this so-called disturbing news was?"

"No. She told him that she'd been Paul Singletary's lover right up until his death. In fact, she claimed that she'd been with Father Singletary the night before he died, that they'd slept together at her flat."

"Hardly the stuff blackmail is made of. Unless she's married. She's looking for money?"

"Yes. She told Reverend Apt that Singletary owed her a large sum, and that she was not looking for anything more than what had been promised her. She also hinted that if she revealed her past—and present—she could uncover much unpleasant news about Singletary's involvement with her and with other causes and institutions, yes, that's what she said: causes and institutions."

" 'What had been promised her'? In return for what?"

"She wouldn't be specific with Apt. She suggested that he call her in a few days. He's naturally reluctant to do that, which is why he contacted me. He wants *me* to call her."

"I suppose you'll know a great deal more after that call. How can I help?"

"I thought perhaps *you* might make that call."

"Why me?"

"To be candid with you, Mac, the major con-

cern here is to keep our client, the Church of
England, as far away from scandal as possible.
Far away. The fact that this firm and I have
been closely linked for many years with the
church makes me a part of this institution, too,
makes it a bit sticky, if you catch my drift. Also,
I thought direct contact might be useful to you
in your investigation."

Smith rubbed his eyes. On the one hand, he
was not interested in trying to resolve an apparent blackmail attempt by Miss Clarissa Morgan.
He had other things to do, including enjoying
his honeymoon. On the other hand, if she had
been as close to Paul Singletary as she
claimed, she could be a valuable source of information, one he didn't want to walk away
from.

"It's an odd request but all right, Jeffrey, I'll
call her."

Woodcock gave Smith notes he'd made during his meeting with Reverend Apt. Written on
the bottom were Clarissa Morgan's name and
telephone number.

"You will let me know what comes out of the
conversation," Woodcock said as he helped
Smith put on his raincoat.

"Of course. I'm not sure I'll call her today, but certainly by tomorrow. You'll hear from me."

The maroon Ford dispatched by Lambeth Palace to pick up Smith was too big to navigate Duke's tiny courtyard. The driver left the car on narrow St. James's Street, the tires on its right side up on the sidewalk, and walked Smith to it from the hotel. "Having a good stay, sir?" he asked as he opened the door.

"Yes, very. I always do when I'm in your great city."

They crossed Lambeth Bridge and pulled up in front of the main entrance to the palace.

"Will you be waiting for me?" Smith asked.

"Yes, sir, I was told to wait."

Smith was greeted at the door by a woman who introduced herself as the bursar. She led him to a small, comfortably furnished study, where the Reverend Malcolm Apt was waiting.

"Welcome to Lambeth Palace, Mr. Smith," Apt said.

"Thank you for seeing me," replied Smith. "And thank you for providing a car. It really wasn't necessary."

"Our pleasure. I hope you don't think we

have a fleet of automobiles at our disposal. We don't own the autos, but we have a rather good arrangement with a local car hire."

"It was a very comfortable ride, although I think a large Ford is a little inappropriate for London's narrow streets."

"I've told the car-hire company that very thing. I suppose their attitude is that when driving a dignitary, a large vehicle is in order. Please, sit down." He pointed to a cream-colored couch in the center of the room. A two-shelf bookcase ran along part of the wall opposite where Smith sat. Above it was a window that faced the chapel. Walls and ceiling were covered in oak paneling; a set of gold drapes covered another wall, in front of which was a chair that matched the sofa. Apt sat in it.

"This is called the Old Paneled Room," Apt said. "It was originally Archbishop Cranmer's study, but that goes back a few hundred years."

Smith laughed. "Everything in England goes back a few hundred years. When was Archbishop Cranmer in residence?"

"Fifteen thirty-three. He stayed around quite a while, more than twenty years. He presided over the special commission in 1543. That was when the London clergy took the Oath of Supremacy."

"There was some controversy surrounding it, wasn't there? Something to do with Sir Thomas More?"

"You have an excellent memory for history, Mr. Smith. Sir Thomas More was the only layman invited to the commission. He refused to take the oath giving the king powers over the church. So did the bishop of Rochester. They walked out, and paid dearly for their decision. But, Mr. Smith, as much as I enjoy talking history with you, I'm certain your schedule doesn't allow it."

"Unfortunately, it doesn't." Smith pulled from his jacket the letter of introduction to the archbishop of Canterbury from Bishop St. James and handed it to Apt. Apt placed half-glasses on his nose, read the letter, removed the glasses, and said, "I'm afraid it is quite impossible to meet personally with the archbishop. I assure you, however, that every aspect of our conversation will be transmitted to him, and I will relay to you his responses."

As cordial as Apt was being, Smith didn't like him. He reminded Smith of miscellaneous middle-level managers in corporations who reflect the power of their bosses, or secretaries to physicians who bask in their employers' inflated sense of lofty calling. He also had the feeling that Apt had the ability to talk for an hour about things that had no bearing upon the purpose of any meeting—like Jeffrey Woodcock. British genes, or public-school training?

Smith got to the point. "I've come to London for two reasons, Reverend Apt. The first, at least the one that prompted the trip, was to take my wife of a few months on a honeymoon."

Apt smiled weakly. He did not offer congratulations.

"The second reason has to do with the murder of Reverend Paul Singletary."

"What tragic news that was. It saddened all of us, including the archbishop."

"It's my understanding that Paul Singletary had a meeting with you the day before he died. Is that correct?"

Apt adopted a thoughtful expression. He rolled his fingertips over his thumb and narrowed his eyes. "Yes, I suppose it was. I'm trying to fix the time of Reverend Singletary's death. Yes, we met the day before."

"It is my assumption that the purpose of the meeting was to discuss Word of Peace."

"Among other things."

"Did Reverend Singletary get to speak with the archbishop?"

"No, he did not."

"Why did Reverend Singletary feel it necessary to speak with the archbishop? Was he disappointed when he couldn't?"

"Yes. I was not especially pleased to be the one to tell him that the archbishop's enthusiasm for Word of Peace had diminished in recent months."

"None of us likes to be the bearer of bad news. Why has the archbishop's enthusiasm diminished?"

"A number of reasons. Some of the movement's leaders are not to the archbishop's liking. Then, too, there is the matter of money."

"Money given to Word of Peace?"

"Yes." Apt sighed. "We may be a religious institution, Mr. Smith, but finances do play an important role in how we conduct and manage our faith. We, too, must deal with a bottom line."

Smith thought of George St. James, who

seemed always to be in the pursuit of funds. He also wondered whether Apt was hinting at some possible financial indiscretion. He decided to be direct: "Was Paul Singletary under suspicion by you or the archbishop concerning use of Word of Peace funds?"

Apt answered quickly. "No, although Reverend Singletary, for a man caught up in questions of poverty—among other things—was not what you'd call the most frugal of men." Apt's expression said clearly to Smith that this phase of the conversation was over.

"It's my understanding that Reverend Singletary had intended to return to Washington two days after his meeting with you," Smith said. "Obviously, he returned a day earlier than planned. Do you have any idea why?"

Apt formed a tent with his fingertips and said over it, "No idea whatsoever. In fact, I asked how long he was staying, and he told me he was visiting the countryside. Yes, what he said exactly was 'your limpid countryside.' I remember it well. I hadn't heard anyone describe our countryside as limpid before."

"I'd say it's an apt description." Smith decided not to add the usual "no pun intended."

"Do you know where in the country he intended to visit?"

"No, I really don't."

Smith didn't believe him. "I remember from conversations with Reverend Singletary that he was especially fond of the Cotswolds. Did he ever talk about his love of that area with you?"

Apt shook his head.

"Did Reverend Singletary say anything to you that would give me an idea of what he might have done after his meeting with you, whom he might have seen, had dinner or tea with, perhaps gone to the theater with?"

Another flat negative.

Smith leaned back on the couch and shook his head. "I'm afraid this may have been a wasted meeting, Reverend Apt. Of course, I enjoyed meeting you, but I was hoping to gain some insight into Reverend Singletary's movements while he was here. I'm sure you can understand how that could be helpful in solving his murder."

"You are an investigator, Mr. Smith?"

"As Bishop St. James's letter indicates, I am a professor of law at George Washington University. My wife and I have been attending services at the National Cathedral for some time, and I am a personal friend of Bishop St. James, and was a friendly acquaintance of Paul Singletary. In fact, Reverend Singletary officiated at my wedding." Smith stood. "You've been very gracious with your time, Reverend Apt. I appreciate that."

"Please call on me at any time, Mr. Smith. Would you like a tour of the palace? I could arrange to have someone take you right now."

"Tempting, but I have other commitments. Thank you for offering."

Smith's driver returned him to the hotel. As he got out, he said, "Thank you very much. By the way, my name is Mackensie Smith." He extended his hand through the open driver's window.

The driver smiled and shook Smith's hand. "Pleasure to serve you, Mr. Smith. Name's Bob."

There was a message at Reception from Annabel: *Taking tea with Mr. Quarle at the Ritz at four. Please join us if you can. Love, Annabel.*

Smith went to the suite and called the Buckland Manor in Broadway. "My name is Mackensie Smith. My wife and I are staying in London but thought it would be nice to go to the Cotswolds for a few days. Jeffrey Woodcock, a law associate, recommended you highly. Would you have a room for two nights beginning tomorrow?"

"Yes, sir, we do."

"Look, this is sort of a honeymoon for us. I'd appreciate the best room you have."

"The Vaulted Room is available. It's our finest."

"Sounds perfect." He gave his credit-card number and hung up.

His next call was to the number for Clarissa Morgan given him by Jeffrey Woodcock. "Miss Morgan, my name is Mackensie Smith. I'm an American attorney representing the National Cathedral in Washington, D.C. I was also a friend of Reverend Paul Singletary."

"Yes?"

"I've been asked to call regarding certain claims made by you to Reverend Malcolm Apt at Lambeth Palace."

There was a pause. "Why would you call me about this?"

"Because of my close involvement with the Washington Cathedral and Reverend Singletary. One of my purposes in London is to try to trace his movements just prior to his return to

Washington and his murder. I understand you were with him the night before."

"Mr. Smith, I find this most distressing. I don't know who the hell you are. You make certain claims, but as far as I know, you're nothing more than a very glib obscene caller."

Smith had to laugh. "Miss Morgan, I may be many things, but certainly not that. Would you be willing to spend half an hour with me? I think this might work a lot better in person."

She sighed.

"I assure you I am what I represent myself to be, and that I might be able to resolve your claim. But only if we talk."

"I'm busy tonight."

"Fine." He thought to try softening her up. And maybe open her up. "My wife and I are going to the country tomorrow, to the Cotswolds. Are you familiar with a hotel there called Buckland Manor?"

"No."

"It was highly recommended to us by a mutual friend. If you're available tomorrow, however, I'll be glad to postpone our trip."

Another sigh. "I am engaged for the next two days."

I'll bet you are. "Then our schedules coincide

nicely. Can we arrange a time to meet the day after I'm back?''

''Why don't you call me then.''

''All right. I look forward to seeing you.''

Smith shaved before walking the few blocks to the Ritz. As he entered the lavish lobby, London's most famous gathering place for tea, he had two thoughts. One was that he would have to finesse Annabel into accepting his sudden decision to leave the city for two days in the country. He hoped she hadn't made too many unbreakable plans in London.

His second thought was that he wouldn't bother waiting for Tony if this Pierre Quarle character kissed *his* hand. He'd take care of the Frenchman's knees himself.

chapter

12

**The Next Day, Tuesday—
Warm Sunshine. Perfect Weather for a
Drive on the "Wrong" Side**

"I don't know the man I married," Annabel said as Smith deftly navigated a series of round-abouts outside Oxford and found the road marked RING ROAD WEST.

"Why do you say that?"

"Because if I had to come up with a list of adjectives to describe Mackensie Smith, 'impetuous' would not be on it. I can't believe you simply decided to spend a few days in the Cotswolds, picked up the phone, and did it."

"I thought it would be a nice change for us on our honeymoon. After all, there is more to the

United Kingdom than London, and this Buckland Manor is supposed to be superb."

She sighed contentedly and watched the
rolling emerald-green hills, hills dotted with pic-
turesquely placed sheep, slide by. She knew
this was more than an impulsive fling in the
country. Mac had told her of his conversations
with Jeffrey Woodcock, Malcolm Apt, and Clarissa Morgan, and that he wanted to poke
around a little at Buckland Manor about Paul
Singletary's weekend there, apparently with
Clarissa Morgan, no matter how much Miss
Morgan might deny knowing the place. He had
promised Annabel, however, that his poking
would consume a minimal amount of their time.
The fact was—something Annabel hadn't told
him—she'd begun to enjoy the "business" aspect of their trip. It added a certain element of
extra excitement and purpose.

She looked at her husband. His expression
was intense—no, concentrated was more like
it—as he shifted gears with his left hand and
met the challenge of driving on the left. There
had been a few harrowing moments in London
as they tried to find the A40 out of the city, but
she'd read the map well, leaving him free to
deal with the mechanics of avoiding double-

decker buses and other city traffic, all having
wandered into the wrong lane.

They stopped in the quaint village of Broadway and strolled its main shopping street. Annabel went into a woolen-goods outlet while
Mac stood outside and watched people pass
by. He leaned against the building, turned his
face to the sun, and closed his eyes. Annabel
interrupted his reverie. "I can't make up my
mind between two sweaters," she said. "Come
help me choose."

Her purchases in the trunk of their rented
automobile—he'd recommended both sweaters—they left Broadway on the road Mac had
been instructed to take when he'd made the
reservation. Ten minutes later they were on a
long, graceful access road leading to the magnificent thirteenth-century manor house called
Buckland Manor. Before they could open the
car doors, a young man and woman came
down the steps. "We've been on the lookout
for you," said Nigel, the hotel's manager.

"Your directions were excellent," Smith said.
"This is Mrs. Smith."

"Welcome to Buckland Manor, Mrs. Smith,"
said Nigel's pretty assistant, Tracy. "Someone

will be out to take your bags. Please, come inside."

Annabel started up the steps but paused. "How beautiful," she said, referring to a stone church next to the hotel. Its rectory was part of the main building.

"Yes, a splendid example of twelfth-century Norman architecture," Tracy said proudly. "You must visit it while you're here."

They were escorted to the Vaulted Room, accurately named because of the way the white ceiling arched up high above. When they were alone, Annabel said, "Mac, it's absolutely magnificent." She hugged him. "I'm so glad you did this." She explored the expansive, tastefully decorated room. The walls were covered in a pale blue paper with a tiny white design. Curtains defining a series of bay windows were the color of cream; a pattern of small roses gave them a nice touch of blush. The large four-poster bed was covered in the same cream-and-rose fabric, as were skirt tables on either side of it. On a table in front of a love seat was a vase of pink gloxinia, a large basket of fruit, and two bottles of Cotswold spring water.

"You make me a very happy bride," Annabel

said as they stood at a window and looked out over pastures belonging to the hotel. Rare Jacob sheep stood like clusters of mushrooms in one; two huge Highland steer leaned against each other in another. "I'm happy we came here," she said. "I knew you were smart, but this was a stroke of brilliance."

"Shucks," Smith said, executing a perfect toe-in-sand. "Thank Jeffrey. Jeffrey, that is."

After unpacking, they sat on the love seat and discussed what they would do during their stay.

"I just want to hang around," Mac said. "I want to ask people in the hotel and the village about Paul."

"Why do you think anyone would remember him?" she asked. "As far as you know, he was only here once, the weekend Woodcock and his wife bumped into him."

"Yes, I know, but I have this feeling that he had more of a connection to this place than that. It's my understanding that he always in-corporated a trip to the country when he was in London on business. He'd told Reverend Apt that he intended to spend the next day in, as Apt recalls, the 'limpid countryside.' And then there's Clarissa Morgan denying she knows of this hotel. Of course, that could just be embarrassment at having spent a clandestine weekend with a priest. I don't know, Annabel, I just wouldn't feel right not following up on it."

"Well, I am very glad you feel that way, because I am beginning to feel utterly relaxed for the first time in ages."

"Good. If there's one thing a honeymoon should provide it's relaxation." He smiled. "Part of the time anyway."

Nigel, the manager, joined them briefly at dinner that night in the hotel's dining room. Smith asked him about the adjoining St. Michael's Church and was told that it served the villages of Buckland and Laverton. Services were conducted by a traveling Anglican priest. "A nice enough chap with an appropriate name."

"What is it?" Smith asked.

"The Reverend Robert Priestly."

Smith smiled. "A classic case of preordination."

"Yes, quite," Nigel said.

"We have a friend back in Washington who's also an Anglican priest," Annabel said. "He's been a guest here."

"What's his name?" Nigel asked.

"Paul Singletary," Smith said.

Nigel smiled. "Of course. Reverend Single-tary has been here on more than one occasion. He and Reverend Priestly are chums."

"I see," Smith said. "I hope we get a chance to meet Reverend Priestly."

"You undoubtedly will," Nigel said. He asked about their plans for the next day.

"I've been reading the guidebooks," Anna-bel said. "I know there's wonderful shopping, but I hate to waste the precious two days we have doing that. I'm a bit of an amateur bird-watcher. I brought my binoculars and a new camera, and picked up a guide to birds of the United Kingdom. Maybe I'll just spend tomor-row walking and looking."

"Sounds like a splendid idea," said Nigel. "We have a special map for walkers. I'll see that you have it straight away."

"Wonderful!" Annabel looked at Smith. "Feel like joining me, Mac?"

"Do you mind if I don't?"

"Not at all. You do your snooping around, and I'll spend the day with nature."

It was over dessert that Mac mentioned a man eating alone at a table at the opposite end of the room. "He checked in right after us," he said.

"Are you especially interested in him?"

"Not at all, although we probably should introduce ourselves. It's like we made the trip from London together. His car followed us pretty much all the way, and he stopped in Broadway when we did."

"Unusual to see a single man in a hotel like this."

"A salesman, maybe, or waiting for someone. Maybe waiting for us."

"Let's invite him to join us for dinner tomorrow night," Annabel said.

"Let's not. This is our honeymoon. The two of us are the right company. Oh, I get it—you jest."

The next morning they enjoyed a sumptuous full English breakfast. Annabel wore a navy-blue sweat suit and sneakers, and carried a warm jacket. It had turned colder overnight, and fog now veiled the verdant countryside.

"Sure you want to walk in this soup?" Smith asked.

"It enhances the charm," she said. "Besides, it will add drama to the pictures I take."

The small automatic camera Smith had bought her for her last birthday joined the binoculars around her neck. In her hand was the simple map provided by Nigel, and the bird book.

"Sure you know where you're going?" Smith asked.

Annabel opened the folded map, and they looked at it together. According to Nigel, much of the route was marked with small yellow arrows posted on trees, although it wouldn't be necessary to look for them until she reached Laverton by paved road. From there, it would be mostly open fields on her way to Stanton Village and up to the old quarry on Cotswold Ridge. It would be downhill from there, Nigel had assured her. He'd also discreetly pointed out that the only public house she would pass on the hike was called the Mount Inn, just outside Stanton. His final suggestion was that since she'd be walking through many pastures, it would be wise to look before she stepped.

Smith looked up at the somber, leaden sky. A gentle breeze swirled the fog around them like steam. They couldn't see the road from the front steps of the hotel. "Why don't you wait until tomorrow for your walk?" he suggested.

"No, this weather really inspires me, Mac.

Please don't worry. I'll be fine. Have you ever seen a more tranquil place in your life? The fog even adds a sense of comfort, like being wrapped in a blanket."

Smith grunted. Her romantic interpretation of the day's weather didn't jibe with his. "Well," he said, "if you're not back in the two hours Nigel says it takes for the walk, I'm sending out the Mounties."

"How exciting. But wrong country. I'll be sure to take my time."

Charlie, Buckland Manor's resident bearded collie, came bounding up to them. "Go inside," Annabel said. "You can't come with me." A note in each room asked guests not to take Charlie for a walk without a leash. Some local sheep farmers didn't appreciate Charlie's penchant for chasing their flocks and had threatened to shoot him if he came on their property again. Annabel opened the front door and the dog slunk inside.

Mac and Annabel kissed lightly, and she started up the long drive leading to the road, turning twice to wave. Smith missed the second one because the fog had obliterated her from view.

He went back inside and warmed his hands

in front of one of three fires kept going day and night in the public rooms.

"Tea, Mr. Smith?" Tracy asked.

"Yes, I'd love some." When he was served, he asked her, "How can I make contact with Reverend Priestly today?"

"I really don't know, but I'll find out."

She returned a few minutes later. "I called the cathedral in Gloucester," she said. "You are in luck. Father Priestly is scheduled to be here today for a parish meeting. He's due to arrive about eleven."

It was eight-thirty. "Good," Smith said. "I think I'll take a ride to some of the neighboring villages. I'll be back by eleven. If you happen to see Father Priestly, please mention I'd like a word with him."

"Certainly. Enjoy your tea and sightseeing, Mr. Smith, but drive carefully. This fog is the worst I've seen in a long time, and I've seen plenty of it."

Annabel walked slowly along the narrow paved road into Laverton. The ancient row houses lining the road were all constructed of the yellow brick characteristic of the Cotswolds. She reached a red telephone booth that was indicated on the map, crossed the road, and climbed over a low gate, using a crude wooden step that had been provided for walkers. A yellow arrow on the fence post pointed in a direction that would take her across a large grazing wold. The fog seemed to have thickened, if that were possible; she could see vague forms of animals in the distance. Sheep, small cattle? It was hard to determine most of the time. The silence and tranquillity were palpable as she hugged the side of a low stone wall that bordered the field. She heard the call of a bird, stopped, and trained her binoculars on trees immediately to her right. A swallow of some kind. She considered looking it up in her book, but decided not to bother. If she did that every time she spotted a bird, she'd get back to the hotel at midnight.

She continued her walk until reaching Stanton, where she stood in the middle of the deserted main road and took in her surroundings. She saw few birds, but one house was more beautiful than the next, and she snapped some pictures. Where are the people? she wondered.

A church, St. Michael and All Angels', stood in the V where two roads intersected. She meandered through the graveyard studded with ancient stones and approached the door. The sound of a car caused her to stop and to turn. A tan Ford Escort driven by a man moved slowly past the church and disappeared around the corner. All was silent again.

Annabel stood in the middle of the damp, musty church and pondered what it must have been like centuries ago when the faithful came to worship on Sunday mornings. How many hands had shaped the stone and fashioned the stained-glass windows? The ends of some of the wooden pews had been deeply gouged by chains that secured sheepdogs accompanying their masters to church. She looked up at the Gothic pulpit and imagined the words spoken from it to the poor, hardworking members of the congregation.

She looked down; she was standing on a large slab of stone with a skull and crossbones etched into it. She crouched and rubbed her hand over the writing. A man named John Ingles had been buried there in 1705. Below his name was written: JUST IN HIS ACCOUNTS; FAITHFUL TO HIS FRIENDS; MILD IN HIS TEMPER; CONSTANT TO THE END.

How nice to be remembered that way, Annabel thought as she retraced her steps to the front entrance, pausing to drop coins into a poor box.

She walked up a short road leading to the Mount Inn. The agreeable, pungent smell of smoke from the inn's chimney almost physically pulled her up the steep incline and into the cozy interior where a few locals drank and shared stories. One man read the local newspaper, the *Village Voice,* which bore no resemblance to its namesake in New York. Annabel sat at a small table across from the fireplace, where logs arranged vertically crackled, sending orange flames dancing up into the flue. An old woman behind the bar asked if she wanted something. It was too early for anything alcoholic, at least for Annabel, so she asked for a cup of tea. Soon she was sipping the steaming, strong brew and felt herself sinking deeper into the chair as she reached a state of mental and physical détente with herself and her surroundings. Everything was so perfect now. She was married to a man she loved deeply, she was able to indulge her love of pre-Columbian art with her gallery, and she was on her honeymoon in this beautiful place. Sometimes things could be perfect in one's life, not often and never for long, but sometimes. This was a moment she would cherish.

She paid for the tea and continued her walk, taking snapshots as she went. Soon, she'd run out of road again and was moving across vast fields, their green grass rendered even more vivid in the unnatural light created by the fog. Everywhere she looked were shapes, shadows, blurred images of livestock, and the economic backbone of the Cotswolds, its sheep. They would suddenly be there, then disappear just as quickly as the fog made them invisible to her.

The walk to the quarry was now uphill, and Annabel felt it in her legs. "You're out of shape, Annie," she muttered, her breath coming fast, her stride becoming more purposeful as she sought the Cotswold Ridge. From there, Nigel had promised, it would all be downhill.

When she reached the quarry, she sat for twenty minutes on a stone wall. Revived, she tried to follow the crude arrows on the hand-drawn map provided by Nigel. A half hour later she knew she was lost in a sea of washed green and surrounded by an opaque fog.

In the distance to her right was a line of black stick shapes. Trees. The ground sloped slightly to her left. Which way back to Laverton? she wondered. She'd never been very good at directions. But she had to make a decision. She decided to go in the downhill direction, away from the trees. Eventually, she reasoned, she'd have to reach something, someone. After ten minutes she paused and looked back at the row of trees. Something was moving up there. What was it? She squinted in an attempt to pierce the fog. *It* was heading her way. Now she could see that it was . . . someone on horseback. "Wonderful," she said aloud and laughed, suddenly thinking of Mac's promise to send "the Mounties." She'd stop the rider and ask directions back into Laverton. But first, she'd take a picture of this scene that was so eerily beautiful. She pressed off a couple of frames as the figure on horseback, shrouded in the wet fog, headed for her.

The figure was now close enough to be distinguishable. It looked to Annabel to be a woman on the horse, a woman dressed in full riding regalia. The horse was huge and powerful. When it was a hundred yards from Annabel, it suddenly broke out of its slow canter and bore down upon her. It took Annabel a second to react, to realize that she was about to be

trampled. She flung herself to one side just as
the horse reached her, its powerful hooves
thundering close to her head, and kicking up
mud and dung as they struck the earth in passing.

Annabel had fallen sharply on her left shoulder and the side of her face. She touched her
cheek. There was blood on her fingertips.
When she sat up, she looked in the direction
the horse and rider had gone. She couldn't see
me, she thought: the fog. "Idiot! You damn near
killed me." She pulled herself to her feet. Her
entire left side was covered with mud. She was
trying to remove some of it when she heard
. . . hoofbeats. The shapes reappeared, the
horse and rider heading for her again. This time
she had more time to react. She ran in the
direction of a stone wall, slipping, sliding, stum-
bling, grasping at the fog as though it could be
used for support. She looked back once and
saw that the rider had directed the horse to turn
after her. Gasping for breath, her lungs and
heart throbbing with pain, she reached the wall
and threw herself over it. The hoofbeats
stopped. A moment's silence. Annabel was
afraid to look over the wall, but knew she had

to. As she began to raise her head, the horse and rider turned and vanished into the fog.

Annabel wasn't sure what to do next. She needed time to pull herself together before continuing, but was reluctant to stay there. When would the rider return? One thing she knew for certain; she couldn't cross any open fields, would have to stick close to fences and walls.

An hour later she sloshed through the deep mud of a Laverton farmer's pigpen, climbed the fence, and reached the center of town. There wasn't a soul on the street. She was still shaking and knew she was wambling as she headed for the marked pathways that would take her back to the hotel. She was almost out of the village when she froze. A large black Labrador, its fangs bared and threatening growls coming from its throat, appeared from behind one of the stone cottages. "Get away, get away!" Annabel shouted. The dog stopped a few feet from her and continued to growl. "No! Get away, I said!" Annabel yelled.

A window in the cottage opened, and a woman stuck her head out. "Don't be yelling at him. He won't hurt you. He doesn't bite."

"Well, you're sure not going to prove that by me," Annabel snapped. "Get him away from me."

The woman called the dog's name. The animal backed off, still growling, and returned to the back of the cottage.

Annabel's legs were jelly, and she had trouble catching her breath, neither condition abating by the time she reached Buckland Manor. She entered the small foyer and collapsed on a bench, starting to sob. Nigel and Tracy ran from the office. "What's the matter?" he asked. "You look a fright."

Annabel looked up at them. "I've had a terrible experience."

"Your face is bruised," Tracy said.

"I know." Annabel looked down at the legs of her sweat suit, which were covered with mud and sheep dung. She trembled, deeply chilled. "Please, I just want to get to my room and take a hot bath. Is my husband here?"

Tracy looked at a clock on the wall. "He took a drive but said he'd be back at eleven to see Reverend Priestly." It was twenty to eleven.

"Come," Nigel said. "We'll help you upstairs."

They brought her tea and a bottle of port.

Once she assured them that she was all right, they left her alone. She soaked in the tub, but as soothing as its warmth was, she could not stop the internal shaking.

Wrapped in the hotel bathrobe, she poured herself some port and gulped it down, then did it again. She also had tea. Soon, the trembling began to subside, and she was able to focus more clearly on what had happened.

There was a knock on the door. "Come in," she said. "No, wait—who is it?"

"Nigel." He came into the room. "Just checking on you, Mrs. Smith. Feeling better?"

"Yes, much, thank you. Is my husband back?"

"No, but we're keeping an eye out for him. He'll have been slowed up in the fog. We'll send him up the moment he arrives."

"Thank you. You're all very kind."

"Anything to be of help. We feel distressed that we sent you out like this, and it turned out to be such an awful morning. What did happen to you, Mrs. Smith?"

Annabel leaned her head back against the love seat. "I'm really not sure," she said, "but I'll be happy to share it with you once I've figured it out myself."

"As you wish." Nigel lighted the gas fireplace and said he would be available for anything she needed.

Mac Smith parked on the street side of St. Michael's opposite the hotel and near the church's main entrance. He assumed that Priestly would be in the church holding his parish meeting. Smith was a few minutes late. If Priestly was not there, he'd look for him in the hotel.

The church was empty. And cold. Dank. Smith peered up at the high ceiling created of wainscoting that had been intricately decorated. The unworldly, fog-filtered light from outside passed without purposeful effect through large stained-glass windows depicting Baptism, Marriage, and Extreme Unction.

Might as well check at the hotel, Smith thought as he walked toward the rear door. He would not have stopped, would not have seen anything more, if the interesting ornate carvings on the high backs of some of the pews hadn't caught his eye. He stopped and ran his fingers over the carvings, and glanced down and saw a shoe—a man's black shoe. Smith bent over. His eyes traveled up the length of a man's black trousers, then to the torso and its clerical collar, and finally to the head. His mouth and eyes were open. The man was, Smith judged, in his mid-forties, certainly no older than fifty. His gray hair was short, a crew cut, actually. Just above the ear on the side of the head that faced up was a long, oozing wound that had intruded deeply into the skull. A bloodied instrument of death lay on the pew's bench. Smith sensed that he hadn't been dead long, maybe only minutes.

Smith left the church and found Nigel in his office.

"Mr. Smith, your wife is upstairs. She's quite all right, but she evidently had a harrowing experience on her walk this morning."

"Is she hurt?" Smith asked, starting for the stairs.

"No, no, but shaken. She asked that I send you up the moment you arrived."

"Thank you."

"Did you meet up with Reverend Priestly? Has he been very delayed?" Tracy called after him.

Hearing that Annabel had suffered some

mishap had caused Smith to forget for the moment what he'd just discovered in the adjacent church. He paused at the foot of the stairs and said, "Yes, I think I did. He's in the church now. And he's very dead."

chapter

13

Washington, D.C.,
The Same Day: 7:00 A.M.—
The Beginning of a Fat Fall
Wednesday in the Nation's Capital

"Calm down, Mrs. Waters," MPD Homicide chief Terrence Finnerty said. Present in an interrogation room were a department stenographer, another detective from the Singletary murder task force, and Mrs. Waters's son, Brian.

Evelyn Waters had been crying and praying ever since detectives had picked her up at her house an hour earlier. She looked surprisingly the way Eileen St. James had described her. Finnerty was impressed; usually, they never looked the way witnesses said they did.

"Mrs. Waters, there is nothing to be this upset about," Finnerty said. "If you don't calm down, we'll be here all day."

Her son, Brian, said, "My mother is a very religious person, Captain Finnerty. She's also very fragile, as you can see."

"Yeah, I know all that, but if we can't talk to her, we'll get nowhere."

Brian sat on the edge of the table next to his mother and placed his hands on her shoulders. "Mom, please, try to pull yourself together. You aren't in any trouble. They just want to ask you some questions to help find whoever killed the priest."

She took a rapid series of deep breaths and vigorously shook her head. "How could you do this to your own mother?"

"Mom, I couldn't see you living the way you've been ever since you discovered that body. I did it because I love you. These people aren't out to hurt you. They just want you to help them." He said to Finnerty, "She's been a wreck ever since that morning. I didn't know what else to do but call you."

"You did the right thing, Mr. Waters. Try to convince her she's doing the right thing."

No matter how upset someone is, there is just so much energy of despair, just so many tears in the tank. Eventually—it was only minutes but seemed like hours to Finnerty—Evelyn Waters gained enough composure to apologize, and to indicate that she would try to answer his questions.

"What I'd like you to do, Mrs. Waters, is to remember exactly what happened that morning from the time you entered the chapel to when you discovered the body, went up to the bishop's dressing room with the bishop's wife, and then left. Take your time, and don't worry if you forget things. We'll help you."

She looked up into her son's eyes. He was a nice guy, Finnerty decided, a little wimpy maybe but okay. Brian Waters touched his mother's shoulder again and gave her a reassuring smile. Finnerty pegged him to be in his late twenties. They'd had a chance to talk a little before bringing his mother into the room. He'd dropped out of college and was working as a salesman in an auto dealership on Wisconsin Avenue, not far from the cathedral. He lived with his mother; she had been widowed for eight years. According to the son, his father's death sent his mother into religious immersion. She attended six o'clock mass almost every morning at the cathedral, made most noontime masses in the War Memorial Chapel, and spent her time away from church reading the Bible and listening to religious broadcasts. "Did she often go to that little chapel by herself at odd hours?" Finnerty had asked. "When she was especially upset," the son had replied.

"Okay, Mrs. Waters, let's begin," Finnerty said. "I assume you went to the chapel because you were upset about something. Is that correct?"

Mrs. Waters bit her lip against another torrent of tears. She tried to reply verbally, but ended up simply nodding.

"What were you particularly upset about that morning?"

"I . . . it all seemed so hopeless."

"What did?"

"Life . . . my life . . . everything happening in the world. He has to come and stop it."

"Who has to come and stop it?"

"Jesus, the son of God. He's our only hope for salvation. I'd been up all night and . . ."

When she didn't continue, Finnerty asked her why she'd been up all night.

"I couldn't sleep. I had on my movies."

"Movies?"

Her son spoke for her. "She buys videotapes from religious organizations, from radio and TV evangelists. She watches them when she can't sleep."

"I see," said Finnerty. "Go on, Mrs. Waters. Did something on one of the tapes especially upset you?"

She shook her head.

"Then why did you come to the chapel? What time did you come to the chapel?"

She looked up at her son.

"Go ahead, Mom," he said. "You didn't do anything wrong."

She raised her hands as though to indicate the futility of trying to remember the precise time. "Seven, yes, maybe seven-thirty."

"In the morning."

"Yes."

"Did you drive there?"

"No. I walked."

Her son answered. "She doesn't drive, and when we looked for a new apartment in the neighborhood a few years ago after my dad's death, it made sense to be within walking distance of the place where she spends so much of her time. It's also near my job."

"Okay," Finnerty said. "How many times a week do you end up in that small chapel, the Good Shepherd one?"

Another fluttering of the hands in frustration with the question.

"Had you been there earlier in the week, the day before you found the body, two days before?"

"No. Yes, two days before. I went there at night."

"What time at night?"

"Eleven."

Finnerty knew she'd guessed at that time, and renounced trying to pin her down. It really wasn't important. He said, "Okay, Mrs. Waters, you walked into the chapel. First, you had to enter the cathedral. Did you come through those doors just outside the chapel?"

"Doors? What doors?"

"There are doors that separate the inside from the outside. Just inside those doors is the chapel."

For the first time she exhibited an emotion

other than despair. "Yes, of course I came through the doors. How could I get to the chapel if I didn't?"

Finnerty was pleased that she'd snapped at him. Could be a sign she would get through the rest of the interview without more sobbing and invoking the name of God. "I came in to pray," she said softly.

"Did you see the body right away?"

Oh, God, Finnerty thought, my mention of "body" has turned on her faucet again.

"Please, Mrs. Waters, I'm trying to be gentle and to use the right words, but you must—"

Her son now demonstrated a sternness that hadn't been there before. He said with grit in his voice, "Mother, *stop* it and answer the questions."

She looked at him as though he'd physically assaulted her, but his tone had its effect. She looked at Finnerty and said, "No, I did not see the body right away. When I go to that chapel, I sit in the back pew."

"The one immediately opposite the door?"

"Yes."

"And so you walked into the chapel and sat in that back pew. Was there anyone else in the chapel?"

"No, only . . ."

"Only what?"

"Only . . . him." She found the strength to say, "The body!"

"Did you notice the body as soon as you sat in that pew?"

"No. I prayed . . . for a long time. Then I went to the altar."

"To do what?"

"To be near it."

"I see. Go on."

"Then . . . then I happened to look at the little pew against the wall, and I saw him."

"Mr. Singletary."

"Somebody. Yes, Father Singletary."

"What did you do then?"

"I was shocked. I thought he was alive. I said something to him."

"What did you say to him?"

"I said . . . 'Excuse me,' I think I said. Then I saw his head, and I started to scream."

"That was when Bishop St. James came in?"

"Yes."

"Did you stay in the chapel long with the bishop?"

She shook her head. "No. He took me away."

"Upstairs, to his room?"

"Yes." As the memories of that moment in Good Shepherd Chapel flooded her, she began once again to cry, softly this time, childlike.

Finnerty raised his eyebrows at the stenographer. She nodded that she'd got everything. He said to Mrs. Waters, "I know this has been tough for you, but I appreciate your coming here." To her son he said, "Thanks."

"I thought it was best for her," Brian Waters said.

"Why don't you take your mother home. We'll want to speak to both of you again, so don't go anywhere."

"Fine." Brian took his mother's elbow and helped her from the room.

"Captain, there's a long-distance call for you," Finnerty's secretary said through the open door.

"Long distance? Who's calling?"

"Mackensie Smith. He's calling from England."

"I'll take it in my office."

"Bored with your honeymoon, Mac?" Finnerty said upon picking up the receiver.

"Hardly," Smith said. "I'm calling because there's been a murder here that I think could have bearing on the Singletary case."

"How so?"

"A parish priest in Buckland has been murdered in the small church next to our hotel. His name was Robert Priestly. I found his body about an hour ago."

"How do you figure it means anything to the Singletary case?"

"A couple of things. First, Singletary and Priestly were friendly. Second, Singletary probably came out here to see him. Third, he was killed by a blow to the head. This time the murder weapon was on the scene."

"Yeah? What was it?"

"A candlestick."

"Come on, Mac. What do you think happened, the person who killed Singletary here in Washington flies over to England and kills this priest in this town of . . . what was the name?"

"Buckland."

"Don't make sense to me," Finnerty said.

"Murder seldom makes sense, but suit yourself, Terry. I thought it was worth calling you about. Remind me not to bother in the future."

"Okay, Mac, hold on. I appreciate you making a long-distance call and all that. By the way, I just got finished interrogating Evelyn Waters. She's the lady who found Singletary's body."

"Did she shed any light on what happened?" Smith asked.

"Not yet, but it's good to know who she is. When are you coming back?"

"Soon. Who is she?"

"Just Mrs. Waters. Nice lady, kind of pathetic, a religious nut."

"Well, I'm glad one piece of the puzzle is in place. I'll check in with you when we return."

"Hey, Mac, you say *you* found this priest's body? I thought you were on your honeymoon. What are you doing over there, playing cop?"

"No, just happened to be in the wrong place at the wrong time. I'll talk to you when the call is cheaper."

chapter
14

London,
Friday Afternoon—
The Fog Persists

Smith and Annabel sat at their table in the small bar at Duke's. Gilberto had served them Grahams 1945 port as a farewell gesture; their flight back to the States would leave in four hours.

"She's disappeared," Mac said. "After calling her number all day yesterday, I got hold of Jeffrey Woodcock. This morning we went to her apartment—flat, I guess it's called here—and it was empty. The landlord let us in. The place was bare, not a trace."

"That sends a message, doesn't it?" Annabel said.

"It sure does. This Clarissa Morgan puts the
arm on church officials at Lambeth Palace. She
claims she's owed money because of Paul Singletary. The church contacts Woodcock, and
Woodcock has me call her. She's hardly what
you'd consider friendly on the phone, but she
does promise to get together when we get
back. She obviously can't pursue her claim—
call it blackmail—if she can't be found."

They'd driven back to London two nights
before, after having been interrogated in Buckland by local authorities, and after spending
another two hours in the sheep meadows
where Annabel almost lost her life.

Their decision to return to the scene was
made an hour after Smith had gone to the room
to comfort his wife, and to find out from her
what had actually happened. She gave him a
full account, but his lawyer's instincts and training caused him to follow up on her answers,
sometimes to the point of angering her.

"I'm not on a witness stand," she'd snapped
twice. Both times he apologized but pressed
forward, attempting to wring every bit of infor-

mation from her. Once, when she balked at his questioning, he said, "Annabel, there is a murdered priest in the church next to this hotel, and someone apparently tried to murder you. Come on, now, go over it again while it's still fresh in your mind."

"It will always be fresh in my mind," she said.

"I know, but humor me. You were relieved when you saw this person on horseback coming out of the trees in the distance. Did you yell?"

"No. The rider seemed to be heading in my direction. I figured I'd wait until whoever it was came close enough for me to ask directions. I snapped a couple of pictures and—"

"You snapped 'a couple of pictures'? Of the rider?"

"Yes. Damn, I forgot about that. Worse, I don't have the camera."

"Where is it?"

"I think I tossed it as I tried to get out of the horse's way."

Smith glanced to a table on which her binoculars rested. "You have your binoculars."

"Yes, they were around my neck. I'd shoved the camera in the pocket of my jacket and took it out to take the pictures. It was such a beautiful scene. I thought the fog would add something special to it."

Ten minutes later, after Annabel had exhausted her memories of the event, Mac said, "We have to go back and get that camera."

Annabel nodded. "I know. I was waiting for you to say that. I hate to."

"You don't have to come. I'll round up some people and—"

"Don't be silly, Mac. I'm the only one who knows where I was." She smiled. "I *think* I know where I was. At any rate, I'll do my best. I just hope the woman on that horse didn't come back and grab it."

Mac and Annabel huddled with Nigel and Tracy over the walking map Annabel had used, and identified an area where the near-miss might have taken place. Nigel assigned as many members of the hotel staff as he could spare. Some had cars, and they drove in a caravan to a point that precluded having to retrace Annabel's long trek on foot. The fog hadn't lifted, but as Annabel stood in the center of one of the fields, she said, "Yes, it was right about here." She pointed to the wall she'd thrown herself over, and indicated the trees from which the rider had emerged. Smith, Annabel, and the hotel workers fanned out. Within minutes, a kitchen worker held up the camera, a wide grin on his boyish face.

They returned to the hotel and sat in one of its public rooms with local police. Mac replayed the circumstances surrounding his discovery of Reverend Priestly's body, and when that subject had been exhausted, it was Annabel's turn to describe what had happened to her in the sheep pasture.

"I understand you took some snapshots of the wayward equestrian," the investigating officer said pleasantly.

Annabel looked at Mac. "Yes, that's true."

"I also understand you returned and found the camera, Mrs. Smith."

"Yes, we were very fortunate."

"I'm afraid you'll have to leave the roll of film with me."

"Inspector," Mac said, "I understand why you want it, but it has significance for us, too. Do you have photo-processing facilities at your headquarters?"

The inspector shook his head. "Afraid not. We send it all up to London."

"Fine," Smith said. "Can we arrange to have two sets of prints made in London, one for you, one for us?" He smiled. "It would be nice to have something to remember this lovely day in the Cotswolds."

"Fair enough," said the officer.

Mac rewound the film and removed it from the camera, then handed to the officer, who, in turn, gave it to one of his men with instructions to have it driven to London immediately. Mac gave the officer their Washington address and was assured a set of prints would be sent there by courier.

"Hate to say it," Annabel murmured, "but the pictures probably won't amount to much with all that fog. I did have fast film, though."

After the authorities had left, Mac and Annabel sat with Nigel and Tracy. Mac brought up Paul Singletary again. "What did he do when he was here?" Smith asked Nigel.

"Relaxed, I suppose," Nigel said. "He had a favorite room, one facing the gardens behind the hotel."

"He was here one weekend with an attractive woman named Morgan. Do you recall that?"

"Yes, I do."

"Did they share the same room?"

Nigel grimaced. "I don't think it is appropriate

for someone in my position to reveal such information."

"And I respect your discretion," Smith said, "but we're talking about two murders here, first Reverend Singletary's, and now your local parish priest's. Mrs. Smith and I are here in the United Kingdom on our honeymoon, but there is another purpose for this trip. I am serving as legal counsel to the National Cathedral of Washington. Father Singletary, who was murdered there, was a friend. He officiated at our wedding in August. Bishop St. James of the National Cathedral asked me to look into Reverend Singletary's movements while he was here in England. He was in London the day before he was murdered, but told people he would be spending the next day in the country, presumably here, before returning to Washington. That obviously didn't happen, because he was murdered the next night."

"I see," Nigel said.

"Was that the only time he came here with a woman?" Annabel asked.

Tracy said, "Yes, I think it was."

"Did they see anyone else while they were here?" Smith asked.

"No, they kept very much to themselves,

which would be expected," Nigel said. "Except, of course, for Reverend Priestly. As I told you, they were chums."

"Because they were fellow priests?"

"More than that. I overheard them talking one day in the library," Nigel said. "They evidently went back a long way, perhaps to university."

"Anything else you remember about the conversation you overheard?"

"Not really."

"Did Reverend Singletary and Reverend Priestly get together the weekend Singletary was here with Miss Morgan?" Annabel asked.

Nigel and Tracy shrugged. "I don't recall," Nigel said.

"Well, you've been very generous with your time and information," Smith said. "I think we'd better head back to London."

"Mr. and Mrs. Smith, I can't tell you how upset we are that your initial visit to Buckland Manor involved such horrible experiences. Being the one to find the body of Reverend Priestly must've been a ghastly occurrence. And you, Mrs. Smith, almost being killed by an irresponsible equestrian is appalling. We've never had anything like that happen before.

Please accept our apologies for the two days you've had to endure. And come and stay with us again as our guests—on the house, I think you say."

Smith smiled and shook the young manager's hand. "It's a wonderful house. Aside from priests being murdered and my wife almost being run over by a horse, we enjoyed our stay very much. Ideally, we'll come back one day and have the sort of tranquil vacation you're used to providing."

Mac and Annabel were early for their flight and settled into the Clipper Club at the airport. Mac called Jeffrey Woodcock and asked, "Anything new on Miss Morgan?"

"No, Mac. Most unusual, most distressing."

"Do me a favor, Jeffrey. See if you can find out if Reverend Priestly was involved with the Word of Peace movement."

"Shall do, Mac. Again, horrible what happened to Annabel. Please give her our warmest regards."

"Could have been worse. A hell of a lot worse. She might have ended up permanently planted in that field in the Cotswolds."

chapter
15

**Washington, D.C.,
That Evening—Chilly**

They arrived at Foggy Bottom too late to spring
Rufus from the kennel. The grating electronic
voice on the answering machine informed them
that there were eleven messages. Mac noted
the names and numbers on a yellow legal pad.
Some could wait; calls from Bishop St. James,
Terry Finnerty, and Tony Buffolino would be
answered immediately. He called the bishop
first.

"Welcome back, Mac. Good trip?"

"Depends upon how you look at it, George.
Annabel and I had some fine moments, al-

though the whole thing was not what you'd call without incident." He told the bishop of Annabel's strange experience while walking in the fields, and of the murder of the parish priest, Robert Priestly.

"That's horrible!" St. James said. "You say he was killed in the same manner as Paul?"

"A blow to the head, only this time the weapon, a candlestick, was left at the scene."

"I see. Was there any connection between Paul and this Reverend Priestly?"

"You didn't know about him?"

"No."

"There was a specific link between them. They evidently knew each other pretty well, and often spent time together when Paul was in England. I'll fill you in on this tomorrow. I have a class in the morning but thought I'd come by the cathedral after that. I should be there about noon."

"They have you working on Saturday."

"A makeup class. The price you pay for a honeymoon. See you tomorrow."

Smith failed to connect with Finnerty, but reached Tony Buffolino at the Spotlight Room. "You called while I was away?" Smith said.

"Yeah. When did you get back?"

"A little while ago. What did you get on Reverend Singletary?"

"Mac, I spent a pretty good hunk of time on it."

Smith asked when they could get together.

"How about tonight?"

"No, Tony, we're beat." It was eight o'clock in Washington, one in the morning London time. "How about tomorrow afternoon?"

"Can't do it, Mac."

Smith put his hand over the mouthpiece and said to Annabel, "Feel like a little nightclubbing?"

Her expression was what Smith would have expected if he'd suggested a walk in a foggy Cotswold sheep pasture. "Just for an hour," he said.

She shook her head, and Smith knew she meant it. He said to Buffolino, "Annabel is exhausted, but I'll be there in a half hour."

"Great."

"Is there a place we can talk quietly? I really don't feel like hearing what you've learned while your impressionist does obscure personalities."

"I got an office in the back. Lousy view of the stage. See ya."

"You don't mind, do you?" Smith asked Annabel after hanging up on Buffolino.

"Absolutely not," she said. "I'm going to take
a hot bath and unpack. Frankly, I think you're
crazy, but I'm beginning to wonder why that
would surprise me." She came to him, wrapped
her arms around his neck, and kissed him.
"Don't be long, Mac. You have your class first
thing in the morning, and I have to get cracking,
too. Let's cuddle up for a good night's sleep."

"With even half of that invitation, I'll be back
quicker than I planned."

There weren't many customers in Tony's
place, and the show hadn't started, for which
Smith was grateful. Three bored musicians
played slow music with a backbeat. A couple
danced.

"A table, or do you prefer the bar?" a
sunken-cheeked young woman wearing minimal clothing asked.

"I have an appointment with Mr. Buffolino."

"You do? I'll tell him you're here. What's your
name?"

"Smith, Mackensie Smith."

Alicia Buffolino appeared from the rear of the
club. For a second, Smith wasn't sure it was
Alicia. She had always worn her auburn hair

long, and was fond of tight shiny toreador
pants, and tight shirts scooped low at the neck.
Now she'd had her hair cut into a trendy bob,
had applied a considerably lighter hand to her
makeup, and wore a nicely tailored rust-colored
suit and white blouse with a bow at the neck.
"Good to see you, Mac," she said, kissing him
on the cheek.

"Nice to see you, too, Alicia. Forgive me if I
make no sense. We just got back from London,
and I'm still operating on their time. Is Tony
here?"

"He's in the office going over bills. We have
more bills than customers. Come on back."

If Alicia and Tony hadn't called it an office,
Smith would have assumed they were in a
storeroom. Except for a small, genuinely distressed desk, a chair that had suffered too
many heavy sitters (and maybe a hand-gre-
nade attack), and a leaning tower of battered
black file cabinets, the rest of the room was
piled with boxes. Buffolino sat at the desk going
through a swirl of papers. The minute Alicia
opened the door he stood up and said, "Hey,
Mac, good to see you again." To Alicia: "Get a
chair for Mac, would you?"

She returned with a folding metal chair that

she noisily snapped open. "Anything else, Your Majesty?" she asked before slamming the door behind her.

Buffolino shook his head. "Man, she gets more difficult every day."

Not long before she's former wife number three, Smith thought. "So, Tony," he said, sinking into the chair, "tell me what you've found out about Paul Singletary."

Buffolino reached into the bottom drawer of the desk and pulled out a folder. Written on the cover was MAC SMITH. He slid the top piece of paper across the desk to Smith, who put on half-glasses and read it.

"Whattaya think?" Buffolino asked.

"Pretty thorough," Smith said. "A lot of it I know, but there are some interesting items in here. This reference to his military service. Where did you get that?"

"I got a friend in military records in St. Louis. She gave it to me over the phone."

"I'm not sure I understand this joint commission Reverend Singletary was assigned to. It says here he served aboard a destroyer that had been outfitted with sensitive, classified gear, and that the crew was made up of American, British, and French naval personnel. What else do you know about that?"

"What you see is what you get, Mac. What caught my eye was how short a time he served, less than a year. I guess clergy don't get put on extended assignments."

"I'm not sure that's true, but it's worth checking into. There's no reference here to the type of discharge he was given."

"I asked my friend in St. Louis about that. She said the only notation in his file was 'Discharge: Official.' "

"I've never heard of that designation before, but I suppose all discharges are 'official,' " Smith said.

"I'll check it out," Buffolino said, scribbling a note on the folder. The other papers in the file were not as neatly organized as the first, and Buffolino read from them. Smith stopped him when he got to Singletary's travel itinerary back to Washington the day of his murder. "You say he arrived at two-thirty in the afternoon at Kennedy Airport in New York, and took a shuttle to Washington from LaGuardia. That would place him back here at approximately five o'-clock."

"Right."

"Anything else about his trip home?"

Buffolino smiled. "Yeah, there is. Seems he was accompanied by a foxy lady."

"Really? Another friend in strange places tell you that?"

"As a matter'a fact, yeah. I got this gal I used to see once in a while . . . between marriages, of course . . . and she works in crew scheduling. I told her I needed the names of the steward-esses who worked the flight from London to JFK that Singletary was on, and she gave them to me."

"They're not called stewardesses anymore, Tony, they're called flight attendants."

"They're all 'Coffee, Tea, or Me' to me. I called some of these stews—attendants, and told them straight out that I was an investigator looking into the murder of Reverend Paul Sin-gletary, which happened at the National Cathe-dral. I told them that it was very important that if they remembered anything about a priest on that flight that they share it with me. It took me five calls before I connect with this—" He glanced down at a note on the paper. "Her name is Anne Padula. She tells me she remem-bers him very well."

"Why?"

"Why what?"

"Why would she remember him? How many passengers are on those flights, two hundred, three hundred?"

"Yeah, probably, only this Anne Padula got to talking to the reverend. She told me she spotted him the minute he walked in because he was a very handsome guy, especially for a guy in a collar. She told me she wasn't the only female on that flight who gave him a look more than once, including the lady sitting next to him."

"Sitting next to him? I thought he traveled with a woman."

"Well, this stewardess didn't know that right away. What interested her was that they seemed to strike up a friendship pretty fast for a couple'a people who just happened to sit next to each other on a jumbo jet. Then she gets talking to both of them and she gets a sense that even though they came on the plane separate, they knew each other from before. You know, women like this Padula have pretty good instincts, especially working with the public all the time. Anyway, she tells me that she becomes convinced that they came on board separately for deliberate reasons."

"Did she describe this woman to you?"

"Yeah, she did, only she really didn't remember what she looked like as much as she did the reverend. She says this woman was kind of cool-looking, black hair, very fair skin, maybe talked with a British accent. Had big shoulders, she says."

Smith grunted. "She couldn't be sure about the accent? Not hard to recognize a British accent."

"Yeah, except the lady didn't say much. In fact, the lady seemed annoyed that a pretty stew was talking to the reverend."

"Interesting," Smith said. "Did you find out anything else from this flight attendant?"

"That's about it, Mac."

"Did you learn anything about Singletary's movements between the time he arrived in Washington on the shuttle and when he was murdered in the cathedral that night?"

Buffolino shook his head.

"Did your flight-attendant friend notice how Singletary and this woman left the plane? Did they leave together? Did she happen to see them in the terminal, maybe out at a cab stand while she was waiting for a crew bus?"

"Nope. That's all she could tell me, only I

figured it was pretty impressive. How many times do you find anybody who actually remembers somebody?"

"Not often," Smith agreed. "What else do you have?"

"Let's see." Buffolino looked at his notes. "Nothing except—there's an interesting turf war goin' on with this case."

"How so?"

"MPD . . . Finnerty . . . you know him pretty good . . . Finnerty and the MPD start out investigating the murder. It's being handled like any D.C. homicide."

"Where is the jurisdictional dispute?"

"Well, here's where it gets interesting. MPD sent guys to Singletary's apartment. Routine, right?" Smith nodded. "But I hear from some friends I got in the department that anything having to do with Singletary's apartment, personal life, clothes—all of it has been put under wraps by another agency."

"Which agency? The FBI?"

Buffolino shook his head and smiled again. "The navy." Buffolino glanced down at his notes again. "Naval Investigative Services, to be exact."

"Because of the time he spent in the navy,

short as it was?'' Smith was almost talking to himself.

Buffolino shrugged. "Beats me, but that's the word I get. And these." He pulled a sheaf of clippings from the file folder and slid them to Smith. "I figured you'd want to keep up on what the press has been saying while you were gone."

"Much obliged, Tony. Good thinking."

"Yeah, sometimes I think pretty clear . . ." His brow furrowed, and he looked toward the door. "And sometimes I don't."

There was a loud knock on the door. "Yeah?" Buffolino yelled.

Alicia poked her head in. "It's time for the show, Tony."

Buffolino looked up at a black-and-white kitchen clock hanging precariously from a nail. "Excuse me, Mac, I always introduce the show."

"You don't have to," Alicia said. "I can do it."

Buffolino stood and waved the notion away. "Nah, people in a joint like this want to see a guy be the MC. Right, Mac?"

Smith wisely said nothing.

Through the closed door came the ragged roll of a snare drum and the crash of a cymbal.

Then a cranked-up amplification system blared Buffolino's welcome to Tony's Spotlight Room. He told a few bad jokes before introducing a singer who'd come "direct from Las Vegas," and who was "destined to be one of America's great singing stars."

The trio vamped her on, and she launched into a frenetic version of "Everything's Coming Up Roses." Smith grimaced; he was glad Annabel was home soaking in a tub. He wished he were.

Buffolino returned to the office. "Anything else for me?" Smith asked.

"That's about it. Want me to keep going?"

"Yes, I do. I want you to find out whether a woman named Clarissa Morgan was in Washington the day of Paul Singletary's murder. It's likely that she was the woman with him on the flight from London. I also want you to start running some background checks on various cathedral personnel, as you get time. Start with a Canon Nickelson, the music director, and do a couple of the clergy, Reverend Jonathon Merle and Reverend Carolyn Armstrong, maybe a few other names I'll give you later."

"Carolyn? That's a *priest*?"

"A beautiful one, as it happens. We're talking

Episcopal here, Tony, not Catholic. I also want you to see what you can find out about this naval-intelligence interest in the case. While you're at it, see if there is anything going on at MPD that hasn't been publicly announced. In other words, keep digging on all fronts, and keep me informed."

Buffolino had a way of asking for money without having to say it. Smith had brought a check with him; he handed it to his oddball investigator.

"Thanks, Mac. You in town the next couple of days?"

"Absolutely."

"Good. I'll be in touch. How's your pretty wife?"

"Annabel is splendid, thank you. Tired from the trip, but good. How's that boy of yours?"

"Billy? He's doin' real good. Looks like the cancer is in remission. I keep my fingers crossed, though."

Smith stood. "Good, good. I have to leave, Tony. I'm teaching a class at eight tomorrow morning." They shook hands. "Nice work. Keep it up."

When they reached the door to the club, Buffolino asked whether Mac wanted to stay for the rest of the show—complimentary, of course. Smith looked back at the singer, who was doing a version of Judy Garland with "Over the Rainbow." Some men at the bar leered at her. Two couples danced—moved together was more accurate. Light reflected from a revolving mirrored ball danced off them like photokinetic confetti. "I'd love to, Tony, but the trip took a lot out of me. Give me a call tomorrow." He stepped out onto K Street, lowered his head, and walked quickly to his car.

chapter
16

**Washington, the Next Day—
Horizontal Rain**

"How was your honeymoon, Professor Smith?" Joe Petrella asked.

"Busy but pleasant," Smith replied. The class laughed. He hadn't realized what he was saying, or what they were inferring, and he was tired and out-of-sorts. Not having had time to adequately prepare for class added to his grumpiness.

"The woman who found Reverend Singletary's body came forward while you were gone," Joy Collins said, excited.

"Yes, I heard."

April Montgomery, his thin, pale, exception-
ally bright student, asked, "Did you spend part
of your honeymoon in London investigating
what Reverend Singletary did there the day
before he died?"

Smith removed his glasses and leaned his
elbows on the lectern. "What would lead you to
that conclusion, Ms. Montgomery?"

She wiggled her nose and said, "I read that
Reverend Singletary had been in London the
day before he died, and it struck me as an
interesting coincidence that you chose to take
your honeymoon in London at this time."

Smith couldn't help but smile. "Did it?" he
said. "All right, let's take another fifteen minutes to discuss the murder of Reverend Paul
Singletary." He was less annoyed at this intru-
sion than he'd been last time. It would consume
some of the time he'd have trouble filling with
course materials. And the kids might even help
him reason things through.

"I said my honeymoon in London was busy
but pleasant. Half was untrue." He told the
class about Annabel's coming close to being
trampled to death in the field, and about discovering the body of Reverend Robert
Priestly.

"Wow!" Joy Collins said. "Some honeymoon."

Smith laughed gently. "Yes, it was not run-of-the-mill. Now, let's harness the considerable intelligence in this room and come up with any possible connection between the murder of a Reverend Paul Singletary in Washington and the murder of a Reverend Robert Priestly in England, both in church, and, not by the way, Priestly was also killed by a blow to the head. The only difference is that the murder weapon was left behind in Reverend Priestly's case. It was a heavy brass candlestick that was covered with blood—Reverend Priestly's blood, of course—and had been left on a pew next to the body."

Smith studied his students' faces as they sought to forge a defensible link between the two murders. Ms. Montgomery was the first to offer an opinion. "It could have been sheer coincidence," she said.

"Yes, that is a distinct possibility," Smith said. "Oh—sorry. I should add, too, that Reverend Singletary and Reverend Priestly were friends. Not only had they followed the same professional calling, they evidently went back quite a way, perhaps to their college years."

"It's unlikely that the same person committed the two murders," another student said. "I can't conceive of the spontaneous murderer of Reverend Singletary flying all the way to England to kill his friend. Doesn't make sense to me."

"Somebody else said that, also. Doesn't make sense to me, either, but would the murders have had to be done by the same person? And remember, Paul Singletary was part of two worldwide organizations, with members on many continents," said Smith.

"Two?" said Joe.

"The Anglican-Episcopal-Protestant church," Joy Collins said, calmer and more reflective now.

"And . . . ?" Mac asked.

"Word of Peace," April Montgomery put in.

"A conspiracy."

"Possibly," Smith said. "But what would be behind a conspiracy to murder two priests?"

"Hatred for the clergy," said Joe Petrella, the student who had voiced a similar observation during the previous discussion.

"Could be," Smith said, "but that's too lurid, too tabloidish for me. At least for the moment."

Smith was asked, "Do you think it was the

same murder weapon? I mean, the weapon that was used to kill Reverend Singletary was never found, from what I've been reading."

"That possibility has been raised with the British authorities. Naturally, they're doing a thorough analysis of the weapon, although chances of finding any physical evidence that would link it to Reverend Singletary's murder are remote."

"Has anyone checked to see whether a candlestick is missing from the National Cathedral?"

Smith said, "MPD has been looking for every candlestick on the premises. The shape and nature of the wound to Reverend Singletary's head could certainly have been made by such an object."

"You said your wife was almost killed in a field, and that it appeared to be deliberate because the horse and rider returned and went after her again. What connection does that have with the priest's murder?"

"That is a puzzling aspect. We have to be open to the possibility, as April is, that there was no connection—though murderous intent was in the air."

"Maybe the same person who tried to run

down your wife killed the priest, although I can't imagine what they would have had against her, either," Bob Rogers said.

"Maybe," said April Montgomery, "the person had something against *you,* Professor Smith."

A Boeing 707 with U.S. NAVY painted on its tail banked over Annapolis and picked up a compass heading of 225 degrees until entering the airspace of Andrews Air Force Base. The navy lieutenant commander at the controls received permission to land, and soon the four-engine aircraft taxied up to a long gray limousine with tinted windows. A boarding ramp was rolled to the side of the plane. The door opened, and two uniformed military personnel came down the steps, followed by a gray-haired man wearing a tweed suit and carrying a tan raincoat over his arm who seemed to lean slightly to his left as he walked. A naval officer who'd been in the limousine approached the visitor when he reached the bottom of the steps and extended his hand. "Captain Ely, U.S. Navy, Mr. Leighton. Hope your flight was smooth."

"Yes, quite," Leighton said. "Damned foggy in London. Wondered if we'd get off."

Captain Ely escorted the assistant director of MI5's "B" Division to the limousine, and climbed into the backseat with him. The driver had received his instructions before the plane's arrival and immediately drove off, taking Maryland Highway 4, also called Pennsylvania Avenue S.E. He stayed on the road after crossing the District of Columbia line until they reached the historic Washington Navy Yard on the Anacostia River, a seventy-five-acre spread known for much of its history as the Naval Gun Factory; it dated back to President John Adams's purchase of the site in 1799. They drove along narrow roads defined by old gray stone buildings, past the Navy Memorial Museum, one of the longest buildings in the world, and past the Marine Corps Museum and Submarine Museum before pulling up in front of an administration building. Their credentials were checked at a desk inside the door, and a phone call was made. "You can go up now," Leighton and Ely were told. A few minutes later they entered the office of Rear Admiral Stuart Zachary, chief of operations for Naval Investigative Services. With him were Rudolph Kapit of the FBI's counterespionage division, CIA representative Rob-

ert Wilson, and Louis Malvese of the State Department's European Section.

"Good of you to send a plane for me," Leighton said after Ely had left and the others had
settled around a large circular table in a corner
of the spacious office.

"We appreciate your agreeing to come on
such short notice, Mr. Leighton," Admiral Zachary said. "We thought it was important enough
to do whatever we could to expedite this meeting, especially in light of the death of Reverend
Priestly in Buckland."

"Yes. Tragic affair," Leighton said. "The
local authorities have been most cooperative.
We're receiving daily reports on the progress of
their investigation."

"That's good," Zachary said.

"How long can you stay in Washington, Mr.
Leighton?" the FBI's Kapit asked.

"That depends entirely upon you," Leighton
responded. "I'm here at your request."

Malvese, of State, a short, square man with
a pugnacious face, said, "I don't think this
meeting would have been necessary if recent
events hadn't occurred. There seem to be a lot
of loose ends—too many of them, for my taste,

to let them slide. These operations always make such simple sense when they're conceived, but then they take on their own damn life. I promised my boss I would come back from this meeting with a clear view of where we are and where we're going." He looked at the others. "I hope I won't disappoint him."

"The report the agency received last night was confusing, Brett," Wilson said. He knew Leighton well; they'd cooperated on a number of projects over the years. They bore a striking resemblance and might have been mistaken for brothers except for their accents, which they'd once explained away to someone by claiming that their parents divorced shortly after their births and had raised one of them in the United States, the other in Great Britain. The woman who'd noted their resemblance believed the story, which provided the two men with a good laugh after the party.

"Frankly, I'm not especially interested in your reports," Malvese said in a voice that matched his bellicose face. "This whole affair has greater diplomatic implications than your reports consider."

Admiral Zachary said to Wilson and Kapit, "Let's bear in mind, gentlemen, that this is still an NIS operation. We appreciate what help the CIA and the FBI have given us, but it remains our ultimate responsibility."

Leighton smiled to himself at the tension among the four men. How typically American, he thought, to spend so much time defending their positions, justifying their existence, and never fully cooperating to get the job done. True, enough of that went on in British intelligence, but those incidents somehow seemed to be resolved earlier in the game, had less impact upon final solutions. He took out a long, thin brown cigarillo. "Mind if I smoke?"

They did, but all shook their heads no.

Leighton lighted the cigar with an elegant flourish and savored its taste. "Well," he said pleasantly, a smile on his lined, ruddy face, "where do we begin?"

Admiral Zachary answered the question. "Let's start with Clarissa Morgan. What is her condition?"

"Splendid," Leighton said. "Miss Morgan is quite well, I assure you."

"I'm not particularly interested in her health," said Zachary.

"No, I expect not," Leighton said.

"What went wrong?" Kapit asked.

Leighton arched his sizable eyebrows. "What went wrong?" He said to Wilson, his CIA friend, "I think I covered that subject in my conversation with you last night."

"Which doesn't answer the question," Zachary said, making no attempt to hide his annoyance.

"Let me assure you that Miss Morgan is quite secure, and will no longer play an active role in this matter."

"Not good enough," Malvese said.

Bob Wilson stepped in. "Brett, let me try to summarize the concerns of the others. Reverend Singletary was murdered here in Washington at the National Cathedral. Your Clarissa Morgan accompanied him from London the day he was killed. Your people have acknowledged that. Now, it is our understanding that she returned to London and attempted to blackmail the Church of England. That seems to be highly irregular behavior for someone in your employ."

Leighton laughed softly and drew on his cigarillo. "As I said moments ago, Miss Morgan is secure. No longer in our employ but in our care."

"Meaning what?" Kapit asked.

"Meaning that we are in the process of re-
solving her indiscretions and making sure that
her impetuous and unprofessional, to say nothing of greedy, behavior will not be repeated. We
view her as purely a local personnel problem.
No concern of yours."

Malvese's laugh was not born of merriment.
"No concern of ours, you say? Infiltrating Word
of Peace was a joint project, as I understand
it. We gave our okay at State because it was
presented as a—how was it put?—a 'benign'
covert exercise designed only to gather
information. There are now two dead priests,
and a woman operative from British intelligence holding up the Church of England for
money. Benign? Damned malignant if you
ask me."

Leighton was tempted to say he *hadn't*
asked the combative little representative from
the State Department. He allowed the urge to
pass and asked Admiral Zachary, "Did your
examination of Reverend Singletary's videotapes provide you with what we hoped it
would?"

"No."

"Pity. I had the utmost faith in our source of
information regarding this matter."

"Miss Morgan?" Zachary asked.

"Among others. We know that certain tapes, which looked like ordinary commercially recorded cassettes, were given to Reverend Singletary by his friend Reverend Priestly, late of the British Navy. Late of everything, I suppose. Now I get the impression that either they've disappeared or you've found them and nothing incriminating was on them."

"How do you get that impression?"

"By the look on your faces and by what is not being said." His voice took on a sudden lilt, and he smiled at Admiral Zachary.

"No offense, Mr. Leighton," Kapit said, "but your information may be as unreliable as your agent. We know that Singletary and Priestly exchanged sensitive information when they were together in that joint naval exercise, and we also know that the contact continued for a period of time after that. We do not, however, have any hard evidence that it was a sustained involvement over the course of years. We've exhausted every resource we have to trace the videotapes you claim were in Reverend Singletary's possession. He had many—but not the ones for which we were looking."

"Which doesn't necessarily mean, Mr. Kapit,

that they weren't in his possession. Perhaps there is something you've overlooked."

The admiral shook his head. "No, Mr. Leighton, I have to go along with Kapit."

Leighton sighed and sat back, crossed one long tweed-clad leg over the other. He didn't buy what they were telling him, not in the least, but if he was annoyed, it was more a matter of their transparent denials than of the tapes themselves. "Well," he said, "the reality seems to be that the videotapes passed by Reverend Priestly to his cause-driven friend, the Reverend Singletary, have been lost, have disappeared, have perhaps been recorded over with some of your American . . . sitcoms. Singletary was to have used them to thwart American military plans, perhaps, since the cause of peace, or the poor, or the environment always seems to go with an antimilitary stance. And they were to be transmitted to others in the Word of Peace organization. Does that really matter? The technology represented on those tapes has little relevance to today's sophisticated weaponry. Antiquated equipment, already compromised, already replaced, videotaped by amateurs like Priestly. That's all that was on those tapes. Of course, we thought it worth-

while to recover them once Reverend Singletary died, but they are no longer important to
us—or to you, I might add. Just a matter of
tidying up loose ends."

Leighton's CIA friend smiled. The English-
man had a way of politely speaking down to
whomever he was with, regardless of their rank
or position. Most impressive was that those
same people listened.

Leighton surveyed the faces at the table
before continuing, "It would have been nice to
have the tapes, but they would have had considerably more value when Reverend Singletary was alive, helped to keep him in line. The
question now is how his death compromises
our effectiveness within this bloody so-called
peace movement."

"It seems the loss of Priestly would pose a
bigger problem in that regard," Kapit said.

"Not really. Priestly was a decent chap who
served his purpose in a peripheral way. He did,
after all, introduce Miss Morgan to Reverend
Singletary as instructed. A regular Cupid. He
was, you see, our man." Leighton stubbed out
his cigarillo.

"And strictly another personnel problem you
resolved locally," Kapit said.

Leighton didn't respond. Immediately. Then he said, "We did not."

"Where is this going?" State's Louis Malvese asked. "That's what I need to know."

Leighton shrugged. "I thought you might answer that," he said.

When no one did, he added, "Tell me about this Mackensie Smith."

"What about him?" Wilson asked.

"He seems quite in the midst of the muck, wouldn't you say?"

Kapit said, "Mackensie Smith is a former criminal attorney who chucked his practice after his wife and son were killed in an auto accident. He later joined the faculty of George Washington University's law school."

"He certainly doesn't act as I would expect a professor to act. He found Priestly's body. He was at the hotel in the Cotswolds checking on Singletary's every move. He's friendly with a solicitor in London named Jeffrey Woodcock, who numbers among his clients the Church of England. Woodcock gave this Smith Clarissa Morgan's number and asked him to call her, which he did. Why?"

No one had an answer.

"She called us immediately, and we followed

up. Seems Smith claimed to be on his honeymoon. Not a bad cover."

"He was married in August at the National Cathedral by Reverend Singletary," Kapit said. "They were friendly."

"Did he meet with the Morgan woman?" Wilson asked.

"No. He was on his way into the country for a few days. She told him they'd meet when he returned."

"But they didn't."

"Of course not. By the time he returned to London with his bride, Miss Morgan had vacated her premises."

"And gone where?"

"To a secure place."

"The Cotswolds?" Kapit asked.

Leighton's only reply was a tiny smile.

There was a period of silence at the table, broken when Louis Malvese said, "I must have one direct answer, Mr. Leighton."

"Yes?"

"It seems we are not to meddle in your local personnel problems."

"That view is certainly appreciated, Mr. Malvese."

"But what about *our* local personnel problems?"

"Specifically?"

"Reverend Paul Singletary."

"Your question?"

"Did you, or anyone in MI5, have anything to do with his death?"

Leighton lighted another long, thin brown cigarillo. He used the smoke as though it had some medicinal power to clear his thoughts and to help formulate an answer. He looked across the table at Malvese and said through the blue haze rising from the cigarillo's end, "We all had something to do with the demise of Reverend Paul Singletary, at least spiritually. Did we terminate the reverend? No. Did someone from his precious Word of Peace organization? We rather think so."

"Clarissa Morgan?" Bob Wilson asked.

"No," said Leighton. "She wasn't involved in the peace movement aside from keeping us abreast of its activities through Singletary."

"She accompanied him to Washington, was here when he was killed."

"So were you, I assume."

"But I didn't kill him," Wilson said.

"Did your agency?" Leighton asked.

"The CIA? Brett, come on."

Leighton's amused expression caused Wilson to sit back and smile. Nothing absurd about termination on either side of the Atlantic.

A half hour later, Admiral Zachary asked, "Ready for lunch?"

"Famished," said Leighton.

"Good. Please follow me. We've arranged for a nice spread."

She sat in a small, sparsely furnished room in a row house near Battersea Park—fittingly, some would have said, the site of the world's most ambitious and successful home for stray animals. Across the Thames was the Royal Hospital.

"Time to go," said the young man. He had been assigned to her when she was brought there the previous night. "The call came."

"What if I won't go?" she asked, a defiant smile on her lips.

"I don't think that would be wise, Miss Morgan."

"Wise? What do you know of wisdom?"

"Please, just come with us. Don't cause trouble."

"I wouldn't think of it," she said. "Got a fag?"

"Later. Come on. My patience is running thin."

"Do you have a girlfriend?" she asked him.

"I do."

"Are you in love with her?"

"Come on. Let's go."

"I loved him very much. Can you understand that?"

"Who?"

"Reverend Singletary."

"Reverend?"

"Yes. He was handsome and intelligent and good. I loved him. He's dead."

"Oh. Sorry. Please."

"Your Mr. Leighton with all his proper reserve and sense of duty doesn't understand that."

He said nothing, just stood and waited for her to rise from the cot.

"I was supposed to betray him. Then I fell in love. A nasty complication for your Mr. Leighton and his kind. Are you his kind?"

He reached for her.

"Don't touch me," she said, her voice more of a snarl, sufficiently threatening to cause him to withdraw his hand.

He tried a more ingratiating approach. "No great reason to complain, you know. The islands are very beautiful. I plan to go there on my honeymoon."

"Do you? How sweet. I detest heat. My skin is sensitive. I break out in a rash whenever it is hot."

"Miss Morgan, you're causing *me* to break out in a rash. . . ."

"What if I won't go? What if I tell you and your Mr. Leighton to go straight to hell?"

"Miss Morgan, I—"

"Will I be done away with? Will I be 'terminated' like poor Reverend Priestly?" Her laugh was blatantly bitter. "How lies multiply, like stray cats. Will you beat my head in with a candlestick holder to make it appear that there truly is a madman roaming the globe in search of skulls to crush? What fools we've turned out to be." Now she smiled sweetly at him. "Do you enjoy being involved with fools? Did you join up, as I did, thinking you were about to be initiated into a brain trust out to save the British Empire? Poor thing, and so young."

He'd had enough. He left the room and returned with two other men.

Clarissa laughed. "Need help, do you? Well,

no need. I shall retire to the British Virgin Islands with grace and a sense of relief. I shall consult the best dermatologist I can find there and ask him for a proper cream for my rash." She stood, straightened the folds of her skirt. "I hope you and your bride suffer a terminal case of heat rash on your honeymoon."

A car was parked in front of the house. As her young guardian of the past few hours opened the door for her, she said, "And please tell your Mr. Brett Leighton and his MI5 that I think he and it are bloody bastards, and I hope they all rot in hell."

chapter
17

Forecast: Rain Through the Weekend —of Course

Smith was early for his noontime meeting with Bishop St. James, and used the time to wander in the cathedral. There were a number of tour groups being led by Visitors' Services volunteers. Smith couldn't help but smile at the wonderment on the faces of the children being guided through the massive, imposing cathedral. Then he was sobered. Were they aware of the murder that had taken place there? He hoped not. He'd read in a sidebar story that ran with the continuing coverage of the Singletary murder that requests for cathedral tours had increased since the killing. How unfortunate, yet how human, was the tendency of people to be drawn to violence and sorrow. And scandal. Ford's Theater. Chappaquiddick Bridge. Maybe it wasn't the enjoyment of bad things. Maybe it was more a matter of affirming that things were still okay for those who hadn't suffered. Probably not, was the conclusion Smith invariably came to, but it always made him feel better to rationalize away the alternatives.

He stopped at the Good Shepherd Chapel and stood alone in the center of the small room, looking through the window at the gently flowing Garth Fountain. That the peace of such a sanctuary should be violated by murder was deplorable. There were places where violence was not only commonplace, it was expected. To walk through Washington's inner city was to be constantly on guard. But for violence to happen here, in a space reserved for contemplation and prayer?

He looked at the altar. There was nothing on it except a tiny vase of wilting yellow flowers. His thoughts returned to the small church in Buckland where he'd discovered the body of Reverend Priestly. He saw again, in his mind, the candlestick that had been used to murder

Priestly. Such an obvious instrument of death in a church setting. But no weapon had been conveniently left behind here. The Washington police, according to their statements, had examined every cross, chalice, and candlestick in the cathedral. None showed any signs of having been used to end Singletary's life. Could they have missed anything? The cathedral was so large and contained so many "hiding places"—for objects *or* for people. To focus, as Smith was, on finding a churchly weapon not only represented seeking the proverbial needle in a haystack, it was uncalled for. Would he be dwelling upon it if there had not been the coincidence of an Anglican priest's being murdered in a church thousands of miles away? Of course not.

Smith left the chapel and descended the greenish stone stairs leading to the crypt floor.

A sign for visitors pointed the way to the Bethlehem Chapel. Smith stopped every few feet to take in his surroundings. There was another flight of steps to his left. He moved on; a men's room was on his left, then an oak-paneled wall that went up six or seven feet. Above the paneling was a clock visible from the hallway. Just before the wall began was a door with a sign: WASHINGTON CATHEDRAL ACOLYTES. A series of glass display cases came next. They contained antique crosses and other gifts from churches around the world.

As he progressed toward the Bethlehem Chapel, Smith passed a door labeled BISHOP'S GUESTS, then the door to the choir room. Immediately across from it was the entrance to the chapel.

Smith looked back up the hall before entering the chapel. How far was it from Good Shepherd to the Bethlehem Chapel? One hundred and eighty feet, maybe two hundred. A reasonable distance to drag a body, although there was that flight of steps to contend with. Not many of them, though. Certainly not out of the question for the murder to have taken place in any of the cathedral's quiet, secluded corners.

But why? he asked himself. In the first place, why speculate that the body had been moved? The police seemed convinced of it because of the lack of blood in Good Shepherd. A reasonable deduction, certainly, but the lack of blood only suggested that the murder might have happened elsewhere. The much larger question for Smith was: Why move the body? To create the impression that anyone, from anywhere, might have done the deed, since the chapel was open twenty-four hours a day? Why else? Then again, why bother?

As he stepped into the chapel, his eyes went immediately to the Indiana limestone altar. A woman carrying a vase of flowers came from behind it. She approached the communion rail, genuflected, and stepped up to the altar, where she gently placed the flowers between two tall, graceful brass candlesticks, each holding a long, slender white candle. She took great care to be sure that the vase was precisely centered between the candles. Content that it was, she returned to the communion rail, faced the altar, and genuflected again, then started to leave through the door through which Smith had entered.

"Excuse me," Smith said. The loudness of his voice surprised him; they were in a stone boom box.

The woman turned and smiled. "May I help you?" she asked.

"Yes, perhaps you can," said Smith, approaching her. "My name is Mackensie Smith. I'm about to have lunch with Bishop St. James."

"Yes, Mr. Smith, I know who you are."

"I was interested in the routine of dressing an altar," said Smith, "particularly in this chapel. Are you a member of the Altar Guild?"

"Yes, I am."

"Is it the guild's responsibility to take care of the items on the altar—the flowers, the candles, things like that?"

"Yes, we take care of those things."

Smith looked at the altar again and smiled. "It looks beautiful. The flowers are lovely. So are the candles."

"Yes, they are."

"Is the Altar Guild responsible for keeping the candlesticks shined?"

"In a sense, yes. Sometimes we polish them ourselves, although that's generally left to the maintenance staff. We keep an eye on them, though, and when we see one that needs attention, we point it out to them."

"Do the same candlesticks always remain on the same altar? Are those holders up there designated for the Bethlehem Chapel?"

"Oh, no, it would depend upon the service to be celebrated."

"Of course it would. Do you happen to know whether that set of candlesticks has been on this altar for a while?"

"No," she said pleasantly. "They were put there just this morning."

"What about the ones that were there before?" Smith asked.

"They're in the back of the altar. It's a big area, and some things are left there, but never for long. I put the candlesticks that were on the altar back there myself." She laughed. "You certainly have a deep interest in candlesticks, Mr. Smith."

Smith joined in her laughter. "Well, candles always add so much to the visual beauty of a service. I sometimes think of earlier times when candles were the only source of illumination."

"I think about that, too. Of course, they do have even greater symbolism. Some think that two candles represent the divine and human natures of God, but I prefer to think that lights on the altar signify the joy we receive from the light of Christ's Gospel."

"That's nice," Smith said. "Would it be permissible for me to go behind the altar?"

"Of course. I'll turn on the lights."

They stepped behind the altar, and Smith looked at the vault to his left. The woman explained that the first bishop of Washington,

Bishop Satterlee, and his wife were interred there.

Smith's attention next went to a pair of candlesticks on a table. "Excuse me," he said, picking up one of them and lightly running his fingertips over the entire rim of the base, then doing the same with the other. He had a feeling the woman was looking at him strangely. He said pleasantly, "Yes, I do have a deep interest in these things. I'm a collector of sorts. My wife has a gallery." He knew it wasn't necessary to explain his actions, but he did anyway. He checked his watch. "Time to meet with the bishop. You've been very kind. Thank you."

"Any time, Mr. Smith." She hesitated, and he leaned forward to encourage her to say what she was holding back. "Mr. Smith, I know you were a friend of Reverend Singletary's, and that you are helping the cathedral in this matter. Is there anything new? Will they ever find the person who killed him?"

"I don't know," Smith said. "All we can do is hope and pray like everyone else that his killer will be brought to justice. Thank you again. I am late."

When Smith walked into the bishop's study,

it was immediately apparent to him that St. James was agitated. No, distraught and angry more aptly described his mood. Smith mentioned it to him as they sat down for a lunch of onion soup, egg salad, and popovers, served by a member of the kitchen staff.

St. James locked eyes with Smith. "It's probably not for a bishop to say, but it's been one hell of a morning," he said. "I can do without such mornings."

"Care to share it with your rabbi here?" Smith asked.

"I have to share it with somebody. I've spent most of this morning with two of my canons, Merle and Armstrong."

"They must have said something out of the ordinary to upset you so."

"They certainly did. You know, Mac, from the moment of the initial shock of Paul's murder, my concern has been to protect this cathedral from any scandal that might result. You know that, don't you? You understand how important that is to me."

Smith nodded.

"I sometimes wonder if I would do anything to protect and preserve the cathedral's image, perhaps to a fault."

"That's always possible, George. Have you—done it 'to a fault'?"

St. James sat back and pushed his plate away. He sighed and chewed his cheek as he formulated what he would say next. Smith decided to help him along. "Tell me about the conversation you had this morning with Merle and Carolyn Armstrong."

St. James took Smith's lead. "How do I begin? At the beginning, of course. As you know, the police questioned everyone who was in the cathedral the night of Paul's murder. There doesn't seem to be any doubt, does there, that he was killed the night before the body was found?"

"That seems to be firmly established."

"Reverend Merle told the police that he was not in the cathedral that night."

"And?"

"And he has been contradicted."

"Who contradicted him?"

"Reverend Armstrong. You know her, I believe."

"Not well, but Annabel and she have become friendly over the past few months. They've been working together on the mission fund-raiser that's being held at Annabel's gallery. Why would Reverend Merle have lied about being in the cathedral? He'd have every right to be here."

"I don't know, but he continues to maintain that he was not here. He says Reverend Armstrong is mistaken. I think the police tend to believe her, Mac. They've been back twice to speak with Merle."

"You can't blame them for that, considering the conflicting testimony. What do *you* think, George? Was Merle in the cathedral and is he lying, or is Reverend Armstrong lying, or mistaken?"

"I have no idea. Jonathon assures me that he was not here that night, and I have no reason to disbelieve him. On the other hand, I have no reason to question the honesty of Reverend Armstrong." His smile was pained, and he slowly shook his head. "It almost doesn't matter who is telling the truth. The result is that instead of my clergy pulling together and closing ranks in the interest of protecting this cathedral, they are now squabbling. It would be bad enough if they did it privately, but Carolyn Armstrong has made it plain to the police that she is certain Jonathon was in the cathedral that night. Their behavior is so destructive."

"Yes, but there isn't much you can do about it."

"I'm well aware of that." St. James hadn't meant to snap at Smith. He apologized.

"No apologies needed, George. You've been under the gun ever since this happened. This kind of pressure takes its toll. What concerns me is why either of them might lie. Does Merle think that if he denies that he was in the cathedral, no one will consider him a suspect? Or, is he lying because . . . ?"

"Exactly what I was thinking, Mac. Is he lying because he has something to cover up?"

Smith put his finger in the air. "Or is there a reason for Armstrong to lie about Merle? Could this be an attempt to get some kind of shot at him?"

"I almost don't want to know. Eat something, Mac."

Smith laughed. "Before it gets cold? It's already cold, which is what egg salad is supposed to be." He ate some of the salad and half a popover.

St. James appeared to be having difficulty finding a comfortable position in his chair. There was more going on in the bishop's mind than this conflict between his two canons,

Smith knew. St. James eventually got up and went to a window overlooking the cathedral close. He stood erect, his hands locked behind his back, his upper body moving with each deep breath, the body language of a man summoning up the fortitude to face a further unpleasant reality.

"The egg salad is good, George, but I prefer conversation," said Smith.

The bishop gave Smith a strong, definitive nod of his head. "You read people pretty well, don't you, Mac?"

"Sometimes. I think this might be one of them. Come, sit down." After St. James returned to his chair, Smith said, "All right, you have a potential problem because of the conflicting stories of two of your canons. What else happened this morning that has you so uptight?"

St. James let out a baleful sigh. "Just about everything has me upset, Mac, all having to do with Paul's murder. Reverend Armstrong's accusation about Merle being in the cathedral that night wasn't the only thing she brought up this morning. I'm meeting this afternoon with a Korean gentleman named Jin Tse. I met with him immediately after Paul's death. Mr. Tse

was anxious . . . I suppose I can't blame him
. . . that the cathedral's support of the Word of
Peace movement not diminish because of
Paul's passing. I assured him it wouldn't, although I must admit I was not acting out of
deep conviction. Frankly, I don't like Mr. Tse,
and although I can't quarrel with the stated purpose of Word of Peace, I have had many un-
easy moments about it. These movements
sweep up people with all sorts of motives, and
Word of Peace seems better supplied with self-
seekers than peace-seekers. It occurred to me
when you mentioned the murder of Reverend
Priestly in England to ask whether he had any
connection with the movement."

"Not that I know of, unless his friendship with
Paul is an indication. Why do you ask?"

"Do you think it's possible . . . ?"

Smith waited for the bishop to complete his
thought.

"Do you think it's remotely possible that
whoever murdered Paul had some connection
with Word of Peace?"

"Of course it's possible, George, and I've
pondered that. It's also just as plausible that
Paul was murdered by someone not *from* Word
of Peace, but who was an enemy of the group."

Smith narrowed his eyes. "You obviously are doing more than speculating here. What triggered this question?"

"I believe the purpose of the meeting this afternoon is to encourage me to delegate someone to take Paul's place in the movement."

"Who gets the nod?" Smith asked.

"I could be cruel to both parties and assign Reverend Merle."

Smith laughed. "Merle? He doesn't strike me as the type to get involved in liberal causes."

"Exactly. That's where the cruelty comes in. It certainly wouldn't be fair to Word of Peace, either. The obvious choice is Reverend Armstrong. She was very much in sympathy with the movement and Paul's connection with it." He lowered his eyes. "At least I thought she was until this morning."

"What did she say to change your mind?"

"She told me that she'd warned Paul only a few days before his death to be careful of the people from Word of Peace. She told him—at least she claims to have told him—that some of the people were evil zealots who would not allow anything or anybody to stand in their way."

Smith shrugged. "She's right, of course. Extremists on any side of an issue tend to be myopic. Did she name anybody in particular?"

"No. Unfortunately, I had to leave the room at that moment to take a long-distance call from my son, who was on the phone with his mother. When I returned, she was pacing the room and anxious to leave. I asked her to elaborate, but she said she was too upset."

"Did you believe her, George? Do you think she actually did warn Paul?"

"I certainly believed her then, or at least took it as a simple statement of fact. Sitting with you always changes my view of such things. I must admit that you create in me a certain cynicism, or at least skepticism, when it comes to believing people. Not very healthy for a bishop."

Smith pushed back his chair and stood. "Maybe healthier than you think. Jesus had plenty of reason to be cynical and skeptical about some of his so-called friends. Look, George, I'd like to have a few words with Reverend Armstrong. Is that okay with you?"

"I suppose it is, although I wouldn't want her to think I divulged information from our private conversation."

"Don't worry about that."

"I just realized sitting here how selfish I've been during this lunch. You went through some horrendous experiences in England, and I haven't even mentioned them. How dreadful to have discovered that priest's body, and to have had Annabel almost killed."

"It was upsetting at the time, but I suppose we can dine out on the stories for a while. Funny, before I arrived here I spent some time dwelling on the possibility that a candlestick was used to kill Paul. I suppose I wouldn't have become this fixated on it if Reverend Priestly hadn't been killed by one. I just can't get it out of my mind."

"Because both were priests and were murdered in a church?"

"That probably has something to do with it, although I won't try to defend the notion. It's like the shrinks say. Tell someone not to think of a pink elephant, and that's all you can think of. Are you sure the police had access to every candlestick in the cathedral?"

St. James extended his hands in a gesture of helplessness. "How could I possibly know? I have many duties, but the candlestick inventory isn't one of them."

"I would hope not. I just thought you might be

aware of another place within the cathedral that the police might have overlooked."

St. James shook his head. "No. I have to assume they were thorough. Besides, any object could have been used to kill Paul. Any object."

Smith thought of Jeffrey Woodcock's tendency to repeat, and the fact that George St. James never did. But he had now. For emphasis, obviously. "Well," Smith said, "if you think of something or someplace that might have been passed over in the investigation, let me know. In the meantime, I have some things to attend to, including a wife who would probably like to see a little of me this weekend. I plan a Sunday with the phone off the hook and my shoes never leaving the closet. Thanks for lunch, George. Tasty."

Smith returned to the cathedral's nave and wandered its imposing dimensions, stopping to reflect upon the seven-feet-six-inch-tall white Vermont marble statue of George Washington. He paused in the St. Paul tower porch, dedicated to the memory of Winston Churchill; in Glover Bay, which celebrates the first meeting of those interested in building a national cathedral in Washington, held at the home of Charles

Carroll Glover in December, 1891; in Wilson Bay, which contains the body of former president Woodrow Wilson, the only American president to be buried in the District of Columbia. Then Smith looked up for a long time at the Space Window, a stained-glass jewel high above the south aisle. The plaque said it had been created by Rodney Winfield, and was designed around a piece of lunar rock presented to the cathedral by the *Apollo XI* astronauts. No matter how many times he visited the National Cathedral, there was always something else to observe, to learn from, to wonder at.

He started to leave by the south transept, but couldn't resist the urge to visit the Good Shepherd Chapel once again. He stood outside—a young couple was praying in one of the pews. Smith backed away and retraced his steps to the Bethlehem Chapel. As he looked in at the altar, he heard a noise behind him. He turned and saw that the door to the choir room was slightly open. It suddenly closed.

Smith knocked on the door. No one responded, although he could hear a piece of furniture being bumped, then heard a door open and close. He turned the handle on the door, and it opened. He stepped into the choir room and looked around. It was empty. He quickly walked to the only other door, which led to the outside. He looked through the glass in the door, and saw a young boy running in the direction of the St. Albans school. Smith couldn't be sure, but it looked like the young choirboy who'd sung so beautifully at his wedding, and who'd become ill during Paul Singletary's funeral. Why does he seem so frightened? Smith wondered.

He returned to the door through which he'd entered and opened it a crack. He could see directly across into the front of the Bethlehem Chapel. He opened the door farther and put his head out, looking to his right down the hallway leading to the set of stairs that went up to the Good Shepherd Chapel. The stairs were empty; nothing seemed amiss.

He wasn't even aware of the drive home. His mind was too filled with questions.

chapter

18

Monday Morning— Sunny, of Course

At 6:00 A.M. Monday morning, Smith sat in the small study in his house in Foggy Bottom and peered at a pile of briefs his students had written. He'd just got up, was in his robe and pajamas. He'd decided to block out as much of the day as needed to read the briefs, and then to visit his mother at the Sevier home. He looked forward to spending time with her; he didn't look forward to the briefs, but they went with the territory.

Rufus paced the room in his customary manner of communicating his needs to his master.

"In a minute," Smith said as he turned on a small, powerful battery-operated shortwave radio that was tuned to the BBC. He often did this, if only to be able to offer a different analysis of world news at lunch. Could seem pretentious, but he liked the calm and reach of the British Broadcasting Corporation. He listened to the comforting, careful, assured voice of the British newscaster's report on events in the United Kingdom, and was disappointed there was no mention of the Priestly murder. Then, again, he reasoned, why should there be? Priestly was nothing more than a local parish priest in the Cotswolds, hardly the sort of crime victim who would interest broadcasters in the major cities.

He opened his telephone book, found Jeffrey Woodcock's number, and dialed it. It would be approximately eleven o'clock in London. Miss Amill put him through.

"Mac, good to hear from you. Have you settled back in to your Washington routine?"

"No, but I'm in the process. Jeffrey, heard any more from Clarissa Morgan?"

"No, although I understand she has left London. Good riddance, I say."

"How did you find that out?"

"Reverend Apt at Lambeth called me, said he'd received a call from her. She's no longer pursuing her claim, and was leaving London. I think she said she was leaving the country, as a matter of fact."

"Apt told you that?"

"Yes. Meant to call you. I was delighted, relieved, as I'm sure he was. Bloody nuisance, that kind of conniving woman. I'm sure her claim had no merit, but these people can make problems for others, wouldn't you say?"

"Yes, they certainly can. Have you heard anything new about the murder of the priest in Buckland?"

"Just smatterings. Dreadful that you had to discover the body. Dreadful. Hardly British hospitality at its finest. No, I think the last report I heard was that the local authorities had no leads. Probably have dropped the case by now. Obviously, some demented person, some lob who happened upon Priestly and killed him for whatever he had in his pockets, poor fellow."

"Had he been robbed?" Smith asked.

"I don't know. I just assume he was. Would you like me to check? I'd be happy to check."

"Yes, I'd appreciate that." Smith gave Woodcock the name of the lead investigator in

Buckland who'd questioned him and Annabel. "By the way, Jeffrey, did you have an opportunity to find out whether Father Priestly had been involved with Word of Peace?"

"Glad you reminded me. Yes, as a matter of fact I did. Seems he was, at least according to one of the chaps from the organization here in London. Not heavily involved, though. Attended a meeting or two. About it."

"Appreciate the effort, Jeffrey."

"No bother, no bother. Terribly early for you to be up and around, isn't it?"

"I'm an early riser, although this is a little early even for me. Couldn't sleep. Lots on my mind, Jeffrey. Besides, I have a ton of work to do today, and thought I'd get a jump on it. Best to Judith. I'll call again in a few days."

Smith sat back in his leather swivel chair and pondered the conversation. How remarkably similar both murders were. Each priest was hit on the side of the head with what seemed to be an object of roughly the same dimensions. Both were alone in a religious facility, and in both cases it was assumed that the murderer was nothing more than a demented drifter, a derelict, a total stranger who happened upon them. "Can't be," Smith grunted.

Rufus had given up subtle communication. The Dane placed his large head on Smith's leg and growled, wagging his tail at the same time to make sure Smith knew it was not an act of aggression. Smith looked down into the beast's eyes and smiled, roughed up the hair on its head. "Okay, I wouldn't appreciate it if you kept me from heeding nature's call. Come on, we'll go out in the back."

Minutes later, mission accomplished, and Rufus's food disappearing from a large stainless-steel bowl on the kitchen floor, Smith poked his head into the bedroom. Annabel was still asleep. "Hey, I thought you had a busy day, too."

A tousled mane of red hair came up off the white pillow, and a sleepy voice said, "I do, but not *that* busy. What are you up so early for?"

"I always get up early. You know that. I walked Rufus and fed him, and talked to Jeffrey Woodcock in London."

"About what?"

"About whether there'd been any further news on Priestly's murder. I listened to the BBC, but they didn't cover it. I'm getting in the shower. What does your day look like?"

Annabel sat up in bed and shook the sleep

from her head. "The accountants are coming in this morning, and that fellow I hired starts today. Let's see, I really have to start getting ready for inventory . . . oh, and I'm meeting with Reverend Armstrong at four o'clock."

"You are? I had an interesting conversation with George St. James about her."

"Concerning what?"

"Concerning the fact that a few days before Paul was murdered, she expressed her concern to him not only for the image of the cathedral because of its backing of Word of Peace, but because she was concerned for Paul's safety as a result of his involvement."

Annabel swung her legs off the bed and stood. All sleep was now gone. "She told that to George?"

"Yes. I told him I wanted to have a conversation with Reverend Armstrong. Maybe you could do it better and easier."

Annabel slipped on her robe and slippers and went into the kitchen to pour a cup of coffee. Smith followed. "What do you want me to ask her?"

"I don't know, but be subtle about it. George is concerned that Armstrong not think their private conversations are being spread to other people. Maybe just getting into a talk about Paul and Word of Peace will cause her to bring it up."

"I'll try," she said.

It was busier at the gallery than Annabel had expected. The carpenters working on the renovation of the additional space were noticeably behind schedule, which upset her. She didn't show it; instead, she was cordial and urged them to work a little faster—applying honey instead of vinegar, an approach she usually found more effective than complaining.

The new person she'd hired for the gallery, a young man just out of American University's fine-arts program, seemed more interested in demonstrating his academic knowledge of pre-Columbian art than in listening to what Annabel had to say. That, too, annoyed her, but she kept her feelings in check and suggested he find a quiet corner to read the catalog of pieces currently on display in the gallery.

In the midst of this, she had to sit down with her accountants, who were critical of her handling of the new bookkeeping system they'd implemented. And no wonder.

By the time four o'clock rolled around, she

was happy to see everyone leave, and to welcome Carolyn Armstrong to the gallery.

"It's been a crazy day here," Annabel said. "I haven't even had a chance for lunch and was about to order something in. Join me?"

"No, thank you, I had lunch."

Annabel ordered a salad for herself, and two cups of tea. The women settled in her office and, once again, Annabel was quietly taken with Carolyn Armstrong's natural beauty. One thing was different this time, however. The priest was visibly nervous, something Annabel hadn't seen in her before, but it was there, unmistakable and disconcerting. Armstrong's serenity had always added an extra dimension to her appeal.

"First of all," Annabel said, "the good news. They're running behind on the renovations next door. They assured me today that they would finish in time for your exhibition and I have every reason to expect they will, but it's going to be close."

"Why is that good news?"

"Because everything else is worse. But you don't want to hear about my bookkeeping problems."

"I'm sure it will all work out," Armstrong said.

"I have two more artists for the show." She handed Annabel biographies of two Washington artists whose work she felt was worthy of being included.

"Yes, I know this person," Annabel said. "She's *very* good. She'll be a real addition to the show. I'm not familiar with this other name."

Armstrong filled in the man's background, and Annabel was reasonably pleased with this second choice. Not absolutely original, but okay.

There were myriad details to go over concerning the upcoming exhibition, and they worked steadily to resolve them over the next hour. It was now dark outside; the pinspots Annabel had softened with dimmers gave the gallery a warm, inviting glow. She was locking the front door and turning a small sign to indicate the gallery was closed when Armstrong came from the office and examined the valuable works of art on display. "So beautiful," she said.

"Yes, I love coming here," Annabel said. "I find a lovely sense of quiet and solace when I'm here . . . and when contractors aren't."

Armstrong, whose attention was focused upon a black basalt feathered serpent on a

Lucite pedestal, said without turning, "I've been looking for quiet and solace ever since Paul's death." She faced Annabel. "I always found those things in my faith, in being able to use the quiet sanctuary of a church to ask for them from God." A rueful smile came to her face. "It hasn't been working lately."

"Yes, I think I can understand," Annabel said. "Something that senseless and tragic is a pretty powerful force to overcome. I have many moments during the day when I think of Paul, of my wedding day. Of course, I didn't know him nearly as well as you did."

Armstrong looked back at the black serpent. Annabel came up behind her and stood silently, then asked, "Would you enjoy an early dinner together, or a drink?" The other woman had begun to cry. Annabel couldn't see her face, nor was there any sound, but the telltale movement in her back and neck revealed her sobs. Annabel tentatively placed her hand on the priest's shoulder. "Come on," she said, "let's go and have a bite. I just ate, but it was only a little salad. For some reason I'm hungry again."

Armstrong turned and pressed her eyes shut, opened them, and managed a small smile. "Yes, I think I would like that. I'm not due back at St. Albans until eight. Are you sure you have the time?"

"Of course. I just have to call my husband." It sounded good to say that.

Smith had just returned from visiting his mother at Sevier House. Annabel told him of her plan to have a quick dinner with Carolyn Armstrong.

"Fine," he said.

"How was your mother?"

"Good, although she got a call from a British journalist in Buckland who's doing a story about the Priestly murder."

"Why would he call *her*?"

"About me. The English tabloid press will try to track anybody down, anywhere—at least by phone. He asked for an interview, and she told him she didn't give interviews. Or read them." Smith laughed.

"Did you finish reading all those briefs?"

"Yes. Some were pretty good, one was excellent, most of the rest were ho-hum, one or two positively illegal. Have you had a chance to talk to Carolyn Armstrong about Paul?"

"No, but I suspect that will come up. She has to be back at St. Albans by eight. I should be home around then. There's leftover chicken in the refrigerator, and some frozen dinners."

"I'll manage just fine," Smith said. "Desolate, but fine. Enjoy your dinner. Love you, Mrs. Smith."

"Me, too, Mr. Smith."

Annabel Smith and Carolyn Armstrong left the Georgetown Bar & Grill at seven-thirty and said good night on the sidewalk. Annabel was happy to see that Carolyn's spirits were elevated. She'd become animated, even verbose, during dinner, and seemed anxious—no, "desperate" was a more accurate description—to talk to Annabel about anything and everything, including Paul's murder.

Annabel was eager to get home to share the conversation with Mac, but the minute she walked through the front door, she knew he wasn't there. She went to the study and read the note he'd left on the desk: *Have gone to MPD—Reverend Merle has been taken in for questioning—George called and asked if I would go—hope dinner was pleasant and productive—back as soon as possible.*

He called a half hour later and said he expected to finish up shortly and would head straight home.

"Have they arrested Merle?" Annabel asked.

"No, just brought him in for questioning. He came willingly, but it's good I was here. I'll fill you in."

Annabel sat at the desk and made notes of what she remembered from dinner. She turned on CNN, but when there was nothing of local interest—aside from national and international politics, subjects which, in Washington, were considered local news by many—turned to a local newscast. There was a brief item about Jonathon Merle's having been taken in for questioning, although the wording of the report made it sound as if he'd been arrested.

She kept looking at the clock; Mac was a lot later than he'd indicated he would be. Finally, at almost eleven, he came through the door and received his customary exuberant, face-washing, stand-up greeting from Rufus.

"Where have you been?" Annabel asked.

"Tell you all about it as soon as I've taken the beast out. You didn't, did you?"

"No, I did not." She loved Rufus, but never enjoyed being dragged through the streets of

Foggy Bottom by this powerful, albeit magnificent, four-legged animal.

Upon his return, Smith poured himself a brandy, a Nocello for Annabel, and joined her in the den. "Who goes first?" he asked.

"You," she said. "You show me yours, and I'll show you mine."

They both laughed. Smith then recounted for her what had occurred at MPD. Merle had been asked late in the afternoon to make himself available for questioning. Initially, he'd balked, but changed his mind after conferring with Bishop St. James and went with two detectives to MPD headquarters on Indiana Avenue. The questioning focused on two things: First, the inconsistency in his story about being in the cathedral the night of Singletary's murder. He stuck to it, claimed he'd retired to his apartment across the street in the Satterlee Apartment Building, where he spent the evening preparing a sermon he was to give the following Sunday. He had no one to verify that, nor could he explain why Reverend Armstrong would claim to have seen him in the cathedral that night. She was mistaken, Merle said, although Smith commented that the way Merle put it left little doubt in anyone's mind that he felt she was deliberately lying.

The other line of questioning had to do with rumors that Merle's personal dislike of Paul Singletary was intense. Merle did not deny that, although he repeatedly said that his feelings about Singletary—about any other human being, for that matter—could never be strong enough to wish him bodily harm.

"How did the police accept his answers?" Annabel asked.

"In their usual delicate way, with lots of sighs, raised eyes, grunts, and moans. I don't think they seriously consider him a suspect, but you never know. I'm just glad I was there as his counsel."

"That was your official role?"

"Yes."

"Then you're in all the way."

"I now have a client named Reverend Jonathon Merle, if that's what you mean."

"Damn!" she said.

"We'll see what develops next. Enough of this. Tell me about your dinner with Carolyn Armstrong."

"Well, let's see. We had dinner at the

Georgetown Bar and Grill. I had a club sandwich, she had a salad with smoked chicken.''

"I wasn't looking for the menu,'' Smith said.
"Did you have a chance to get into the conver-
sation she'd had with George the day before
Paul's murder?''

"It came up. She said that she'd warned Paul
early on about his involvement in Word of
Peace. She said she asked him to get out, but
he sort of laughed it off.''

"Was she specific about any of the people in
Word of Peace who might have been a threat
to his life?''

"No, although I had a feeling that there could
be a person or two whom she knew more about
than she was willing to share with me. Nothing
more than that, Mac—a feeling. Anyway, I
asked plainly whether she thought someone
from Word of Peace had murdered Paul. She
said she thought it was a possibility, but then
she focused more on Merle.''

"I don't wonder,'' Smith said, "the way she
was quick to tell the police that Merle was in the
cathedral. What did she base her feelings on?''

"Mutual dislike. It wasn't easy for her to be
this critical of a fellow priest, but she was can-

did. She told me that Merle was a warped and evil man, paranoid, jealous of Paul, and a man she felt was sufficiently unbalanced to have done such an act."

"You might say that Merle has a real enemy there."

"He sure does. What do you think?"

"About Merle, or about Word of Peace? I suppose they're all players in the game, not to be summarily dismissed, but I don't know. I wish I did."

They changed and climbed into bed. Annabel browsed through a lovely book Smith had bought for her, *The Artist in His Studio,* while Mac picked up where he'd left off with material for his next class at GW. Just before they turned off the lights, Annabel said, "There's one more thing I should mention about my dinner with Carolyn."

"What's that?"

"She was madly in love with Paul, and I think it even went beyond that. I think they were in the midst of an affair, a very serious one, when he was killed."

"She said that?"

"She didn't have to. Trust me. Good night, Mac. Sleep tight."

chapter
19

**The National Cathedral,
5:00 A.M. the Following Morning
—Frost on Everything**

His eyes were fixed upon the sword embedded in the heart of the Blessed Mother, rendered in tempera over gold leaf. The profound sorrow on the face of Mary Magdalene, who knelt at the feet of the Blessed Mother, radiated out into the Chapel of St. Joseph of Arimathea.

He lowered his eyes and leaned farther forward, his long, angular frame hunched over the wooden communion rail. Lips moved in silent prayer. It was cold in the chapel, perhaps because of the symbolism of Christ's death as well as the natural early-morning chill contained by the stone walls.

He looked up again, and his lips stopped moving. St. Joseph of Arimathea, he thought, the Jew who took Christ's brutalized body into his sepulcher because there was room there, and because there was room in his heart, too, for the crucified martyr.

Opaque, sunken eyes moved to other depictions on the mural behind the altar. Dominating the center was the Christ of Good Friday who had given His life so that others—so that we could enjoy an everlasting life through His grace.

"Forgive me, Father, for I have sinned," he said, embracing the richly polished wood of the rail as though to squeeze understanding and compassion from it. "Forgive me, Father, for I have sinned."

A cough. He looked over his right shoulder at one of two sets of carpeted stairs. No one. The maintenance man who'd cleared his throat as he started to enter the chapel had seen the figure at the communion rail and quickly backed out. You learned certain rules when working in the National Cathedral, among them that prayer was more important than polishing and was not to be interrupted. Maintenance chores could always wait.

Reverend Jonathon Merle made the sign of the cross and slowly stood, using the rail for leverage. Although he was no longer in a submissive prayer position, his concentration was as total as it had been when he was on his knees. He searched the faces on the mural. For what? Did they understand? he asked himself. Were they more than inanimate figures of garish paint and gold leaf? Could they hear his pleas for help? Did those beautiful figures function as conduits to *Him,* or was there a more direct communication?

Merle jerked his head left and right, looked up at the arched masonry ceiling thirty-nine feet above, supported by the substantial stone pillars more than twenty-seven feet in diameter. This was a chapel he avoided when possible, so depressing was its theme. The other chapels rang out with the joy of salvation: the Bethlehem Chapel dedicated to the birth of Christ; the Resurrection Chapel a triumphant proclamation of Christ's having risen in victory. But this chapel was different, with its Norman altar, its green-and-brown stone floor like that of a Roman amphitheater, the attempts by the muralist, Jan Henrik DeRosen, to mitigate the horrible theme of crucifixion through the use of colors so vivid that they only masked what any true believer felt.

Merle went to the center of the chapel and stood on the stone floor. Now he was shaking with anger; it was as if he were there in the scene depicted in the mural, had been there on that infamous day. How dare they, he thought, and his shaking intensified. His fists were clenched at his sides, and his head slowly moved back and forth. There was no cough this time, but Merle sensed that someone was looking down upon him from the top of the stairs. He looked in that direction and saw the maintenance man quickly walk out of view.

"Don't let this happen to me," Merle said to Him. Merle cried inwardly, but his eyes remained dry.

Then he stood ramrod straight, and his mouth pressed into a tight line. He walked up the stairs at the opposite side of the chapel, left the cathedral through the south transept, and sat on a bench in the Hortulus, the "Little Garden," centered on a ninth-century French baptismal font. He sat there until the sun had risen and Bishop St. James would be in his study.

"Yes, Jonathon?" St. James said after Merle had knocked and had been invited to enter.

Merle sat in a chair across the desk from the bishop and stared at him.

"Jonathon, is something wrong?" St. James asked. "You look deeply troubled."

"I . . ." Merle started to say, then fell silent.

St. James got up and came around to the priest. He knew it had been an ordeal for his canon to be interrogated by the police. He leaned back against the edge of his desk, folded his arms across his chest, and tried a little humor. "Are you upset because I never followed through on my offer of a Chinese dinner?" He instantly realized it was inappropriate, and certainly not effective. Merle looked ready to cry at any minute, but there was such an aridness to him that it seemed inconceivable that there could be moisture within.

"Does this have something to do with Paul's death?" St. James asked.

Merle sat perfectly still for what seemed an eternity. Then, with an almost indiscernible movement of his head, he nodded that it did.

St. James drew a deep breath and allowed his body to slump. Was he about to hear that Merle had murdered Paul? He silently said a quick prayer: Dear God, please do not let it be that. But he also had to honestly admit to himself that he had wondered from the start whether Jonathon Merle had killed Singletary. The animosity between them was overt. Devout as St. James knew Merle to be, and yes, good and decent, the bishop also recognized an enigmatic force within the priest, the sort of force that seemed endemic to social misfits, to those seemingly decent and good people who do dreadful things, who gun down fellow workers at a plant, or who follow their inner demons to cleanse the world by murdering prostitutes.

"Jonathon, you know you can trust me. Whatever is weighing so heavily on you can be handled more easily if it's shared."

Merle had been looking down at his hands, clasped in his lap. He raised his head and peered into the bishop's eyes with an intensity that could be interpreted as seeking understanding or revealing his distrust.

"Tell me, Jonathon," St. James said, forcing a smile and placing both hands on Merle's bony shoulders. "Tell me."

Merle spoke in a monotone. "I was treated like a common criminal. I sat in a room where the dregs of society sit, and was subjected to the same scorn. The only difference is that they deserve it. I do not." He leaned forward. "You should have seen what happened. You should have seen their expressions when I honestly answered their questions. They looked at me as the Blessed Mother looked at the Romans who put Him on the Cross. They saw nothing but guilt, nothing but degradation. It was humiliating."

"Yes, it must have been," St. James said. "Sorry I wasn't here when you returned. I was glad that Mac Smith was with you."

"Not all the time. He came later."

"Yes, of course he did. He didn't know you had gone to be questioned at first. Wasn't he a help once he got there?"

"A help? He is one of them. He does not understand that a man like me, a man like you, answers to someone above their worldly views."

"Mac Smith is a good man, Jonathon."

Merle sighed, and his head fell forward.

St. James returned to the chair behind his desk. "Jonathon, I understand the pain you're feeling, and I have considerable sympathy for it, but is that all that has brought you here this morning? Is it simply the pain, the humiliation, of having been questioned at police headquarters?"

Merle's head came up. "No, there is a much heavier burden upon me."

"And what is that burden?"

"That . . . I have been forced to suffer such debasement and degradation while the one who should bear it walks free."

St. James sat up straight. "What do you mean? Are you saying that you know who killed Paul?"

Merle's face opened up, blossomed as though he had awakened from a deep sleep. "Yes," he said.

Again, Bishop St. James had hoped it would not come to this. Did the priest sitting across from him really know? If so, was he about to point his finger at someone within the cathedral, someone who, if guilty, would bring disgrace to the institution he loved so much? He didn't ask for a name.

"She is a slut," Merle said.

"She is a . . . a slut? Jonathon, to whom are you referring?"

"Reverend Armstrong."

"Oh, my God," St. James said, bringing his hand to his face and rubbing his eyes.

Merle was now more animated. "Don't you see? She shared his bed. She slept with him, fed his carnal instincts."

St. James flapped his hands in the air as though to obliterate everything that was happening at the moment. "Jonathon, you are saying that Reverend Armstrong and Reverend Singletary . . . had an affair?"

The smile that crossed Merle's face was the first that morning. "Of course," he said. "Everyone was aware of it. I knew about it long ago. Didn't you?"

"No, I did not, and I am not sure I believe it now. How can you make such an accusation? Do you have proof of this?"

Merle's smile widened. "Oh, my dear friend and bishop, it has been going on under your nose for so very long."

St. James abruptly went to the window and looked out over the close. "Are you saying that not only did Reverend Armstrong and Reverend Singletary have an affair, but that she murdered him as a result of it?" His hand gripped drapes that had been parted to allow the morning sun to enter the study. His eyes were closed tight: Please don't say yes, he prayed.

But Merle affirmed in a voice that had gained volume, "Yes, that is what happened."

Bishop St. James released his grip on the drapes and turned to face his priest. "I pray that you are wrong, Jonathon."

"I have been offering that same prayer ever since it happened," Merle said. "Unfortunately, my prayer has not been answered."

The aloofness behind Merle's statement angered the bishop. He gave Merle a hard look and said, "If you have any evidence to support what you are saying, Jonathon, you must come forward with it to the proper authorities. I'll stand with you, but you must have evidence, must have proof, before you make such accusations."

Naturally, it had occurred to the bishop that Merle's statements might represent nothing more than giving tit for tat. Carolyn Armstrong had implicated Merle in the Singletary case, at least to the extent that she claimed he was lying about his whereabouts the night of the murder. Was this a misguided attempt to get even? More disconcerting was the question of whether this was a way of turning the spotlight from himself to Armstrong because . . . because perhaps he *had* been in the cathedral

that night, and . . . and *had* murdered Singletary.

No. That contemplation was too painful. The
bishop said, "Mackensie Smith has been extremely helpful in every aspect of this unfortunate situation. He functioned as your attorney
during most of the questioning at police headquarters. He is a friend of mine and of this
cathedral. I would like you to tell him what
you've told me. I trust his judgment. Will you do
that, Jonathon?"

"Yes."

"Good. I'll call him now."

Merle stood and started for the door.

"Please stay until I've reached Smith and
have arranged for you to get together."

"I have work to do, Bishop. You know where
to reach me. Thank you for your time."

After Merle had left and closed the door, St.
James sat in his chair and tried to sort out what
had happened. There was such anger in the
man; his parting words had been uttered with a
wind-chill factor of minus sixty. Was there any
truth to what he'd said? St. James tried to pray
but was incapable of it. What would he ask for,
what sins would he confess? Instead, he
picked up the phone and dialed Smith's home.

chapter
20

**Later That Morning—
The Frost Has Melted, but It's Still Chilly**

Choirboy Joey Kelsch and his mother sat with other mothers and children in the waiting room of his pediatrician, Dr. Gabe Griffith. Joey had been cared for since birth by Dr. Abraham Goldin, who'd retired six years ago and sold his practice to the young Dr. Griffith and two associates. They'd built it into one of Washington's thriving pediatric partnerships. Some mothers of children who had been Dr. Goldin's patients weren't sure they liked the new, younger, and decidedly trendy pediatricians, but few had abandoned ship. The long waits that were never the case with Dr. Goldin were balanced by not having to seek out a new physician in another part of town, arrange for records to be transferred, and all the other inconveniences inherent in a change of doctors. Besides, this new group of Young Turks were local celebrities of sorts. Dr. Griffith wrote a column for a weekly newspaper, and conducted a talk show on one of the cable channels. Claiming Dr. Gabe Griffith & Associates as your pediatric group conferred panache akin to that of having the Gene Donati Orchestra play your wedding or François Dionot cater your bar mitzvah.

Joey and his mother waited almost an hour. Finally, a nurse said with studied pleasantness, "Joey, Mrs. Kelsch."

When Dr. Griffith finished examining Joey, he said, "Looks in great shape to me. A fine, healthy young man." Mrs. Kelsch's expression told the doctor his evaluation had not appeased her.

"Tell you what, Joey, how about going back into the waiting room while I chat with your mom for a few minutes?" Griffith said.

Joey didn't hesitate. He was gone within seconds.

"You said he's been acting strange lately," the doctor said. "In what way?"

"I don't know, Doctor, it's hard to pin down. Joey has always been high-strung and hyperactive, but ever since—" She looked up at the ceiling as though wanting to affirm that what she was about to say had validity. Evidently, she decided it did, because she continued, "Ever since Reverend Singletary was murdered at the cathedral, Joey has been a different boy. He sulks a great deal, and sometimes is downright arrogant and nasty."

"Well, you're right, it could have something to do with that event. Was he close to Reverend Singletary?"

"Not that I'm aware of. He certainly knew him because of going to school there and being active in the choir, but he never talked about Father Singletary to my husband or me. It's as though that event changed him." She told the doctor how Joey had vomited while singing a solo during the funeral.

Griffith, who was sitting behind his desk, ran his fingertips through a carefully arranged set of gray-black curls and shook his head. "I wouldn't worry about this, Mrs. Kelsch. Joey is a sensitive boy and has probably taken a great deal of this to heart. He also has the demands of school, peer pressure, and all the other things that work on a youngster of his age. No, I wouldn't concern myself about it."

"But you aren't living with it, Doctor," Mrs. Kelsch said.

Griffith smiled. "That, of course, is very true. Tell you what, Mrs. Kelsch. If you think it's sufficiently serious, maybe Joey should see a psychiatrist, talk it out, deal with whatever it is he's feeling about Reverend Singletary's murder. I can refer you to some excellent ones."

"A shrink for Joey? No, I think that would be more destructive than helpful."

"Well, that's the only advice I can offer. I'm a pediatrician, not a psychiatrist. Think about it. If you decide to give it a try—and some of the people we work with are top-notch—I can arrange an appointment. By the way, anything new on the reverend's murder?"

"I have no idea, Dr. Griffith," she answered. "My husband and I discussed taking Joey out of the cathedral school, maybe placing him in another private school just to get him away from there."

"That's a decision only you and your husband can make, but I wouldn't be too hasty about it. Keep an eye on him, and talk to your husband about getting Joey some professional counseling. Have a good day, Mrs. Kelsch."

Joey's mother tried to make light conversation as they drove home in their new red Volvo wagon, but Joey would have none of it. He sat in a defiant shell against the passenger door and would not respond to his mother's questions and comments. His withdrawal made her increasingly angry, and by the time they walked through the door of their home, she was screaming at him. He immediately went upstairs and slammed his bedroom door.

Maybe Dr. Griffith was right, she thought as she fixed herself a cup of herbal tea in the kitchen. Maybe he does need counseling, some sort of professional intervention. Lord knows, she and her husband had been unable to reach him. That's what shrinks were for, to reach people.

She carried her tea upstairs after having decided to suggest to Joey that they see a counselor. She knocked on his door; there was no answer.

"Joey, it's your mother."

When there still was no response, she tried the door, but he'd locked it from the inside. She banged on it with her fists. "Joey, open this door immediately! This is ridiculous, and I will not stand for it." She beat on the door again even harder, and the teacup and saucer in her left hand fell to the floor, the tea creating an instant brown stain in the thick white carpet.

She heard the lock turn and the door opened. Staring up at her was her only son. She had seen anger before on his face, but nothing to equal this. His eyes filled, and he screamed, "Leave me alone! You don't understand!" He pushed by her with enough force to propel her against the wall and bounded down the stairs. She heard the front door open and slam shut.

"My God," she muttered as she picked up the cup and saucer. What should she do?

She walked into his room and looked around. Was he using drugs? The thought sent chills through her. No, of course not. But people said that parents who assumed their children would *never* use drugs were often the most disappointed ones. She should have raised that possibility with Dr. Griffith. But Joey? At the age of ten? Ridiculous.

Still, she opened each of his dresser drawers and searched beneath what clothing was in them. Most of his clothes were in his room at the cathedral school. She reached up in his closet and ran her hands over the shelf, looked under the bed, riffled through books and papers and magazines. Then she glanced up at the wall above his bed, where a National Cathedral calendar had always hung. It wasn't there; it had been torn to shreds, the pieces strewn over his pillow.

She returned to the kitchen and sat at the table. Dr. Griffith had said that academic pressure might be contributing to her son's erratic and unacceptable behavior. Was that what the torn calendar meant, that he no longer wished to attend the cathedral school? Maybe it *was* time to change schools. She'd talk to her husband about that as soon as he returned from his business trip to Denver. Why wasn't he here now? She'd call him that night in his hotel and bring it up, even though he hated those kinds of discussions when he was away. He'd have to listen now. This was serious. This was their only son.

Canon Wilfred Nickelson, the National Cathedral's musical director, seldom came home for lunch. Although he, his wife, Jennifer, and their three daughters lived in a rented house only a few minutes' drive from the cathedral, Nickelson preferred to take lunch in local restaurants. Jennifer often commented that they would save a considerable amount of money if he ate lunch at home, but he never did. The fact was that Nickelson and his wife did not get along especially well; the less time spent with her the better, although he was a relatively devoted father who found time to spend with his family on weekends and in the evenings.

This day, however, he walked through the door precisely at noon.

"Willie?" Jennifer shouted from the kitchen in the rear of the small house.

"Yes, it's me."

She'd been kneading dough for bread; she often baked her own. Jennifer Nickelson was proud of her baking prowess, and had won some area bake-offs. Her hands were caked with flour, and an apron covered her from neck to knee. "What are you doing home?" she asked.

"I have something on my mind, Jen, and I think we ought to discuss it now."

Her eyes widened. "Sounds heavy. Are you sure I want to hear this?"

"It doesn't matter whether you want to or not. You're about to."

She muffled an angry comment and returned to the kitchen. He followed and sat at a small table. "Sit down," he said.

"In a minute, as soon as I finish this."

"Jen, sit down now."

Her husband would never be characterized as easygoing. She'd learned to live with his temperament over the years of their marriage, although some of her family had rebelled by finding excuses for not spending time with Wilfred Nickelson. Jennifer wiped her hands on her apron, filled a pan with warm water, and put her bowl of bread dough on a rack over the pan. Then she took a chair across the table. "What's going on, Willie? You sound as though you're about to announce the outbreak of World War Three."

He managed a smile, which she knew did not come easily. She looked into his eyes and saw something quite different from any expression that had ever been there over the course of their marriage. Usually there was blankness, anger, or cold control. This day, however, she discerned fear, or at least deep concern, in his eyes. She placed her hands on his on the table and asked, "Willie, what's wrong?"

If his smile was forced, his laugh took even more effort. "Wrong?" he said. "Absolutely nothing. In fact, everything is right. How would you like to move to San Francisco?"

"How would I like to *move* to San Francisco? I like San Francisco. I loved that trip we took there a few years ago. How would I like to move there? I wouldn't."

"Why not?"

"Because I like it here. The girls go to school here. We have friends here. Besides, I'm not a fan of earthquakes." She, too, forced a laugh to lighten things.

"Well, Jen, earthquakes or not, we are about to move to San Francisco."

She slumped back in her chair and looked at him as though he were an alien who'd dropped in from another planet. "Willie, what do you mean we're about to move to San Francisco? We live here. You work here."

"Not for long. I've been offered a job as music director at St. Paul's in San Francisco. I took it. We're moving there in a week."

She tried to respond but was incapable of

words. Instead, she went to the counter and peered at the bread dough that had begun to rise in the bowl.

"Jen, did you hear me?" Nickelson asked.

"Yes, I heard you," she said in a flighty voice, a voice she often lapsed into when confronted with a confounding situation.

"Jen, sit down again and listen to me. I mean business."

"Yes. That's the problem: I know you do. I just want to make sure—"

The sound of his fist making contact with the table jolted her.

"Damn it, sit down."

She did as she was told, although she did not look at him. He said, "Jen, I hate my job at the cathedral. I've been wanting something else for a long time, and now I have it." He took her hands this time as he said, "What a wonderful opportunity! How many times have you said you don't like Washington, hate the heat in the summer? Think about it, Jen. I'll have a whole new situation that I can be enthusiastic about, and you and the kids can enjoy that beautiful weather out there, enjoy the Bay Area. We need a change, Jen. We desperately need a change."

It took a moment for her to summon up the courage to express what was on her mind. "Willie, I could understand if you had wanted to find another position and we'd talked about it. I think it's wonderful that you've found something that pleases you more, but why so suddenly? You said they offered you the job. That means you must have asked for it."

"Yes, of course I did. I learned of the opening through another music director here in Washington, called, put together a résumé and sent it out, and they want me. Isn't that wonderful?"

"And you never included me in any of this?" Hurt filled her voice.

"I'm submitting my resignation to Bishop St. James this afternoon. I'm supposed to be out in San Francisco in a week. I promised them that. That means you and the girls have a fast job of packing to do. Call a mover this afternoon. They're paying for the move, so don't worry about cost. Just get it done so that we can be out of here no later than a week from now."

"Willie, what will the Bishop say about giving him such short notice? That isn't right."

"Don't worry about that. He'll understand. He'll *have* to understand. Now, I have to get back." He went to the refrigerator and pulled out a plastic container of tuna-fish salad Jennifer had made the day before for the kids. He smeared salad on two pieces of bread, wrapped it in foil, and took it with him to the foyer, where he shoved the sandwich into his raincoat pocket. Jennifer stood in the kitchen doorway.

"No turning back, Jen," he said, pointing his finger at her. "I expect movement on this when I get home tonight." Then, as though he realized he was being unnecessarily belligerent, which would be counterproductive, he smiled, came to her, kissed her on the cheek, and said, "We'll have a wonderful life together in San Francisco."

chapter
21

The Next Morning, Wednesday
—Indian Summer

Bishop St. James's call to Mac Smith the previous morning had reached only Annabel's voice on their answering machine. It wasn't until late in the afternoon that Smith returned the call and heard about the bishop's conversation with Jonathon Merle, and that Merle was willing to repeat and elaborate it to Smith. They made an appointment for nine the next morning.

Smith was precisely on time, as was his habit, and sat in the bishop's study with St. James and Merle. Merle told Smith what he'd told the bishop.

"Reverend Merle, what you say is interesting, of course," said Smith, "but as an attorney, I have to question the validity of it." Merle started to respond, but Smith quickly added, "I'm not questioning your truthfulness. I understand that what you say comes out of conviction, but you've told me nothing that would stand up as tangible evidence. Was Reverend Armstrong in the cathedral the night of Reverend Singletary's murder?"

"Yes, she was."

"How would you know that?" Smith asked. "You said you weren't here that night."

If Smith had thought to catch Merle in an inconsistency, he failed. The priest said calmly, "That evening she was scheduled to counsel a group of young couples who are planning to marry, and to prepare a slide presentation in the auditorium upstairs, off the conference center."

"Reverend Armstrong freely admits she was here the night of the murder," said St. James. "She told the police that."

Smith said to Merle, "Why would Reverend Armstrong counsel young couples here in the cathedral? She's assigned to St. Albans. Are they all planning to be married in the cathedral?''

Bishop St. James again answered the question. ''Yes, they are, but there's no need to wonder why clergy from St. Albans perform tasks in the cathedral. All clergy assigned to St. Albans also conduct a great deal of their business here. We have separate buildings and what are basically separate congregations, but there is a great deal of interchange between the two.''

''I see,'' Smith said. He turned back to Merle. ''Do you know how late Reverend Armstrong stayed in the cathedral?''

''You mean the night of Singletary's murder?''

''Yes.''

''Why don't you ask her?''

''I intend to, of course, but since you seem to know a great deal about her movements that night, I thought you might save me some time.''

''I don't know exactly how late, but it had to be at least ten.''

''Why?''

''Because . . . because the slide presentation was extensive.''

"You've seen it?"

"No, but I've been told about it." Merle was not quite as composed as when the conversation started. Earlier, he'd stared blankly at Smith as he answered questions. Now his eyes were in motion, and he picked at the skin on the palm of one of his hands. Rather sharply, he said, "Why are you asking me questions like this? I thought you were my attorney. You sound the way the police did, accusing, distrustful."

"Not at all, Reverend Merle, but I promised Bishop St. James that I would help if anyone from this institution were to be accused of Paul Singletary's murder. You're pointing a finger at Reverend Armstrong. All I want to do is to ascertain what tangible facts you have to back up *your* accusations. The police will be much tougher."

Merle leaned forward. His lip curled in anger, and he pointed a long, bony finger at Smith. "You want tangible evidence?" His mouth unfurled in a victorious smile. "Here's one piece of it. A week before Singletary died, I was privy to a conversation between him and Carolyn Armstrong. They didn't know I was listening. I suppose they assumed no one was able to overhear them. They were wrong."

"Where did this conversation take place?" Smith asked.

"By the Garth Fountain outside of Good Shepherd."

"Where were you that you could hear this conversation?"

"In Good Shepherd. I'd gone there to pray. The window was open, and I heard them. At first, I ignored them, but when I heard voices rise in anger, I went to the window and looked out. They were standing next to the fountain."

"Hard to hear conversations out there with the water running," Smith said.

"It wasn't running. The fountain was down for repairs."

"What did you hear, Jonathon?" St. James asked.

"I heard her accuse him of betraying her, of being unfaithful to her."

Smith glanced at the bishop before asking his next question. "You say she accused him of being unfaithful to her. Did she get more specific?"

"Yes, as a matter of fact, she did. She accused him of having an affair with another woman—she didn't say who that was, nor did I wish to know, but she was very clear about it."

"And you understood from the conversation that Reverend Singletary was intimately involved with Reverend Armstrong at that point."

Merle's laugh was sardonic. "What would *you* deduce from that, Mr. Smith?"

Smith nodded, conceding the point. "Did Reverend Singletary say anything in his own defense?"

"He told her to stop being childish, told her that she did not own him and that he was free to do what he wished."

Smith sighed. "Again, Reverend Merle, interesting but hardly reason in itself to accuse Reverend Armstrong of Reverend Singletary's murder."

"They ended their conversation this way, Mr. Smith. Armstrong told him that if she couldn't have him, no other woman ever would."

Smith said, "I appreciate your telling me this, Reverend Merle. Was there anything else said, or done, during that conversation that would lend credence to the notion that she is Reverend Singletary's killer?"

A look of exasperation came over Merle. His

voice matched it. "Even if there were, is anything else needed, Mr. Smith? Just remember.
Reverend Armstrong is a pathological liar. Just
remember that. She and I could never work
together as . . . closely as she did with Singletary."

Smith was about to tell him that from a legal
perspective a great deal more was needed, but
he decided he wasn't there to give a lecture on
jurisprudence. That was for his class at GW. He
thanked the priest again and watched him
leave the room.

"What do you think, Mac?" St. James asked.

"He may know more. But I think that a *motive*
has been established for Carolyn Armstrong to
be a suspect, nothing more. Merle was certainly known to have disliked Singletary, which
gives him a motive, too. I told you I intended to
speak with Reverend Armstrong. I didn't do
that, but Annabel did. They had dinner together."

"What came out of that dinner?"

"Nothing substantive, although Annabel left
it convinced that Reverend Armstrong certainly
had been intimate with Paul. Madly in love is
more like it. Let me ask you this, George. Since
we're discussing motive here, is there anyone

else in the cathedral who would have had a motive, no matter how minor, for killing Paul?"

St. James pondered the question before saying, "I don't think so. Of course, none of us go through life without run-ins with other individuals. Paul had his share. I recall him berating one of our maintenance people once. I forget what it was about."

"How long ago was that?"

"Months."

"Is that individual still employed by the cathedral?"

"Yes, but don't read more into this than it deserves. I'm talking about an isolated incident."

"Did you mention this to the police?"

"No, I don't think so. I never thought about it until now."

"Somehow I can't imagine Paul berating anyone," Smith said. "I'd better have a word with this maintenance man." The bishop gave Smith his name. "While we're coming up with suspects, is there anybody else to add to the list?"

"If having a minor squabble qualifies you for the list, I suppose there would be dozens of people. A harsh word here or there, a momentary fit of pique. Canon Nickelson certainly was not personally fond of Paul."

"That so? Why?"

"I could never really put my finger on it, Mac. Something to do with Nickelson's wife. There had been rumors, briefly, that Paul had become involved with Jennifer Nickelson. I confronted Paul about it. I remember it clearly. He laughed and assured me that there was absolutely no truth to the rumors, that he liked Mrs. Nickelson as a person but that they had never done anything more than shake hands. I believed him, of course. Still, the rumor persisted, and I was told that Canon Nickelson was furious about it."

"Did you ask Nickelson about it?" Smith asked.

"No. I felt that would be in bad taste. Frankly, Mac, I've always been aware of Paul's reputation as a bit of a womanizer, but there isn't the slightest doubt in my mind that he had nothing to do with Jennifer Nickelson. Besides, it's all about to become academic."

"Why?"

"Nickelson resigned today."

"Really? From what I've seen—and heard—he does an excellent job."

"Yes, he's a talented musician. He'll be difficult to replace, although what really upset me was that he gave only a week's notice—six days, actually. It puts us in quite a bind."

"It must. Did he give any reason for such a hasty departure?"

"Something to do with a sick family member in San Francisco. But that's not the reason. He's taken a job out there as musical director for St. Paul's."

"Just like that?"

"Just like that."

"Aside from the situation with Paul, how did Nickelson get along with others here at the cathedral?"

St. James sighed. "He wasn't particularly liked. Strange when you think about it. Here's a man who is able to draw the finest musical performances from everyone, yet is unable to draw friendship or affection from those same people. No, he did not make many friends while here." He laughed. "Our students refer to him as Willy Nickel. They occasionally complain to me about him, but children often do that when having to deal with someone like Nickelson who demands the best of them."

Smith stood and stretched. "Give me a bit more of your evaluation of Jonathon Merle. I know you don't particularly like him, but is he what you would term a balanced, rational person?"

St. James's face clearly said he wished that question had not been asked. He answered it this way: "We all enter into this calling, this vocation, because we have been touched by something that cannot be explained by scientific methodology. We become priests and nuns because we believe deeply in something that no one can prove even exists. There is, of course, the Ayn Rand theory of self, which says that a nun becomes a nun because she is uncomfortable with the secular life, and satisfies her selfish needs while, at the same time, doing good. She's happier, and the lepers are treated. It's a nice theory, but with all due respect, Ms. Rand's view does not satisfy me. Maybe it holds water in some cases, but not all.

"The problem is that because this work, this calling, draws people who are bound up in some degree of mysticism, it often appeals to certain individuals who are not especially rational or grounded in a sense of reality." He raised his eyes and shook his head. "I wish I weren't saying this, because it is blatantly unfair to Jonathon. He's a good man and a fine priest.

He believes fervently in his calling and his faith
. . . but perhaps, on occasion, he believes a
little too strongly and is intolerant of any devia-
tion from it. He can be zealous about that to the
same extent that Paul was about his work with
social programs. And he has his own problems,
which keep him from the perfection he seeks in
himself. And others."

"Yes, I understand," Smith said. "I have to
go. Thanks for your time, George. I'll be in
touch."

After Smith left his meeting with the bishop
and Merle, he went home to wait for Tony Buffolino to arrive. Buffolino had called the night
before, saying he had some interesting information. He arrived, showing signs of his old
excitement.

"First of all, Mac, you told me to check into
the backgrounds of the two Reverends Merle
and Armstrong. What I came up with ain't exactly a moon landing, but I think it's worth passing on."

"I'm all ears," Smith said.

They sat at Smith's kitchen table. Smith had
made coffee and placed a plate of jelly dough-

nuts between them. In a moment or so, Buffolino was on his second. "First of all, this Merle is a pretty dull character."

Smith laughed. "I suppose you could call him that. Uptight, upright, but not a barrel of laughs. Is that all you've found out about him?"

"Yeah, except for one interesting period in his life that wasn't so dull."

"What period was that?"

"The two years he spent in a loony bin."

Tony's tendency to use the cruel vernacular often riled Smith, but he knew that if he raised an objection he would only prompt a debate over calling a spade a spade, as Buffolino called it, or telling it like it is.

"Go on," Smith said.

Now Buffolino referred to notes, and gave Smith the dates of Merle's confinement to a mental institution in Ohio. It had taken place fourteen years ago, and the official reason for his confinement was "schizothymic personality." He fumbled the first word.

"Technical term for schizoid," Smith said. "Any information on how his treatment went, and the prognosis?"

Buffolino shook his head and helped himself

to another doughnut. "These are pretty good, but I'm not too hungry. No prognosis, but he put in a good two years, that's for sure."

"Okay, Tony, next."

"Next, this beautiful Reverend Carolyn Armstrong. A nice lady, it seems to me."

"Why do you say that?"

"Well, she came out of a tough life. She looks like class, but she's been over some bumps. I mean, she was born illegitimate and dumped by her mother. Grew up in a series of foster homes down in Newport News, and even spent time in orphanages. I didn't think they had them anymore."

"I suppose they do. Hmmm. Not an easy beginning for a young woman. But she certainly seems to have pulled her life together."

"Yeah, she sure has. She started pretty young trying to get it together."

"What do you mean?"

"She was in a beauty contest when she was sixteen."

"Beauty contest? Did she win?"

"Sure did, Miss Newport News."

"Did she go on in the beauty-contest business? Did she win other titles? Was she Miss America?"

Buffolino shook his head. "Nah. She's good-lookin', but no Elizabeth Taylor."

"Anything else about her?"

"A lot of boilerplate, nothing that matters where this case is concerned. I do have one thing on another front, though."

"Please."

"The police have what they consider a pretty good suspect."

Smith's eyes widened.

"You know that woman who found the body, that Mrs. Waters?"

"Sure."

"Well, she's got a son named Brian."

"So I gather."

"It seems this Brian Waters used to live in Newport News, too."

"Which means what?"

"Which means I have no idea whether he ever knew Reverend Armstrong, but I do know he was arrested twice for assault. No convictions."

"MPD likes him as a suspect?"

"Yep."

"Then why would he have come in with his mother—walked right into the police's hands?"

"Because," Tony said, "—maybe I'll just finish this last one—he knew they'd find his mother somehow. She was hysterical and would have eventually turned herself in or gone back to Mrs. Bishop, and the guy figured better the heat should be on his mother, with him the good guy, than on him. Besides, one of those assault charges in Newport News had to do with him knocking around a priest down there."

Smith poured himself more coffee and drew a deep breath. "How hard are they working him, Tony?"

"Hard enough to have brought him in twice for questioning. My friend told me they consider this guy a head case. But he comes off like a very nice and normal human being."

"So why did they turn to him? Oh, I guess I know."

"Why?" Tony said, surprised.

"Because he's a car salesman. They check on anybody in certain occupations."

"Just like on Italians or guys with beards. Car salesman—so he knows how to make nice to people. But my friend tells me that the elevator doesn't always reach the top floor with Brian Waters. Want to know something else about him?"

"I want to know anything you know."

"This guy is right of John Birch. He belonged to one of those neo-Nazi groups in Newport News, one of those hate organizations."

"Does he have any affiliation like that here in Washington?"

Buffolino shrugged. "Beats me. Haven't finished checking yet. But this is a guy who ain't destined to love a guy like Singletary who's talkin' all the time about the rights of the blacks and Hispanics and the poor, not a character who has already punched out one priest. You get my drift?"

"Yes. What's your friend's line on Brian Waters? Do they think they have enough to arrest him?"

"Not yet, but they're digging. I mean, the guy lives with his mother a couple of blocks from the cathedral. She's a religious fanatic, he's a fanatic in another way. Hey, I could come up with worse scenarios."

"Yes, Tony," Smith said, "you could."

Later that afternoon, he attended a faculty meeting at the university. Smith considered such meetings to be necessary evils or, at best, ritualistic necessities that had to be indulged. Everyone, sociologists said, needed a hangout at which to spend time in friendly surroundings

and with people who shared a common purpose and background. Meetings were like that,
Smith had decided years ago: they represented
a need to gather together and affirm that everyone was involved in the same pursuit, more or
less, and actually could get along, at least
within the conference room.

The meeting lasted a lot longer than he'd
anticipated or needed; this nothing new, it
never seemed to fail. He left just in time to
make a date he'd arranged earlier in the day
with an old friend, Cameron Bowes, who'd
been Voice of America's CIA liaison for the
past ten years, and with whom Smith kept in
touch. Smith had few close friends in government agencies, but Bowes certainly headed
the short list.

They met in the lobby of the Four Seasons
Hotel in Georgetown, where a pianist in a tuxedo played show tunes as background for
Washington's movers and shakers in their
comfortable little corners, large ferns providing
"cover" as they talked about big things. Cameron Bowes was a slender, almost diminutive
man, with silver hair, a face filled with lines, and
interesting angles, and who wore expensive

clothing like a model. He was also an unfailingly interesting companion over a drink, erudite and well-read, a man whose interests transcended the day-to-day demands of his VOA position.

After they'd been served drinks by a young woman in a floor-length green-and-yellow jungle-pattern gown, Bowes said, "A toast to the end of summer in Washington and to the Redskins. Your evaluation, Mr. Smith, of our favorite team."

"I haven't given much thought to it, Cam. I suppose I'll get into the season when it's almost over, provided they make the play-offs."

"Spoken like a true sports fan, although I think you're going to be very disappointed if you're waiting for that. Tell me, Mackensie, what's new on your plate aside from having committed your considerable legal talents to an entire institution of higher religion?"

Smith laughed and sipped his bourbon. "What do *you* hear about murder most foul in the National Cathedral?"

"Spooky places, cathedrals. I've toured all the biggies around the world. Not that I consider myself an aficionado of temples of worship, but my wife seems to think that a trip *anywhere* is wasted without spending at least some time in them. This Singletary was a controversial guy.''

''Yes, he was, although a lot of the controversy may have been unjustified. Hell, wanting to improve the lot of his fellow man and wanting world peace shouldn't spur controversy. Agree?''

''Sure, but there are lots of people who don't. They prefer to see the situation remain exactly as it is, a growing number of rich people worrying about their capital gains, and a growing number of poor people trying to find money to feed their kids breakfast before they go to school so that they can learn what a capital gain is. Or capital. Anything new in the investigation?''

Smith shook his head and looked around the room. There were a number of familiar faces, faces that ended up in the newspaper now and then. He suffered one of those assaults of ambivalent feelings that sitting in such a place sometimes triggered. On the one hand, he liked being there, was at home in places of power. On the other hand, he knew so much of it was a sham, more a play than a reflection of real life. We're all players, the bard had said. Sometimes Smith enjoyed his role of the moment; it was after he'd got offstage and was home with time to reflect that he knew he really didn't like playacting very much. Not for himself.

Bowes seemed to have drifted into his own private thoughts, too. He said absently, "How deeply involved have you gotten in Word of Peace?"

Smith heard him but didn't react immediately. He was still analyzing his feelings about being there. He turned and raised his eyebrows, shrugged. "Not involved at all, although it keeps looming as a consideration where Singletary's murder is concerned. Why do you ask?"

"Well, Mac, Word of Peace has not gone without the Company's attention. Interesting assembly of characters in Word of Peace, lots of fine people with unassailable motives, a few others whose motives don't stand up to scrutiny."

"Is that so?" Smith said.

"How close are you to the bishop, Mac?"

"We've been friends for a long time."

"Then you have his ear."

"Yes, I think so."

"Why don't you give your friend the bishop

some good advice. Why don't you tell your friend that he should disassociate himself as quickly as possible from anything having to do with Word of Peace.''

Smith smiled. Among many things he liked about Cameron Bowes was that after an opening of amiable indirection, directness became part of the package. ''Tell me more, Cameron. Tell me why I should advise him to do that.''

''To avoid scandal, to avoid more controversy, to avoid further involvement in a mixed bag of good news–bad news people.'' Bowes looked around the large, lavishly furnished lobby before leaning close to Smith and murmuring, ''Word of Peace has been infiltrated by damn near every intelligence organization in the world. When the movement started, it was pure, if you can call any movement pure. But it immediately attracted all sorts of global hustlers who use movements like this the way Wall Street rainmakers smell a takeover and jump in with junk bonds, et cetera. It's a classic case of cause and effect—or, start a cause and get several effects. The good guys come first, then the bad guys, then the good guys working undercover.''

''I can't believe I'm hearing this from you.''

"What's so difficult to believe?"

"That you would assign black hats and white hats so easily. Intelligence organizations aren't always, to use your simple phraseology, 'good guys.' Anyhow, who are our major players?"

"The CIA, among others. The navy's in. The British have an even greater presence."

"Any special reason?"

"The Church of England." Bowes finished his drink. "They got suckered in like the National Cathedral did because of the passion and commitment of people like Paul Singletary."

Smith asked, "Should I be looking at Word of Peace as the place to find a murderer?"

"They're as good a place to look as any. Don't tell me you haven't thought about that."

"Of course I have. Any aspect of Paul Singletary's life has to be looked at, and I'm sure everyone with some official connection to this case is doing just that. But I've been looking into narrower possibilities. Somehow, Cam, even though Paul was deeply involved in the movement, I can't conceive of his being killed because of it."

As another round was served, Bowes stopped talking. When the waitress had gone, he said, "Ever hear of a Korean named Jin Tse?"

"Yes. Bishop St. James mentioned him to me. Jin Tse seems to be the point man for Word of Peace here in Washington. Singletary told the bishop about him, and after the murder, Jin Tse sought out the bishop to be sure of the cathedral's continuing support."

"Mac."

"What?"

"Jin Tse is not good news. Jin Tse works directly for Korean intelligence. He's also a known assassin." Bowes mentioned two political assassinations that had taken place over the years.

"Jin Tse did those?"

"That's our best information."

"Maybe he 'assassinated' Paul Singletary," Smith said.

"Maybe. Rest assured that possibility is being given very careful consideration."

"This has all been very illuminating, Cameron."

"What are friends for, if they can't illuminate their favorite people? Want to know what I think?"

"Only if you'll be honest with me about your source of thinking."

"What do you mean by that?"

"I mean that I would like you to differentiate between what you've read in the papers like any other citizen, from what you're telling me man-to-man, as a friend, and what you're telling me because of the Company's interest in this case. By the way, I assume the CIA's file on this has gotten pretty thick."

"Yes, and it includes material on Reverend Singletary's murder. I happen to know that by now a portion of it also has to do with Mackensie Smith."

Smith started to say something, but Bowes continued, "Every move you've made since you became involved is known to those charged with following this case. Quite an interesting honeymoon you had in London."

"That, too, huh?"

"Uh-huh. I don't want to belabor this, Mac, but we're talking big stakes here. If Word of Peace was involved in any way in Reverend Singletary's murder, it shouldn't take a genius to figure out that they will stop at nothing to achieve their goals, whatever they are, and that includes demonstrating an absolute lack of reverence for a law professor at George Washington University and his pretty wife. Be careful, Mac. There's a war going on. Singletary was only a skirmish."

chapter
22

**The Next Morning, Thursday
—Still Pleasantly Warm**

If the FBI had not decided to arrest overnight a number of people in Washington involved with Word of Peace, the small story in the morning paper about the cathedral case would have been given a more prominent position on page 1, perhaps at the top, run in 24-point Helvetica bold. Instead, it was relegated to the bottom, its headline in 14-point Geneva, and in italics.

The lead story was the FBI's sweep of Word of Peace leaders, including Jin Tse and some of his associates. Others caught in the net included a breakaway Catholic priest, the black leader of one of D.C.'s urban coalitions for the poor, a West German businessman, a South American embassy official, and a faith healer from Oklahoma who had somehow established a mission in Washington under the auspices of Word of Peace. Charges ranged from fraud to extortion, spying to conspiracy.

"Read this," Mac said, handing the paper to Annabel. She sat on the edge of the bed, and the widening of her eyes mirrored her reaction to what she was reading. "Wow!" she said, tossing the paper on the bed.

Smith had given Annabel a reasonable account of his conversation with Cameron Bowes at the Four Seasons, but had deliberately skipped the warning Bowes had issued. As he reflected upon it after parting from Bowes, he became increasingly concerned. Bowes was a straight shooter, not a bigmouth; he played it as close to the vest as any employee of a sensitive agency was expected to do. That he'd brought the subject up at all gave it, at least in Smith's eyes, considerable weight. He hadn't mentioned it to Annabel because he didn't want to concern her, although he would continue to be concerned about her, but he knew she wouldn't buy that decision. She'd want to know about any danger to him. She wanted to be a "partner," but only a limited partner, she'd told him. That didn't mean unduly upsetting your partner. Did it?

"How do you think this relates to Paul's murder?" Annabel asked. The story had ended with a note that Paul Singletary, the murdered Episcopal priest, had been actively involved with Word of Peace. The final line of the article directed readers to a parallel story about new developments in the Singletary case at the bottom of the page.

The headline on the smaller story read MURDER WEAPON FOUND? According to Chief of Homicide Terrence Finnerty, an anonymous caller to the police late the night before had directed them to the National Cathedral's Children's Chapel, where, according to the caller, the instrument used to kill Reverend Paul Singletary would be found. The police responded to the tip, removed two candlesticks from the altar, and, according to Finnerty, discovered that the base of one was dented in a pattern consistent with Singletary's head wound. Laboratory analysis revealed that a fragment of hair matching the deceased's was found, and that a miniscule residue of human blood of the same type as Reverend Singletary's was on the holder. There were no fingerprints. Examination of the holder involved the use of a mass spectrometer and other sophisticated forensic devices. The police had no knowledge at the time of the identity of the anonymous caller, except that it was a male.

When Annabel finished reading that story, she asked Mac, who'd slipped into sweats in preparation for a brisk morning walk, what he thought of it.

"Hard to tell at this juncture," he said, "but I have this nagging feeling about one thing."

"What's that?"

"That whoever put the holder on that altar and called the police is intimately connected with the cathedral, really knows it."

"You mean the murderer? No, it wouldn't have been the murderer who put the holder in that chapel and then called the police."

"I wouldn't think so. Why would a murderer successfully hide the weapon for this amount of time, then put it out in the open for the police to find?"

"Unless it served the person's purpose. If Paul's murder was not connected with the cathedral but the killer wants to have the investigation focus more intensely on cathedral people, it isn't a bad move."

Smith immediately thought of Brian Waters, the son of the woman who'd discovered Singletary's body, and who, according to Tony Buffolino, had become a prime suspect. He'd told Annabel about his conversation with Buffolino.

"Could be Waters," she said, as if reading his mind.

"Could be a lot of people, Annabel. I'll call Finnerty later and see if I can learn anything else. In the meantime, I'm ready for some air. I'll be back in forty-five minutes. Will you be here?"

"Probably. I'm not opening until ten."

They kissed, and Smith started for the kitchen, where Rufus's leash hung by the back door. He stopped in the doorway and turned to look upon this beautiful female creature who was his wife. He'd shared almost everything with her—should he tell her about Bowes's warning? He had to. "Annabel, I filled you in on what Cameron Bowes had to say last night, but I left something out."

She raised an eyebrow questioningly.

"Cam said he thought Word of Peace was a

dangerous organization. He told me it's been infiltrated by many intelligence organizations, including people like Jin Tse, who, according to Cam, is not only linked to Korean intelligence, but is a political assassin. He also told me that the CIA has built quite a file on Word of Peace, and that you and I have prominent space in it. Even our honeymoon was tracked."

"That's horrible," she said. "What the hell did they do, put cameras in our hotel suites?"

"Probably not, but they certainly knew our movements in London. The reason I'm telling you this is that if there is some threat to us by virtue of my being involved with the cathedral and Paul's murder, I want to keep you as far away from it as possible." As he said it, he thought of his mother in Sevier House. Could she also be in danger because of him? No rational person would think so, but a reporter had tracked her down—or was it a reporter?—and there was a well-documented lack of rationality when it came to zealots and cause groups, to say nothing of intelligence organizations, including the CIA and MI5—and not forgetting Cosa Nostra and Colombian drug czars. None of them played by the same rules as the rest of the mostly rational folks. When groups like those decided the chips were down and the stakes were high enough, it was women and children first—forget about lifeboats.

Smith shoved his hands in the pockets of his blue nylon windbreaker. "I don't know how much credence to give what Cameron said, but he's always played it straight with me. I think he told me those things because he truly considers me a friend, and I can't ignore what he said."

"How much danger are we in?" she asked.

"I have no idea, Annabel, but we do know someone tried to run you down, trample you to death, in that sheep field. I know we've been watched. And now this bunch from Word of Peace has been arrested and charged with a laundry list including subversive activities, misuse of funds, money laundering, and God knows what else. Maybe you ought to go away for a while."

Annabel laughed. "Mac, that's grade-B black-and-white-movie stuff. We're not on late-night TV. Go away? Where would I go? *Why* would I go?"

Her response nettled him, and he responded angrily, "Sorry if I come off as grade-B material, Annabel. I suggested it because I love you."

Oooops, she thought. She crossed the room, wrapped her arms around him, and gave him a long and intense hug. "Mac," she said into his ear, "you are anything but grade B. To me, you are the all-time leading man. I didn't mean anything by it. Still, I'm not leaving you."

"Please," he said, "don't ever leave me."

"Have a good walk. I love you."

"And I love you, Annabel Smith." He turned to Rufus, who was sitting at attention. "Come on, beast, let's go sniff up the neighborhood." He looked back at Annabel. "One thing's for sure, Annabel, nobody would mess with us with Rufus around."

"Sure," Annabel answered. "Any stranger with a gun and a dog biscuit wins. Go."

Smith's brisk walk with Rufus always gave him time to think, something he did better with legs moving and fresh air pumping into his lungs and circulating to his brain.

The first fifteen minutes were characterized by exuberance for dog and master. The middle quarter-hour found dog still charging ahead while master grappled with a damnable set of conflicting thoughts—questions, really—about recent weeks in his life. By the time the two were on the last leg of their morning circuit of

Foggy Bottom, dog had slowed down and was panting, and master had come to the conclusion that everything, including the walk, had gone on long enough. His only commitment to Bishop St. James had been to give his friend unofficial legal advice, and to perhaps serve as counsel should the accused murderer come out of cathedral ranks. That should have been it. Instead, he'd found himself playing investigator again, discovering the body of a priest in the idyllic Cotswolds, almost losing his bride in a sheep pasture, and now being warned by a friend who was up on things in the nation's leading spookery that his involvement might cause harm to him and to those he loved. "For what?" he asked himself aloud as he opened the front door. "Enough!"

"Enough what?" Annabel yelled from the living room.

"Enough of this life. I'm a college professor, damn it, not a gumshoe! Let the police find out who killed Paul, and if it's somebody I care to represent, I will."

She appeared in the doorway. "What brought this on?"

"A walk with the beast and time to think. I'm sorry about all this, Annie. It's my fault, getting us into something like murder. You and I are esteemed members of the academic and artistic communities of Washington." He proclaimed it with exaggerated pomp, his hand on his heart. She started to giggle. "Therefore, the dirty business of murder and murderers shall henceforth be left to those of lesser stature and baser instincts."

"Bravo!" She applauded. "But what about Reverend Merle?"

"I did him a favor. He's not my client." He bowed. "Time for this sage to shower, which I understand places me closer to God, and to bestow my infinite wisdom upon my class of misguided achievers. Gimme a hug and a kiss, baby." He wrestled her into the living room and fell on top of her on the couch.

"You've gone mad," she said, gasping.

"I have, and I love every minute of it."

She rammed the heels of her hands against his chest and slid out from under. "Do you think you can sustain this burst of affection until tonight?"

"Do I have to?"

"Yes, and I look forward to the evening." She stood. "Now, learned professor, go get clean and teach. We need the money."

■ ■ ■

Smith didn't wait for his students to raise questions about what they'd read in the papers and seen on television. He announced, the minute he stepped to the podium, "Let us take what has become our daily fifteen minutes to discuss murder at the National Cathedral. You know what I know via the free press. Any comments? Any suggestions? Brilliant insights?"

Everyone in the room offered at least two of the above in the next ten minutes or so, but none of their speculations caused Smith's mind to turn down a new alley with a light of revelation at its end. He shared with them one small bit of information he'd received as he was leaving the house. Jeffrey Woodcock called from London to say that the slain priest, Robert Priestly, had indeed been robbed. His wallet had been taken, and it had been found in a public trash can in the picturesque village of Chipping Campden. Whatever cash had been in it was missing; everything else seemed to be intact.

"So?" April Montgomery asked.

"So, it means that the murder of Priestly now differs in two ways from the murder of Singletary. Not only was the same type of murder weapon, which could have been coincidental, left at the scene in Priestly's case, and not in Singletary's, but robbery might have been the motive. It certainly wasn't where Reverend Singletary was concerned. His wallet hadn't been touched.''

"Meaning that two different killers were involved," Joy Collins offered.

"Meaning only that such a possibility exists." Smith asked what their reaction was to MPD's announcement the night before that the possible murder weapon in the Singletary case had been found. Their collective reaction pretty much paralleled his and Annabel's—namely, that the circumstances under which the weapon had been found were more interesting than the weapon itself. Bob Rogers, who tended to be the most reticent of Smith's students, suggested that whoever placed the candlestick in the Children's Chapel and called the police obviously knew who the murderer was and had been hiding the weapon in order to protect his or her accomplice.

"Then why would this person come forward now and lead the police to the weapon?" Smith asked.

"Maybe they had a falling-out," Joe Petrella said.

"Possibly, but why just lead the police to the weapon? Why not place an anonymous call and inform the police of the murderer's identity?"

"Maybe they didn't have that much of a falling-out," April Montgomery said, the hint of a rare laugh in her voice.

Smith smiled and changed the subject to the FBI sweep of Word of Peace.

April said, "I knew you'd bring that up. If you hadn't, Professor Smith, I would have. Reverend Singletary was involved with that organization. It seems to me that any one of those lowlifes arrested last night could have killed him."

Smith raised his hands into the air. "Wait a minute," he said sternly. "Simply because a movement dedicated to something worthwhile is tainted by certain individuals is not cause to paint that organization with a broad black brush."

"I agree," said Joyce Clemow. "But do you think Reverend Singletary might have been doing something . . . well, dishonest, or destructive, or even disloyal?"

"No, I do not think that is much of a possibility. I think Reverend Paul Singletary was a good man whose goodness led him, at times, into situations he would have been better served by avoiding." Smith looked at his watch. "All right, on now to the subject of effective plea bargaining."

As Smith was about to leave the building, Dean Jaffe's secretary handed him a three-page fax that had arrived from Jeffrey Wood-cock in London. It was a column in a British tabloid. Woodcock had scribbled on top of the first page, *"Thought you'd be interested in this, Mac."*

The article began:

The brutal, grisly, bloody murder almost two weeks ago of an Anglican parish priest named Priestly in the peaceful Cotswolds raised little interest outside of local authorities there. But this reporter and this newspaper have recently learned that the deadly blow to Priestly's head might not have come from some lob looking to empty the priest's pockets of his meagre belongings, despite the fact that the slain clergyman's wallet was found days later in a neighbouring village. To the contrary, the wielder of the life-

taking candlestick could well have represented an intelligence organization, even
our own esteemed MI5, whose service to
the Crown has not been without incidents of
snuffing out life for the "greater good."

Highly-placed sources who have agreed
to speak with this reporter only on the condition that their names not be revealed
claim that the Reverend Priestly lived a life
far more exciting than administering last
rites to dying sheep farmers. In fact, according to these highly-placed sources, Reverend Priestly had been asked to leave the
military service under questionable circumstances early in his career. A copy of
Priestly's military discharge papers ob-
tained by this reporter lists the reason for
his severance from the service as "official,"
a term often used by military authorities to
get rid of a troublesome person without saying anything good or bad about him.

Seems Priestly's dirty deed had to do with
a joint naval exercise between British and
U.S. troops. According to our highly-placed
sources, the Reverend Priestly, a decidedly
left-of-center chap, walked away with some
extremely sensitive videotapes on which

the latest military technology was demonstrated in living colour. Our sources tell us that he passed those tapes on to a friend who shared his bleeding-heart tendencies. The identity of that friend is unknown, although this reporter is in the process of tracking him down.

The article went on to outline in sketchy terms more of Priestly's background. Then it got to Word of Peace.

The Reverend Priestly was involved in a number of causes, local and international, most notably Word of Peace, a group whose professed purpose is to bring about peace on earth, but whose members evidently had less spiritual things on their agenda. A number of leaders of the movement were recently arrested in Washington, D.C., and charged not only with using funds raised for peace to line their own pockets, but with harboring a sizable nest of political operations. An Anglican priest named Paul Singletary, who was murdered in Washington's National Cathedral, was a leading voice in the organization. Whether he would

have been arrested, too, must remain con-
jecture, but our highly-placed sources assure us that he was a close friend of the
slain Cotswolds priest, and we have further
learned that he served with Reverend
Priestly during that joint naval exercise.
Whether Singletary was, indeed, the friend
to whom Priestly passed the classified videotapes is unknown at this time. It is known,
however, that Priestly had recently indicated to a close friend—perhaps Singletary,
who visited with him in the Cotswolds only
days before his own murder—that he was
about to make public what he knew about
the flim-flam going on within Word of Peace.
That, of course, would be sufficient reason
for that organization, or at least someone
from it, to silence him forever.

But there is more. Other highly-placed
sources have informed this reporter that
Reverend Priestly had been recruited by our
own intelligence organization, MI5, and that
he did its bidding to avoid having his unsav-
oury military indiscretions exposed. Was the
Reverend Priestly about to blow the proverbial whistle on MI5?

Stay tuned.

Smith finished reading the fax, shoved it into his briefcase, and headed home. He and Annabel had discussed how little they really knew about Paul Singletary. But if there were even a modicum of truth to the suggestion that he'd passed classified tapes, he'd been a total stranger.

Clarissa Morgan watered plants in the villa on Virgin Gorda that had been rented for her. She then left the low white house carrying a small yellow carry-on bag, which she placed on the passenger seat of a white Toyota Corolla that had been leased for her. She opened the driver's door, paused to look out over the shimmering azure waters that surrounded the British Virgin Islands, got into the car, and drove slowly around the island until arriving at Beef Island Airport, where she parked and entered the terminal. She knew she'd been followed by the same man in the Toyota minivan who'd been her shadow since her arrival in the BVI. She didn't care, had never bothered to find out who he was. It didn't matter. She knew *why* he followed her, and *who* had told him to. That was enough. It was all enough. "Enough!" she'd said to herself two days ago after returning home from dinner at a local restaurant. "Enough!"

"Your flight is delayed, Miss Morgan," the petite, pretty native ticket agent said.

"How long a delay?"

The agent looked at her computer terminal. "Probably only a half hour."

"Not so bad," Morgan said, thinking that for Air BVI it represented being ahead of schedule. "Thank you. I think I'll have some tea."

The ticket agent watched the woman cross the small lobby and thought, Nice to deal with a visitor who doesn't take a delay as a personal affront.

The man who'd been standing near the door approached the agent. "I overheard you telling that woman that her flight was delayed. Is that the flight to New York?"

"No, it's to San Juan."

"But it connects to flights to New York."

"It can. It connects with many flights."

"Thank you."

The man, whose cheeks bore the spidery red lines of a heavy drinker, looked around the lobby as though in a state of confusion.

"Is there something else I can help you with, sir?" the agent asked.

He was startled at her voice. "No, no, thank you very much." He walked in the direction of the small concession stand that sold coffee, tea, and sweets. He stopped a dozen feet away and watched Clarissa Morgan as she was handed a Styrofoam cup, paid the attendant, and went to a bench against the wall. Once seated, she looked at him and smiled. He turned away, glanced back, then went outside.

A half hour later Clarissa Morgan gave her boarding pass to the attendant, climbed the drop-down stairs, and disappeared through a door. The man went to a public phone. He pulled a dozen scraps of paper from the pocket of his soiled safari jacket, cursed, dropped several others to the ground, picked them up, cursed again, and found what he was looking for. He put on glasses, leaned close to the phone's dial pad, and slowly, tentatively, punched in numbers. The operator came on the line, and the man gave her a long series of numbers. "Collect," he said. "Make it collect. Tell them this is Dedgeby from the BVI." His accent was Cockney. He waited for several seconds, and then heard the sound of a phone ringing. After four rings a crisp voice said, "Yes."

"A collect call from Mr. Dedgeby in the British Virgin Islands."

"Hold on." After a minute of static and crackling, the person said, "Go ahead."

"Give me Control."

"Hold on," the man on the other end said. Seconds later another voice came on the line. "Mr. Dedgeby. What do you have?" The Morgan woman. She's getting on a plane for Puerto Rico."

"Is that so? Perhaps she has friends there."

"I don't know anything about that," Dedgeby said, wiping perspiration from his brow. He didn't like making a living watching other people. It was too demanding. But it paid well. Besides, it was that or jail. He preferred spending his days and nights in one of the local places, drinking rum. You couldn't do that when you were told to watch somebody, had to be on tap all the time, waiting for them, spying on them, taking away time better spent with friends over some Pussers.

"Mr. Dedgeby."

"Yes, I'm here."

"You say she's boarding a flight to Puerto Rico. Has it left yet?"

"No, it's bloody well still here. These people don't know how to run an airline. Probably sit out there in the heat for another hour."

The man on the other end said, "Thank you for the information, Dedgeby." A loud click broke the connection.

Dedgeby got into his battered minivan. It threatened not to start, but it eventually did, and he drove off, talking to himself, a smile on his face. "Bloody glad she's gone. Hope she never comes back."

"Leighton here," Brett Leighton said into the phone.

"Sir, we received a call from Dedgeby in the BVI."

"Yes? What did he have to say?"

"Miss Morgan has boarded a flight for San Juan, Puerto Rico."

"I see. Is that her final destination?"

"Dedgeby didn't know, sir."

"Yes. Well, thank you for calling." He hung up.

Two hours later Brett Leighton, wearing a new tweed suit tailored for him at P. A. Crowe in a way that accommodated his slightly left-ward leaning posture, boarded a Concorde flight to New York. Once settled, he removed a piece of paper from his inside jacket pocket on which was written a flight itinerary, commencing in the British Virgin Islands and terminating in New York, with a two-hour layover in Puerto Rico.

"Foolish woman," he said quietly.

The man seated next to him turned. "Pardon?"

Leighton smiled. "Nothing, sorry to disturb you. Nasty habit I have of talking to myself at times. Shan't do it again."

His seat companion smiled, too, and went back to his magazine.

Foolish woman, Leighton thought, silently this time. Involving women in such projects was always a mistake, in his judgment, and he'd expressed that view to his superiors on more than one occasion. Too emotional, too impetuous. Too likely to fall in love with the one person they shouldn't. Here she was, promised a chance to stay alive if she'd just stay put. Well, he could have put someone on her in San Juan, but he believed that he knew where she was heading.

"Cocktail, sir?" a flight attendant asked.

"Yes, I think that is much needed. I've taken to talking to myself," Leighton replied pleasantly. "Gin, a double, and please withhold the ice."

chapter
23

That Afternoon—
Indian Summer Fading Fast

Upon returning home from class, Smith placed a couple of calls to Terry Finnerty at MPD. He was informed on the first one that Finnerty was away from his office but would return shortly. Smith left his number, but decided not to wait for Finnerty to return his call. He tried again twenty minutes later. This time Finnerty was there.

"Congratulations, Terry," Smith said, "on picking up the murder weapon."

"Sometimes you get lucky."

"I read that you got a tip from an anonymous caller."

Finnerty chuckled. "Nothing but good citizens out there."

Smith ignored the cynicism. "It was a man who called?"

"Yeah."

"What did he say exactly?" Smith asked.

"I'll read it to you. 'You'll find the weapon used to kill Reverend Singletary on the altar in the Children's Chapel in the National Cathedral.' "

"Couldn't have been plainer than that," Smith said. "As I recall, the person who reported Singletary's body was a woman."

"That's right."

"Any doubts about the candlestick?"

"Whether it's really the weapon? Nah. No question at all."

"Thanks for your time, Terry. Just wanted to keep in touch."

"That's what a good lawyer is supposed to do, keep in touch for his client."

"I don't have a client, or have you decided to charge Merle with the murder?"

"No comment."

"What about Brian Waters?"

"What about him?" Finnerty's voice suddenly changed. He'd been relaxed, almost jovial, with Smith. Now, at the mention of Waters's name, he tightened. "What about him?"

"I got an idea you might be more than casually interested."

"Butt out of this, Mac."

"I didn't mean to upset you, Terry. I heard a rumor that— "

"Yeah, yeah, you heard a rumor. What you heard was garbage from that wacko you got working for you, Buffolino."

"I wouldn't call Tony a wacko."

"You call him what you want. I say nobody's home there."

Smith wasn't in the mood to argue Buffolino's relative sanity. "I just thought in light of the anonymous tip about the candlestick that it could have been someone like Brian Waters."

"Brilliant deduction, Sherlock. Great minds think alike. I have to go. Nice talking to you, Mac." He hung up with enough force to make the point that the conversation had, indeed, ended.

After walking Rufus, Smith left just as Annabel was arriving. "Where are you going?" she asked.

"The cathedral. I want to check on something. How come you're home?"

"I left some papers in the den. What are you checking on?"

"Something that's been nagging at me since the last time I met with George. I won't be long. You?"

"I'll be home for dinner. You?"

"Not only will I be home for dinner, I intend to cook it."

"How wonderful. I married the Legal Gourmet. What's on the menu?"

"A big surprise. See you tonight."

When he arrived at the cathedral, two MPD patrol cars were parked immediately outside the south entrance. There was also a van marked METROPOLITAN POLICE DEPARTMENT—FORENSIC UNIT.

Smith entered the cathedral and looked around. The usual tour groups were being led through the massive church by volunteers. Smith went into the War Memorial Chapel, where a member of the Altar Guild was dressing the altar. He looked into the Children's

Chapel over yellow MPD crime-scene tape. It was empty. Two new candlesticks rested upon the small altar. He closed his eyes and tried to imagine what had occurred that fateful night. Had the murderer actually killed Paul in the Children's Chapel and dragged the body all the way to Good Shepherd? Probably not, but the idea was not out of the question, either. The entire cathedral was a potential scene of the killing. Distance could not be used to rule out any possibility.

Or had the murder actually taken place in Good Shepherd, the assailant bringing the murder weapon all the way to the Children's Chapel? Why would anyone do that? Then again, why would the person who'd called the police choose the Children's Chapel in which to place the murder weapon? Did that location have relevance, or was it simply the most convenient place? Most important, where had the dented candlestick bearing traces of Singletary's hair and blood been stashed all this time? And why?

Smith crossed the nave and went down the stairs leading to the lower level, where the Bethlehem, Resurrection, and St. Joseph chapels were located. He went to the Bethlehem's door. Another yellow crime-scene ribbon blocked access. Inside, a Forensic team was going over the floor of the chapel with some sort of electronic gear. The man operating the unit was dressed in a white lab coat. His eyes were glued to a screen on which eerie green lines were in constant motion. "Terry Finnerty here?" Smith asked over the yellow tape.

One of the Forensic men looked up. "He's upstairs with the bishop, I think."

"Thanks."

Smith knocked on the door to St. James's study. "Come in," the bishop said.

St. James was seated with Finnerty and two members of the cathedral chapter, and Smith joined them in a semicircle of chairs around the bishop's desk.

"Didn't think I'd see you," Finnerty said. "I was just telling the bishop why we've sent in a Forensic team to go over other areas. We figure that whoever murdered Singletary did it outside the little chapel where he was found, but not *too* far away. Make sense to you?"

"I've been thinking that for a while." Smith hadn't meant to upstage Finnerty, but the sour look on the detective's face indicated he had.

Smith decided not to mollify him; he'd thought of it before the detective assigned to solve the murder had, so let it be.

St. James managed a weak smile, sighed deeply, and shook his head. "When will this be over?" he asked.

Smith nodded at Finnerty. The wiry little detective said, "That's what the politicos have been asking us. That's why we're back here extending the investigation, you might say. They're putting the arm on my boss, so he puts it on me. Chain of command. Anyway, Bishop, I know you don't like having us around, but it's the only choice we have. They want action. Besides, they invested megabucks in new equipment and like to use it."

One of the chapter members told Smith that an emergency meeting had been called for six that evening. "We hope you'll be there, Mac."

"I don't know, I think I—"

"We know you're busy, and that this is not your 'job,' if I may call it that, but your presence is comforting to all of us," said another chapter member.

"I'll see what I can do about shifting a dinner appointment I made for this evening." That shift wouldn't be easy.

Finnerty and the chapter members soon left, leaving Smith and St. James alone.

"I'm surprised to see you, Mac," the bishop said.

"I didn't mean to barge in, but—"

St. James shook his head. "Here I am being dishonest again. The fact is, I did expect to see you, if not today, certainly within the next few days. You know, don't you?"

"About the candlestick? About the call to MPD telling them it was in the Children's Chapel? Yes. I didn't know as fact, but I had a pretty strong feeling. Your language was too specific to be that of a layman. The only question I have is, why?"

"Yes, that would be the logical question. First, let me tell you how I learned of it. I was passing the Children's Chapel two days after the murder when a member of the Altar Guild, who was rearranging things there, stopped me. She said she had discovered something she thought I would want to know about."

"She'd found the candlestick."

"Exactly, although she didn't know the significance of it. She pointed it out to me because its base was damaged, and thought I might want to have it replaced. I remember laughing, saying something about how the bishop of the National Cathedral has to keep his finger on everything. She is a good woman, and she was embarrassed. I realized I had said the wrong thing. She'd only stopped me because I happened to be there. At any rate, Mac, I went to the altar and looked at the candlestick. I knew somehow the moment I touched it that it was the weapon used to kill Paul. My next thought was that if I was correct, it might somehow give weight to the possibility that he'd been murdered by someone from the cathedral staff.

"Having handy, immediate access to it suggested someone standing near the altar, where laypeople almost never go. Knowing that in the cathedral there are hundreds of candlesticks, I saw no need to get rid of it. The dent was small. A whole lot of things came to my confused mind, but, as always, I guess I wanted no further damage done to the cathedral and its people or to the work of God we're trying to do here. So, foolishly, I hid it, replaced it, and went back to breathing again. Full of guilt, of course."

"I understand your motivation, George, but why didn't you just get rid of it if that was the way you felt?"

"I replaced it on the altar and hid it in my house, but after talking to you about the murder of that priest in England, I knew I might at some time have to make it available to the authorities . . . no matter what the consequences. I suppose I wanted to hedge my bets, as they say." He saw the puzzled look on Smith's face and added, "With Him. I mean, it was bad enough that I didn't report it, but to physically destroy evidence would have gone beyond even my limits of wrongdoing."

Smith sighed and gave his friend a reassuring grin. "Yes, George, destroying it would have been a more serious act. Not that this isn't. By the way. Did the woman who pointed out the damaged holder see you remove it from the altar, make the swap?"

St. James almost laughed. "I certainly hope not. I mean, I assume she didn't. She walked away. As I said, she was embarrassed."

"Is it possible that someone else might have seen you?"

"Unlikely. There were people in the cathedral, but I think I was quick and careful. I was startled for a moment, though, as I was leaving the chapel."

"What startled you?"

"One of our maintenance men was standing just outside."

"Just outside the chapel?"

"Yes. He's a disagreeable sort, always slinking around someplace or other. Some of the staff have complained about him, but no one can find cause to dismiss him. He does his work."

"Is he the same one I talked to after you told me he'd had an altercation with Paul?"

"Yes," St. James said quickly.

"I didn't like him much, either," Smith said. "He told me Paul was always 'on his back,' always being critical. I don't believe that."

"Nor do I. At any rate, he was loitering about the chapel when I took the candlestick, but I'm almost positive he wasn't looking in when I did it."

"Let's hope so. I may talk to him again. I'm glad you called the police, George. As far as I'm concerned, we may be able to think that it never happened."

"Thank you, Mac, but I'm not sure your forgiveness is enough. I've let this entire cathedral down with my foolish, irresponsible thinking."

Smith shrugged. "Don't be too hard on yourself, George. Yes, you made a mistake. You were risking prosecution to serve other purposes. What it says to me is that you're human."

St. James managed a smile. "Yes, I suppose we all are. Flawed. Misguided. Meaning well and doing foolish things. But that was the idea, wasn't it, when He created us?"

"The biggest flaw is in people who don't recognize that they're flawed. You'll work this out with yourself—and with Him, who risked prosecution, too. In the meantime, I'd like to bring up something that's been on *my* mind."

"Are you about to confess something, too? I am in that business, after all."

Both men laughed quietly. Smith said, "I came to a conclusion this morning that I really have to bow out of this case."

"I'm sorry to hear that," said St. James, "but I'm not surprised. This has been a considerable imposition on your time and talents, and everything you have done to this date will always elicit gratitude from me and everyone else at the National Cathedral. I mentioned to the chapter members who were here earlier that I thought we should find money in the budget to pay you."

Smith shook his head and waved his hands.

"No, money has nothing to do with my decision, George. I've spent a little for a private investigator, but no matter. I've done this out of . . ." He smiled. "Well, out of my respect for you and our friendship, out of an abiding belief in this cathedral, and a regard for Paul, and . . . and out of my own sense of guilt, I suppose. You mention money for my services. I'm sure you're aware that I only show up here at weddings, funerals, Easter, and Christmas, and I don't always make the latter two. Let's just consider anything I've done to be a down payment on delinquent tithing."

"As you wish, but don't be so hard on yourself. You spend more time here than simply on those occasions."

"Strictly because of a pragmatic interest in certain events. I don't get down on my knees very much."

"From what I've always heard, you never did, to anyone."

They shook hands, and Smith said he would try to return for the six o'clock meeting.

"No, Mac, no need. I'll explain to the chapter why you are no longer able to be involved."

"Thanks for the offer, George, but I'd rather tell them myself." What he didn't add was that he wasn't sure he would follow through on his decision. In fact, he knew he probably wouldn't, but it had felt good saying it. At least he could tell Annabel he'd tried. And suggest that late dinners were more romantic.

He worked out at the Yale Field House and arrived home at four-thirty. There was the usual variety of messages on the machine, but the last one was less usual. It stopped him cold: "Mr. Smith, this is Clarissa Morgan. I trust you remember me from our brief telephone conversation in London. Sorry to have broken our date, but circumstances seemed to dictate it. I would appreciate a chance to meet with you as quickly as possible. No need to fly to London. I'm here in Washington. I'm reluctant to tell you where I'm staying and have it recorded, but I will make an attempt to contact you again, possibly this evening. Thank you."

"Ah, yes," Smith said as he slumped in the leather chair behind his desk. Rufus put his head on Smith's leg. Smith rubbed his ears, then looked into his friend's large, watery eyes. "Looks like things are about to get interesting, buddy."

chapter
24

Later in the Day—
Stormy Weather Ahead

It was the sort of domestic screaming match the neighbors had got used to since Nickelson and his family rented the small house in the subdued lower-middle-class neighborhood. It was worse in summer; then the windows were open and the sound carried farther and was louder. But even with the windows closed, the force of Nickelson's voice respected no barrier as simple as windowpane or door. You heard it, and sometimes it seemed so intense, so steaming with anger, that you considered calling the police. In fact, you did on a few occasions, and they came and calmed another domestic dispute. No need to haul the husband away, especially not the musical director of the National Cathedral. No blows had been struck, just angry words exchanged between a husband and wife. Nothing new to the D.C. police, or to police in any other city, for that matter.

It was business as usual this late afternoon for the Nickelsons' next-door neighbor. She'd been breading chicken for her family's dinner when the first salvo was fired.

In the other house, Nickelson shouted again, "I told you we were leaving in a week, Jennifer. Nothing has been done! Absolutely nothing!"

"We are not going to San Francisco," she said.

"Damn it!" He sent a row of books from a low bookcase flying to the floor. "You will do what I say." Each word was punctuated with a stab of his index finger.

Jennifer Nickelson turned on her heel and stomped into the kitchen. Their daughters were upstairs trying to do homework. Now they pressed their ears to the bedroom door. Sometimes they fell on their beds and squeezed pillows tightly about their heads.

Downstairs, Nickelson followed his wife into

the kitchen. "You have an obligation to me, and don't you ever forget it," he said.

She wouldn't face him because she didn't want him to see the tears silently rolling down her cheeks. She tried to control her voice—and her trembling—as she said, "You have no right to put us through this." She slowly turned and extended her hands in a gesture of pleading. "Will, are you so insensitive that you don't see what you're doing to us? Asking us to pick up and leave so quickly is unfair. Please try to understand how disruptive this is to the children, to me."

"I don't *care*," he exploded. "I said we were leaving, and we will leave when I say." His face was flushed with anger, and Jennifer backed away. While he'd never struck her, she always felt he was capable of it, sensed that if the rage boiled to a certain level it would spill over the rim and obliterate any sense of reason, cause him to do things he would not ordinarily, naturally do.

He was capable of exhibiting violence against inanimate things. How many times had those books flown off that shelf, or the table been slammed against a wall, a fist rammed through Sheetrock? They'd patched holes in the wall in every house in which they'd lived. Once, Jennifer had laughed when their oldest daughter baby-sat for a family that was considered a bastion of domestic bliss, a perfect couple. The daughter came home and reported that there was a hole in the bathroom wall where the husband had punched his fist through it. "I suppose there's a hole in the wall of every family in America," Jennifer had said lightly to one of her friends at lunch. "Better the wall than the wife," her friend had replied.

Early in their marriage, the thing that was most difficult for Jennifer to reconcile with her husband's irrational anger was his profession. He was, after all, the Reverend Canon Wilfred Nickelson, an ordained minister. A priest. Jennifer had been brought up in a religious household, her experience with clergy confined to the local Presbyterian minister, a gentle, ineffectual soul who never raised his voice, and who devoted most of his sermons to the forgiving, loving nature of God. Jennifer responded positively to him; her father was an alcoholic subject to fits of rage that included physical attacks upon her mother, and occasionally upon Jennifer and her younger brother. When she met Wilfred Nickelson, she saw in him the same passive kindness that her minister possessed.

Besides, Wilfred was very good-looking and loved music, which Jennifer did, too.

It seemed like only minutes after they were married that his volatile side emerged—about what, she could not remember; few of the issues that sent him into fits of screaming and table-pounding were remembered.

Now, fourteen years later, she faced him in the kitchen with a determination that she hadn't felt before. She would not pack up her family within a week and move to San Francisco. That was asking too much. Any rational person would agree with her. Her mother had agreed when she told her about it, and so did her brother. "Let him go by himself, and you follow later" was their advice.

"Will, we cannot leave here that quickly. It is unfair to the girls. If we must move, why don't you go to San Francisco and get settled, find us a place to live, and we'll follow when it's more convenient."

She thought she'd presented this idea nicely, but all it did was set him off again. He accused her of betrayal, of standing in his way, of threatening to break up the family and keep his daughters from him. She felt sorry for him at that point, so misguided were his reactions. She took a few steps toward him and extended her hands. "Will, I love you. We all love you, but . . ."

His anger had not abated, but he lowered his voice and thrust his face at her. In a way, the lowered, almost whispered voice projected even greater menace. "What is it, Jen, can't you leave him?"

She dropped her arms and stared at him blankly. "Leave who?"

"Him. Your precious Paul."

She tried to say something, but all that would come from her lips was incredulous laughter. "Will, how can you still . . . ?"

He grabbed her by the arm and squeezed, his face now inches away.

"Stop it, you're hurting me. The girls will hear. Stop it, let me go!"

He propelled her against the sink. "Can't leave his ghost?" His voice was a snarl.

She started to cry, turned her head away from him. He strengthened his grip on her arm and shook her; now his voice peaked. "He's dead! You can't have him anymore." He grabbed her other arm and shook her violently, her head snapping back and forth as he repeated over and over, "He's dead! He's dead!" And then he hit her, the first time ever, the back of his hand against her eye, his knuckles breaking skin above it.

Upstairs, the Nickelson girls lay on their beds in the fetal position, pillows pressed tightly against their ears.

Nickelson released the grip on his wife and put on his coat. "I will never forgive you for this," he said. The front door slammed shut.

She walked on quivering legs to the kitchen table and fell heavily into a chair. Her first thought was to go upstairs and comfort the girls, but at this moment she wasn't physically capable of it. Besides, they'd see her and only become more upset. She touched the bone above her eye; blood returned with her fingertips.

There it was again, the accusation.

It had been that way from the first week of their marriage. He would erupt over many things, insignificant lapses in the housekeeping, or comments from her that he took in the wrong way, but the worst trigger was always his belief that she flirted with other men, was unfaithful to him. He should have known it wasn't true. What was she, someone who used heavy makeup and batted her eyes at passing males? Of course not. He would interpret her natural openness to another man as a come-on, encouraging attention. She'd never meant it that way, and soon found herself going into a shell socially, barely smiling at men to whom she was introduced and avoiding animated conversations. Couldn't he see that she was a devoted wife who enjoyed being a homemaker, a wife who baked her own bread and dressed her children nicely and tried to create a home filled with warmth and happiness for him? He couldn't. It was a character flaw, her brother told her one night when she called in a fit of panic. "He should seek help. Find a good shrink. You shouldn't have to live this way, Jen. He might be dangerous, fly off the handle some night, become violent."

Of course, she did not heed her brother's warnings. Will never struck her or the children, aside from an occasional smack on the girls' rear ends when they'd been naughty. But she also knew her brother was right. Inside her husband was the capability to lash out one day over some innocuous provocation; he could hurt someone—most likely her.

The confrontations between them over Paul

Singletary began the week Wilfred took up his duties as musical director of the National Cathedral. A welcoming party for them was held. Jennifer was excited about her husband's new assignment. To be tapped for the National Cathedral was a distinct honor. As far as Jennifer was concerned, he'd both earned and deserved the position, and she basked in it—quietly, and without overt display. She was proud to accompany him to his welcoming party. She bought a new dress and spent more time than was her custom preening in front of the mirror.

Will was in good spirits that night. They left the girls with a cheerful baby-sitter and went to meet all the wonderful people who would be part of their new lives in Washington, D.C.

Jennifer's first reaction upon meeting Reverend Singletary was that he was a very handsome man, and very nice. He took special pains to make her feel comfortable in the crowd of strangers. He brought her a glass of punch while her husband was chatting in a corner with a fellow clergyman, and immediately she knew Wilfred was aware of that simple act of graciousness. He kept looking over at her as she chatted with Singletary. Soon, he was at her side.

"You have a lovely wife," Singletary said to Nickelson.

"Yes, thank you." He took her arm and guided her away from the handsome young priest to a knot of people, mostly women.

That night, after they'd got into their robes and were sitting in front of the television, she said, "This is all so exciting, Will. Everyone seemed so nice."

"Too nice," he said, his eyes fixed upon the flickering screen.

"What do you mean? Was there someone you didn't like?"

He glared at her as he said, "Jen, I wish you would become a little more worldly. Just because some of them wear a collar doesn't mean they're all goodness and light."

She laughed nervously. "I know that. It's just that on the surface, they all seemed very pleasant and—"

"Stay away from Singletary."

"What do you mean?"

"Just what I said. Stay away from him. He has a reputation as a womanizer."

"I didn't . . . I didn't know that. I was just being friendly. He brought me some punch and—"

"Enough said, Jen. Quiet. I want to hear the news."

It was only the first of a number of scenes between them over Singletary, each displaying more of Nickelson's wrath. Jennifer tried to avoid Singletary whenever they were together at a cathedral function, but found it impossible to be rude to him. It didn't take much; all she had to do was smile and say hello, and her husband's eyes would be on her throughout the evening. Then, once they were home, there would be the inevitable blowup.

When Singletary was murdered, Jennifer was devastated. Her husband's admonitions had created a curious closeness of sorts between Singletary and herself, at least psychically. It was as though they were secret lovers. She'd come to the conclusion that Singletary knew what the situation was and was willing to play along with it, casting glances at her, his smile playful, a twinkle in his eye. A game. It had become a game, and he was an important figure in her life even though they barely said hello to each other.

All of this went through her mind as she sat at the kitchen table. Eventually she calmed down sufficiently to tend to her injury and go up to her daughters, who had resumed their homework. Jennifer forced a smile. "Hi, girls, how's it going?"

Her daughters turned to her with red-rimmed eyes. "Do we have to go to San Francisco?" the younger asked.

Jennifer stood silent, her eyes trained out the window. She responded in a calm and firm voice, "No, at least not right away." Then she hugged each of them and returned to the kitchen, where she filled the house with the sweet smell of baking cookies.

"Glad you could make it, Mac," a chapter member said as Smith entered the meeting room at six o'clock. He'd considered skipping the meeting and staying home in case Clarissa Morgan called again, but decided to take his chances. The meeting could be important, and he'd get back home as soon as it ended.

"Not much of a chore. It was a dinner date I could easily put off." Which wasn't true. He'd suggested to Annabel that they have a late dinner when he returned from the meeting. Her response was to announce that she was returning to the gallery, where she would try to reconcile those ridiculous spreadsheets and bank statements for those ridiculous accountants, and would take care of her own dinner needs, thank you very much.

Smith joined the others at the conference table and waited for St. James to arrive. When the bishop came through the door, his face was drawn and the corners of his mouth sagged. He said nothing, simply took his seat at the head of the table and stared at the tabletop, his hands flat on it, his fingers spread. He eventually looked up. "There is an urgent matter we should discuss immediately," he said wearily. "I just had a call from Mrs. Kelsch. As some of you know, she's the mother of Joseph Kelsch, one of our students and the most gifted singer in the boys' choir."

The bishop paused and said nothing for a moment.

"He sang at our wedding," Smith said into the silence. "He does have a beautiful voice. He was—"

"He's disappeared," said St. James.

There were muffled responses from the chapter members.

"He was supposed to come home after school, but didn't show up. Mrs. Kelsch became concerned and called the school."

"Why assume he's disappeared?" a chapter member asked. "Maybe he went off with a friend for the afternoon. You know how kids are."

"His room was searched. He'd evidently taken some items of clothing and a small suitcase he always kept in his closet. There is also the possibility that some harm has befallen him. Mrs. Kelsch told me he's been extremely upset lately, so much so that she sought the advice of the boy's pediatrician."

St. James looked at Smith, who said, "It probably is too early to assume the worst. But not too early to find him. The police have been called? Do we know who his closest friends are? Would Joey go to a grandparent?"

"Yes. The police have been alerted. One problem seems to follow another these days," St. James said. "Trouble comes in threes. Isn't that the saying?"

"Yes, and without much substance to back it up," said one of the chapter members, though smiling. The man was one of the more cautious members. "At what point do we worry about this in an official sense, Mac? Is there something we should do to protect ourselves legally?"

Smith didn't appreciate the pragmatic question, but ignored that aspect of it. "I suggest we conclude this meeting as quickly as possible and do what we can to help." He surveyed the faces at the table. "I understand this meeting has been called to deal with another aspect of the Singletary case. Has something new developed on that front?"

St. James answered. "Yes. The police have determined that the murder took place behind the altar in the Bethlehem Chapel."

Smith sat back, and nasty visions filled his thoughts. He could see Singletary sprawled on the stone floor behind that altar, and his mind immediately traced what happened after that— candlestick carefully wiped, blood mopped up from the floor, the body dragged down the hallway past the choir room and up that short flight of stone steps to Good Shepherd. Then, or maybe in reverse order, the murderer sought a place in which to discard the murder weapon. Who could it have been? *Damn it, who did this? Let it be over.* He glanced at St. James, who seemed to be waiting for him to say something.

"Sorry, my mind was wandering. I'm glad they've nailed down where the murder took place."

"There's another issue to be raised here this evening," said St. James. "This recent development seems to indicate more strongly, at least to me, that Reverend Singletary was murdered by someone with a connection to this cathedral, not by a stranger. If so, I want to allocate funds for the defense of that person, whoever it might be." He looked at the members of the chapter. "Mac told me earlier today that he could no longer continue in this role. I know he wanted to tell you himself, but—"

Smith interrupted. "Bishop St. James is right. I did make a decision to disassociate myself from this case. A simple matter of time, or lack of it. But I've reconsidered." Smith realized that his change-of-heart announcement came on the heels of the bishop's mention of funds being available to defend the murderer. Bad timing, he told himself. It would sound like money was behind his decision to back off. He said, "If you intend to finance the defense of Paul Singletary's murderer, that's admirable. But not related to my decision. I'll want only expenses. However, if you think that by creating a defense fund you will, in some way, cleanse the image of the cathedral, you're misguided. The cathedral didn't kill Paul. Eventually, people will come to see that."

"Oh, no, Mac," said a chapter member. "It is much more a matter of responsibility. I suppose you could term it taking care of our own."

"If that's the case, I applaud your generosity and sensitivity. Look, I'm not in this as defense attorney. I don't try cases, nor do I want to. My role is advisory. I will find you an attorney, should that need arise, and will do what I can to help that attorney do the job. Whatever money you come up with goes to that attorney, not to me." He finished with "Enough said. Is there any other reason for me to stay?"

"No, we just have some routine matters to take up," said the chapter president.

Smith stood and said to St. James, "Could we speak privately, George?"

"Of course."

Once in the hall, Smith said, "I got a call on my answering machine from Clarissa Morgan. I told you about her, the British woman who'd had an affair with Paul."

"Yes. You said she'd disappeared from London, never kept her appointment with you."

"Exactly. She says she's in Washington and wants to meet with me. I have no idea what it involves, but I'll follow through. I just thought you should be aware of it."

"Mac, let me ask a pointed question you asked me. Have you called the police?"

"Not yet. I don't want them to get to her before I do. Obstructing justice is getting to be an epidemic around here. But I have a hunch she'll open up to me more readily than to Terry Finnerty. And I think she represents the bigger picture, bigger than our police, bigger even than the cathedral."

"Do you think . . . ?"

"George, I don't think anything at this point, beyond that. She sounded anxious, said she didn't want to leave on my machine the location of where she was staying, and that she would call me again. I've got to get back to the house and be there when she does. If she does."

"Of course. Thank you for coming tonight, Mac."

Smith touched the bishop on the arm. "Getting complicated, isn't it?"

"Too complicated."

"Let a few hours pass where the Kelsch boy is concerned, let his folks and the police look for him. Chances are he'll arrive home full of apologies and excuses. If he doesn't show up soon, call me. I'll be home all evening."

St. James sighed. "Again, what can I say but thank you?"

"Try a couple of prayers for all of us, including yourself, and get a good night's sleep. Forgive my choice of words, George, but for a bishop, you look like hell."

chapter
25

A Pelting Rain
in Time for Rush Hour

When Smith returned home, he discovered a note pinned to the front door informing him that his neighbor had signed for a delivery. He went next door, where Mrs. Sinclair handed him an overseas courier envelope. The return address was Scotland Yard. "Thanks very much, Valerie," Smith said to her.

He returned to his house and opened the envelope. The photos Annabel had taken of the figure on horseback had been blown up into eight-by-ten-inch prints. Smith scrutinized the pictures. The fog, and the distance from which

Annabel had taken the pictures, precluded a clear view of the rider's face. What could be discerned, however, was that the rider was fairly big and broad-shouldered yet somehow plainly a woman, although her full British riding getup was almost unisex.

Smith left the photos on the kitchen table and was about to change into more casual clothing when the phone rang. It was Tony Buffolino.

"Hey, Mac, what's happening?"

"What do you mean?"

"I haven't heard beans from you. I mean, I been off the case a little bit, but I'd like to get back on." He spoke in a stage whisper. "Man, this place is drivin' me crazy. I got to get away. Come on, you must have something else for me to do."

"Yes, I might. How are you at finding little boys?"

"Little boys? What do you think I am?"

"Tony, hold the comments and listen to me. Where are you now?"

"At the club, where else? I spend my whole damn life here. That's the problem. Mac, between you and me, I got problems here, and not just with Alicia. Things ain't goin' so good, financially, I mean. I don't know, maybe I should turn this place into another topless joint like the ones on either side. Guys comin' in and out all night, and all the owner's got to do is pay a couple 'a girls. These acts I got here come high. They're all direct from Vegas."

"Vegas, Illinois," Mac said, "and lounge acts from East St. Louis."

Tony laughed. "Come on, Mac, turn me into an honest man again."

"Stay there, Tony. And stay as you are. Don't go topless. I'll get back to you in a couple of hours."

"You want to come down, have a meal on the house?"

"Thanks anyway."

Smith went into the kitchen to make himself spaghetti. Anything was preferable to the "chef" at Tony's Spotlight Room, another assassin. Annabel had left a message on the machine that she was taking her new assistant out for a lifesaving, or life-threatening, dinner: "To tell him he either starts earning his money my way, or he can find another job." Good: she was taking it out on the arrogant assistant.

He filled a large pot with water and put it on the stove, poured mushroom sauce in a saucepan, grated a chunk of Parmesan cheese, and cut a lettuce wedge.

The phone rang; he moved more quickly than he ordinarily would have. Clarissa Morgan was on his mind. That was the call he wanted.

It wasn't she. The dean, Daniel Jaffe, was inviting Mac and Annabel to a party at his house a week from Saturday. Smith's mind wasn't exactly on university party-going. He told his boss it sounded fine to him, that he would check with Annabel, and got off the line.

The water was boiling, and, adding a teaspoon of vegetable oil to keep the spaghetti from sticking, he snapped strands in half and placed them into the water, adding a pinch of salt. He turned the flame low under the saucepan and dashed oil and vinegar on the lettuce. All of this was observed with keen interest by Rufus, who could usually count on Smith to share. This was not always true with Annabel, however. It was a matter of philosophy, of dog rearing. "Of course he begs at the table," she often told Mac. "He begs because you give him something."

"Yes, but now that he's gotten into that habit, it seems a shame to disappoint him."

It was never a serious debate, and the dog

knew it, like a child playing one parent against the other. He was better at it than most kids.

Smith watched the TV news in the kitchen while he ate. The discovery of small but electronically discernible traces of blood on the floor of the Bethlehem Chapel had been announced by the police. While that represented a significant finding, it did not move the investigation closer to identifying the murderer.

He fed a few strands of spaghetti to Rufus by holding them above the dog's head and watching him snap them off inch by inch. It wasn't a terribly humane way to reward the animal's patience, but Smith could never resist it when spaghetti was involved. Then he gave Rufus a real serving in his dish.

He put the dishes in the dishwasher and looked at the clock. Annabel should be home soon, unless her career-counseling conversation had been more complicated than she'd anticipated.

Smith was much on edge, and he knew it. Ordinarily, he was able to settle into his recliner and read on evenings like this when he was alone. Not this night. He found himself pacing the house, stopping only to look at the telephone as though it had a life of its own, or should. He tried reading the newspaper but found it lacking. Television didn't appeal, nor did preparing for his next class.

Then, with a ring that jolted his nervous system and threatened to alert all of Washington, the phone went off.

"Hello," Smith said loudly into the receiver.

"Mr. Smith?"

"Yes. Miss Morgan. I've been waiting for your call."

"I'm sorry to be so elusive, Mr. Smith, but I think it prudent. When might we meet?"

"Any time that's good for you. Do you want to tell me a little about why we're meeting?"

"No, not on the phone. I thought . . ." There was much pain in her laugh. "I thought it might be appropriate for us to meet at the cathedral."

Smith glanced up at a clock. It was almost eight. "At the cathedral? At this hour?"

"I know it sounds an unlikely place, but it would suit me. Will you?"

Smith thought for a moment. The cathedral could do without new late-night visitors. But he mustn't lose the contact. "I suppose so. When?"

"Would an hour from now be rushing you?"

Smith's concern was that he would not be

home when Annabel returned. He'd leave a note. "Yes, I'll meet you at the cathedral in an hour, Miss Morgan. How about the Good Shepherd Chapel—it's open at all hours."

There was silence on the other end, and the thought process she was going through was almost audible. "I'll call you back."

"Miss Morgan, is anything wrong? Can you confirm? Are you—"

A sharp click announced that the conversation was over.

Smith hung up and thought about what had just taken place. There'd been background noise—traffic, some voices. She'd obviously been calling from a phone booth.

He resumed pacing, but was interrupted by a call from George St. James. "Mac, I just received a call from Joseph Kelsch's mother. The police haven't come up with a trace yet."

Smith glanced at his watch. "I have a private investigator who's done work for me. I'm putting him on this. He's . . . he's between assignments and anxious to start a new one."

"How could he help? I mean, if the police haven't been able to find the boy . . ."

"Yes, I agree, except that he is a former

Washington cop. He has resources of his own."

"All right, Mac. Maybe I should call Mrs. Kelsch and inform her."

"Sure, but I don't think it's really necessary. My investigator will be checking quietly. I'll keep you informed."

"Good. Have you heard from Miss Morgan?"

"Yes, twenty-one minutes ago. We were in the process of arranging a place and time to meet when she hung up. I think she was calling from a booth. Maybe ran out of coins. Or courage. She suggested meeting at the cathedral, of all places, but I think she might reconsider. How late will you be up?"

"Late. I'll be here in my office at the cathedral probably until midnight. Carolyn and Jonathon are somehow producing drafts of their report, even though they've accused each other of murder. And I have reports to get out. The world is made of paperwork."

"We'll all end up drowning in it one day," Smith said. "Listen, I want to clear this line. I'll be up late, too, and I'll be here unless I run out to meet Lady Morgan. I'll call you."

Buffolino took Smith's call in his tiny office at

the rear of the club. "I only have a minute," Smith said. "About the missing boy. His name is Joseph Kelsch, Joey." Smith filled Buffolino in on the circumstances surrounding Joey's disappearance, his address, school, parents. Buffolino knew several places where runaway kids tended to go, and he promised to go out looking. "I'll be up late, Tony. Call anytime."

Smith checked the news again. His friend Rhonda Harrison was anchoring that night, and had just begun an update on the FBI's arrests. She said that a statement had been issued by the director of the FBI that the sweep was the result of an ongoing and long-term investigation of Word of Peace. According to the director, the Bureau had worked in concert with law-enforcement agencies from other countries.

The investigation was focusing on two aspects of the organization's activities. One had to do with the diversion of funds to the personal bank accounts of some of those arrested. The other dealt with subversive activities. Word of Peace concealed, according to the FBI's statement, a network of espionage activity, with the organization used as a cover. Sufficient evidence had been gathered to make a strong case against certain individuals within Word of Peace for the passing of sensitive and classified information to their respective countries or to stateless groups.

According to the FBI, those arrested had established an elaborate web of informants who reported on the activities of a wide range of people involved with Word of Peace. Secretaries, postal workers, custodians, and bank clerks received regular payments in return for passing on information considered useful to some of the group's leaders. Meticulous records had been kept and have been secured, and the individuals named in them will be part of the continuing investigation.

Rhonda concluded, "The director took pains to point out, however, that while many individuals have been accused of wrongdoing, the indictment is not directed at Word of Peace itself as a charitable and well-intentioned movement. Many outstanding individuals and institutions have given considerable support to Word of Peace, according to the director's statement, and it was his feeling that a worthwhile organization had been misused by these named in the indictment."

■ ■ ■

As Smith watched television, Brett Leighton walked into the lobby of the small and popular River Inn on Twenty-fifth Street N.W., a few blocks from Smith's Foggy Bottom home. He said to the nicely tailored young woman behind the desk, "I'm here to meet Miss Morgan. Clarissa Morgan. She's a guest."

The receptionist checked. "Yes, Miss Morgan is in room twenty. The house phone is over there." She pointed across the lobby.

"Thank you," Leighton said, smiling. He walked slowly toward the phone, glanced over his shoulder, saw that she'd turned her attention to a computer printer running off a reservation, and he quickly stepped into a waiting elevator. Room 20, he thought. He pushed the button for the second floor, stepped out into the carpeted hallway, and went to the door with *20* on it. He rapped lightly. No response. He knocked again, a little louder this time. Still no sound. "Too bad," he muttered, retracing his steps to the lobby and going out to the street. He turned deliberately and walked north, although unsure of which direction to try.

Had he gone south on Twenty-fifth, he would have come within minutes to a public telephone across from the Kennedy Center for the Performing Arts and seen Clarissa Morgan standing a few feet from it.

After abruptly hanging up on Smith—she'd had the feeling that someone was watching her—she'd gone inside the Kennedy Center and wandered around its massive red-carpeted and white, marble foyer; it was like a cathedral of another sort and purpose, she thought. She was tempted to use one of the public phones in the center, but there were too many people and too much noise to make the call. Eventually, she left the building and returned to the booth from which she'd originally called Smith. Now she was caught in a bout of indecision. She knew Smith lived in the neighborhood; maybe it would be better to simply drop in on him. No, she didn't like that idea. It would have to be another phone call. Where should she suggest they meet? He hadn't seemed to like the idea of the cathedral at first. She couldn't suggest her hotel because she knew *they* would probably know she was staying there. They knew everything. Not that she cared, at least she hadn't up until this point. The hell with them. Damn them all. But it wouldn't be fair to Mackensie Smith to bring him into the midst of something even nastier than he'd already experienced—to say nothing of his bird-watching wife.

The cathedral.

It had to be the cathedral. He'd show up. She didn't know it well, but had been there, had a sense of it. It was so large, there would be many places, like that chapel, where she could meet him, tell him everything. For it was time.

She stepped into the booth and reached in her purse. She had a few shillings, but she was out of American change. She swore softly, returned to the Kennedy Center, and went to a gift shop, where she bought a key ring with a ballet dancer dangling from it. She used a traveler's check and asked to be given a portion of her change in silver. This time she ignored all the well-dressed people milling about. There was safety in numbers. She stepped up to one of the public phones and dialed.

chapter
26

Now Raining Cats and Rufus-size Dogs

Joey Kelsch sat in darkness behind the Jerusalem altar, at the east end of the nave. It was deathly quiet; he wondered whether the sound of his own breathing, which he tried to control, could be heard everywhere, by anyone in the building. Next to him was the small suitcase packed with underwear, jeans, two sweaters, socks, and his favorite Ping-Pong paddle.

He sat on a brilliant blue needlepoint kneeling cushion decorated with sprays of wheat, grape clusters, a spear, and a crown of thorns, symbolic of Holy Communion and the Passion and the crucifixion of Good Friday. He'd taken the cushion from in front of the elaborately carved wooden communion rail that separated the sanctuary from the chancel.

Joey heard movement in the nave and slowly, carefully peered out over the altar; he saw nothing and glanced up. Looking down on him, or so it seemed, was a large carved figure of Christ set in one of three reredos. Quotations from Saint Matthew's Gospel were written on another:

For I was an hungered and you gave me meat; I was thirsty and ye gave me drink; I was a stranger and ye took me in; naked, and ye clothed me; I was sick and ye visited me; I was in prison and ye came unto me.

Farther up was the *trompette en chamade,* Willie Nickel always called them, the imposing pipes of the great cathedral organ.

He looked over the altar again at the nave's vast emptiness. At the far end, more than four hundred feet away, was the west rose window, a soaring circle and an acclaimed tribute to the art of stained glass.

If there *had* been a noise, the source of it was

not visible. Joey sank down onto the kneeling pad again, drew his knees up to his chin, and wrapped his arms about them. He was cold and frightened, and had no idea what to do next. He'd entered the cathedral after having decided he could no longer stay at school. Nor did he want to go home and face the questions, the scolding that were sure to ensue. There was too much on his mind, too many things to sort out, too many decisions to be made. *Damn* Willy Nickel, he thought. If Nickelson hadn't given him that stupid punishment of sorting music in the choir room, none of this would have happened. He would have played in the Ping-Pong tournament and probably won. Instead, he was forced to witness the most horrible thing he could imagine—yet could do nothing about it. There was no one he could trust or turn to and tell what he saw, what he knew. It hadn't been easy calling the police that next morning to tell them a murder had been committed in the National Cathedral. He'd blurted it out fast to the officer who'd answered the phone, and hung up immediately. The policeman thought he was a woman. That's what the newspapers and television said. Joey was glad. After making the call, he had visions of some special machine attached to the phone at police headquarters that could immediately identify boys and where the call was placed and the school of whoever placed it—some supercomputer. He'd heard about voiceprints, and how each person's voice was unique and individual. Yes, he was very relieved when he read they thought a woman had called. But it was a fleeting and minor relief. Because he still knew, still had been a witness to the event.

He began to cry silently. Maybe he would just die there. That would be the end of it. Maybe he would just die and be found behind the high altar the next morning the way Father Single-tary had been found in Good Shepherd. He prayed without sounding the words, ending his prayer with "Please tell me what to do."

He didn't know that the police were outside searching the close for him, or that a man named Tony Buffolino was checking the bus station, or that his parents were at home, his mother hysterical, his father trying to calm her but quietly fearing the worst for their only son. Nor did he know that upstairs in the bishop's study, a meeting was in progress at which Bishop St. James and members of his staff worked on a financial report that was expected in two days at the church's executive council in New York City. With the bishop were Reverends Merle and Armstrong and three lay members of the cathedral chapter.

Damn that Willie Nickel, Joey thought again, clenching his fists. More tears ran down his already stained cheeks.

Mac Smith took Rufus for a short walk in the rain, returned to the house, checked the answering machine, and heard Morgan's voice confirming she'd meet him at the Good Shepherd Chapel. He wrote Annabel a note: *Gone to meet Clarissa Morgan at the cathedral. Don't ask why there. It just happened that way. Maybe we'll finally get to the bottom of this. Wanted to see you but will return ASAP. I love you. Don't worry. Mac.*

He checked his watch: time to go. He'd changed into tan corduroy slacks, and slipped a brown cable-knit sweater over the blue button-down shirt he'd worn that day. He'd also changed from black wing-tip shoes to his favorite pair of tan desert boots. He put on his raincoat, gave Rufus a reassuring pat on the head, and headed for the front door. The ringing phone stopped him.

"Mr. Smith?" a woman asked.

"Yes."

"This is Helen Morrison at Sevier House."

Smith's heartbeat accelerated. "Yes, Miss Morrison. Is my mother all right?"

"No, Mr. Smith, that's why I'm calling. She's taken a bad fall, and we think she's broken her hip. She hit her head pretty hard, too."

Oh, God. "Where is she?"

"The ambulance has just arrived to take her to the hospital. We've made her as comfortable as possible. I wanted to let you know as soon as possible."

"Yes, thank you. What hospital is she being taken to?"

"Georgetown University."

"I'll be there as quickly as I can."

It was nine-thirty. There was no debate in his mind about which obligation to meet. Maybe I can swing by the hospital, make sure Mother is being properly cared for, and then find Morgan, he thought. He'd be late at the cathedral, but so be it.

He half-ran down the street to the garage they rented. Three minutes after he'd driven off, Annabel arrived, noticed that Mac's car was gone, and went to the house.

She opened the door, hung up her coat, and went to the kitchen. Mac's half-consumed cup of coffee was on the table and still steaming. Next to it was the pile of photographs from London. She looked at them carefully; a chill went through her as the memory returned of that day in the sheep meadow.

Usually when she came home to an empty house, her initial response was to go to the study in search of a note Mac might have left her. This night, however, she first went to the bedroom and changed into silk pajamas, a robe, and slippers. She made herself a cup of tea and then strolled into the study . . . saw and read the note.

"Not without me, you're not," she said.

Minutes later she was dressed again and pulling her still-damp raincoat from the closet. She shoved the photos in her oversized handbag and headed for the front door. Instead, she went to the answering machine and changed the outgoing message. "This is your partner, Mac. I'm on my way to the cathedral to be with you. If this is somebody else, leave a message after the beep."

It was raining harder now as she sprinted in the direction of their garage. By the time she reached it and opened the door, her shoes were soaked from puddles she hadn't bothered to avoid. She turned the ignition key. Nothing. Can't be, she thought. It started fine all day. "Come on," she said, jamming her foot down on the accelerator. No sense trying to talk it into action. She stood on the sidewalk, looked up and down the street. No chance of getting a cruising cab at this hour, in this neighborhood, in this rain. She walked to the Kennedy Center, where a performance in the Opera House was letting out, and was able to grab one of many waiting taxis before the throng of theatergoers poured through the doors in search of those elusive vehicles. "The National Cathedral, please," she told the coal-black driver whose name on the posted license read like that of an African king. As he pulled away, she wiped condensation from the inside of the window and looked out. "Stupid," she mumbled. "You may be a brilliant professor, Mackensie Smith, but sometimes you are just plain stupid. Going to meet that woman alone, late at night."

Then she thought, stupid? Who's stupid? She had just left a message on the answering machine that was crazy. No one should use their machine to tell callers that they're out. No woman should announce where she is going, alone and late at night. Especially not a woman whose life has been threatened.

Well, they were partners—and they could share the stupidity prize—if they lived.

Mac Smith stood at the side of a bed in Georgetown University's emergency room. His mother, whose grip on his fingers was pincer-like, smiled up at him and said, "Don't worry, Mac, I'll be fine."

"Yes, Mother, I know you will. Are you in much pain?"

She closed her eyes and shook her head.

"The shot helped," he said.

Eyes still closed, she nodded.

The orthopedic surgeon on call that night entered the room carrying X rays that had been taken of Josephine Smith's hip and head. "A clean break," he said, slapping the still-wet plates up under metal clips and flipping on the back light. His finger traced a dark line on her left hip. "I've seen worse."

"What about the blow to her head?" Smith asked.

"I see nothing on the X ray that would indicate any sort of injury." He leaned over Mrs. Smith and said, "You're going to be just fine."

She smiled. "I know," she said. "I was just telling my son that. You shouldn't have bothered taking an X ray of my head, not this hard-headed old lady. I take after him."

Smith grinned and massaged her hand.

"We'll make sure you have a comfortable night," said the doctor. "Afraid we'll have to do a little surgery on you, however."

"I suppose you do," she said. "Where do I sign?"

The doctor looked at Smith and laughed.

"Be careful what you give me to sign," she said, wagging a finger at him. "This man is a lawyer, and a very good one."

Ten minutes later a hospital administrator came in with a surgical consent form, which Josephine Smith signed with a weak but deliberate flourish.

"How's Annabel?" she asked Mac when the administrator left the room.

"Fine, although she wasn't home when I left. She was having dinner with an employee. I'd better give her a call."

"Tell her not to be concerned about me."

"I'll tell her, Mother, but don't count on it. You do know she loves you very much."

"Which makes me a fortunate old lady. Go on, now, get home to her. I'll be fine. I'm getting drowsy."

Smith looked up at a white clock with black hands. Ten past ten. How long would Clarissa Morgan wait? He kissed his mother on the forehead and said, "I'll stay until you're asleep. Then I'll go home, but I'll be back first thing in the morning."

He went out to the nurses' station, where the doctor was making notations on a chart that had been created for Smith's mother. "You'll operate tomorrow?" Smith asked.

"Yes. I've already scheduled the O.R. for eight o'clock."

"How long does this kind of surgery take?"

"A couple of hours. I think we can fix your mother up just fine, although she will have a long period of convalescence."

"Yes, I'm sure. Thank you very much, Doctor. I know she's in good hands. I'll stay with her for a while."

When he finally did leave, Smith's focus was on getting to his meeting with Clarissa Morgan, and he forgot about his intention to call home. He went directly to his car, sat back, and had a sudden urge for a cigarette he hadn't had in fifteen years, told himself what happened to his mother could have been worse, and drove from the emergency-room parking lot in the direction of the National Cathedral.

While it had made sense in the beginning to seek refuge in the cathedral, and to choose the Jerusalem altar because it was the least likely place anyone would come at night, it now occurred to Joey Kelsch that he couldn't just sit there for the rest of the night—for the rest of his life. He'd heard voices, some of them outside and amplified. They sounded like the police. Were they searching for him? That thought caused him to shudder. If they really searched for him, they would certainly find him, even if it took a day or two, and they would ask him lots of questions. They'd hear his voice and maybe remember the voice of the person who'd called to report Reverend Singletary's murder.

He had to find someone, tell someone.

Bishop St. James. He was a nice man who would listen, and would protect him.

Joey stood and peeked over the altar. Outside, powerful lights came and went, piercing stained glass and throwing bizarre, grotesque patterns of color over the nave's stone grayness. Joey decided to leave his suitcase where it was, but he did pick up the kneeling pad and slowly came around from behind the altar with it. He paused, went to the communion rail, and laid the pad from where he'd taken it, in front of a plain block of wood that represented Judas; the rail was made up of eleven other carved blocks, each bearing the figure of a saint.

He tiptoed away from the rail and down the long center aisle, passed the elaborately carved oak choir stalls, and reached the crossing—the cathedral's center—its four gigantic sustaining piers rising up almost a hundred feet, though it seemed to Joey they went to heaven. He had always been impressed with how big the cathedral was, but at this moment it seemed to have grown tenfold, as if it had suddenly been filled with helium gas and expanded like a ponderous gray balloon. He'd never felt so tiny before, a speck upon the floor. He looked down; he was standing on the Crusader's Cross, the cathedral's special symbol.

He seemed so small and alone. Then, somehow, it was as if he felt a presence, but not a scary one, just a kind of all-encompassing and powerful one. He couldn't see a face, but he knew it was there, gentle, smiling, sort of saying, "Everything will be all right, Joey. Go now and do what you must."

He walked to the south transept and down a set of steps to the gift shop and information center, where he knew there was a pay phone. He pulled a small notepad from his rear pocket and opened it to where pieces of paper were inserted. One of them was a list of cathedral clergy and their office and home numbers. They were all there, including the bishop. His heart raced as he found a quarter in his pocket, lifted the handset, and inserted the coin. When he heard the dial tone, he squinted at the touchtone pad and carefully punched in the bishop's home number, hoping not to make a mistake. It was his only quarter.

"Hello," Mrs. St. James said.

Joey gulped.

"Hello, who is this?"

"Ma'am, is Bishop St. James at home?"

"No, he's not. Who's calling?"

"Ma'am, this is Joseph Kelsch. I go to school here."

Had Eileen St. James been visible to him, Joey would have seen her stiffen at the mention of his name. She said, "Yes, Joseph, how nice of you to call. Where are you?"

"I'm . . . I really need to see the bishop right away. It's very important."

"I'm sure it is. Are you near the cathedral?"

"No, ma'am, I'm—" A searchlight swung past the window, its beam bathing the small black alcove in harsh light. Joey's grip on the handset tightened, and he stopped breathing.

"Joseph, please tell me where you are. I'll have the bishop come to you right away."

"I don't know. . . . Could you tell me where he is, please, and I'll go to him."

Mrs. St. James realized she was going to lose contact, and decided to give him what he wanted. "The bishop is in his study in the cathedral, Joseph. He has a meeting, and he's going to work very late. You could go see him there."

"Thank you, ma'am."

There was a pause.

"Deposit fifteen cents for an additional three minutes."

Joey hung up and flattened against the wall as the light once again intruded upon his safe place. He'd never been to the bishop's study, but he knew where it was. He started to leave the alcove but the light came back again and illuminated everything. He crouched below the small booth that housed the telephone and tried to decide what to do next. Was he doing the right thing by going to see the bishop? Maybe he should just go home and forget about it—*try* to forget about it. And so he remained there, huddled and tense, and thought about it.

Clarissa Morgan's message on the machine had confirmed the time and place for them to meet. "The Good Shepherd Chapel," he had said, reasoning that it was sure to be open—the murder had not changed cathedral policy in that regard—and was indoors. No sense having either of them waiting outside in the drenching cold rain pouring over Washington. He was aware of the macabre aspect of meeting there, but it still struck him as a logical place. Also, he wanted to detect any sign of resistance.

Clarissa had agreed.

Now, as she sat alone in the chapel, her mind was filled with conflicting thoughts. She was growing angry at Smith for not being there. It was getting late. Was this some nasty way of getting even with her for skipping out of London on him? No, he wouldn't be that childish. He was a grown man, and a respected attorney and professor. Something must have happened. She'd wait, but not more than another fifteen minutes.

Simultaneously, she thought of Paul. Whenever she did, her emotions shifted between sadness and anger. He was so prone to becoming involved with the wrong people—always the wrong people. She'd pointed that out to him repeatedly, but he never listened. Oh, he placated her from time to time, told her that he was seriously considering disengaging, but he never did, and she'd reached the point where only ultimatums were left. How many of those she had issued him, the most recent when they'd flown together to Washington from London.

His announcement came as a total surprise to her the morning after his disappointing meeting at Lambeth Palace. She'd gone out early to the greengrocer's, leaving him sleeping in her bed. When she returned, he had showered and dressed.

"I have to go back to Washington immediately, Clarissa," he'd said.

"I thought you were going to the country today."

"My plans have changed."

She asked why, but he was evasive. Because she was a neat and orderly person, it was not difficult to ascertain when something in the flat was out of place. He'd obviously used the telephone while she was out. It must have been a call that prompted his sudden change in plans.

"I'll go with you," she said.

"I prefer that you don't."

They fought about it, and eventually he gave in, albeit without enthusiasm, and made two reservations. He'd remained angry until they'd settled in their seats and the flight was over the Atlantic. Then he became more agreeable once again. Clarissa recalled that his change in attitude coincided with the pretty little flight attendant's flirting with him. Her lips tightened. He was such a fool for a pretty face and trim figure, so easily seduced by red lips and pert breasts. She knew; she hadn't had any problem seducing him. Then, of course, it had been a deliberate act that had nothing to do with being attracted to him, nothing to do with wanting to establish a real intimacy with this surpris-ingly handsome man of the cloth. But it had progressed, as those things sometimes do, until she was in love with him, madly, desper-ately, insanely in love with him.

The tightness of her mouth softened almost into a smile as she thought of Brett Leighton's warning to her about that very thing. "Re-member, Clarissa," he'd said, "we simply want to know everything he's doing in Word of Peace. We simply want to know who he's in-volved with and what they're doing. Keep it at that, Clarissa. It's a job, one you might even find pleasant, but nothing more than a job."

She'd laughed at Leighton that day, which made him angry. By then, she'd done his bid-ding before and had seduced those men he wanted seduced so that secrets and informa-tion might be transmitted over pillows damp with love. She'd already become jaded and wanted out when she took on the "Singletary assignment" as one last job. After love tran-scended simple lust, she wanted Paul to take her out of the game that had become dis-tasteful, wanted him to love her, too, to com-mit himself to her. Which he said he would do, but he had not lived long enough to carry it off.

And so what was left?

Very little.

It was getting later.

chapter
27

Wetter Yet

George St. James ended his phone conversation with his wife and said to those with whom he was meeting, "Thank God. That was Eileen. She received a call from Joey Kelsch a few minutes ago."

"Wonderful," said one of the chapter members. "Where is he?"

"The boy wouldn't tell her. He insists upon seeing me. She told him I was working here late. I suspect he'll be by soon."

Canon Wilfred Nickelson, who'd been packing personal belongings in the choir room, had stopped off to leave a forwarding address with the bishop and clear up a few other details, and heard St. James make his announcement. "You say he'll be here soon?" Nickelson asked.

"Unless he decides not to come."

"Excuse me," Nickelson said. "Sorry to have interrupted."

"You know, Wilfred, we will miss you," St. James said. Nickelson's announcement of his hasty departure had only added to St. James's generally depressed mood of late. It had been suggested that a big going-away party be held for Nickelson, but a thunderous lack of interest on the part of the cathedral staff caused St. James to offer a modest one, which Nickelson had declined. But the call from Eileen had lifted his spirits. At least the problem of a missing student would soon be over. He suddenly found it easier to forgive his choirmaster.

Nickelson appeared to be flustered by the kind words. He was well aware that his short notice had not sat well with St. James or with others in the cathedral. He said, "Thank you, Bishop. I'll miss you, too."

As Nickelson left the study, Annabel's African king turned off Wisconsin and drove into the cathedral close. She had expected to arrive at a virtually deserted cathedral at this hour. Instead, there were MPD cars everywhere, and lights played over plantings on the grounds.

Annabel paid the driver and stood on the steps of the south transept, wondering where Mac would have arranged to meet Morgan. The time would have helped determine that. The cathedral was locked after dark unless a special religious event was taking place. He might have opted for an outside rendezvous. No, not in this weather. She pulled her raincoat collar up around her neck and wished she'd had the good sense to bring a hat and umbrella.

Mac would probably—and she knew she was trying to project herself into his mind—would probably have suggested meeting in the Good Shepherd Chapel because of the easy, twenty-four-hour access to it. It dawned on her that she would not have to circumvent the cathedral to reach the outside door off the garth. Because of all the activity, every door to the cathedral was open. She could take an interior route.

As she was about to go through the south entrance, she spotted Chief of Homicide Finnerty coming out of the Herb Cottage, a gift

shop selling herbs harvested from the cathedral gardens. "Chief," she shouted, coming
down the stairs.

"Mrs. Smith. What are you doing here?"

"Looking for my husband. What's going on?"

"Searching for a missing boy."

"What missing boy?"

"Joseph Kelsch. Mac didn't tell you?"

"No. I haven't seen him."

A uniformed officer came out of his squad
car and ran up to them. "Chief, the kid is okay.
Headquarters just got a call. The kid called the
bishop's house and has arranged to meet him
tonight."

"Jesus," Finnerty said. "We spend the night
getting soaked out here and the kid calls up?
Terrific."

Annabel looked at him incredulously. "Isn't it
wonderful he's been found?" she said.

"Yeah, usual runaway stuff and I've got a
whole squad out here catching pneumonia."

"By the way, why are *you* here?" Annabel
said. "I thought you were in charge of Homicide."

Finnerty put his hands on his hips and looked
at her as though she'd mispronounced a simple
word. "Mrs. Smith, because of the reverend

getting it, I've picked up this cathedral as per-
manent duty. Anything happens here, they call
me no matter what—murder, a kid sneaking off
to a dirty movie without telling his parents, a
pickpocket working communion, I get it, and I'll
be glad when I don't. Excuse me, I want to pull
my men off and go see the bishop."

Annabel watched the little detective swagger
away, barking orders as he walked. She went
up the stairs, entered the cathedral, and tried to
get her bearings. She knew where the Good
Shepherd Chapel was, but was confused for
the moment about how to get there. She considered returning to the outside, but the inces-
sant sound of rain changed her mind. She
started across the dimly lighted nave, the
squishing sound of water being squeezed out
of the crepe soles of her shoes coming back at
her loudly, as though tiny microphones in the
laces were picking it up and amplifying it
through speakers in her ears.

She paused at the crossing and looked down
at the large Crusader's Cross. To her right was
the high altar; she could not know that Joey
Kelsch had returned there and was sitting on
his suitcase, pondering whether to fulfill his
promise to the bishop's wife. She looked left

and squinted to better see across the vast expanse of nave that reached to the west rose window.

Would Mac and Clarissa Morgan be in Good Shepherd? It was only an assumption on her part, of course, but why assume anything? There was a way to find out, and she set off again, her pace faster. She reached the steps and descended.

A single candelabrum on the hallway wall spilled a drop of light through the chapel's open door. Annabel approached, wishing the sound from her wet shoes could be muffled. She stood outside and listened. No voices came from within, but there was movement. Annabel thought of Paul Singletary slumped dead just beyond the door.

She could see only one pew; faint, mottled light from the window illuminated its emptiness. A sound of slight movement came from the high-altar end of the chapel that was out of Annabel's line of vision. She drew a deep breath and stepped through the door.

Standing with her back pressed against the altar in the chapel was a tall, broad-shouldered figure. The silouhette was oddly familiar. Light through the window shone on the left side of her face; the right side was in shadows, a theatrical mask of good and evil. The woman was tense; her right hand was jammed into her raincoat pocket, and her eyes were wide.

"Miss Morgan?" Annabel asked.

The other figure's deep sigh filled the small space. Her body then physically and visually lost its tautness, and she half-smiled. "Mrs. Smith. Yes, I am Clarissa Morgan."

"Sure you don't want me to keep a couple of officers around?" Finnerty asked Bishop St. James. He'd found him in his study, where the meeting was still in progress, and called him into the hallway.

"No, thank you," St. James replied. "They might scare the boy off."

"You don't know where he called from?"

St. James shook his head. "My wife said it was definitely a phone booth. Could have been any one, a mile away or here, for all I know. Anyhow, I think he'll show up. My wife said he sounded committed to seeing me."

"Okay, your call, Bishop. We'll keep an eye out for him. If we spot him we'll—"

"If he doesn't show up here in a reasonable amount of time, I'll let you know. In the meantime, all I can do is thank you for your quick and professional response."

"Thanks," Finnerty said. "That's our job." He didn't consider searching for lost kids *his* job, but it seemed the thing to say. "Hey Bishop," Finnerty said suddenly, pointing to a high open window at the end of the hall through which rain was streaming, "you got a ladder or chair? I'll get one of my men to close up that window before we go."

"Oh, for Pete's sake," the bishop grumbled, "the custodian should have been around hours ago, when the rain started, to close any open windows. No, don't bother one of your men. I'm sure he'll be around soon to close that window—and to mop up that puddle."

"Well, okay," Finnerty said. They shook hands, and Finnerty left and headed for his car.

St. James returned to his study, where the two lay chapter members were preparing to leave. The work had gone more smoothly and quickly than St. James had anticipated. The report needed only finishing touches, which Merle and Armstrong were working on, civilly but with a distinct distance.

Once the chapter members were gone,

St. James yawned, then said to his two clergy, "I'd call it a night, too, but I have to be here for Joey. If he shows up."

Merle said, "No need to do that, Bishop. You never can tell when that might be. Reverend Armstrong and I will be here for a while, to complete this document. If you have something else to do, go ahead and do it. Catch a few winks. We'll get in touch with you the minute he shows up."

St. James sat behind his desk and considered the offer. Merle had his kinder moments. The bishop was fatigued; it had been a long day and night, and he sensed he was coming down with a cold, maybe even the flu, which he'd heard was taking on the proportions of an epidemic in the Washington area. He'd tripled his intake of vitamin C that day in the hope of fighting off whatever was brewing inside. He'd got soaked late in the afternoon, and there was still a dampness to his clothing that passed through his skin and assaulted his bones. Besides, despite their recent differences, Merle and Armstrong seemed to be reasonably cooperative with each other, and with him. He said, "I really want to be here when Joseph arrives, but I could use a little time at home, maybe a hot bath and a cup of Eileen's tea. How long will you stay?"

"Probably another hour," Carolyn Armstrong said, looking up and smiling. "Go take that bath and enjoy the tea."

St. James stood and stretched. His muscles ached, and the prospect of sinking into a hot tub became almost overwhelming. "I think I will, but I'll be back in less than an hour. If he shows up, please call immediately."

As St. James prepared to leave the cathedral, he had a spasm of second-guessing. Joey Kelsch had specifically told Eileen he wanted to see the bishop. Would the boy bolt when he arrived at the study and found only Reverends Merle and Armstrong there? St. James reasoned Joey wouldn't—rationalized it, actually. Both canons were well known to all the students in the school. There shouldn't be any problem. Besides, they would call him, and he would return as quickly as possible, even if it meant cutting short his soak. He buttoned up his raincoat and went out into a blowing rain, forecast to be "occasional," that had become a District of Columbia monsoon.

■ ■ ■

Tony and Alicia Buffolino sat in their storeroom-cum-office at the rear of Tony's Spotlight Room. Outside, the band, now reduced to a piano player and drummer, labored through their repertoire of songs that all sounded alike for the entertainment of a half-dozen customers who all looked alike. On the desk was a tall pile of bills and a spreadsheet Alicia had worked up earlier in the day.

"It's no use, Tony," she said. "We can't pay these bills—we can't even pay the entertainers anymore." The piano player and drummer were the sole source of entertainment that night.

"Yeah, yeah, I know. Maybe we could do some kind of special promotion. Or, if you'd let me bring in a couple 'a strippers, say, it would be different."

"Absolutely not," Alicia said. "I will not have women taking off their clothes in my club."

"Your club?" Tony guffawed. "This joint was my idea, and all you do is get in the way with No this, No that."

"That isn't fair, Tony."

"Yeah, well maybe I'm not fair, but this place ain't fair, either. We gotta have a gimmick, like the song says, or find some way to get people in here and keep them alive and around before they go out or pass out. We could go topless, maybe."

"You could go topless. All you seem to be interested in is what you've always been interested in. This place is turning you into some kind of lowlife. I thought you were better than that."

"Yeah, I thought I was better, too. But those bills are telling me somethin', that nothin's getting better." He thought, yes, he had been better somehow, when they first met. He had been working for Mac Smith and life had started over. Now it was turning over, headed for the bottom. He flared up at her: "Well, I thought you were better, too. Whatta you know about this business, a waitress."

She clenched her fists and said, in a burst of sheer frustration, "All you were was a cop, Tony Buffolino, and that didn't work out, either." Her look of disgust and despair hit him like a blow before she slammed the door on her way out.

He slumped in his chair and shook his head. What had he got himself into this time? Another marriage, and a business partner who didn't understand how things worked. He could make something of the club if he didn't have to listen to her. But he also knew—and had trouble admitting even to himself—that maybe he wasn't being square with her. Maybe she was right; he was an ex-cop who'd been bounced off the force and who decided to become a big-shot club owner—and couldn't even meet the payroll. Some big shot.

He needed to talk to someone who understood him, who'd support him. During a previous conversation with Mac Smith, Tony had lapsed into a round of complaints about Alicia and the state of their marriage. Smith had suggested they see a marriage counselor.

"A shrink?" Tony had said. "What's a shrink gonna do, put us on a couch together?" He laughed. "Hey, maybe that would help."

"Don't be so cynical about counseling, Tony," his professor friend had said. "Alicia seems like a nice person. She's obviously crazy about you, which I suppose casts suspicion on her judgment, but I don't think you want to lose her. Remember, she's Number Three."

Buffolino had told Smith he'd think about it, which he did. He'd suggested to Alicia that night that maybe he'd be willing to go to a counselor, and she'd responded enthusiastically. But they hadn't gone any further because, as

Tony had to admit to himself, he couldn't bring himself to make the call, and wasn't about to let Alicia choose the person who would attempt to help pull their marriage together. If they saw a shrink, it would be his guy.

Dumb, he thought as he sat dejectedly in the battered office chair. Smith had been right; he didn't want to lose her. Tomorrow, he'd suggest she pick a counselor and make an appointment. Tomorrow. Couldn't make the call this time of night unless it was to cops, the hospital, or the local funny farm. Sometimes they all seemed to be one place.

He picked up the phone and held it in front of him. Who should he call? He had to call somebody, get out of here, at least for the evening. There was no show to introduce, so he wasn't needed. He considered calling one of his ex-wives, but they were both a source of pain out of the past. Right. Mackensie Smith. He'd call Mac and schmooze with him awhile. But the machine said:

"This is your partner, Mac. I'm on my way to the cathedral to be with you. If this is somebody else, leave a message after the beep."

"Huh?" He'd never heard that kind of message from Smith's machine before. He dialed the number again, got a busy signal, waited, then once again tried the number and got the same message from Annabel.

He hung up and frowned. What was Smith doing at the cathedral at this hour, in this weather, and why was Annabel going to meet him there? What had she called herself? His "partner"? Partner in what?

Buffolino had canvassed a number of places where runaways tended to go. He'd come up empty. All he'd learned was that the boy had been reported as missing to the police, and that Terry Finnerty was leading a squad on a search of the cathedral grounds. Why Finnerty? He was Homicide. Did this kid have something to do with Singletary's murder?

It was all too much for Tony to ignore, particularly in light of his desperate need to get away from the club, the bills. He put on his old raincoat and slouch hat and walked into the club, where Alicia was berating the piano player for having taken his break too soon. "Forty on, twenty off," she said.

"We played forty-five last set," the pianist said, downing a glass half-filled with amber liquid.

"I'm leaving," Tony said.

"Where are you going?" Alicia said.

"I got somethin' else to do."

A blast of rain hit his face as he went outside. He ducked quickly into one of the two topless clubs that flanked Tony's Spotlight Room and looked around. The room was packed with men who ogled a tall, lithe young woman wearing gloves, high heels, a bored look, and absolutely nothing else.

"Hello, Tony," the club's owner said. "Want a seat?"

"Nah, just checkin' out the competition."

The owner laughed. "Doin' pretty good, huh?"

"Yeah, congratulations, I got to go." To kidnap some customers, he thought, pulling his coat together.

"I can't understand what happened to my husband," said Annabel, who sat with Clarissa Morgan in the two-person pew at the front of Good Shepherd Chapel. "I hope he hasn't had an accident. The weather is dreadful."

"It can be even worse in England, in London or, say, in the Cotswolds," Morgan said.

"Yes, I suppose it can be. The last time we

were there, I had an experience I'll never forget." Annabel looked at Morgan. She pulled the photographs from her purse and handed them to the other woman. Morgan's expression said many things, including a silent statement that she didn't need photographs to know about Annabel's nearly being trampled to death. She glanced at the pictures, then gave them back to her.

"That's you on that horse, isn't it?" Annabel said.

"Yes. I owe you an apology for that, Mrs. Smith."

Annabel shifted so that she more squarely faced the beautiful British woman at her side. "Why? I didn't even know you."

"That's correct," Morgan said, clasping her hands on her lap and looking down at them. "I was told to do it by my employer."

"Your employer? What employer would tell you to kill somebody you didn't even know?"

Morgan denied Annabel's assertion. "I didn't intend to kill you, Mrs. Smith. I was told to frighten you, rough you up, make you and your husband decide you had better things to do than snoop around sheep pastures and churches. We couldn't get to him, frighten him off, but if you were threatened, he'd be more likely to pull out."

Annabel leaned against the back of the pew and looked at the depiction, above the altar, of the Good Shepherd cradling the lamb. "I'm sorry. I don't understand violence."

"Better you don't, Mrs. Smith, better you don't understand many things surrounding Paul's death."

"Maybe you're right, but I'll reserve judgment about that. Who were you working for? Who told you to scare us off?"

"I'd rather not say. The organization represents interests far larger than you and me." She sighed and said with a sense of relief, "I no longer work for them. That's why I'm here, to see that no one else is hurt." Annabel's next questions received only evasive, noncommittal answers. She thought about Mac. Where *was* he? Did the organization to whom Clarissa referred intend to do harm to Mac, to her? she asked.

"They do what they feel they must," Clarissa said. "We don't count for very much."

"Did *they* . . . did they kill Paul Singletary?"

Clarissa raised her head, the long, perfect

line of her jaw, nose, and forehead turned into a lovely silhouetted cameo in the light from the garth. "In a sense," she said.

"Did you kill him?" Annabel asked.

Morgan said nothing.

"You had an affair with him. Did you do that because your employer told you to?"

"Yes."

"How dreadful."

Clarissa turned and stared at her.

"I mean, for Paul," Annabel said. "Did he ever know?"

"No, never. I would never have done that to him. You see, Mrs. Smith, I came to love him very much. It didn't happen at the beginning. At that point it was just another assignment, the sort of assignment I'd become quite expert at. But then something happened that had never happened to me before. I committed the cardinal sin . . ." She laughed bitterly. "What an interesting choice of words. Possibly I should say canon sin. In any case I committed the sin of losing sight of why I was with him, losing myself to him in every way."

"And?"

"And he lost his life because of it, I believe."

Both women tensed as they heard the doors

leading to the outside swing open. Mac Smith stood in the chapel doorway. Annabel immediately went to him and wrapped her arms around him, wet raincoat or not. "Thank God you're here," she said. "What happened? I got your note, but—"

"Mother took a fall. Broke her hip."

"How terrible. Is she all right?"

"She's fine. She's at Georgetown University Hospital, resting comfortably. They're doing surgery on her tomorrow." He looked over Annabel's shoulder and saw the woman seated in the pew. She hadn't looked in their direction, as though not wanting to intrude upon their privacy.

Smith said, "Miss Morgan. Sorry I'm late. There was a family emergency and—"

She turned. "I heard. I'm sorry about your mother."

Smith moved to the altar and looked down at her. Annabel remained in the doorway. "I'm sorry we missed each other in London, Miss Morgan," Smith said, "but I'm glad you're here and called me. The question obviously is, why? What brings you to Washington?"

Clarissa Morgan sat deep in thought as Mac and Annabel waited silently. Then the woman

looked up at Smith and said, "I came here because I wanted to do something decent for
once, Mr. Smith."

"Go on."

"You see, I've caused a great deal of pain
and suffering for many people. I'm not that old,
but I've spent much of my adult life lying and
cheating and not really caring about the results.
That happened with Paul. I lied to him. I
cheated him. I manipulated him into a situation
in which he lost his life. I would like to atone for
that." She looked around the chapel. "I suppose this is a fitting place for the atonement of
Clarissa Morgan."

"I don't think place matters when someone
is trying to unload a heavy conscience," Smith
said.

"No, I suppose not."

"Are you talking about your attempt to blackmail the Church of England?" Smith asked.

"Oh, goodness, no. I saw that as my way out.
But it was a silly attempt, ridiculous actually,
very amateurish. I should have known better. I
thought that by accumulating a goodly sum of
money quickly, I could take myself away, disappear, but that wasn't to be. They paid me well,
but—"

"*Who* paid you well?"

"Your wife and I have gone into that a bit."

"Except I have no idea who it was you were working for," Annabel said.

Mac and Annabel, looking at Clarissa Morgan from their respective vantage points, were surprised to see her begin to cry.

"Can I get you something?" Smith asked.

"No, please, just . . . could you leave me alone for a few minutes? Paul's death does this to me at the oddest times. I'd just like to be alone here." She touched a handkerchief to her eyes. "I might even pray. I haven't done that since I was a child."

Smith nodded at Annabel. "We won't be far," he said.

They went out into the hallway and shut the door. Annabel grabbed his arm, whispered, "Mac, I think she killed Paul."

"That thought ran through my mind. But . . . did she say anything specific?"

"No, damn it, she has this elusive way of talking around things, but for a moment I was gripped with the belief that she killed Paul. She's a very troubled woman. She seduced him on the order of somebody she calls her 'employer,' whoever that is. She talks like a spy, a regular

Mata Hari, entrapping men for this employer or organization. That must be it. She must work for an intelligence organization, and she seduced Paul for some purpose of theirs."

"Cam Bowes was pretty direct about the heavy involvement of intelligence agencies in Word of Peace. What do you think, Annie, that she set Paul up to be killed, or actually did it herself?"

"I don't know, but she is capable of taking physical action—of several kinds. Clarissa Morgan was the person on horseback in the Cotswolds."

Smith grunted. He wasn't surprised. Clarissa Morgan knew when they would be in the Cotswolds, and where they were staying, because Smith had told her. "Look, I'm not happy you're here," he told Annabel, "although I can understand why you are. I'm going back and see if I can get her to tell me what she came all the way to Washington to say."

"What do you want me to do?"

"Find a phone and get George. Tell him you're here and that you need a safe place to park for a while."

"All right," Annabel said. "Please be careful, Mac."

"I will."

"I'm sorry about your mother."

"Happens to people that age. The doctor said it was a clean break and should heal nicely. She'll be fine, I hope. What I want to make sure is that *you* stay fine."

He watched her go up the stairs. She turned, then disappeared from his view.

In the choir room, Canon Wilfred Nickelson placed the final piece of music personally owned by him into a box and put the cover on it. He heard footsteps in the hall and opened the door slightly. Reverend Merle was about to enter the Bethlehem Chapel.

"Finish the report, Jonathon?" Nickelson asked.

"Yes."

Fifteen minutes later, Joey Kelsch tentatively looked around the edge of the high altar. He saw nothing, no one. Suitcase in hand, he left the sanctuary and chancel and made his way along the wall to the stairs leading to the bishop's study. He moved as carefully and quietly as a cat. More than anything, he did not want to meet a single person before reaching the bishop. Once, when he thought he heard footsteps, he stopped and ducked behind a pillar, but he decided he had imagined the noises.

He walked down the short hallway and stopped in front of the study. A typewritten note hung on the door: *Joseph—I'm waiting for you in the Bethlehem Chapel. Please meet me there. Bishop St. James.*

Joey didn't know what to do. He'd assumed—counted on—the bishop's being in his study as his wife had promised. Joey didn't relish the thought of going back down to the crypt level, but didn't see any other choice. The bishop must have had business that took him there, and if Joey didn't show up, he might offend the one person in whom he was putting his faith.

The note was tacked to the door with a yellow pushpin. Joey yanked the note loose and put it in his pants pocket. Nobody else should know he was there. He was frightened, but also relieved. It would soon be over. Then maybe everything would be the way it was before, and he could enjoy his life again.

He'd just passed the entrance to Good Shepherd Chapel when someone loomed large in the doorway. There was a light on behind the person. "Joey," Mac Smith said. The boy froze in his tracks. The voice had been a man's, but all Joey saw was the face of a woman. He bolted from where he'd been anchored to the floor and raced down the stairs, stumbled and sprawled on his belly at the bottom, his suitcase flying across the hall and hitting the wall. He scrambled to his feet and continued down the hall toward the Bethlehem Chapel. He ran so fast he almost went past the door, but stopped by grabbing the frame and pulling himself back. He looked inside; the chapel appeared to be empty. He looked up the hall and saw two people, the woman he'd seen through the doorway of Good Shepherd, and a man. They stopped at the foot of the stairs and watched him.

He stepped inside the chapel and went to the middle of it, next to the communion rail. "Bishop St. James," he said, his words echoing back at him. "It's Joey Kelsch. I got the note."

Smith and Clarissa Morgan went on to the chapel but paused in the hall; they could not be seen from within, but they could hear.

"Bishop, Bishop, it's Joey."

"No need to be afraid, Joey," a voice said. Joey turned in its direction. Someone stepped from behind the altar.

"Where's the bishop?" Joey asked, his voice breaking.

"He'll be here in a minute, Joey. He asked me to talk to you first."

Suddenly, Joey was a caged animal. He turned in a circle, his eyes open wide with a plea for help, his small body starting to shake.

"Come here, Joey. Come to me."

"No . . . I want the bishop." He turned and went for the door through which he'd entered, but another person stood in it. A tight whine came from Joey's throat.

The figure at the altar took several additional steps into the sanctuary and glared at the person standing in the doorway. "What are you doing here?"

"I've come to right a wrong," Clarissa Morgan said.

Mac Smith took a step forward so that he could look through the door. Morgan entered the chapel and stood in direct confrontation with Reverend Carolyn Armstrong.

A male voice sounded from the back of the chapel: "Come here, son, it's all right."

Smith looked in for the source of the voice. Canon Jonathon Merle stood in the middle of the aisle. "You have nothing to fear from me,

Joseph. Come." He extended his hand and beckoned with long fingers.

As Joey backed away from Merle, Smith heard footsteps behind him. He turned and saw Canon Wilfred Nickelson coming down the hall with purposeful strides, his face hard. Nickelson stopped when he saw Smith. Smith cocked his head and stepped back, leaving room for Nickelson to pass. Nickelson appeared to have been heading for the chapel, but he turned and went back up the hallway, pausing once to look over his shoulder, then bounded up the stairs toward Good Shepherd.

Smith wheeled to get inside the chapel. Joey had sunk to his knees and was sobbing. Clarissa Morgan went to the boy, looked down at him, then stepped up onto a small rise in front of the communion rail. Directly behind it was Carolyn Armstrong.

"How dare you come here!" Armstrong said.

"How dare *I* come here? I think I have more right here than you do, Reverend." She stressed the last word; her scorn was palpable.

Armstrong took a step forward, her face only a few feet from Morgan's. "How could you set foot in this chapel after what has happened?"

Smith could see that Morgan was smiling,

and in contrast to Carolyn Armstrong's overt anger, which caused her to shake, was composed and very much in control of herself. She said, "Paul loved me, and you couldn't bear that, could you?"

Armstrong was mirthless. "Loved you? He detested you, only he didn't know it. You deceived him, used him, and when you couldn't use him anymore, you killed him."

Morgan looked again at Joey Kelsch, who still crouched on the floor, trying to make himself as small as possible. "You seem to have quite an effect on this young boy. He's absolutely petrified of you."

"He's an emotionally disturbed child. Get out of here! The sight of you disgusts me."

The uncharacteristically loud voice of Jonathon Merle now filled the small chapel. He had walked up the aisle until reaching Joey, then said to Carolyn Armstrong, "Who is this woman who violates this chapel?"

Clarissa Morgan said, "Ah, Reverend Merle. Paul told me about you. He described you perfectly. How sad he had to spend so many of his days with hypocrites."

Merle made a move toward her.

She said, "Don't you dare touch me. I don't

intend to suffer at your hands or anyone else's, as Paul did."

"I'll call Security," said Merle.

"By all means." Morgan came to the closed communion rail, lifted the hinged portion, and threw it back with such force that it threatened to break. Armstrong, shock on her face, stepped back until she met the edge of the altar. Morgan came through the rail's opening and took one slow, small, deliberate step. "You couldn't bear the thought that he loved another woman," she said. "You have this facade behind which you hide, the uniform of God, your privileged place before altars, yet you couldn't forgive him, or me, that we were in love."

"Love? He didn't love you!" Armstrong screamed. "He hated you. He saw a pretty English face and your . . . experienced sexual favors, but he never loved you!" Her body went into a tremor, and she lowered her head, wrapping her arms about herself. "He never loved you. He loved me, but you wouldn't let him see it."

Tony Buffolino had come through the door leading to Good Shepherd, heard the voices downstairs, and found his way to the chapel.

He stood with Smith and watched the scene being played out at the altar.

Merle said, "Reverend Armstrong, come with me. This woman is demented."

Morgan said, "You hated Paul. Paul told me so. Why are you defending her?"

Armstrong snorted. "Defending me? How absurd."

"How can you claim to be a messenger of God when you know what you did? You killed him, murdered him in cold blood." Morgan took another step toward Armstrong; they were less than two feet from each other.

"I'll get Security," Merle said, and turned.

The women ignored him. "Paul returned to Washington a day early because of a phone call from you," Morgan said. "He told me on the plane why he was coming back, and he promised to end his relationship with you so that he and I could find a life together."

"That's a lie," Armstrong said, extending her arms behind her and placing them on the altar.

"He told me that you were insanely jealous of us, that you'd threatened to smear him and ruin his reputation as a priest."

"That's not true. I hated the fact that he was

involved with a woman like you, a user, a woman who cared nothing for him except what you might get from him. I told him that many times."

"Yes, you did, and he didn't believe it. He also never hesitated to tell you about me, about his feelings for me. I suppose it was cruel of him to do that, but I'm glad he did."

Clarissa Morgan knew that Paul never really loved her, but she also knew that he felt increasingly, desperately trapped by his relationship with Carolyn Armstrong. It was something she did not admire about Paul, his tendency to talk freely about other women. He'd talked about Armstrong a great deal on the plane, and Clarissa had begged him to disassociate himself from her, to give himself a chance to see whether he did—could—love *her*. He promised her he would give himself that chance. He wasn't allowed to live long enough to follow through on that decision.

Hearing movement behind her, Morgan turned. Merle was walking toward the crouched, shaking Joey Kelsch. The boy looked up into Merle's eyes, then looked at Morgan as she said loudly, as though addressing a crowd, "She murdered him!"

Joey shoved his hands against Merle's legs, scrambled to his feet, and ran toward the rear of the chapel. Merle lost his balance, then started after the boy.

"Watch out!" Buffolino yelled from the door.

Carolyn Armstrong had lifted a brass candlestick from the altar and was coming at the other woman with it. Morgan whirled, tensed, and pulled herself into a defensive shell, hands covering her head, knees bent.

Smith and Buffolino ran into the chapel. "Get the boy, Tony," Smith called. He vaulted the altar rail and said to Armstrong, "Why not give that to me, Reverend." He extended his hand.

"You don't understand how it was," Armstrong said, her body shaking.

"No, I probably don't, but I'm sure you can explain it."

Then, suddenly, Armstrong raised the candlestick again and threw it at Clarissa Morgan. It missed and ricocheted off the stone floor with a deafening clang. As the sharp sound of metal hitting stone reverberated throughout the chapel and faded, Buffolino came from the rear of the chapel. Joey had tried to hide in a pew, and Buffolino had half-coaxed him, half-dragged him from it. He held Joey by the arm, firmly but somehow gently herding Merle, too.

"Tell them how it happened, Jonathon," Armstrong said in a whisper.

Merle looked desperately at Smith and Buffolino. "I don't know what she's talking about."

"Tell them how after I hit Paul, *you* offered to move his body to Good Shepherd so that it might seem that an outsider killed him. Tell them, Jonathon. You are a man of God. For God's sake, tell them the truth!"

There was silence as all eyes turned to Merle. He didn't seem to know what to do, what to say. He looked from one face to the other, then finally fixed upon Mac Smith. The taut muscles of his gaunt cheeks and chin sagged; his thin lips began to tremble. Slowly, he raised his hands palms-up at Smith in a weak plea for understanding. "I . . . I didn't want to move him. Oh, God, no, I didn't want to do that. It was terrible seeing him on the floor, blood running from his head. It made me sick. I was so sorry— for both of them."

He glanced at Armstrong, then back at Smith. "She didn't mean to do it, Mr. Smith. I know that. God knows that. Singletary could be cruel to her. I saw it more than once." He looked at Armstrong before continuing. "She wouldn't have hurt him if he hadn't driven her to it. How much can a person take? I asked her once to give him up and to be my friend. I told her I could help her forget him and make her happy."

Smith looked down at the floor. This sudden tenderness by the stiff-necked Jonathon Merle, whose severe features were the stuff of caricatures, embarrassed Smith.

Merle continued, "I told her I wouldn't do it, but she pleaded with me. She told me that if the police thought Paul had been murdered by an outsider, they wouldn't suspect her. Even so, I still refused. But then she told me that the cathedral would be ruined if it got out that one member of its clergy had killed another. I believed that, Mr. Smith, I really did, and I took Paul's body to Good Shepherd for that reason."

Smith thought of Bishop St. James and his ill-advised attempt to hide the murder weapon because of the same faulty reasoning. How many wrongs are done in misguided attempts to do right?

Smith said to Armstrong, "I believe Reverend Merle. He's telling the truth, isn't he?"

Carolyn Armstrong's face was tight and bitter. But then her body convulsed as she started to sob. Her hands went to her face, and she sank to her knees in front of the altar.

Merle, too, started to cry, but the only visible signs were large tears that ran slowly down his cheeks and found the corners of his mouth. "There was one other reason," he said, with difficulty. "I love her."

Smith went to Joey Kelsch and put a large hand on the boy's shoulder. "Joey, I know you've been through a lot, but everything is going to be all right."

Joey looked up into Smith's eyes. "I saw him," he said. "I saw him moving Father Singletary the night I was in the choir room."

"Yes, we know," Smith said. "We know now what happened." He spoke to Buffolino. "Make sure neither of them leaves here. I want to make sure this boy gets back to his family. And I want to call Finnerty. On time for once. And he'll be coming back here again tonight."

chapter
28

Two Nights Later—
A Lovely Fall Evening
in the Nation's Capital

"Sad, huh?" Tony Buffolino said.

Tony, Mac, Annabel, and Alicia sat in a banquette along the wall of Tony's Spotlight Room. Alone on the bandstand, a sallow-skinned man with flowing gray hair, wearing a blue tuxedo jacket with sequins, lethargically played a keyboard while an electronic drum machine provided a cha-cha-cha rhythm.

"Well, maybe it was just the wrong idea in the wrong place," Smith said. "Maybe Washington, D.C., just isn't ready for a Las Vegas nightclub. Besides, there's no gambling."

"No gambling? This whole place was a gamble. But you're right, Mac. I had a good idea, but I bet against the house. I was ahead of my time in D.C."

"Exactly," Annabel said.

"Don't be too hard on yourself, Tony," Alicia Buffolino said. She touched his hand and smiled. "It just wasn't meant to be. Besides, I have to take some of the blame here. I wanted you to be more than a private detective following cheating husbands. I wanted you to be a businessman. This was just the wrong business."

Tony grinned at Mac and Annabel. "Ain't she somethin'?" he said.

"Yes, I think she is exactly that, Tony," Annabel said.

"Do you know what the shrink told us this afternoon?" Buffolino asked.

Mac and Annabel raised their eyebrows.

"The shrink—she's a woman, which don't exactly make me happy, but she seems pretty straight—she told me I don't always sound the way I'm thinkin'. She got us into a conversation and taped it on a videocamera. Then she played it back. I got her point. There I was thinking nice things and telling them to Alicia, but when I see myself on the tape I sound mad, like I'm puttin' her down."

Smith smiled, said, "We're all guilty of that at times, Tony. Sounds like you're going to get a lot out of marriage counseling."

Alicia said, "All I want out of it is a good marriage with this knucklehead."

"Hey, don't call me a knuckle . . . Whatta you . . . ?" He broke into a big smile and embraced her. "Yeah, I guess sometimes I am a knucklehead."

The only other person in the club was a Hispanic busboy who also functioned as bartender for Tony and his guests.

"Did you cook up our meal in the kitchen?" Smith asked.

"Nah," Buffolino said, "I had takeout brought in."

The Chinese food was set out in bowls on the table. A sign on the front door said: PRIVATE PARTY IN PROGRESS—NO ADMITTANCE.

Annabel tasted an eggroll and said, "I really feel sorry for Clarissa Morgan."

"Not Carolyn Armstrong?" Smith asked, spooning beef with snow peas onto his plate.

"Of course I feel sorry for Carolyn, but in a way Clarissa's story touches me even more."

She sat back. "I could see myself ending up in that kind of life. I mean, it must have seemed exciting in the beginning, a beautiful young woman being a paid agent for British intelligence, at first merely dating, then later seducing men who have secrets important to the state, living the high life and being paid well on top of it."

"Didn't get her far," Buffolino said through a vast mouthful of shrimp fried rice doused with sweet-and-sour sauce and Chinese hot mustard.

"I know," Annabel said, "and that's my point. She did what she was told to do, and then simply because she fell in love with Paul, they cut her loose."

"Not quite as cruelly as Reverend Priestly was cut down in Buckland," Smith said.

"Why did British intelligence kill Priestly, Mac?" Annabel asked. "I'd have put my money on the murder being the work of someone from Word of Peace."

"Then you'd have won your wager. Maybe you should put in gambling here, Tony. The problem was that Priestly, who once was a Young Turk allied with Paul Singletary, had gone over to MI5. He was no longer trying to pass along useful data and weapons information and such to help Word of Peace; he'd become suspicious of certain characters high up in it and went over to become an agent for the Brits, who fed him bits of this and that. His role now was to get the goods on the bad apples in the peace movement. Problem was that the heavy hitters in Word of Peace got wind of it—twigged to it, as the English say—and wanted to eliminate this source who had become a danger to them. Once Paul was killed here, in such a distinctive fashion, Mr. Jin Tse, who was not only a mover and shaker in Word of Peace but an acknowledged terrorist and assassin to boot, flew to England and hit Priestly in a manner calculated to make it seem that the murders were parallel—to divert attention, obviously, from his organization—since he knew that they *hadn't* killed Paul Singletary.

"But wait a minute, Mac," Annabel interrupted, "how could Jin have known to kill Priestly with a candlestick? At that time nobody but Armstrong, Merle, and, I guess, St. James, knew what the murder weapon used on Paul was."

"I think one other person knew," Mac said, "and George confirmed my suspicion yesterday when he told me that one of the cathedral custodians skipped town the night of the storm, the night the evening news carried the story about the FBI sweep of Word of Peace's petty spys. My hunch, and this is all based on circumstantial evidence until the police can find him for questioning, is that the maintenance man at the cathedral saw St. James switch candlesticks, and make a nervous display of it at that. George is a charming guy and a wonderful bishop, but I assume he's not the smoothest of men when it comes to removing murder weapons. The maintenance guy reported it to Jin Tse, who is smart *and* inscrutable. He saw the opportunity to use a similar weapon in the Cotswolds. As it turned out, he's more inscrutable than smart considering the time he's facing. Of course, Word of Peace might have gotten to killing Paul anyway because of the unwanted attention he'd been attracting with his overactive love life, or at least sex life. Not only that, he was tottering on the edge of being accused of feathering his own nest with their funds. Which he was, in fact. The trips to England to see his mistress; the very expensive security system in his apartment, installed because Paul was beginning to think that his whole life, the whole shaky, secret edifice, could bring him down. Whether he was afraid of MI5 or the CIA or others in the peace organization may never be known—but he wasn't paranoid. Treason is a good reason to be fearful. And he was sincere about almost everything in the movement."

"You mean attempted treason," Tony put it, "don't you? Didn't I hear that the street value of the tapes meant they were not exactly prime stuff?"

"Right. But stealing the wrong stuff and turning it over, or holding it to turn over at the 'right time' to a nation's enemies, is treason whether the tapes were outdated or not. The British only let Priestly get hold of weak material from the start, and he and Singletary held on to it too long. It's like strong narcotics or weak narcotics—it matters to addicts but not to the law. When MIS confronted Priestly with knowledge of his taping and other acts, stuff he had been feeding to Paul, he had an extra reason to be 'turned,' and to work for them. Also, he was beginning to want out, didn't much like using his friends, made the mistake of letting that show. Jin and company figured that he might tell all he knew about Word of Peace, information he'd gotten from Paul, to buy his way clear."

"What I don't understand," Annabel said, no longer attempting to eat, "is why those two priests should have been engaged in intelligence trafficking, anyhow."

"Oh, sure you do. They met when both were in the military, engaged in joint exercises of the two navies, and became good friends. You can almost hear the conversations between them, young idealists, ministers in the military, bemoaning the money spent on weapons while much of the world is dirt poor, deciding over a few beers late at night that they had to do something to help prevent further escalation or nuclear destruction." He frowned. "The problem with those two was that they were naive, inept. Priestly eventually paid the price, as Paul might have, long after most other young idealists have put on pinstriped suits and taken managerial jobs with defense contractors. Really a shame."

"What a world," Annabel murmured. "Believe in peace and work for it, and get killed because of it."

"You are, as usual, too nice. Paul wasn't killed for his commitments but for a lack of them. Especially toward women." He sipped Chinese tea, now cold. "Well, at least they gave Clarissa Morgan the option of leaving England and settling in the British Virgin Islands, which, I might point out, is not exactly hardship duty."

"She seemed so resigned about going back there. This Mr. Leighton . . . what did she call him, her 'control' . . . seems to call all the shots in her life."

"Your expression is almost too appropriate. I propose to call the shots at this table: a toast." He held his glass of Blantons high over the table. Buffolino picked up his glass of Don Q rum and Coke, and Annabel her white wine. "What are we toasting?" she asked.

"First, George St. James and his return to his relatively normal life as bishop of the National Cathedral. Of course, what he prayed wouldn't happen did happen. One of his own was the murderer. Which proves that even for a bishop, not all prayers can be answered. He's gotten some phone calls. One woman said she would no longer contribute to that 'den of iniquity' posing as a cathedral. But he—and the cathedral—will ride it out because they must. We need him, and the cathedral."

"You bet. A great institution, some great people—and an eternally good cause. What's the second thing we're toasting?" Annabel asked.

"The end of a sad, nasty, and upsetting episode in our lives," Smith said. The rims of glasses clinked together. "And," Smith added, "I propose a toast to the National Cathedral getting back to its business at hand, namely setting the spiritual pace for this increasingly hedonistic slice of society."

"Amen," Tony said. "What's that mean?"

"Hedonistic?" Smith said.

"Yeah."

"Caring about your own fanny more than anybody else's."

"Makes sense to me," Buffolino said, raising his glass again.

"What do you think will happen to Jonathon Merle?" Annabel asked.

"Hard to say," Smith replied. "He was an accessory under the law, but I have a feeling they won't go hard on him. He walked in on them right after she'd hit Paul with the candlestick, and bought her rationale that if the body were found in Good Shepherd, it would appear that someone from outside the cathedral had murdered him. He had finally found someone on earth to truly love. Also, Merle is a good soldier. Jonathon believes in the cathedral and what it stands for, and thought he was doing the 'right' thing. He wasn't, of course, but he'll have to answer to a lesser god than he's been used to." Smith shook his head. "Nickelson is a sad case. Because he was convinced his wife was playing around with Paul, he had good reason to think he'd be accused of the murder. Frankly, he's better off in San Francisco, and the cathedral is better off without him."

"His wife would be better off without him, too," Annabel said, "but that's another story."

Buffolino gestured to the bartender. "Another rum and Coke." He also ordered for Mac and Annabel, but they demurred. Buffolino said, "I really feel sorry for that kid, Joey. Man, he must be some mess, running away like that, having seen Merle dragging a body up the hall. Tough on a kid."

"Yes, it is," Smith said. "Interesting that Armstrong was convinced Joey had seen *her* moving the body, not Merle."

"Do you think she would have hurt the boy?" Annabel's concern, even after the fact, was etched in her face.

Smith shook his head. "I don't think so. Killing Paul was not a premeditated act. She was the woman scorned, and she lashed out."

"Whattaya think she'll get?" Buffolino asked.

"I don't know. Susan Kellman is a good attorney, a good choice to defend Armstrong, if I do say so myself. I think they'll probably do well, fairly well. Word of Peace is another matter."

"I'm glad that the cathedral and the Mother Church have disassociated themselves from it," said Annabel.

"I suppose so," Smith said, "but it's kind of a shame, too. We could use more effective peace organizations. Too bad a few factions decided to make use of it for their own purposes."

"More ribs?" Buffolino asked.

"No, thanks. Not those ribs, anyhow," Smith said. He took Annabel's hand and asked, "Dance?"

She giggled. "Here? Now?"

"Yup. Excuse us, Tony."

Buffolino smiled as he watched the Smiths take to the small dance floor.

"What would you like to hear?" the musician asked.

" 'Our Love Is Here to Stay,' " Annabel said.

They danced close, their cheeks touching,

Annabel humming the melody along with the pianist, who seemed to have become inspired by two live, moving bodies. Halfway through the song, Mac whispered in her ear.

"No," she said, pulling her head back and laughing.

"Why not?"

"Do you really think he'll know the answer?"

"Bet you a hundred bucks."

"You're on," she said.

Smith guided her close to the bandstand and said, "Excuse me," to the musician.

The musician leaned over the keyboard, his fingers still working the keys. "What?"

"Do you know your fly is open?" Smith asked.

The pianist laughed. "If you can hum it, I can play it."

Tony Buffolino suddenly appeared next to them. "Mind if I cut in?" he asked.

"Not if she doesn't," Smith said.

She didn't. As they danced, Tony leading manfully, half as tall as she, he told her that he was out of the nightclub business for good, that he wanted to turn over a new leaf with Alicia, and that his best days—and nights—were spent working for Mac. She smiled. Even Tony was becoming nicer. But she hoped there would be few occasions for Tony to get assignments from Mac. Still, looking over Tony's head at her husband, she wasn't so sure.

Later that night, while they sat propped up in bed and browsed through the newspaper—Rufus providing a breathing footboard—Smith asked, "Say, did you really find that phony Frenchman Pierre Quarle handsome and charming?"

"Yes. Didn't you?"

"No. He had bad breath."

"I didn't notice."

"You were blinded by the accent, and your nose shut down."

"I was not. Mac, are you jealous of me?"

"At times."

"Don't ever be. I am your woman, and will be for the rest of my life."

"Then I won't be . . . jealous. All the time. Just stay away from Frenchmen with halitosis. And especially from any man without it. If you don't—"

"What will happen if I don't?"

"He becomes a meal for the beast. Right, Rufus?" He cued the dog with his right foot.

The Dane growled and shifted position. Smith and Annabel turned off their reading lights.

"Good night, Professor," she said.

"Good night, Patron of the Arts."

"Never again."

"Never *what* again?" Smith asked.

"Two never-agains. First, never hire an assistant who thinks he's smarter than you are but turns out to be merely impossible. And two, never get involved in murder."

"You can count on that. I'll never get caught up again in any murder in a national cathedral."

"Yes, I'm sure you mean just that. Good night, Mr. Smith."

"Good night, Mrs. Smith."

ABOUT THE AUTHOR

MARGARET TRUMAN, the author of nine successful mystery thrillers, was born in Independence, Missouri. She now lives with her husband, Clifton Daniel, in New York City.

They have four sons and two grandchildren.